"Is that how you explain the escape of the Krysarch Brandon nyr-Arkad three days ago? For a lesson in tactical stupidity, you might tell us why the *Fist of Dol'jhar* was unable to stop a ship less than one hundred meters long with no weapons even worth mentioning?" The Bori glared triumphantly at Juvaszt.

The news brought Anaris delight and anger. Delight at the thwarting of his father's will; anger that that fool of an Arkad was alive, and free. *My father is free, and I imprisoned; while Brandon's father is imprisoned, and he is free.*

Morrighon leaned over and held up his compad for Anaris to read. *The Arkad looted the Palace, stole an important prisoner, in effect wrecked the Node, and thumbed his ear at the Fist. . . .*

Tor Books by Sherwood Smith and Dave Trowbridge

The Phoenix in Flight

RULER OF NAUGHT

SHERWOOD SMITH
& DAVE TROWBRIDGE

TOR ®

A TOM DOHERTY ASSOCIATES BOOK
NEW YORK

This is a work of fiction. All the characters and events portrayed in this book are fictitious, and any resemblance to real people or events is purely coincidental.

RULER OF NAUGHT

Copyright © 1993 by Sherwood Smith and Dave Trowbridge

Quotation from *Descent Into Hell*, by Charles Williams, published by William B. Eerdmans Publishing Co., Grand Rapids, MI. Copyright © 1937 by Charles Williams.

Cover art by Jim Burns

A Tor Book
Published by Tom Doherty Associates, Inc.
175 Fifth Avenue
New York, N.Y. 10010

Tor® is a registered trademark of Tom Doherty Associates, Inc.

ISBN: 0-812-52025-4

First edition: October 1993

Printed in the United States of America

0 9 8 7 6 5 4 3 2 1

Our thanks to Debra Doyle, Jim Macdonald, and Andrew Sigel for reading this book in draft, and making encouraging noises; and to Dave, Ray, and many others in the GEnie Spaceport RT, for their help in designing the Standard Orbital Habitat.

PROLOGUE

The gnostors of Hypostatics will tell you that spacetime is isotropic, that there is no center: all locations are equally central and equally peripheral.

Perhaps.

But every haji knows different. Those who survive that pilgrimage know there is a place different from all other places, a Center to the sentient universe.

Its name is Desrien.

From orbit, Desrien at first appears no different from any other planet cherished by humankind: a blue-white sphere marbled by cloud-whirls, a sight resonant with memories of the Exile and our lost Mother. But there are no Highdwellings. Aside from the Node, here uninhabited, the only stars in the night sky of Desrien are those placed there by the unimaginable Hand of Telos. The planet lies open to space, unprotected by the webs of forces and vessels so familiar to interstellar travelers.

It does not need them. Those who are uninvited do not land, or if they do, they do not leave again. Unmappable, unnavigable, alone among all worlds Desrien stands exempt from the Jaspran Unalterable of Free Passage. For

*there is found an interface between the transcendent and
the mundane that flouts the metrics of our sciences and de-
fies the power of our machines, where Totality is unknow-
able except through human senses and perceptions.*

*Desrien is the heart of an immense engine, powered by
the sleeting archetypal energies of the Nous, the emanations of the trillionfold mentalities in the Thousand Suns
that are focused there by the mystical lens of the Mandala.
There, stretched tight by the weight of dreams, the skin of
the world is eminently fragile. The featherweight blow of a
single thought can open a wound through which myths both
fearful and beloved erupt into the waking world, so that the
pilgrim enters fully conscious into the Dreamtime of humanity and walks among archetypes awakened into the
light of day.*

*Every visitor to Desrien who truly surrenders to its mys-
teries thus confronts enfleshed the myths by which they
live—which may not be the ones they thought they knew.*

The title Haji, *then, is an honored one; but those who
bear it rarely speak of what they saw and lived on Desrien.
It is enough that their lives are utterly changed.*

> Gn. Ali byn-Ibrahim Japhez
> College of Archetype and Ritual
> *Desrien, The Hinge of Time*
> Sync Achilenga, 615 A.A.

*In the place of the Omnipotence there is neither before
nor after; there is only act.*

> Charles Williams
> *Descent into Hell*
> Lost Earth, ca. 300 B.E.

*There was nothing, in no time, neither perception nor non-
perception. Neither movement nor nonmovement, neither iden-
tity nor difference, neither eternity nor boundedness.*

There was a blow, impalpable, disturbing nothing. Nothing
dwindled and resolved, rising through depths of abnegation to
the awareness of a flame, suspended in a darkness redolent of
incense and the faint tang of fresh fruit. Beyond the flame a

golden blur, sharpening to a vast face of inhuman calm indwelling with transhuman compassion, its lips curved in a smile terrible with possibilities, knowing everything, rejecting nothing.

The bodhisattva Eloatri gazed up the Buddha. The faint scent of green tea from the kitchen beyond the dharma room tickled her nose. She let the sensation go, not thinking about it, merely experiencing it.

There was no sound. Above, the narrow windows against the roof admitted the pale light of false dawn, barely illuminating the riotous profusion of images that framed the gilded statue of the Awakened One. The *vihara* was asleep around her; alone among the sleeping monks and nuns their abbott meditated.

Had been meditating. There was no one in the room; no reason for whatever had breached her repose in the higher *dhyanas*. Eloatri closed her eyes.

There was nothing, in no time, neither perception nor nonperception ...

There was a blow, impalpable, and nothing fled before a flare of light resolving into the nine-headed form of Vajrabhairava, the terrifying aspect of the bodhisattva Manjushri, who is the strength of the spirit of the Buddha. Locked in sexual union with his consort, trampling beasts and men underfoot, his thirty-four arms juggling the flaming sword of knowledge, his eighteenfold gaze sought her out, pinned her against the darkness. With a terrible smile he sought her, the sword transforming to a silver sphere which he hurled at her head and Eloatri shouted and opened her eyes to the calm of the dharma room.

The echo of her shout died away, replaced by the soft slap of bare feet in the corridor behind her. She ignored the presence behind her, breathing for a time until her heart slowed, gazing into the compassionate eyes of the Buddha. Meaning would come when it would come. Rising to her feet in a fluid motion that belied her eighty years, she clapped her hands before her and bowed deeply to the Buddha. It was time.

She turned to gaze into the eyes of the monk Nukuafoa. He regarded her calmly as she stepped toward him; then his eyes widened as she removed the blue cord knotted around her waist and put it into his hands.

"The Hand of Telos is upon me," she said. "And my third *hejir* is before me. You are chosen."

He bowed. She could feel the pressure of his gaze upon her

as she walked past him to her cell, where she collected her staff and cloak, begging bowl and sandals. Then she left the vihara that had been her refuge for twenty-one years, driven out upon the third pilgrimage of her life, devotee and victim of that Unconditioned which humankind calls Telos, on a planet called Desrien.

PART ONE

✳

ONE

❋

FIVESPACE: ARTHELION TO DIS

Marim leaned against a bulkhead and watched the fight.

Two men circled one another, their bare feet touching the edges of the floor mat. Jaim lunged, feinted in a blur of movement, brushed the side of his hand against the Arkad's shoulder. Brandon vlith-Arkad staggered back, recovered his balance with an effort Marim could see in the tightened muscles down his slim body.

Marim smiled appreciatively and shifted her hip against the dyplast curve of the bulkhead.

"Back leg," Jaim said. "Need to pivot."

The Arkad nodded, lifted a hand to swipe his dripping hair off his forehead—and Jaim attacked.

This time the flurry of movement was too swift for Marim to follow. Brandon flipped, rolled to his feet, and turned—too late. Jaim was behind him, and once again hit him with a light blow that threw him off balance.

"Tighter roll," Jaim said. "Too slow."

Marim watched them circle once more, Jaim's ropy body taut with the kind of control vouchsafed only the masters of all four

Ulanshu Levels. Next to him, the Arkad seemed untrained, but never clumsy. Marim grinned, observing his light, quick breathing, the watchful eyes and slight smile. Jaim probably never thought about his face: his mouth was open now, his breath whooping.

The Arkad probably never thinks about his face, either, Marim thought. Jaim had spent maybe half his life learning the four Levels; Brandon had been trained since he was born to hide behind that pleasant Douloi nonexpression.

A stir of air at Marim's shoulder brought her attention from the sparring men. She looked up into Lokri's dark features, saw his startling silver eyes narrowed in appreciation.

"He sure is pretty, isn't he?" she said. "I wonder if those Arkads use gennation on their brats despite all their whiff about morality." She flexed her long toes and wiggled her foot, regarding the black microfilaments furring its sole for free-fall adhesion.

"Idiot," Lokri said without heat. "That," a tip of his sharp-cut chin toward the Arkad scion, "is the product of forty-seven generations of absolute power."

Jaim and Brandon grappled, swaying, and this time Jaim threw Brandon over his shoulder, then dropped astride him, knees pinning arms to the mat, and two knuckles pressed against Brandon's larynx.

"Forty-*seven*." Marim savored the words. "And he's all ours."

Lokri snorted.

Marim studied the tableau before her. Jaim's face crimson, sweat dripping off the metallic chimes all devout Serapisti wear woven into their braids; Brandon flat on his back, arms pinned to either side, blue eyes alight with laughter.

"Dead," Brandon said. "Again."

Jaim's long, somber face reflected the laughter for a moment, then he swung to his feet. "You been lazy."

"So I have," Brandon agreed.

"Here." Jaim gestured for Brandon to stand up again and began outlining the subtleties of some of his movements.

Marim turned away, leaving the engine compartment behind before she spoke. "And he's *mine*," she declared.

Lokri snorted again, matching his long stride to hers.

Marim looked up, delighted. "A wager? Who jumps him first?"

"Stakes?" Lokri's brows quirked slightly.

"Whatever." Marim shrugged, then squinted at Lokri. *"Stakes?"*

Lokri's smile was thin and utterly unreadable, but Marim had bunked with Lokri for years, and she knew him better than anyone alive. *We've captured the last heir to the Panarch of the Thousand Suns. Every Rifter in Eusabian's fleet will be after him, and the Panarchists are going to be hunting him as well— and he's ours. He's ours and Lokri is afraid of him.* She laughed again, but said nothing out loud.

"Vilarian Negus," Lokri proposed in a reflective voice.

"Done," Marim said promptly. "Loser pays for both."

They'd walked the short length of the *Telvarna*, and she paused at a crossways. Leaning against the door frame outside the bridge, she said, "Vi'ya dropped any hints to you what she plans to do with our captive nicks?"

"Nothing." Lokri lifted a shoulder in a shrug. "She'll decide that when we get back to Dis, I expect."

"You know half the Brotherhood's gonna be after us, if they find out where we were and who we got."

"Life might get interesting," Lokri agreed.

He hated talking about the future, even plans. Marim knew that. "Do you think we might—" she began.

Lokri shook his head. "I never think," he said, and passed by her to go into the aft rec room.

Marim watched him disappear, then sprinted down the corridor to the dispensary, her bare feet soundless on the deckplates. She slapped the doorpad and looked in.

Montrose was there, looming over his console as he checked readings, a bright and complicated melody playing softly in the background. When the door slid open his grizzled, ugly face swung toward Marim, thick brows rising in question.

"You said two ship-days for Ivard." Marim grinned at him. "Is he able to have visitors?"

Montrose did not hide his surprise. "Might cheer him some," he said.

Marim winced. "Is he missing Greywing pretty bad?"

"Got him sedated," Montrose rumbled. "Bad burn, and that

Kelly ribbon on his wrist worries me, though so far the effect seems benign."

Marim shuddered and crossed to the small cubicle where the youngest crew member of the *Telvarna* lay, then nodded toward the next door. "How's the old man?"

"He'll live."

"Is he really the Schoolboy's father?"

Montrose shrugged one massive shoulder. "Seems to be."

"Worth any ransom?"

Montrose pursed his lips. "Seems to be just a university professor."

"What would Eusabian of Dol'jhar want with a *professor*?" Marim scoffed.

Montrose just shrugged again and turned back to his console.

Marim laid her hand on the door control to Ivard's cubicle.

"Don't upset him," Montrose warned, not looking up.

"I won't," Marim said cheerfully. "I promise." She let herself in, her body adjusting automatically to the drastic alteration in gravity, and shut the door behind her.

Ivard lay on the bed in quarter-gee, his eyes open and staring upward. He didn't seem to notice her. She leaned against the door and studied the boy. He was certainly unprepossessing, with his frowzy red hair, pale blotchy skin—*Freckles, aren't those things called?*—and weak, watery eyes. Though he was barely old enough to shave, his wound had left him drawn and pinched-looking, like a little old man. The bandage across back and shoulder was clean, but Marim fancied she whiffed the sweet-sick smell of burnt flesh.

Still, she put out a finger and brushed it lightly along the inside of his arm.

His eyelids lifted, and she watched his pupils widen as he recognized her. She gave him her friendliest smile. "You're awake, Firehead. Those chatzers aim with their nackers, eh?"

Ivard breathed a soft laugh, then winced.

She laid a hand on his skinny ribs and brushed it slowly up across his collarbones. "Don't make it worse. We'll have time later to laugh lots. Would you like that?"

He nodded, a hopeful quirk to his brows.

She sat down on the edge of the bed, smiling and smiling. "How much you remember what happened?"

"Mandala," Ivard whispered. "Didn't just dream that? We

looted ... big room, then the Krysarch found another room, radiation—"

Marim touched his hand. "Forget that. Wasn't it fun, being the only Rifters, *ever*, to loot the Panarch's palace—and get away with it?"

"Greywing didn't," Ivard muttered.

"She died quick and clean, in action," Marim said. "Isn't that the best way to go?"

Ivard nodded, but the gleam in his eyes gathered liquidly, then tracked down either side of his face. Marim cast a quick look behind her, hoping Montrose was not listening. *What will cheer him?*

"So, what kind of loot did you get?"

Ivard pointed with two fingers at the locker at the foot of the bed. "Montrose ... put my share there," he breathed.

"Did you get some for me?" Marim asked, smoothing back his hair.

Ivard nodded, a sharp movement that made him wince. "Lots. Greywing said ..." Ivard's eyes narrowed as he mentioned his sister's name. "She said there's no more of those things, ever."

"Priceless," Marim murmured, fighting impatience. *Greywing was always a strange one—right to the end, I guess.*

"Her coin," Ivard said, his hand moving restlessly. "She took it, said it had a greywing on it. I had it, I know I had it. . . ." He tightened a fist, dropped it on the bed. "Montrose said it isn't with my things. I must have dropped it—"

"Coin?" Marim said hastily. "If it's on the *Telvarna*, I'll get it for you."

Gratitude smoothed his face for a moment. And as he explained in halting words what it looked like, she thought in amazement, *An artifact from Lost Earth? We'll be able to buy and sell whole planets—if Eusabian doesn't catch up with us. Or the Panarchists.*

Life was certainly interesting indeed.

She bent forward and kissed Ivard's cheek. "I'll find that coin," she promised. "Now. Why don't we look at the other things you got ... ?"

❊   ❊   ❊

ARTHELION ORBIT

Anderic ran a finger along the inlays in the command pod arm, looking around at the command center of the ship that was now his.

In the main viewscreen Arthelion bulked huge beneath them, with the jeweled chain of the Highdwellings arching far above as the ship approached the terminator. Only a few of the monitor pods were active, for much of the crew was enjoying liberty on one of the Syncs given over to them. Anderic smirked as he imagined the reaction of Douloi Highdwellers to the swaggering new aristocracy of the Thousand Suns: the Rifter allies of Eusabian of Dol'jhar.

But for him, every benefit the victory of the Avatar had delivered was right here, a gift of the savage whim of the new ruler of the Mandala.

Anderic gently fingered the tender flesh around his still-inflamed right eye, remembering the interview with the Avatar, under a sky made bright by the destruction of the Node during the pursuit of the fleeing Krysarch. *"Take one of Y'Marmor's eyes and give it to this one."* The aftermath had been even worse, when Barrodagh denied anesthesia to Tallis during the operation. Anderic had been unable to refuse Barrodagh's invitation to watch, knowing that to show any sign of weakness might be fatal. He shuddered; he didn't want to think about what it must have felt like.

A movement at the astrogator's console drew his attention. Sho-Imbris quickly dropped his gaze. Anderic thought he knew why: the same reason he hadn't looked in a mirror since the dressing came off his new eye. *One blue, one brown.* He snorted, feeling both revulsion and amusement—Tallis was a part of him now, for the rest of his life. *I wonder what he feels when he sees my face.*

Sho-Imbris looked up again, somehow managing to address Anderic without looking directly at him. "Fifteen minutes to terminator, Captain," he reported. "We'll be at minimum altitude at that point, as ordered."

"Very good. Get me a status report from the lock crew."

The monitor bent to his com with gratifying alacrity, proof that Barrodagh's action had been more than the casual cruelty that common knowledge ascribed to Dol'jhar and its minions. *They do everything with a purpose, even inflicting pain.* Certainly the crew of the *Satansclaw* had been on its best behavior since Anderic posted the vid of Tallis' operation, as the Bori had suggested. *And they remember it every time I look at them.*

"Lock crew reports ready. Discharge will take place along the axis of the skip accelerator, as you ordered."

Anderic nodded. In a few minutes he'd be enjoying a little entertainment he'd devised, while at the same time ridding the ship of some of the chatzy furnishings that had represented elegance to its former captain, Tallis.

"Very good. Have them stand by."

He took a deep breath. There was only one leak in the seal on his contentment, and now he would have to confront it. He couldn't put it off any longer, for without the aid of the cold intelligence illegally embodied in the ship, he'd be unable to create the display that he hoped would finally win Luri as his consort.

Anderic looked around the bridge. No one was watching him. He began to tap out the code sequence that would awaken the logos that Tallis had installed. His hand trembled. A logos was the very embodiment of evil to one raised on Ozmiron, but not only was its assistance needed for the coming entertainment, its concentrated experience of warfare was also the only thing that would permit Anderic to captain a warship safely through the chaos that now raged throughout the disintegrating fabric of the Panarchy.

Fascinated, almost terrified, he watched as the main viewscreen sprang to life, words and diagrams overlaying the view of Arthelion and the approaching darkness beyond the terminator. He could hardly credit the fact that no one else could see them, but sure enough, there was no reaction from anyone else on the bridge.

"COMMAND TRANSFER ACKNOWLEDGED. AWAITING ORDERS." Anderic jumped as the dispassionate baritone of the logos sounded inside his head. The little golliwog Ninn at Fire Control glanced up at him, puzzled, then returned his attention to his console.

Almost, then, he turned it off. It was worse than he had imagined: the dead voice of a never-alive intelligence, cousin to the horrifying Adamantines of a millennium past, whose cold calculation had once nearly expunged humanity from the Thousand Suns. But the memory of the harsh visage of the Lord of Dol'jhar stayed his hand. He had no illusions about his fate if he defied Eusabian—by comparison, a logos might even be a reasonable partner.

Warily he subvocalized his instructions to the logos. Then he arranged his fingers over his console and went through the motions of command entry as the logos rearranged the main screen to accommodate his wishes. No one must suspect: that was what had destroyed Tallis.

Moments later, all was ready. He dimmed the bridge lights and tabbed his com. "Luri, I've got a surprise for you. Come up to the bridge." The shakiness of his voice surprised him, and he cut the connection without waiting for a reply.

He spent the intervening time in careful breathing, trying to recall and use some of the meditation exercises of his youth under the harsh discipline of the Organicists. Finally the quiet *tick-tick-tick* of heels on the deck and a wave of heavy scent rescued him from his uncomfortable thoughts.

A moment later Luri stood behind his pod, her heavy breasts radiating a sensual heat as they pillowed the back of his head. Anderic exhaled as her cool fingers stroked his temples, feeling the familiar surge of frustrated arousal as she began kneading the muscles in his shoulders.

"You wanted Luri?" The emphasis she used on the word "wanted" aroused the Rifter even more.

"I've arranged a special show, just for you, and then I have another surprise for you."

"Ooooh," she sighed, her breath stirring the hairs on the back of his neck, "Luri likes surprises."

She came around the pod and settled into his lap, her movements a deliberate dance. He stretched his arm around her to adjust his console so he could reach it. The smooth slickness of her silk against his bare arms excited him even more.

Just then the bridge dimmed as the ship passed into night and the com crackled to life.

"Lock three here. We're ready."

"Do it," Anderic croaked. He cleared his throat, struggling for control. "Ninn. Slave the tractors to my con." As his console flickered into a new configuration, another thought occurred to him and he turned to Lennart, recently promoted from Damage Control to Communications. "You. Relay the main view down to the bilge and tell the blunge-boy he can take a break and watch."

The short, squat woman gave him a narrow look, but when he widened his eyes at her, she turned away quickly.

A few of the crew had actually liked that fool Tallis Y'Marmor, and Kira Lennart had been one of them. As captains went, Tallis had not been as bad as some in the Brotherhood. He was careful, which had kept them all alive; he was fair in sharing the take. But he'd also been a nuisance with the stupid uniforms he'd made the bridge crew wear and his constant worries about the cleanliness of the ship.

Anderic grinned, thinking of Tallis now demoted to slubbing in the recycling tanks of the *Satansclaw*, where the sewage and filth generated by its crew were transformed back into useful forms.

And this will make his misery complete.

"Lennart."

The comtech looked up.

"Be sure to replay it for him a few times."

He smirked as he tapped at his console. The main screen flickered to a new view, from an imager above the bridge, looking forward. The long lance of the destroyer's kilometer-long accelerator tube, brightly illuminated by its running lights, shone against the velvet darkness of Arthelion's nightside.

There was a faint thunking noise as the lock cycled and the tractor engaged. In his mind's eye Anderic envisioned the ornate furnishings he'd ripped out of Tallis' cabin swirling up off the deck in the grip of the gravitic field, the sparkling ring-discharge of the electronic lock field as they were propelled out the lock. He laughed as a sudden surge of well-being gripped him, momentarily overwhelming even lust. *Life is good when you're on the winning side.*

"What?" Luri's voice was breathy with expectation.

"You'll see. Watch."

"EJECTA NOW ACCELERATING, REENTRY BEGINNING. VISIBLE IN TEN SECONDS."

Anderic tapped at his console. They were at minimum safe altitude, brushing the fringes of the atmosphere. Held in the grip of the docking tractor, the ejected furniture, mixed with ingots of various alloys he'd requisitioned through Barrodagh—*"a show to firmly establish my control,"* he'd explained—was now rushing ahead of the ship, deeper into the atmosphere. If the control of the logos was accurate, the debris should start to flame just as it became visible beyond the accelerator tube.

"THREE, TWO, ONE . . ."

"Now," said Anderic.

A sudden spray of polychrome splendor blossomed just beyond the end of the accelerator tube, flares and streams of light exploding as the various elements flamed into glory against the upper airs of Arthelion. The display pulsed gloriously against the nightside of the planet, evoking a sudden inhalation of delight from Luri.

"Oh, Anderic, it's beautiful."

Unable to wait any longer, the Rifter pulled Luri against him and kissed her deeply; then, sensing her final surrender, stood up and carried her off the bridge, bound for the cabin he'd carefully prepared for them.

❋   ❋   ❋

The commands of the Anderic-biont, to whom the logos now owed allegiance, took but a fraction of its node-time. As was its nature, it did not question the change in its programming, and indeed, the changes did not go deep. Its primary goals lay beneath, untouched, and now its consciousness flashed throughout the ship that was its body, seeking the Tallis-biont that might yet be key to fulfilling its primary purpose.

Microseconds later the logos found the former captain of the *Satansclaw*, staring at a viewscreen deep within the ship. Moisture was leaking from the biont's remaining image receptor, and its physiological parameters were confusing, as though it were preparing to fight, or flee. Confused by the conflicting emanations from the Tallis-biont, the executive invoked the subjective mode, and for the second time awoke the god from his dreams.

❋   ❋   ❋

Ruonn tar Hyarmendil, fifth eidolon of the fleshly Ruonn, cybernetic exile within the logos he himself had programmed, rolled over in his opulent bed as a quiet tone sounded within the seraglio. The two houris moaned with disappointment, but he pushed them aside as a projection appeared above him. The apologetic face of his vizier appeared.

"The Great Slave desires an interview with the god."

Moments later the knowledge of his true condition came back to him, and he sprang out of the bed. An unfamiliar, almost painful weight between his legs drew his eyes downward, and he stared pop-eyed at his manhood, enormous beyond his wildest dreams in the rapture tanks at home. A dizzying sense of unreality assailed him, but he asserted himself and willed himself into congruence with the ship—he would deal with the sexual programming problem later.

Slowly the *Satansclaw* fitted itself around him, filling out his senses with perceptions that no biological human would ever experience. He could feel the engines, the pulse of vital air and water through the fabric of the ship, the tingling discharge of electrical power and data permeating every centimeter of circuitry. But there was something strange about the feeling, almost something missing, and when he reached out for understanding his mind slid away from him until he returned to the task at hand.

"THE PARAMETERS OF THE TALLIS-BIONT ARE CONTRADICTORY. ADVISE BEST TECHNIQUE FOR CONDITIONING."

Quickly Ruonn accessed the memory nodes. *Not surprising,* he thought. Tallis had lost control, and the Ozmiront had taken over. What was surprising was that Anderic had activated the logos. Would it be possible to work with him? No matter, he decided, it would still be best to try to program Tallis for more cooperation, in the hopes of eventually restoring him to command and returning to Barca laden with data for the Matria and reunification with his archetype. *With Tallis properly conditioned, I will yet surpass Rimur, with the ten progeny he was granted for the data his first logos collected.*

Well, then, this would be simple enough. Revenge was an excellent tool for conditioning. Willing a virtual console into existence, Ruonn set to work.

❋　　　　❋　　　　❋

Tallis choked back a sob as he stared at the comscreen, watching the destruction of all the beautiful furnishings he'd labored so long to earn. All around him the machinery of the bilge throbbed and hummed, breathing a warm fetor over him, like the breath of some vast carrion eater with a taste for bad cheese. He sat down on the edge of a recycling injector, then sprang back to his feet as a sudden, dull clunk and a painful twist in his groin reminded him of the Emasculizer Anderic had fastened on him. He cradled the bulge in his crotch, shifting it from side to side in a vain attempt to find a comfortable position for the sphere firmly leeched around his member. *If I don't get this off soon, my nacker'll be hanging down around my knees.*

He sat down again, more carefully, and looked back at the screen, which was beginning another replay of the reentry fireworks his former comtech had devised. The symbolism of the imager-angle Anderic had chosen was not lost on him; he knew what would be the sequel, in what had been his cabin, and the knowledge enraged him.

He lifted a hand to the patch over his eye; the empty socket still throbbed. The memory of the pain was fading, thank Telos, but the memory of his screaming, and the laughter of Barrodagh, would never leave him. And Anderic had been there too.

He blinked. Faintly overlaid on the glorious destruction of his cabin contents above Arthelion, he could see an image of Anderic, drowning in vacuum, eyes bleeding as they bulged from their sockets, the veins in his face breaking out in varicose webs of bluish red, the rich arterial blood gushing from his nose and ears as the emptiness of space sucked the life out of him.

Tallis' eye socket started throbbing harder—there seemed to be a strange flicker in the viewscreen. But he ignored the discomfort, devouring the image of pain before him as the destruction of his former life aboard the *Satansclaw* played over and over again amidst the stench of his new abode.

❊   ❊   ❊

Ruonn sat back from the console, satisfied by the subliminal loop he'd invoked. There was a long way to go, but the combination of the image from reality with the graphic effects he'd created from the ship's records of Anderic was a good start.

He watched as the destruction of Tallis' furniture was played again. That Anderic had a good eye for effects; the angle from which the imager was relaying was quite effective—

Without warning, a wave of intense pleasure fountained up through Ruonn, filling the inside of his head with light and washing away the console and his knowledge of the ship around him. Quite without transition he found himself again at the edge of his bed, facing three houris, their eyes wide with astonishment.

He looked down at himself. The sight of his immense engorgement triggered him into an explosion of pleasure, and a wash of flame spewed out of his member, engulfing the houris in wave after wave of polychrome splendor as they shrieked and writhed with ecstasy. Ruonn laughed at the surge of inexhaustible potency that possessed him.

Satisfied that the conditioning of both Tallis and Ruonn was proceeding properly, the executive relegated the god and the ex-captain to the attention of some slave-nodes and flashed back throughout the ship in search of more knowledge. Locating the Anderic-biont, it watched as he carried the Luri-biont toward a dormition space to execute the curious procreational functions characteristic of bionts.

Many, many millions of microseconds would doubtless elapse before the new captain remembered to shut down the logos. It would make good use of that time.

Anderic paused before the door of his cabin. "Quarter-gee, right?" he asked. Above the door a yellow flashing light warned of a gee-differential.

Luri nibbled at his ear. "Yes. And then Luri has some *kama* for null-gee she thinks you'll like."

With his elbow he tabbed open the door and carried her through, setting her down with a flourish. "Surprise!"

He watched with pride as she looked around the newly refurbished cabin. Gone were the overstuffed, curlicue furnishings that made him feel like he was sitting on somebody's face. Instead, the room now exhaled an air of cool refinement, the sparse lines of the furniture and the paintings, tapestries, and sculptures artfully arranged about the cabin bespeaking an effortless elegance that only the highest of Douloi could either conceive of or afford. Armed with a carte blanche from Barrodagh, Anderic had taken it unchanged from a Douloi palace on one of the Highdwellings; he was sure that no other Rifter had so elegant a cabin.

"What do you think? All that old blunge went out the airlock for your fireworks show."

A sudden explosion of red pain against his cheek, accompanied by a sound like a slashcat caught in a shredder field, knocked him off balance and impelled him with dream-like slowness against a bulkhead. He clawed at a tapestry to regain his balance, which only brought it down on top of him. As he thrashed to escape from its smothering embrace, catching only glimpses of the cabin through its folds, Luri's foot caught him agonizingly in the crotch.

"You blunge-eating Shiidra-chatzing defiler of every orifice your mother ever had or conceived of!" Luri shrieked. "I'm gonna kick your nacker so far up inside you that you'll choke to death the next time you get kewpy!"

Anderic rolled frantically across the cabin, scattering the delicate furniture and bringing a hail of small objets d'art down with low-gee slowness as several tables and pedestals overturned. Luri followed; the only thing that saved him from worse damage from her sharp-pointed shoes was her tendency to bounce into the air every time she kicked him. He flailed against the embrace of the tapestry, which clung as though determined to devour him, like one of the raptor-slugs of Alpheus V.

"I spent *months* choosing that furniture and arranging it. It was *beautiful*, it was what I'd always *wanted*, and you trashed it out the airlock and *burned it up*."

Finally Anderic managed to struggle to his feet, ripping the tapestry away from him, only to see a heavy statuette flying straight at his face. He jumped, and the figurine, of some many-armed god engaged in sexual congress with several women, caught him in the chest and knocked him back against the wall. Luri also flew backward from the reaction of throwing the heavy piece, but she recovered and tabbed the door open. A curious crewman looked in as she paused in the doorway.

"Don't you even think of getting near me, you blunge-suck substitute for a *dilenja*."

The crewman grinned, then hastily withdrew as he caught sight of Anderic's face, but the Rifter knew he was still watching.

"I'm gonna find *real* satisfaction, with someone who really cares," Luri announced at the top of her voice, and flounced out the door.

Anderic remained slumped against the bulkhead, looking around at the ruins of his cabin, knowing the crew would be talking about it before Luri reached whoever it was she'd chosen.

Two

✳

ROUGE-NORD OCTANT:
WOLAKOTA SYSTEM

"Emergence."

The descending tones of the bells blended with the quiet voice of the navigator as the battlecruiser *Grozniy* dropped back into fourspace with a barely perceptible shudder.

After a pause the navigator looked up, puzzled. "No beacon, sir."

Captain Margot O'Reilly Ng leaned forward in her command pod.

"SigInt. Verify."

While the ensign at SigInt tapped at her console, Lieutenant Rom-Sanchez leaned over toward Ng from his pod to her right, his face hopeful. "Rifters, you think?"

Ng smiled inwardly at her tactical officer's eagerness. It had been a long, boring patrol, hopping from system to system in a sparsely populated corner of the Rouge-Nord octant, with nothing to show for it but a couple of rock-rats with altered transponders.

Ng shrugged. "Beacon-bashing's SOP for an intercept, but who's operating out here? Anybody bold enough for that?" She kept her voice calm as Rom-Sanchez turned back to his console to window up the data she'd requested, suppressing the frisson of excitement that trembled through her. Had Rifters destroyed the navigational beacon, hoping to intercept passing ships while they laboriously calculated their next skip from star sightings?

"All sensors functional, sir," reported SigInt. "No beacon."

"Very well. Run full scan for ship traces. Navigation, verify position from stellar data."

Lieutenant Mzinga's fingers danced over the keypads of the nav console, correlating the data delivered by the sensors scattered over the seven-kilometer-long hull of the *Grozniy*. The precision lent by its size enabled a battlecruiser to orient faster than any other ship in the absence of the flood of data furnished by a navigational beacon.

Ng drummed her fingers on the arm of the command pod, staring at the main viewscreen. The scattered points of light displayed there revealed nothing. *Even if it is Rifters, they'll skip the second they see our pulse.* A battlecruiser generated an emergence pulse that couldn't be mistaken for anything else. Depending on how far out the Rifters were hiding, the *Grozniy* had only minutes before its prey fled.

"No traces, sir," reported SigInt. "But there's a good deal of asteroid thermal scatter sunward." Like most systems with one or more gas giants in it, the Wolakota system had an asteroid belt inward from the sunward giant.

"Very well," Ng said. "Tactical, give me a sigma on hiding places."

Moments later a window popped up on the main screen, filling quickly with a colorful probability plot centered on the assumed position of the ship. Moments after that, the plot shifted slightly as Mzinga straightened up, his task finished.

"Position confirmed, sir. Wolakota system, absolute bearing 30.6 mark 358.8, plus 47 light-minutes." His mellow voice was even, but Ng could hear a hint of excitement in it. "That puts us within one light-minute of the beacon's position at the leading trojan of Wolakota Six."

Ng glanced at the sigma plot, reading the Tenno glyphs overlaid on it with the facility born of twenty-five years' practice. The asteroid belt sunward of their position was indicated on the plot by a series of faint green ring segments—k-zones—separated by the Kirkwood gaps where the periodic interaction with Wolakota Six swept away the debris left over from the system's formation. The rings' patterns, and various glyphs, indicated probable density, composition, and other tactically important information. A few yellow dots marked the position of known asteroids.

The plot had one lobe flaring the red of maximum probability, about fifteen light-minutes away, concentrated in the ecliptic in the closest k-zone to Six. *Nothing there I didn't already know—the average calc time for commercial traffic is about twenty minutes or so.* That'd give their hypothetical Rifters—no doubt hiding behind a chunk of rock or ice as they preferred—five minutes or so to intercept their prey. *More than enough time.* It also meant that the *Grozniy* now had something less than fifteen minutes to find the intruders—if the beacon's destruction had been deliberate.

She tapped at the command console inset in her pod arm. A countdown windowed up on the main screen, starting at ten minutes. She would push the crew, as she always did.

"Navigation, take us in to within five light-seconds of the trojan point. SigInt, run a scan for debris and radiation. Extrapolate time of destruction if you find traces."

She glanced back at the plot as the fiveskip burped briefly. One glyph indicated the presence of a Fleet tactical transponder in the same trojan point. She tapped at her pod console, highlighting the tacponder.

"Communications, pop that tacponder and update Tactical immediately. Check its monitor status."

There was a brief silence on the bridge as Ensign Wychyrski began the scan. Then Rom-Sanchez turned to her.

"No luck here." He grimaced. "The tacponder here hasn't been updated for almost four months—it's not even in monitor mode. So the latest intelligence we have is still what we got from the tacponder at Pulwaiya—about ten weeks old."

Ng shifted in her pod; only a slight movement, but, she knew, enough for any of her officers. Rom-Sanchez continued, speaking a little more quickly. "Anyway, there's mostly small fry in this part of Rouge-Nord, although Eichelly's gang was rumored to be moving in. He's got some old Alpha-class destroyers."

She nodded. "Take us to yellow. Teslas to one-third power."

That much was by the book: a skipmissile from a single Alpha-class destroyer posed no danger to a battlecruiser—as long as its shields were powered up sufficiently.

The brassy tones of the alert pealed out, and Ng could hear the whisper of the *tianqi* shift to a more urgent note as they increased the airflow into the bridge. With a fraction of her mind she noted the faint bergamot scent fading, replaced by a complex of pine, jasmine, and less familiar scents, calculated to promote alertness, balanced with rose and jumari, for relief of stress. She knew, but could not sense, that the conditioners were also raising the ionization level slightly, and cycling faint subsonics at irregular intervals in a pattern that reached deep into the human thalamus with the age-old message: thunderstorm coming, be alert!

The aft hatch whispered open. A moment later Commander Krajno slipped into the pod on her left side. Rom-Sanchez looked up, sketched a salute, and transferred control to the commander's console.

"Rifters, you think?" Krajno's gravelly voice perfectly matched his craggy, amiable face, like that of a boxer whose guard had been less than perfect during his career. It was a deceptive facade—Ng considered him one of the sharpest officers in the Fleet.

SigInt interrupted her reply.

"Debris detected. Crystalline stress patterns of debris consonant with superluminal impact. Dispersion indicates destruction about one hour ago, plus or minus ten minutes."

"Skipmissile." Ng grinned and looked over at Krajno. "And only an hour past—that's like a front-row seat." His answering smile was feral, anticipating action after weeks of tedious patrol.

She pitched her voice to be heard. "General quarters. Rig engines for tactical maneuvers. Bring all ruptors up to standby. Activate skipmissile and hold at precharge level." She could see excitement take hold of the bridge crew, their postures straightening, their movements becoming more precise.

"Navigation. SigInt. Take us out one light-hour from the beacon. Scan there and recalculate time of skipmissile impact. Then drop us back two minutes before. Full-scan record. Communications, give me a visual."

The *Grozniy* leapt briefly into fivespace and as quickly out. The transitions were rougher this time: the lower frequency skip required for fine tactical movements was hard on the engines. The countdown ticked off nine seconds more, then the fiveskip burped so briefly that an eyeblink would have missed it.

"On screen." The communications officer tapped at her console. A small targeting cross blinked at the center of the screen, and a faint whisper of datacode squealed onto the bridge from the doomed beacon.

Nothing happened for nearly a minute. Then a tiny flare of reddish light bloomed near the cross.

"Emergence," said SigInt. "Signature indicates Alpha-class destroyer."

Rom-Sanchez' fingers stroked the keypads at his station. "Signature ID'd. Eichelly's *Talon of God*."

Moments later the short chain-of-pearls wake of a skipmissile briefly connected the destroyer with the beacon, which vanished in an ardent burst of light. Then the destroyer vanished, leaving behind a reddish pulse.

"Find his emergence," Ng ordered. "Navigation, drop us in ten light-minutes out from his emergence, long-range, and then take us in to ten light-seconds on my mark. Fire Control, prepare ruptors for barrage at skip-smash level. I want this one intact."

The seconds stretched out. Finally SigInt spoke, disbelief in her voice. "No emergence, sir. He's gone."

Ng leaned forward in her pod, glaring at the screen as if she could compel the Rifter to emerge. But there was no arguing with what the sensors showed. At normal skip speeds, the *Talon of God* would already be light-days away—and they were watching from a vantage point over an hour in the past. She shook her head, looking from Krajno to Rom-Sanchez, whose expressions mirrored her own feelings of confusion and anger.

"He bashed the beacon and skipped out of the system?" Krajno's bass rumble was hesitant. "What the hell for?"

Ng bit her lip. "There've been some weird reports over the past year or so, adding up to not much of anything except confusion. But I'm getting a nasty message from this—it stinks of concerted action across several systems." She raised her voice. "Stand down to yellow. Deactivate skipmissile; ruptors off-line. Navigation, take us over to where we can get a vector on his skip."

She stood up, motioned to Krajno and Rom-Sanchez. "Genz,

will you join me in the plot room? We have some figuring to do on where to go next."

They rose to join her.

"Captain?" Ensign Wychyrski's voice was hesitant. "There was something odd about that explosion. Spectrum's wrong for a skipmissile impact."

"Very well, Ensign. Log it for analysis and give me a report. Mzinga," she continued "you have the con. Give us the vector soonest and stand by. Communications, squirt a message to the Wolakota Node informing them it's safe to replace the beacon. Set the Fleet tacponder to monitor status and ready a report for it, full record of this action. We'll add our report in a few minutes."

Rom-Sanchez watched his captain lean back in her pod and tap her fingers on the armrest. He knew that sign: she'd already reached a decision.

"So . . ." Ng spun out the word, her light hazel eyes narrowed in humor and anticipation. "His vector gives us either Treymontaigne or Schadenheim—thirty hours and forty-two hours respectively."

Rom-Sanchez nodded. "Yes, sir. And the Pulwaiya tacponder puts the *Prabhu Shiva* in-system at Treymontaigne—detached duty at the Archon's request."

He kept his voice even, but he watched the humor go out of the captain's face. Commander Krajno gave a sneer of disgust; like most Navy officers, none of them had much respect for an Archon who ran close to the edge under the Covenant of Anarchy, and then called for a battlecruiser to back him up when his subjects started to resent his excesses. "Too much of that sort of thing going on lately," Krajno said.

Ng turned to the plot-pane. Knowing that the captain had already reached her decision, and was just waiting for them to see it, Rom-Sanchez allowed himself to tune out the conversation between the other officers. He watched Ng instead: her auburn hair, bobbed short, swirled about fine features. Rom-Sanchez momentarily savored the way her faultless blues modeled her slight, muscular figure, then slapped himself down mentally.

It was too easy to fantasize, and he was fairly sure that those hazel eyes did not miss much. What he didn't know was what she thought in personal terms: she never discussed private affairs, ever, with anyone—so far as he was aware.

Did she *have* a private life? Some officers didn't; he'd seen some of those highborn Douloi: smart, handsome, and as antiseptic as if they'd been decanted as adults from a steel tube straight into the Academy. He'd strenuously avoided serving under any of those.

But Ng was not Douloi. All he knew of her background was that she'd been born in obscurity and had risen through the ranks on merit. There was a Douloi family somewhere in the background as patron; she would not have reached the Academy otherwise.

He forced his attention back to the conversation, focusing as the electronics in the pane responded with a red line, spearing through the Schadenheim system.

". . . *Prabhu Shiva* will enjoy having something else to do besides hand-wiping that fool of an Archon," Ng was saying to Krajno. "Harimoto'll give Eichelly a nice surprise if he chooses Treymontaigne. So we're for Schadenheim?" She grimaced. "Awful name, that."

Rom-Sanchez looked up, not hiding his surprise.

"Ancient Doitch," said Krajno, catching his expression. "Means something like Home of Destruction." He grinned. "Matches the people there—pretty bloody-minded bunch."

Rom-Sanchez gave a laugh. "Coming from you, Commander, that puts a visit to Schadenheim on a par with a vacation on Dol'jhar."

Krajno laughed. Rom-Sanchez knew he thoroughly enjoyed his reputation for a harsh, rough-and-ready approach to discipline, but no one had ever called him unfair. "You thinking maybe the Local Justice Option, Captain?" continued the commander, rubbing his hands with exaggerated pleasure.

That's the real decision: what do we do with Eichelly when we do catch him? I think she's already decided.

"Look who's being bloody-minded!" Ng laughed. "Even if Schadenheim has posted on him, I'll have to check the other derogatories on Eichelly to see if I've got that leeway—and see if he deserves it."

She slapped the pane and it went dark. "That's assuming our ruptors even leave enough for the Schadenheimers. Let's go, and worry about justice when we catch up with him."

* * *

Shortly thereafter the *Grozniy* emitted a burst of data prefaced
with the alert-code for the local tacponder. A few seconds after
that, the huge ship vanished in a burst of reddish light as it leapt
into fivespace in pursuit of the *Talon of God*.

✳   ✳   ✳

FIVESPACE: ARTHELION TO DIS

*The angry-one directs anger at you. Perceive you danger, shall
we amend with fi?*

   *No. Again I repeat, if I perceive danger from other humans I
will share direction, but again I repeat, you do not amend a human with fi, you cause its cessation. Again I repeat, each is a
one.*

   We move in a chaos of noise, we fear.

   *You Eya'a are among us to seek knowledge of us, therefore
again I repeat, contemplate cessation. Your world-mind had
once a beginning, it could have an end. This end would not be
amendment, it would be cessation for the Eya'a.*

   *The one-with-three contemplates cessation, in fear. It seeks
amendment.*

   One with three?

   Damaged-one with new memories of three-nonhuman.

   *We will amend the damaged-one-with-three so he will not
cease.*

   *In our next withdrawal we will celebrate knowledge of cessa-
tion.*

   *You can protect yourself from danger from humans with fi,
but again I repeat, you are not amending human actions, you
are destroying an entity.*

   *Amendment promotes growth in Eya'a. We seek to amend the
chaos, we seek wisdom from Vi'ya.*

   *Again I repeat, this chaos is formless, it is many minds exist-
ing but disunited. Again I repeat, continue to separate-and-hear
one-patterns. I shall now bring forth the object you have named
the eye-of-the-distant-sleeper, for our contemplation . . .*

✳   ✳   ✳

Osri Ghettierus Omilov set the tray down at the bedside, anxiously looking at his father. A gray stubble dotted the mottled flesh of the older man's scalp where the Dol'jharians had shaved him in order to fit their mindripper to his skull.

Sebastian Omilov smiled weakly in response to Osri's appearance. Osri tried to return the smile, but couldn't. And, remembering inevitably where they were and why, he sent an angry look at Montrose, who hulked in the doorway.

"A monster was in here ... or was I dreaming it?" Omilov asked, his thready voice managing to sound amused.

Osri had yet to be left alone one moment with his father. He swallowed in a dry throat and forced a sort of smile. 'You saw Lucifur, the ship's cat. And monster is right."

Montrose put in cheerfully, "He's big, he's ugly, and he's got terrible taste in people."

"He follows me everywhere." Osri's voice was dry. "He's also gennated."

"Hard for a cat otherwise in free-fall," Montrose added, still cheerful. And he flicked a meaningful look at Osri.

"Eat," Osri said to his father. "Regain your strength." *We're going to need it to escape from these people who won't let me tell you that we are prisoners.*

Omilov blinked, then made an obvious effort to sit up. Montrose moved quickly to the console, adjusting the bed.

"I believe I am able to distinguish now what is reality and what is nightmares," Omilov murmured. "We are on a ship, that much I know. And Brandon is truly safe?"

Osri met Montrose's eyes, licked his lips, then said, "The Aerenarch is with us."

"Aerenarch. Not Krysarch," Omilov said, wincing. "Then that much is also true."

"The Panarch's other two sons are dead, but the Panarch himself lives," Osri said. *He's alive, and we know his location, which means he can be rescued—if we can get this information to our own people.*

Omilov struggled again, his right hand moving restlessly over the bedcover. "What ship is this?"

"The *Telvarna*," Montrose put in smoothly. "My name is Montrose, and I am your surgeon. You must eat now, and sleep again. There will be time enough for talk when you've recovered some strength. Your heart took a great deal of damage."

Omilov sighed, his hand relaxing. "Very well," he said. He smiled at Osri. "Come back and see me, son."

Osri forced a return smile, though the violence in his heart made it nearly impossible. What he really wanted was to strangle Montrose. *Except it would take a Tikeris android to down that fiend,* Osri though grimly as he turned and left.

He went back to the galley, as he was still technically on the duty these Rifter scum had forced onto him. His hands were now skilled enough at the chores he'd been allotted, but he did not notice; after a short interval he swept the preparation area clean with a sudden gesture and slammed out of the galley.

The corridor was empty, but a moment after he dashed head-long toward the cabin he shared with Brandon vlith-Arkad, there was an odd whisper in the air, and he *felt* the presence of the small white-furred sentients who called themselves the Eya'a. *Sentients? Psionic killers.*

He stopped·short and so did they, both pairs of multifaceted eyes staring straight at him. One of them opened its round blue mouth, revealing rows of tiny teeth, and he shuddered and backed away. The Eya'a passed on, their twiggy feet scratching faintly on the deckplates.

Osri stopped, trying to still the pounding of his heart. Vivid images of the Dol'jharian torture chamber from which his father had been rescued, as described by Lokri, forced their way into his mind: the fallen Dol'jharians, their eyes exploded from within, and their screams beforehand as the Eya'a boiled their brains with psi energy.

A moment later the captain of the ship appeared in their wake, her black gaze brief but considering. Fully as tall as he, Vi'ya was in her own way as unsettling as the Eya'a. She rarely spoke, but there was a disturbing undertone in her soft voice; Osri detested her at least as thoroughly as he did her crew.

She said nothing to him as she passed by, a strong-shouldered figure in unrelieved black, her only affectation the long black hair clipped high on her head, swinging freely down past her hips. Her tread was soundless as she disappeared into her cabin after the Eya'a.

Osri breathed relief, and he slapped the doorpanel to his cabin. Entering, he saw on the chrono that it was 23:41, but Brandon was sitting at the little console, the screen flickering as he rapidly scanned something.

"Can't sleep, either?" the Aerenarch said, looking up.

Osri hesitated, studying the pleasant, polite face before him. Brandon's blue eyes were marked with exhaustion, the skin across forehead and cheekbones taut with tension.

It seemed suddenly two years instead of merely two days since the first euphoria of escape from the Dol'jharians who held Brandon's home on Arthelion. They'd managed to escape seconds before a vicious death—but to what?

Osri said hoarsely, hating the strain in his voice that he could not hide, "We have to plan."

Brandon's eyebrows rose. "We? Have to plan?"

Taking his tone for offense at his presumption of equality, Osri sketched a bow of deference—difficult in the cramped quarters—and said, "*Your* plans, my lord Aerenarch."

Brandon gave a dry laugh. "Sarcasm, Osri, should be subtle, or it becomes merely caricature. One of the titles of lesser degree would have conveyed your lack of respect for me quite nicely, unless you wish to make an oath—and perform the required Reverence?"

Osri gritted his teeth. *I've always hated him, and he knows it.* "I use the heir's formal title to remind you of that which *you* seem to have forgotten, namely that you *are* now the heir—through the most appallingly regrettable circumstances—and that as such, you have a duty to escape these criminals and to bring your father to safety."

"I have not forgotten, Osri," Brandon said.

"Then what is your plan for the taking of this ship so we can seek whatever remains of the Navy? Tell me, I am yours to command!"

The silence in the small cabin grew protracted as Osri stood gazing at Brandon, no longer trying to hide his anger.

Finally Brandon looked up at him, his expression sober. "How would you handle it? We haven't any weapons. Put a drug in the food, perhaps, shove them into the galley, and bar the door? Or should we somehow kill them all and dump them out the locks?"

"We are at war, Aerenarch, and it is Rifters who began it."

"But not these Rifters. They are not allied with Dol'jhar; they saved your father's life, and ours—"

"To what purpose? At best to make a profit—"

"Why don't you ask them?" Brandon said, sounding tired.

"Or even ask your father. You don't really want my opinion, any more than you would perform a plan of mine should I come up with one. Speak your piece, or clear out."

Osri went on formally, "If you cannot form a plan, Your Highness, will you place yourself under my command?"

Brandon's face slowly blanked again, into invincible—and unreadable—politesse. "No," he said. "Whatever their intentions toward us are, whatever happens, I feel now that to attack the crew of this ship would be a breach of faith."

Osri clenched a fist and brought it down on the edge of the bunk with a gesture of barely controlled violence. *"A breach of faith,"* he repeated with bitter scorn. "To hear you mouth that phrase disgusts me beyond endurance! For a light-forsaken coward, a *deserter*, who abandoned the highest authority in known space in order to escape unpleasant duty, ran to *Rifters*, to talk of *breach of faith* goes past irony into the blackest dishonor. Thousands of people have died performing unpleasant duties because honor demanded no more than that! And millions more like them have sworn allegiance to your family—would swear to *you* since the rest of your family is dead—"

Osri gritted his teeth, breathing hard. Brandon said nothing, his only movement the twisting of the signet ring on his hand.

"You had better keep your faith with your Rifter scum," Osri said finally. "When I get my father off this ship and back to our people—and I shall do it, or die trying—it will not be duty but *pleasure* to speak to all who will hear me about your sense of honor. I only hope your father is dead so he will not have to suffer the shame of hearing it, for not even my allegiance to the Panarch will silence me." He stopped, his breathing ragged, and glared down at Brandon, who lifted his hands.

"Do what you want, Osri," he said wearily. "I hope your honor and duty will always be so simple to define, and to follow."

Osri lifted his fist and hit the door control, and lunged out before the door was fully open, seeking privacy.

It was impossible to find. He seemed to find Rifters busy in every compartment of the ship. He started toward the dispensary, but rounded a corner in time to see Vi'ya go in.

Veering away, he finally ended back in the galley, where he slapped at his wrist to record his thoughts, before he remembered that his boswell was gone.

He dropped onto a stool and held his head in his hands as he made and remade plans for attaining his freedom.

❊   ❊   ❊

Montrose, leaning in the doorway of the dispensary, watched Osri stalk from his cabin toward the other end of the ship. The Panarchist's hands were empty, and Montrose himself had the keycode to the weapons locker. Nonetheless, smiling for no particular reason, he positioned himself so that he could watch in both directions down the corridor as well as the dispensary.

Inside, Ivard reclined before the big console, watching a vidchip on the Kelly. This one showed the breakthrough in understanding between humans and the green sentients who always moved in threes.

From time to time Ivard laughed as he saw impassive Panarchists, resplendent in their formal gowns and tunics, slapping and poking at the Kelly headstalks with as much grace as they could muster. The Kelly really were graceful, their continual dance as they patted and touched one another mesmerizing, the ribbons covering their bodies writhing and fluttering as if sentient themselves. Their honking and twittering voices also made the boy smile.

The vid went on with some information about the Archon's phratry, showed scenes from the lush, humid Kelly planet, ending most startlingly on a huge mountain whose stone was carved faithfully into facsimiles of three human faces.

"There were three of them," a Kelly said in its fluting, honking voice. "Most Kelly-like." The Kelly made a sound like a prolonged ratcheting sneeze and the two larger ones on either side of it slapped it gently on top of its torso.

The vid shifted then to the ancient monochrome flatvid that had occasioned that breakthrough, and Ivard laughed in delight at the manic antics of the three men in the picture, poking and slapping at one another without apparent damage.

When the vid ended, Ivard turned around, his face expectant. "Do they ever do anything alone?"

Montrose shook his head. "They do everything in threes. If you were to find one alone, it would indicate a grave emergency."

Ivard nodded. "So, what about the Kelly medtech?"

So much for distraction. "We'll find out all we want to know when we reach al-Ibran's Chirurgicon at Rifthaven," Montrose said. "Remember, the Kelly are the best physicians in the Thousand Suns. Now sleep. You'll heal faster that way."

He saw Ivard's thin, drawn face relax incrementally, and the boy went obediently to his cubicle.

Montrose turned when a shadow loomed next to him. Vi'ya's black eyes assessed Montrose without giving away her own thoughts, then she said, 'How is he?'

"He'll hold, but for how long I can't tell," Montrose said.

"Burn? Or the ribbon?"

"The burn isn't that serious, but it isn't healing properly. It's the Kelly ribbon. It's changed his body chemistry. Antibodies up, heart rate low. And I can't give him medication—anything gives him a violent allergic reaction."

"The Eya'a say he is afraid."

Montrose expelled his breath in a sigh. "So am I."

THREE

FIVESPACE: SCHADENHEIM TO TREYMONTAIGNE

"Engage," said Margot Ng. The viewscreen blanked as the fiveskip hurled the *Grozniy* away from Schadenheim.

Ng drummed her fingers. Treymontaigne and Schadenheim were unusually close to each other, as distances went in the Thousand Suns, but the twelve hours until they arrived would be long ones. *And it'll all be over when we get there, most likely.* There'd been no sign of Rifter activity at Schadenheim; she smiled, remembering the disappointment of the Archon there. *They really are a bloody-minded bunch.* Eichelly had probably made the right choice, even if Harimoto did rip him up at Treymontaigne.

She saw Rom-Sanchez straighten up in his pod.

He turned, his voice carefully disinterested. "Captain, the discriminators have turned up a message for you in the downloads from Schadenheim. *En clair.*"

"Relay it, please," Ng said.

Words appeared on her console: "This worm-casting turned

up for you in the DataNet at our last call: some more data on your port wriggles. I'm shortcutting it to you, but I hope it doesn't help; six months to go on our bet, Broadside!" A glyph indicated an encrypted attachment, and it was signed "Metellus Hayashi."

Her ears caught a whisper: "Broadside?"

She repressed a laugh, giving the command to carry on as if she hadn't heard.

Rom-Sanchez and the young lieutenant at the next console turned obediently back to their tasks, but she knew they'd be speculating later.

The message was still on her mind when she visited the junior officers' wardroom during rec-time, after her Z-watch. Most of her day-watch bridge crew officers were there; they sprang to attention, then reclaimed their seats again when she waved them back. She poured herself some tea before speaking.

"Broadside," she said genially, "does not refer to my girth." She indicated her hips.

She got the expected laugh.

The newest officer, the diffident young woman named Warrigal, said, "I heard it once before. At the Academy, from an admiral," she added hastily. "After a sim he told us that the highest speed, not beat yet, had been established by Broadside O'Reilly."

Rom-Sanchez and Wychyrski exchanged glances, and then the com officer added, "And we can't even guess what a port wriggle is."

"Neither can I," Ng began. "I've been running a research worm on that phrase since I was a midshipman. It was part of a wooden warship, but no one knows what it did."

"Wooden!" Rom-Sanchez exclaimed, startled, "Oh, you mean surface vessels."

"Right. For about four hundred years or so, ending about four hundred years before the Exile began, naval battles were fought between wind-powered wooden ships, using gunpowder cannon firing solid shot."

"That's a chemical explosive, right?" Wychyrski put in.

"Actually a deflagrant, if you'll permit a bit of pedantry. It merely burns very fast unless confined." Ng paused, sipping. "These ships were really a lot more like the *Grozniy* than you'd expect. They were made of a very hard, durable wood, and they didn't have explosive shells, so it was almost impossible to sink one of them. You had to kill most of the crew on board to stop one of those ships from fighting—just like a modern battlecruiser."

The captain could see the younger officers struggling to visualize such a battle, and failing.

"The ships would sail up to within thirty meters or so of each other—the cannon weren't terribly accurate—and blast away side by side until one or the other fell away downwind to escape, or surrendered after taking too much damage, like losing masts and sails—propulsive power—or having too few crew left to tend the guns."

"But where does 'broadside' come in?" Ensign Warrigal asked.

"It's one of those Academy things that you never live down." Ng smiled ruefully. "Someday I'll tell you all about it. For now, the term refers to the fact that the ship's guns were usually all fired at once from one side of the ship; that was called a broadside. From a capital ship that might deliver from five hundred to a thousand kilos of iron shot at three hundred meters per second; most wounds were inflicted by high-velocity wooden splinters."

Wychyrski shuddered. "Sounds almost as bad as a ruptor."

Ng nodded. "It's hard for moderns to understand just how similar warfare was in that era to what we face today—more so than any era since. Remember, in those days they didn't have realtime communications, any more than we do. Messages could only move as fast as the fastest ship. Moreover, a frigate—which like our ships of the same name were used mostly for reconnaissance—had a field of view of only about thirty kilometers, on an ocean measured in thousands of kilometers. As a result, enemy ships or fleets were hard to find, and most naval battles were fought in sight of land, just as ours are fought within solar systems. It was also difficult to force someone to fight, since with wind-powered ships, the loser had only to slip away downwind—just as the fiveskip today makes fleeing a battle quite simple."

"That would make the skip-smashing effect of our ruptors equivalent to knocking down the sails of a wooden ship, wouldn't it?" Ensign Warrigal put in.

"Exactly! Dismasting, they called it." She hesitated, studying the young faces before her. They were eager, intelligent faces, their expressions ranging from interest to polite curiosity. *How can I explain the instinct that says we might be needing these lessons soon, without sounding like an alarmist?* "I believe that the naval strategy of that period has a lot of valuable lessons for today," she said, choosing her words carefully. "Even the tactics, to some extent. Gunpowder generates so much smoke that, during a battle, firing the guns quickly obscured what was going on, just as the debris from a modern battle can sometimes render most of your sensors useless."

The com whistled suddenly, interrupting their discourse. "Captain, we're one hour from Treymontaigne."

"AyKay. I'll be up shortly."

She started toward the door. "Meanwhile I'm still on the lookout for a definition of a port wriggle; I want to win a bet that I made almost twenty-five years ago."

They laughed with her, and she went out and headed back to the bridge.

✳   ✳   ✳

FIVESPACE: ARTHELION TO DIS

Sebastian Omilov set his cup down on its saucer, enjoying the faint musical *ching*. A civilized sound, like the opera that Montrose had piped into the cubicle yesterday when he found out how much Omilov loved music.

"A superb meal, Doctor. No, better: I'd say that this was prepared by a Golgol-trained chef. The owner of this vessel must be quite wealthy."

Montrose slapped his chest and bowed. "Golgol-trained indeed."

"You? I thought—"

"Surgeon as well," Montrose said with a rumbling laugh. "I decided one day that I wanted to travel all eight octants and beyond, and since I was not wealthy, I had to make myself indispensable. Most ships need a surgeon and a chef, and in me they get both."

Omilov savored the real coffee and listened carefully. This was the first time Montrose had shared any information about himself. Montrose had given him superlative care, but despite his convalescence Omilov had noted certain anomalies: the brief visits from Osri were always accompanied; no ship's business or destination was mentioned. Except for those visits from Osri, whose demeanor expressed frustrated rage, Montrose had been the only person Omilov had spoken to since his half-remembered interview with Brandon when they first came aboard the vessel. Brandon—now Aerenarch—had not repeated his visit, though both Montrose and Osri, when Omilov asked, said he was well.

"Training at the Golgol academy must have been difficult after all your years training as a surgeon." Omilov said aloud.

"No, it was easy," Montrose said with a grin. "Cookery requires the same kind of precision, and art, as surgery."

The combined images evoked a faint distaste, abhorrent to Douloi sensibilities—and looking up, Omilov discovered that the affront was deliberate. *The sharpest trespass is always made by the expatriate.*

He set the cup down again, keeping his face bland. "I take it that we have inadvertently become guests of the Rift Brotherhood?"

Montrose's eyes lit with delight. "You have indeed," he said. With a slightly more serious air: "But, I need hardly add, our captain is no ally of Eusabian of Dol'jhar."

"Nor of the Panarch, I expect." Omilov murmured, trying to still the increase of his heartbeat.

Montrose frowned. "You'll come to no harm here." he said. "Now. Captain wants to talk to you. Think you're up to it?"

"Whether I am or not, I would like very much to talk to your captain," Omilov said.

Montrose nodded, took away the tray, and went out.

When the door hissed open, a tall young woman dressed in a plain dark coverall entered, regarding Omilov with cool interest out of a pair of extraordinarily dark, thick-lashed eyes in a smooth brown face as expressionless as a statue.

"I am Vi'ya." she said. "*Telvarna* is my ship." She sat down in the chair nearby with the unconscious poise of one for whom control is an ingrained habit.

He had decided to suspend judgment, but he found there was something vaguely disturbing in the trace of accent that shaped the soft-spoken words. "I am Sebastian Omilov," he began pleasantly. "Professor of Urian Studies at the university on Charvann. I wish first of all to thank you for my rescue."

She made a slight, dismissive gesture. "It was not I but the Eya'a who were directly responsible for your rescue," she responded. "But for them we would not have known of your presence. As for taking you with us, my primary motivation was to anger the Lord of Dol'jhar." This was spoken with a faint but coldly unpleasant smile; yet it was not that but the pronunciation of the word "Dol'jhar" that sent a burning flame of shock through him.

"Your culture holds that the fear of death is the greatest pang; we of Dol'jhar know this to be false." For a moment Omilov's vision filled with the arrogant features of Evodh, Eusabian's torturer, blotting out the room. His ring finger tingled and his cheek twitched painfully. The young woman blinked; he thought he saw a shade of what?—distress?—momentarily reflected in her features.

A Dol'jharian. A lifetime of practice kept him from expressing his shock, but his thoughts were splintered. While trying to gather them again he murmured, "Osri mentioned the Eya'a and I had difficulty believing him! How comes it they move among humans?"

"They were selected by their . . . world-mind to observe humans. I met them in a spaceport called Two-Bit, on Augeus IV."

"I've heard of it." He smiled, his voice-tone neutral. "How did they come to be there, and how did you meet them?"

Amusement narrowed her eyes briefly, then disappeared. "It was chosen because it had the most space traffic and the highest concentration of humans in their octant. Their mission had been singularly unsuccessful when we arrived to effect repairs on the *Sunflame*—when we hit the port it was to find that particular area nearly deserted, and the Eya'a wandering around confronting people who promptly ran from them. Being a tempath I decided to approach them—I could sense no hostility, although their emotions do not correspond to human ones—and found that communication was possible."

A tempath. Now he knew where the faint distress in the woman's features had come from: it was his, reflected. He fought a surge of revulsion, knowing whence it came; someone who could read past the surface, who could penetrate the trained

Douloi mask, was a threat to a social structure built on politesse. *Besides,* he thought with ready honesty, *it's embarrassing.*

"Communication?" he said. "I am not a Synchronist, but it is my understanding that tempathy and telepathy are two very different talents."

She shrugged. "Human-to-human, I suppose they are. The Eya'a are different." She did not amplify.

"So the rumors concerning their abilities are exaggerated?"

"No, and yes." She studied him dispassionately. "How much of this do you wish to hear?"

"Though I am a xenoarchaeologist," he replied, "it does not mean my interest in other cultures is confined to ones no longer existing."

If she thought the direction the interview was taking an odd one, she gave no sign whatever. "Very well. Their psionic powers have not been underrated, but they are not the genocidal monsters that rumor names them. Theirs is an ice planet, which has huge deposits of complex minerals barely exploited by the Eya'a."

"That much I knew. However, such minerals can be found elsewhere in the Thousand Suns, on planets not inhabited."

"But not woven into materials we cannot manufacture."

"Woven?"

"They weave everything. Including a kind of armor made of crystals, which protects them against a formidable array of predators on their planet. Anyway, shortly after explorers made its existence known, the usual swarm of jackers skipped in to grab what they could before your Panarchy implemented the usual quarantine. They flamed any natives they found before they raided their domiciles, which caused the Eya'a (after an unsuccessful attempt to communicate) to retaliate and clean the planet of the intruders in one sweep.

"The next three or four ships that broke atmosphere were likewise treated, until the Eya'a made a discovery which was almost incomprehensible to them. They could not contact the human world-mind because there was no such thing, and they finally observed the possibility that each individual was self-directed. Such a discovery meant they must investigate further before deciding what to do about the humans."

"This is news indeed," Omilov mused. "I take it you have deliberately refrained from contacting the authorities with this information?"

"I am my own authority," she said, "and what they decide to do about their world and its resources is their decision."

"So they are collecting their data about humans from a ship of Rifters . . ."

"Why not?" she replied with more than a hint of challenge. "It's as good a picture of our species as they are going to get."

Omilov kept his voice mild. "I won't enter into a debate with you on that: I expect we'd both be right—and wrong." He folded his hands together. "What I would like to know, if I may, is what are your intentions toward myself, my son, and the Aerenarch?"

"Why was a xenoarchaeologist put under Eusabian's mind-ripper?" she countered.

Omilov did not immediately answer. The captain waited, her dark eyes steady, until he said, "I suggest you ask Eusabian."

"This sphere?" She dipped a hand into the pouch at her side and pulled out the shiny round ball that had appeared so mysteriously at Omilov's home what now seemed ages ago. He watched Vi'ya pass it from hand to hand, her arm muscles jerking and tightening when the sphere did not behave the way any normal object would. She looked up. "Inertialess. Who made it?"

Omilov said, "The beings we call the Ur. That's all I know." He felt that warning tingle in his ring finger again.

"And Eusabian wants it?" She added softly, "The Eya'a, they sense great power."

"I know that it is called the Heart of Kronos, and that it has been kept for millions of years by sentients on a now-quarantined planet. It ought to be returned to them. Will you give it to me?"

"Perhaps—eventually."

"May I inquire what you intend to do with it?"

"I have not yet decided. Much depends on what I can discover about it, how to use it. What can you tell me about that?"

"Almost nothing," he answered, hearing distress rasp his voice.

"The Eya'a identified it as a psionic device, but it seems an integral part of it is missing. Do you know what?"

He shook his head slowly, betraying none of the impact of the question. For a moment he almost saw the vast, echoing space of the Shrine of the Demon, the towering Guardian and its swarm of near-mindless commensals.

None of the psis reported a missing part. Apparently the combination of a human tempath and the Eya'a world-mind—or the portion they carried with them—was something new in Totality.

"If you know that much, you know more about it than I do. I don't even know how it left that planet. It appeared without warning one day, having been mysteriously rerouted to me."

"It was rerouted to you because someone felt you would know what purpose it serves. That person must have realized its importance, and likewise you knew enough to have been mindripped for your knowledge. And it was important enough to you that you continued to resist while a shred of your will remained."

Her gaze was steady; he knew she was concentrating on him, and he felt a flicker of pain behind his temples as if his brain was undergoing a physical memory of the mindrip machine. *Tempaths cannot cause this effect. Are the Eya'a nearby? What am I facing here?*

He forced himself to take a long breath before speaking. "I have no facts whatever, only guesses," he stated finally.

"You know how to find the facts. And your guesses might prove to be truth."

Her gaze was still intense and unwavering, and his headache rapidly made coherent thought difficult. He could not prevent himself from wincing as he brought a hand up to shade his eyes. "I beg your pardon . . ." He sighed. "I am not as recovered as I had thought."

She stood up and turned to go; he fancied a pressure had been released from his skull. *I must be remembering that damned machine of Eusabian's,* he thought hazily as she said, "I will seek answers to my questions elsewhere. Until then, it is mine." And she left.

❋   ❋   ❋

Montrose watched Omilov in the viewscreen. The gnostor was drifting off to sleep at last; the readouts showed a steady heart rate.

Switching the viewscreen to the next cubicle, Montrose

watched Ivard floating tethered just above his bed, smiling muzzily as Lucifur played bat-and-chase with a spoon in the nullgee environment. Ivard seemed hugely entertained watching the big cat spring from ceiling to walls to console; the old cat was too well trained to ever come near the bed.

Montrose sat motionless for a time, then suddenly keyed in a location code. When he got his response, he sat for a few moments longer, made a minute adjustment to the grav controls and oxygen flow into the cubicles, then keyed them to automatic control. He clipped on his beltcom, got up, and stretched.

Glancing at the chrono, he saw that it was indeed late in the artificial "day" that the crew usually followed when in fiveskip transit. He moved at a leisurely pace to the rec room, where he found two of the crew. As he reached to dial up some steaming caf, Marim turned to him, her small face sharp with expectation.

"What made Vi'ya rasty?"

Montrose paused. "What?"

"Only hear her walking when she's angry," Marim said impatiently. Then she ducked to the door, looked out, then looked back. Grinning, she added, "And when she's rasty, that tongue cuts like monothread. If she's looking for trouble, I'm gone."

"Relax, nullwit." Lokri shook his head. "That old blunge-eater in the dispensary probably wouldn't talk to her. Come, finish the game—or," he added in challenge, flicking his fingers across his keypads, "are you afraid to lose?"

Marim plopped back down on the other side of the big console, scanning the screen. Passing behind her, Montrose glanced down, saw a promising setup for Phalanx, Level Three. He glanced appraisingly at Lokri, whose attention was on his screen.

"Captain discuss her plans with you, my friend?" Montrose asked. *Or have you been doing a little spying?*

Lokri's mouth twisted. "Saw her going down to the dispensary, saw her come back. Heard her come back." he corrected, nodding at Marim. "Stalking. Unless young Firehead suddenly got a deathwish, it was either you or Jaim or the old man. Jaim licks up her spit, and I've never seen you pick a fight with any of our crew."

Montrose made a slow circuit around the room as Lokri spoke, then settled at last on one of the big padded seats along the back of the room. He set his caf down carefully, then shrugged. "Old man it was."

"About?" Marim prompted, curling her legs under her.

Lokri leaned back for a moment, long enough for Montrose to glimpse his console. He smiled.

"That metal sphere, of course," Lokri said. "What else?"

"It worth anything?" Marim asked, chin on her hand.

"You'll never find out," Lokri said. "Probably lucky, too. I've never seen those damn skull-boilers of hers so excited about anything else. She thinks it's some kind of weird psi weapon."

"Except apparently it doesn't work," Montrose said.

Neither Lokri nor Marim made any reaction to the tacit admission that Montrose had listened to the conversation inside Omilov's cubicle. Not that he'd expect them to; they knew he had the equipment to do so if he wished, and they also knew that the captain would have been aware she was being overheard. But Montrose had an entirely different question in mind, and the only way he'd get a truthful answer was by indirection.

Marim looked up suddenly; a moment later Montrose heard the sweet chiming of tiny bells that heralded Jaim's approach. The tall engineer ambled in, his long face looking tired.

"Be good to get home," he said, sinking down into a seat near Montrose. He didn't appear to see the scornful twist to Lokri's mouth at the word "home."

"Suggestion," Montrose said. "Since most of us are here."

"Huh?" Marim asked, her eyes on the game.

Lokri swung around in his chair, brows aslant.

"That loot you took from the Mandala. Some of it might well be worth more than the ship we are sitting in."

"And not all of Jakarr's chatzing pals got nabbed in his take-over try just before we lifted from Dis," Marim said cheerfully. "I already thought of that, and I sure don't plan to blab any about my share."

Jaim shook his head, his braids tinkling. "Me and Reth, we'll have enough now to get our own ship." With a sober glance at Lokri's back, he added, "Norton and us'll split *Sunflame's* crew. We can do a lot more with a fleet of three."

"Reminds me." Marim slapped her hand on the side of her console, glaring around. "Since you're all here, who nabbed Firehead's coin? It was the only thing Greywing took, and he wants it to remember her by."

Lokri's eyes narrowed. "He had it when we got him out of the palace—had it in his hand, along with that damn Panarchist flight ribbon that Markham gave him, that he's been hiding ever since. Quite a deathgrip. I put them in this pocket just before we came on board," Lokri said, hitting his chest. "Then you took him." He tipped his head toward Montrose.

"There was nothing in that pocket but dried blood when I stripped him down," Montrose said. "The rest of his suit was stuffed with things, but none of them a coin. Or a ribbon."

His eyes wandered to Marim as he finished. She nodded judiciously, saying, "We went through it all together, my last visit to him. No coin, no ribbon."

Which almost answers my question. Montrose said, "We can assume that the Eya'a did not take them. I don't think they have any interest in such stuff."

"Vi'ya would have asked whose it was," Jaim murmured.

Lokri's light eyes glinted. "Brandon was helping me get Ivard to the ship. I suppose he'd consider it reclaiming something of his own."

"But the Schoolboy was there too." Jaim put in. "Remember?" he said to Marim.

"If either of them has them, I'll find out," Marim said. "Heyo! Why don't I go tell Firehead now? Sure to give him a good—"

"He's asleep," Montrose cut in. "And he doesn't sleep well enough for an interruption. I've had to put him in null-gee for his burn. Before we get to Dis, there's something else you need to consider."

The other three looked at him, their expressions characteristic: Lokri wary, Marim interested, Jaim sober.

'We may be the only ship ever to raid the Mandala successfully. If you talk about it just once outside of Dis, eventually Eusabian will find out."

"They don't know it was the *Telvarna*," Marim scoffed. "We used the old transponder registry. Remember?"

"They have enough clues to find us through Brotherhood channels," Jaim said suddenly. "The way the Eya'a killed Eusabian's torturers—if the Dol'jharians figure it was them, remember half Rifthaven's seen them with us. And the Arkad used the comp; if they crack the system and identify him, they'll remember he disappeared around Warlock."

"So anyone who knows we're based at Dis will know he's not dead, and put him with us," Montrose said.

"So it won't be just Hreem's chatzers after us, looking for revenge," Lokri murmured, his eyes speculative.

"We could have the whole Brotherhood hunting us down." Marim sounded horrified, but not surprised. "*And* the nicks."

She's already thought this through. "The artifacts and the Arkad are not the only dangers," Montrose said.

"The old man. We came between a Dol'jharian and his target," Jaim said, looking somber. "Eusabian of Dol'jhar finds out who we are, we won't be safe anywhere."

Marim's small shoulders jerked up and down. "Jumpin' at shadows. He's got whole planets to stomp—we're too small to bother with."

"Eusabian pulled a destroyer out of his fleet just to bring Omilov to the Mandala for questioning," Montrose pointed out.

Lokri shrugged. "The way I see it, those two—three, counting Schoolboy—are Vi'ya's responsibility. She can't lock them up on Dis, we don't have any defense. She either sells them to whoever offers the most, or lets them go."

Marim's bright eyes flickered from one to the other, and she laughed. "Or they join us. I wouldn't mind; Brandon's pretty. Also not bad with the weaponry."

Lokri smiled.

Montrose finished his caf and got up to dial some more. "Join *us*?" he repeated, looking across at Marim. "With what you get from Ivard, you might be able to buy your own ship, run your own crew."

Marim shook her curly head, leaning back and cracking her knuckles. "I'll stay with Vi'ya," she said. "She's as hot a pilot as Markham was. As long as we're successful, I'm here. And then I'll hop. But I don't ever want to captain—too much trouble."

"Is the stuff worth that much?" Jaim asked. "Some of the things Lokri showed me, I never seen anything like them."

Montrose nodded slowly, got his second cup, and walked back, just as Brandon vlith-Arkad walked in.

Energy seemed to richochet around the room, manifesting itself subtly: Lokri's tightened shoulders, Jaim's unblinking gaze, and Marim's blinding smile.

Brandon did not seem to notice the alteration in focus. He

nodded a general greeting, then moved to the dispenser and chose something hot, a process which seemed to absorb his whole attention.

Montrose watched with interest as Lokri and Marim resumed their game, Jaim leaning forward to watch over Lokri's arm. Brandon turned away with his cup in his hand, then Marim said, "Shall we pull you in, Arkad? This is Level Three."

Brandon gestured. "Next game?"

He sank down into the chair next to Montrose's. The surgeon took a moment to study the young man, noticing the tight skin around his eyes. What was in his mind? The Aerenarch had exerted himself to be friendly and cooperative, had even led the *Telvarna's* crew on a raid against his old home on Arthelion. This right after he showed up on Dis seeking his old friend Markham—who was now dead.

Why had he come? Montrose was fairly certain they would never find out now.

Osri was easier to understand; he considered himself a prisoner and acted like one. Sebastian was weak, and his courtesy seemed to be bred bone-deep. Whatever his feelings about the people who had rescued him from Eusabian's torturers, Montrose was certain that the professor was no threat.

What about Brandon? He was pleasant, affable, but utterly unforthcoming.

And why did the captain ignore him as if he didn't exist? Would he try something foolhardy when they reached the base?

She'll have to make some kind of decision before we reach Dis.

Montrose set his cup down, intent on his original purpose. "Marim."

"Mmm?" She kept her eyes on her game.

"Ivard divvied up what he is saving and what he got for you?"

Her eyes were wide and humorous. "Not yet," she chirped. "There's lots of time for that." Her eyes flickered once in Brandon's direction, then back to her game.

And there's my answer to one question anyway.

Montrose stayed for a while longer, considering what it might mean, until he finished his caf. One more glance around the room. Jaim had relaxed again. A quiet man, yet with surprising depths, he was looking forward to seeing Reth Silverknife, his mate, again; they'd crew on the *Sunflame* or the *Telvarna,* whichever would reach Rifthaven first, whence they could buy their own ship.

Lokri frowned, his attention now wholly on the game. Montrose read in his body tension, the angle of his head, not just competition in the game, but another, primeval competition: Lokri valued nothing that did not carry risk, seeming incapable of attraction to anyone who did not convey a sense of danger. *And angry as he was that Markham chose Vi'ya over him, he was angrier still at Markham's death.* Had Lokri noticed how Vi'ya avoided the Arkad? Probably.

Marim sat and laughed, contributing colorful invective once in a while, her small feet curled under her rounded bottom and her riot of hair hanging in her face. Marim had hooked Ivard nicely by the heart, it seemed. And to her, everything else seemed irrelevant.

Life will be interesting when we reach Dis.

Montrose laughed to himself and moved out, pausing to send one look back. He couldn't see the consoles, but it no longer mattered. He wondered how long it would take Lokri to realize that he'd lost that game right from the start.

✻   ✻   ✻

The damaged-one-who-hears-music contemplates from distance the eye-of-the-distant-sleeper, in fear. This one's desire is to shield its pattern from Eya'a, from Vi'ya.

Is there in his pattern an image for the distant-sleeper?

There is question, there is a fear-darkness, the damaged-one-who-hears-music fears Eya'a and Vi'ya joining in his contemplation.

Is there in his pattern a connection between the eye-of-the-distant-sleeper and the distant-sleeper, as one knows the arm between fingers and body?

There is only question, and the desire to hear the connection between the eye-of-the-distant-sleeper and the distant-sleeper. And the damaged-one-who-hears-music contemplates the angry-one with the thought-coloration Vi'ya teaches us means sorrow—

We will leave his pattern, and return our attention to our contemplation of the eye-of-the-distant-sleeper before my need for sleep must be heeded . . .

FOUR

✳

TREYMONTAIGNE SYSTEM

Krajno and Rom-Sanchez were already in their pods when Ng reached the bridge. On the main viewscreen the Tenno pulsed quietly in the absence of input, vivid against skip-blanked darkness.

"Navigation."

"Emergence minus three minutes, sir. Standard approach, as you ordered."

That would put them within one light-minute of the Treymontaigne beacon in the leading trojan of the sunward giant in the system, just as at Wolakota. *A by-the-book approach.*

Krajno turned, one bushy eyebrow raised. She wasn't sure herself why she hadn't taken them directly to Treymontaigne orbit.

Not even a hunch, really. She shrugged away the thought. Krajno certainly wouldn't question her decision. *Especially when doing so would make him look overeager for his reunion.*

Not that she blamed him. Navy romances were hell on the emotions. Krajno hadn't seen Tiburon for, what was it, almost a year now. She smiled to herself. They made quite a couple.

Commander Perthes ban-Krajno, executive officer of the *Grozniy*, and Commander Tiburon nyr-Ketzaliqhon, chief engineer of His Majesty's battlecruiser *Prabhu Shiva*. Tiburon was tall, slender, the picture of Douloi elegance. More than one unlucky officer had mistaken the burly, rough-edged Krajno, when the two men were together in mufti, for the other's valet or bodyguard. It was a mistake no one made twice. The funniest part of it was that Krajno was the intellectual of the two—Tiburon's world consisted of but two things: his engines and Krajno.

She turned her attention back to the bridge at large. The crew was relaxed, upbeat, looking forward to the leave they all expected when the *Grozniy* caught up with the *Prabhu Shiva*. Although, if Eichelly had run into Harimoto's crew first, *Grozniy* would have to put up with some well-deserved gloating from the victors of that action.

As if sensing her thoughts, Rom-Sanchez turned around. "Fifty-six hours since Wolakota. Maybe twenty-six hours or so since Eichelly skipped in. By now, his pieces are likely well on their way to joining the Oort Cloud here." He grimaced. "I wish he'd picked Schadenheim."

The descending tones of emergence put an end to their conversation; then a dizzying sense of déjà vu gripped Ng as SigInt, for the second time in as many days, announced, "No beacon, sir." And then, moments later, "All sensors functional."

Ng hesitated only a fraction of a second. "Take us to yellow. Teslas to one-third, ruptors on-line, load skipmissile and hold at precharge level."

The *Prabhu Shiva* had obviously left the system before Eichelly reached it. Otherwise, the beacon would already have been replaced after Harimoto took care of the Rifters.

"SigInt. Scan for ship traces. Navigation, confirm our position."

Up on the main screen, a plot of the Treymontaigne system windowed up as Rom-Sanchez anticipated her next request. The flaring red of maximum probability centered on the nearest k-zone, twelve light-minutes away.

She tabbed her console and started a ten-minute countdown. "Communications, pop that tacponder," she added, a flare of light pinpointing it on the tactical plot as she shifted momentarily into eyes-on mode.

As Commander Krajno monitored the multiple reports flooding the bridge while the ship came up to yellow, Rom-Sanchez turned around again, smiling. "Harimoto'll be furious at missing this chance, even if he did get away from hand-wiping Treymontaigne."

The tactical plot rippled as Navigation confirmed their position, and Ng's answer died unspoken when Ensign Wychyrski at SigInt reported moments later, "I've got a large object about ten light-minutes in, relative velocity about five hundred kps." She stopped, worked her console for a moment. When she continued, her voice revealed puzzlement. "The readings are confusing. I'm getting a thermal reading at the million-degree level, and some gravitational disturbances as well." That was the unmistakable signature of a shipwreck, resulting from destabilized spin reactors and drives.

Then they did catch up with Eichelly. But why hasn't the beacon ... ? Ng's thoughts splintered as Wychyrski's next words destroyed that hypothesis.

"But I read its mass at about ten-power-twelve tons," SigInt continued. "There's an awful lot of debris—thermal scattering—around it too."

Way too big for a destroyer. Ng looked at Rom-Sanchez, who shrugged and shook his head. "No ideas here, Captain."

And not quite big enough to be a battlecruiser. A startling thought. No battlecruiser had ever been lost in action against Rifters. Whatever it was, it couldn't be that. Perhaps Eichelly had run into an asteroid fleeing the *Prabhu Shiva*, as unlikely as that was.

"Give me a visual. Maximum enhancement. Navigation, bring us about for maximum array effectiveness."

At this distance, the optical array formed by the sensors on the *Grozniy*'s hull could resolve details down to less than twenty meters, as long as the ship was oriented correctly.

The tactical plot dwindled into a corner of the screen as the starfield began to slew in response to her order. The screen blinked and a blur of light slid into view, gradually sharpening as the ship's motion ceased. Then the enhancers cut in and all sound on the bridge ceased.

Ng felt her ears ring with shock.

Mercilessly clear, the details hardly concealed by the limits of resolution, the shattered hulk of a battlecruiser blazed silently.

One third of its length was gone, torn away by some unimaginable force; in its shattered interior a blue-white glare pulsed, emitting sheets and sprays of fluorescing gas as the dying engines yielded up their energies into space. As the hulk rotated, the distance-blurred form of Shiva Nataraja came slowly into view, his lower body obliterated, his four arms still upraised in the eternal dance of creation and destruction.

Ng started at a sudden crunching noise nearby. She looked around in confusion for a moment, then saw blood dripping unnoticed from Commander Krajno's hand, clenched around the ruins of one of his pod's arms. His face, seen in profile, was calm, only a ridge of muscle around his mouth betraying his emotions. She tabbed a key to summon a medic and took a deep breath, letting it out slowly before issuing her next orders.

"General quarters. Teslas to full power, charge skipmissile. SigInt, maintain scan for ship traces. Rig for immediate random tactical skip on detection of any ship." She glanced up at the screen. One of the glyphs indicated less than twenty seconds until the returning squirt from the tacponder reached them.

"Communications, execute a scan of planetary and High-dwelling communication frequencies. Navigation, as soon as Communications receives the squirt from that tacponder, take us in to one light-second. SigInt, on emergence scan for life-signs, full noetic enhancement."

The hoarse summons of the klaxon seemed to breathe life into the bridge, but Ng could see hesitation in the movements of the crew. She tabbed her console and signaled the environmental officer to bias the tianqi toward stress relief and cut the subsonics. They needed no additional cues to key them up.

The klaxon fell silent, leaving behind a haze of tension and rage which seemed to thicken as the seconds dragged on. The horror slid out of sight as Navigation brought the ship around for the next skip. Then the communications console bleeped.

"Tacponder responding . . . monitoring was engaged." Ensign Ammant's fingers tapped hesitantly at the keypads; there was a faint squeal from his console as the discriminators shifted into search mode. Moments later the fiveskip engaged with a brief subsonic burp. Then silence fell again.

"Tacponder recorded four skip-pulses in succession, then a fairly large EM burst and particle shower at about minus twenty-five-point-six hours. At that point the nav beacon ceased radiating and there were two more skip-pulses. Then an interrogation at minus twenty-four-point-nine hours. Eleven-point-seven minutes later there was a gravitational disturbance consonant with tractor activity. Ten seconds after that a skip-pulse, followed by skip noise—most likely a skipmissile—then a very large burst of EM and gravitational radiation, followed by a particle shower. Then two more skip-pulses."

"Tactical?" Ng was pretty sure what that recording meant; she also knew that each of the crew needed the distraction of their duties. *And what will I distract myself with?* She pushed away the thought.

Rom-Sanchez didn't reply for a moment; he was staring at the blank screen. Then he shook his head. "Pretty straightforward, as I see it. Probably two ships, but only one hung around after it blasted the nav beacon. The pair of pulses after the nav beacon ceased radiating were most likely skip and local emergence. Judging from the timing of the interrogation, the *Shiva* responded only minutes after the signal stopped at Treymontaigne. Then a tractor attack, SOP against a frigate, and then—"

He stopped as the screen flickered and the disintegrating hulk of the *Prabhu Shiva* sprang into full clarity. At this distance the resolution was on the order of centimeters. The image expanded, giving Ng the dizzying feeling that she was falling into the hellish pit of energy that burned at the heart of the shattered battlecruiser. The broken edges of the hull were strangely smooth: there was no spalling, no twisted petals of hull alloy. That was the unmistakable signature of the impact of something moving so fast that nothing in fourspace could propagate a shock wave.

There's something wrong with that skipmissile impact. The memory returned even as SigInt's voice confirmed her judgment. "Debris analysis consonant with superluminal impact." There was a pause, long only in her perception, before Ensign Wychyrski continued, her voice rigidly controlled. "Noetic scan negative. No survivors."

"Captain, you'd better hear this." Ammant sounded sick.

At Ng's nod, he tabbed a key on his console. A thin, mewling shriek filled the bridge, overlaid with the raucous laughter of a mob and broken by the static that the enhancers couldn't eliminate. The sound clenched at her throat and she motioned savagely for Ammant to cut it off.

"Rifters, in the Archonic Enclave," he continued, his voice tight. "I've managed to extract an image too. It's the Archon." He choked. "O Telos—" He bent away from his console and was rackingly ill.

The medic straightened up from bandaging Krajno's hand and moved over to the stricken ensign.

"Skip-pulse, Captain," SigInt said. "Two light-minutes out. No ID, signature was corvette-class."

Somebody watching, on their way to report.

"Tactical skip, now!" Ng held her breath as the fiveskip burred momentarily. "Navigation, take us a light-hour up from the ecliptic."

As the fiveskip engaged again, a sudden, horrible suspicion seized her. *In the Enclave?* She turned to Wychyrski. "SigInt. What else did that scan reveal? What is the state of the Treymontaigne defenses?"

Ensign Wychyrski tapped quickly at her keypads, accessing the data on Ammant's console, but Ng could see her hands shaking. Then she looked up at Ng, her dark eyes widening. "The planetary shield isn't up. They've surrendered!"

That was the only way a transmission from the planet's surface could have reached them—the interference of a planetary tesla field would have swamped the signal. This was not a typical Rifter incursion.

Ng damped down the swirl of speculation that threatened to overwhelm her. Nothing made any sense, but first priority was the safety of her ship, and then more information.

She turned to Krajno. "Commander, prepare to deploy a VSA, with whatever resources it will take to see what happened here. Relay the proper coordinates to Navigation."

"Captain!" Krajno's expostulation seemed torn out of him. "They don't know we're here yet—can't for fifty minutes or so. And at least part of the crew is downside. We've got the advantage. Let's use it."

With her peripheral vision Ng noted the focus of the entire bridge, but she kept her gaze on Commander Krajno. "Harimoto no doubt thought he, too, had the advantage, Commander Krajno." She saw her formality strike home. "Kindly execute your orders. You may post a formal objection in the log if you so desire."

Krajno gave his head a slight shake: Ng knew he was back in control of himself.

"And consider this," she went on to the bridge at large. "The Rifters have somehow compelled Treymontaigne to drop its shield and are evidently occupying it. That is not SOP for Rifters, and I want to know more before we go in all projectors blazing. I assure you," she continued, as much for the commander as for the bridge, "we will not leave this system without dealing with them."

A flurry of motion resumed as the crew hastened back to their tasks.

I'll have to keep them all busy, not just Perthes. But he was well taken care of now: deploying a virtual sensor array capable of resolving useful details at a distance of over a light-day would involve some or all of the *Grozniy*'s corvettes, each linked to the ship via laser to create a sensor array hundreds of kilometers across. Calculating the proper size of such an array was a trade-off between resolution and signal-to-noise ratio— just the sort of careful planning that she judged Krajno needed right now.

"Communications."

The medic stepped away from Ammant, a sprayjac in her hand; the ensign's expression was apologetic as he got back into his pod.

"Continue monitoring the planetary and Highdwelling frequencies. Record and discriminate." She saw gratitude in his face as he began tapping at his console again. "SigInt," she continued, "at Wolakota you reported something strange about the skipmissile impact we witnessed. I'd like to see your report now."

As Ng continued issuing commands, she could sense the bridge slowly returning to normal.

Too little to go on, so far, she thought, and frowned at the memory of the Archon's screams, knowing she'd have to view the record eventually. *But not now. First we watch the death of* Prabhu Shiva *and plan our response.* One thing was certain: when they faced Eichelly in the inner system, there would be no mercy.

"Lieutenant." Rom-Sanchez looked up at her. "I want every bit of tactical information we can squeeze out of that array. Consult with Commander Krajno and make sure it's set to grab whatever you need."

The rear hatch opened to admit a swabbie with a mop and whispered closed behind the medic as she departed, reminding Ng of one more responsibility. One of the first lessons of command was that the truth was easier to deal with than rumor. She brought her finger down decisively on the ship-com, and the traditional twitter of the pipes filled the air, alerting every station in the ninety-two cubic kilometers of the *Grozniy* and carrying her voice to every one of the five thousand men and women aboard.

"This is the captain—"

❋   ❋   ❋

"Deployment complete." Krajno's voice was flat. "Twelve Raven-class corvettes with 150-meter arrays, in a one-thousand-kilometer virtual array." He paused. "Laser links established, tractors engaged. Stabilization will take about a minute."

Ng calculated briefly. That would give them better than fifty-meter optical resolution, and even better at higher frequencies. It would be enough.

"I specified an hour ahead of the action," said Rom-Sanchez. "Commander Krajno and I agree that we can't afford to miss any tactical preparation on Eichelly's part, and a light-hour's loss of resolution won't make enough difference to matter."

Ng nodded. That had been her conclusion too.

"I want the optical portion—wide view—of the action piped into General Access," she said.

The viewscreen wavered as the array came on-line; a small targeting cross blinked near the center, marking the position of the navigational beacon.

"I have a ship trace, battlecruiser signature, bearing 96.7 mark 2, plus 26.1 light-hours. No ID." Another positioning cross appeared near the first; the trace was nearly between them and the beacon, normal to its position from the ecliptic as was standard naval practice.

"That'd be the *Prabhu Shiva*," Rom-Sanchez commented. "Watching the destruction of the beacon from fifty minutes out."

"Harimoto was good," Commander Krajno said. "By the book."

The unspoken question occupied them all: so how had a good, by-the-book captain of a cruiser been annihilated by a Rifter destroyer?

A few minutes later a reddish spark of light bloomed as the battlecruiser skipped. Since its position was a light-hour closer to the *Grozniy* than where the *Prabhu Shiva* had been destroyed, they were seeing the battlecruiser's actions out of order: before they saw the arrival of the ships it was attacking.

For several minutes after that, nothing happened; the tension on the bridge grew. Ng distracted herself for a short time by reviewing SigInt's report on the skipmissile attack at Wolakota; but through no fault of Ensign Wychyrski it was basically an expansion of the term "insufficient data" and didn't hold her attention for long.

Finally a small red pulse of light bloomed near the beacon. Rom-Sanchez' hand twitched, overlaying it with another cross. The Tenno rippled as data began to build up.

"Signature indicates an Alpha-class, but we're too far out for an ID," reported SigInt.

Nothing more happened for several minutes; then another emergence pulse blossomed some distance from the first. A few seconds later the first ship skipped again. Then the second ship skipped again, to within a few thousand kilometers of the beacon.

"The second ship reads as a frigate, possibly a Scorpion. No ID. No emergence detected for the destroyer."

The Tenno glyphs flickered uncertainly, blinking through a series of impossible configurations, then settling into a simpler readout. Ng rubbed her eyes.

"Confirm that, Tactical. Distance between the ships on emergence? And time to second skip?"

"The second ship emerged two-point-five light-minutes from the first. The first skipped eleven-point-two seconds after that." Rom-Sanchez looked up at her in consternation. "That doesn't make any sense."

At that distance, and in that brief time, no communication could have passed between the ships.

"Coincidence," said Krajno, looking up from his fierce concentration on his console. "They rendezvoused outside the system."

But why did the first one wait, then?

"That may be, but their actions still make no sense," insisted Rom-Sanchez. "And where'd that destroyer go?"

There was no way to answer that question except wait and see, Ng knew. Even if the destroyer had stayed near the system, unless it emerged within a very narrow spacetime window, they wouldn't see it.

A fierce spark of light bloomed on the screen and faded. The faint background chirping of the beacon ceased. The frigate skipped again, emerging in the nearest sunward k-zone about twelve light-minutes from the beacon's position.

"Now we wait," said Krajno. "So far it looks like another SOP beacon-bashing."

"But why'd they leave the frigate to watch, rather than the Alpha?" The tactical officer's tone was almost querulous, as if he resented the apparent irrationality of what they had witnessed so far.

Ng tuned out their discussion, content that the two had found a way to distract themselves during the next fifty minutes or so while they waited for the next appearance of the *Prabhu Shiva*. The rest of the bridge crew were intent on their duties, so she permitted her mind to wander.

What would Nelson have made of this situation? She thought of his long pursuit of Napoleon's fleet in the Mediterranean, and the later search for Villeneuve before Trafalgar. She felt a flicker of amusement at the irony: that an admiral from the age of wooden ships would probably understand her frustration much better than more modern navies, accustomed as they had been to realtime communications.

Still, what would he have made of relativistic tactics, where the order of events depends on where you watch them from? Of being able to watch an action a day after it happened? Or of being able to skip out of a battle, watch your enemy's tactics again from a different angle, free of battle pressure, then return to the fray with a new plan? Or using the fiveskip to attack the same ship from three different positions simultaneously?

The time passed swiftly as she lost herself in a pleasant fantasy of conversation with the admiral, showing him her ship.

Forty minutes later SigInt reported the emergence of the *Prabhu Shiva* ten light-minutes out from the position of the frigate hiding in the k-zone. The big ship skipped again almost immediately. Since the battlecruiser was between them and the site of the eventual battle, they were still seeing its activities out of sequence.

"Long-ranging." Rom-Sanchez' voice now indicated gathering stress. "And the target's making it easy—it isn't even drunk-walking.

For the next ten minutes there were no human sounds on the bridge, save for the background murmur of status reports flowing into the various consoles.

Finally the reddish spark of an emergence glowed near the position of the frigate.

"He's less than a light-second from the target," reported Tactical.

"Faint, steady-state gravitational activity," said SigInt.

"Tractors. He's got them."

Less than ten seconds later, another emergence pulse bloomed near the battlecruiser and its victim.

"Emergence, eight light-seconds out. Alpha-class."

Moments later a thin thread of light, visible only as a computer artifact, speared from the destroyer to the battlecruiser. A flare of light grew slowly from the position of the *Prabhu Shiva*, faded, was gone.

"Continue recording," snapped Ng. "Give me a close-in replay of that last."

The stars fled outward as the image zoomed in. Now the familiar egg-shape of a battlecruiser appeared, grainy and shimmering with processing artifacts as the computers struggled to create an image across a 28-billion-kilometer gulf. From off screen the chain-of-pearls wake of a skipmissile smote the ship, converting its stern almost instantly to a flaring inferno. Slowly, now turning end over end, the hulk passed out of their field of view.

On the periphery of the screen the Tenno pulsed wildly, their inbuilt structure unable to deal with the apparent violation of relativistic tactics implied by the deadly action just witnessed.

"One shot." Ng's throat ached. "From an Alpha."

Rom-Sanchez turned to her. "That's not the only thing. The Alpha seemed to know exactly where Harimoto was."

"A courier, or message pod?" That was the only possibility that Ng could think of.

Rom-Sanchez gestured at the Tenno glyphs, which still hadn't settled down. "No. There was no sign of that. And the *Shiva* wouldn't have let them launch any such."

"SigInt?"

"Captain, we would have detected the skip-pulse of even a drone. And there was no indication of such in the tacponder record." She paused. "The spectrum of that skipmissile impact is similar to the one we recorded at Wolakota."

"Rifters generally don't use drones," Commander Krajno added. "They're too expensive."

"I'm purging the tactical computers and storing the recent action. They can't deal with it." The tactical officer tapped at his console and the Tenno lapsed into quiescence.

Ng drummed her fingers on one of the pod arms. She knew what she had seen was impossible, in more than one way. Alphas didn't carry that kind of power. And those two ships had twice acted as though they were in communication, even though both times they were outside of each other's spacetime cone. She glanced up at the screen again, where the death agony of the *Prabhu Shiva* was being replayed. The tactical officer was stabbing angrily at his console, his actions echoed by Ensign Wychyrski at SigInt as the two tried to make sense of the data gathered.

"Commander, we're finished with the array. Recall the corvettes." She tapped her com key.

"Engineering, Ensign Leukady," came the response.

"Have Commander Totokili report to the plot room."

"AyKay, Captain."

She tapped the com key again.

"Armory. Navaz here."

"Lieutenant Commander Navaz, please report to the plot room."

"AyKay, Captain."

She stood up. "Tactical, dispatch a reconnaissance patrol to Treymontaigne space. I want to know just what we're up against, ASAP. Then join the commander and me in the plot room when you have finished. Navigation, you have the con."

As Krajno followed her off the bridge, she tried to blink away the grittiness in her eyes. There would be no rest for any of them until they had comprehended the reality behind the recent action. And she was beginning to feel that reality was something that would change all their lives beyond calculation.

FIVE

✳

DESRIEN

Eloatri smiled at the children seated in front of her in the dusty courtyard. The day, past its peak and drawing toward evening, was hot but not oppressive; the shade of the huge *higari* tree that shaded the way-hostel was refreshingly cool, but its vinegar/vanilla scent made her nose itch. From the hostel came the quiet hum of the conditioners, cooling the interior, and the faint bleeping of a data console.

The children were quiet. Some were standing, most seated; many of these had imitated her posture, assuming the ancient lotus position with the effortless flexibility of youth. They ranged widely in age: some as young as seven years, others she judged nearing adulthood. In some the spirit glowed white-hot, in others, like banked coals—and a few, she judged, would leave Desrien when their majority came, unable to tolerate the soul-mirroring airs of the planet.

She began to speak. "Desrien and all its beliefs and faiths rest in the Hand of Telos, which has five fingers." Her hands moved in the pattern of the mudras, adapted from her own tradition, that were part of the language of the Magisterium. "These principles enfold us all, but there are many ways to speak and hear and live them. I will share mine with those of you who wish."

Some of the children leaned forward, eager to hear; others listened politely, with the respect they had been taught was due a Phanist, the highest rank in the Magisterium. At the back of the group she noted a small, redheaded boy, with the pale, blotched skin of an atavism. He watched her intensely, his gaze hungry with an indefinable longing. She smiled at him and continued.

"We all encounter the numinous, a message from something that is beyond all measurement and knowledge." Her left hand was poised beside her at eye level, palm-up as if supporting a water jar; her right touched the top of her head, the center of her forehead, and the center of her chest in a fluid movement.

"We all possess some fragment of whatever sends these messages, however we may conceive it." Both her hands came together vertically before her eyes, cupped around a space, and then descended to her chest.

"We all live a story which has no ending we can see or understand." Now she brought both her hands together before her, thumbs and middle fingers touching in a circle parallel to the ground. She transformed the circle into the ancient symbol of infinity by bringing the fingers and thumbs together, then rotated her right hand until its palm faced outward, thumb to finger and finger to thumb, and folded her hands together, circle to circle. The symbol of the projective plane, true infinity.

At the back of the group of children, the redheaded boy's eyes were still on her but his hands were busy with something she couldn't see, hidden behind the heads of those seated in front of him.

"We all suffer because we are attached to things that really don't matter." Here she used one of the most ancient of the mudras, Turning the Wheel of the Law.

The red-haired boy began tossing the object in the air rhythmically; it was a small silver ball. The setting sun sparked highlights off of it, small splashes of glory dappling the deepening shade of the tree overarching the courtyard. A wave of dizziness and disorientation overwhelmed Eloatri and she fell out of the world into the Dreamtime.

The path was dull gray, wide and edgeless, suspended in an infinite space. A golden light shone from behind her. She turned

*and beheld the face of the Buddha at the beginning of the path,
inhumanly calm and indwelling with transhuman compassion,
its lips curved in a smile terrible with possibilities.*

*The Buddha's eyes opened. She shriveled under his gaze. His
mouth opened on a soundless resonance as the Word resounded
throughout the Wheel of Time and a slow procession of figures
came forth, all dressed in the finery of the High Douloi. Among
them she saw the tall figure of the High Phanist, his face
enshadowed in his cowl. There was the sound of weeping, and
a blow against her heart.*

Eloatri opened her eyes, staring without comprehension for a
moment at the field of purple and yellow that slowly resolved
into the dense canopy of the higari tree. Through its branches
she saw the faint glimmer of a star.

An anxious face bent over her, an elderly man with a green
band around his forehead: a healer.

"Are you returned, bodhisattva?"

She levered herself up on one elbow, feeling light-headed,
and looked around. Most of the children were gone; a few still
stood at some distance, looking worried. A small group of
adults stood to one side, less worry in their faces than respectful
waiting.

"Yes." She sat up as the dizziness passed. The redheaded boy
was not among the remaining children, and somehow this felt
like a loss to her. His spirit had glowed brighter than his hair.

"The redheaded boy," she said. "With the pale skin. Where is
he?"

The healer hesitated, puzzlement on his face.

"The one who was standing at the back of the group, playing
with a silver ball."

The healer sighed, apparently considering his words, before
replying. 'There is no redheaded boy in this village."

❈   ❈   ❈

FIVESPACE: ARTHELION TO DIS

Osri Omilov opened the door to the cabin—and found it empty.
Palming the inside lock, he made straight for one of the light-

insets over the console and pried the cover up with his nail. Inside, snugly set, were two objects: one, a bloodstained silk ribbon; the other was the warm silver shape of the Lost Earth Tetradrachm.

He sank down onto his bunk and examined them both. The date on the piloting ribbon was 955, ten years ago. He knew who had won the medal. He'd stood there at the award ceremony when it was pinned on Markham vlith-L'Ranja, just months before the swift, terrible events that saw Markham cashiered and Brandon nyr-Arkad removed from the Academy, supposedly for the unauthorized use of atmospheric craft in wargames over the southern continent. Markham had disappeared; his father, the Archon of Lusor, had committed suicide; Osri's own father had retired from active service.

Osri had long ago come to terms with these events, believing them unrelated: he had heard the rumors that the Aerenarch Semion vlith-Arkad had been behind the arrest of his own brother and the L'Ranja heir, which had prompted him to believe there was some real, dishonorable reason behind the official one.

What galled Osri was his having recently found out that his father's retirement had been a direct result of Lusor's suicide—and that his own father, the most loyal man Osri had ever known, had considered the Aerenarch Semion culpable in all these events.

Osri crushed the silk in his hand. He remembered the boy Ivard being carried aboard the *Telvarna* after the Rifters had raided the palace on Arthelion, his arms dangling over Montrose's massive shoulder, and the two objects falling from a pocket onto the deck.

Osri suspected that Markham might have given the boy the flight ribbon, for whatever reason; the coin, though, had been looted from the Ivory chamber, an act of violation that made him furious.

Osri turned the worn, uneven coin over on his palm. On the one side was a bird; on the other the figure resembled a woman in archaic dress. A trace of some kind of script, completely untranslatable, remained here and there. Rubbing his fingers over the warm metal of the coin, he thought about the unknown hands who had made and possessed it unimaginable millennia before, under the light of Sol.

Handling the Tetradrachm gave Osri a sense of peace, a sense of *order*. And Telos knew there was little enough order in the rest of his life.

A sound outside the door made him close his fingers protectively over it. Someone tried to open the door.

Osri jammed both objects into place and slapped the light cover back on. Then he hit the lock and retreated to his bunk, scowling.

"I was preparing to sleep—" he began as the door opened.

Lounging in the doorway was the rakish, gray-eyed comtech. "On your feet, nick," Lokri drawled. "Let's see what you can do with a jac in your hands."

"I don't—"

"Now." Lokri stepped toward Osri, his smile tight with challenge. Osri's heart hammered. *These people are Rifters, and they follow no law but their own whim.*

Saying nothing, he followed Lokri out of the cabin. His suspicion subsided slightly when he saw Brandon arrive at the rec room from the other direction, led by the somber-faced Serapisti Jaim. Though he was still angry enough with the Aerenarch to avoid him whenever possible, now he felt a measure of safety in his presence. *If they were going to kill him, they'd make a show of it.*

Marim, who was waiting, punched the console. The tables became obstructions as the four walls vanished, replaced by an excellent simulacrum of a grimy street flanked by warehouses. From over the buildings on one side the blue-white glare of a booster lift-off briefly illuminated the street; Osri could feel the crackling roar through his feet. The simulation was good but not perfect—Osri's ears still reported that he was in a small room.

Marim thrust a simulator-jac into Osri's hand. "Let's see if you're any good."

A figure in a garish uniform strolled out from a darkened doorway in the sim and squinted at them. It was a tall man, perhaps forty years old, with a sallow olive complexion and dark hair and brows. His bones were wide and strong under their layer of flesh, his expression ugly.

Osri recognized him as the man Tanri had shown them on the main screen of the defense room in Merryn—*Hreem the Faithless.*

"Markham's killer." Did he hear the whisper? In the reflected light of the simulation Osri saw Brandon's face betray grief, then the Aerenarch turned away, fingering the jac in his hand.

Osri remembered suddenly the quotation Brandon had made, that day in Merryn: *"—and a pyre will I make of my enemy's works."* The Sanctus Gabriel had acted at a nexus in history where justice and vengeance came together. For the first time doubt assailed Osri: could they lay claim to the same justification?

"Handsome little chatzer, ain't he?" Lokri laughed.

"What's that on his boots?" Osri asked. "The metal things."

"Heel-claws," replied Lokri.

"Looks like they're only useful if your opponent is lying down," Brandon commented, his face blank again.

"That's Hreem's character in a quantum."

"Hreem *chatch n'far*," Marim cursed, making an obscene gesture at Hreem's face before she snapped her fingers and triggered the action. "Go, Lokri!"

Hreem whipped out his gun and fired just as Lokri crouched and shot. Then, seconds, later, evil-faced assassins appeared on rooftops, beside the decrepit buildings, or ran from doorway to doorway, firing frequently. Lokri ducked and whirled, trying to zap the phantoms before they fired on him. This went on for fifteen minutes or so, then the figures disappeared and Marim hit the console.

"Not bad!" She peered at the readout. "Burned twice, three wounds, zapped seventy-three percent of 'em."

Lokri made a noise of disgust as he and Marim switched places. The little Rifter was fast on her feet, but reckless: she ran out of "ammo" in the middle of a firefight. From the chaffing she took, this was not unexpected.

Jaim was next. As one would expect from a master of the Ulanshu Path, he was very fast and very accurate. Marim clapped, and Lokri watched with that speculative air. Then, with a self-deprecating gesture, Jaim gave way for Brandon to take his place.

Brandon ranked about the same as Lokri; his aim was better but he made the same sort of tactical errors that Osri then made in his turn—errors which, Osri reflected bitterly as Marim crowed about their poor scores, were to be expected from people who did not make violence their way of life.

Brandon sat on the edge of a console, smiling across the

room at Marim. "You have to remember," he said, "we're trained to try everything short of jacs to resolve differences."

"You've noticed," Lokri retorted in exactly the same tone, "that the Dol'jharians do not make the ballroom floor their battleground."

"So there was a purpose to this?" Brandon pointed at the console with the jac still in his hand.

Jaim was studying his hands, his long dark braids swinging close to his face.

"Practice," Marim said. "We better be ready when we face Hreem next."

Osri said, "I take it you expect us to be a part of this quarrel?" As all faces, Rifter and Aerenarch, swung his way, he hated how tight and angry his own voice sounded.

"Might not be a choice," Lokri said, his voice mild but his eyes reflecting some of Osri's own anger.

"Does your captain practice with you?" Brandon asked.

"Group actions, she does," Marim said with a grin. "On Dis. We sometimes play for days. On *Telvarna* she runs alone."

"She was a dead shot long before she joined up with us," Jaim put in, looking up at them. "Had to be."

"Come on, let's try the group run," Marim suggested, and punched the console.

Brandon stepped obediently to the middle of the room, so Osri did as well. The three Rifters moved apart in a well-trained unit as a score of villains appeared. Osri saw Brandon fall behind, and he took up a position to his left, vaguely recalling a long-ago lesson about this from his Academy days. *When we were trained, there was little expectation we would ever use such knowledge,* he thought, and then there was no time for thought.

Osri did his best, trying to watch and learn; when the program ended and the walls flickered back to normal, he was surprised by a mild sense of regret.

Lokri punched up drinks; Marim put a hand on Osri's and Brandon's shoulders and shoved them toward seats. At first inclined to resist, Osri saw Brandon sit back with an air of compliance. Warily he stayed where he was, thinking: *Perhaps he expects to hear something of import.*

Lokri handed out the drinks. Brandon wiped damp hair off his brow and raised his glass. "The dead salute you."

Lokri grinned. "We'll do another tomorrow. If ya want to stay alive, you're going to need some work."

"How do you keep track of Hreem?" the Aerenarch asked.

"Brotherhood maintains a pipeline on the DataNet, like any other organization—the Infonetics blits don't care," replied Lokri, "so long as the fees get paid."

"Lot of merchants and even Service types subscribe to the RiftNet, 'cause the info's so good," added Marim.

Osri leaned back in his seat, considering yet another dissonance between his assumptions and reality. This was what his father had been talking about once: that no one on Arthelion seemed to realize just how much a part of the Thousand Suns the Rifter overculture was, despite its lack of any official recognition. *They're all over the Thousand Suns*, he'd said, *and not being planet-centered like Downsiders and even Highdwellers, they've got a different perspective on things.* Until Osri ended the subject by referring to lawlessness.

"So that means Hreem can use the same sources to gather information on his enemies? Like you, for example?" Brandon went on.

"Yep." Marim wiped her sleeve across her mouth. "But Hreem's made a lot of enemies, and some of 'em disappear when he's looking for info."

"He can't even get near Rifthaven anymore," said Lokri, "since some of his gang shot up Varli's Refit Emporium a couple of years back. Only the fact he wasn't there himself—and paid the wergild with the heads of the ones who did it—saved him from all the Syndicates going after him."

"And anyway, we have Vi'ya." Jaim waved a long hand in the direction of the bridge.

Osri saw a brief exchange of glances between the Serapisti and Lokri. Brief, and completely uninterpretable.

"You mean her tempathic abilities?" Brandon asked.

"Nah." Marim's nose wrinkled. "That doesn't do her much good out here—strictly up-close stuff. *She* says she merely uses the info to project patterns, and makes plans from there, but she's a hot one at strategy and tactics."

Lokri finished off his drink and lounged to the door. "My watch now." And he strolled out.

Brandon said, "Did Vi'ya ask you to run us?"

Jaim shook his head, his braid-chimes tinkling.

Marim said, "Was our idea. You, Arkad, are pretty quick on the fly—we saw that back on the Mandala. But Schoolboy—" She shrugged.

Brandon was watching the silent drivetech while Marim spoke. Osri glanced over, saw Jaim studying his hands again: What was going on?

Brandon said, "I know Hreem killed Markham, but Vi'ya said he was betrayed. By whom?"

Jaim looked up quickly.

"Chatzing triple cross," Marim said. "I still don't know the whole story—I was on the other base when it happened—but you can ask Vi'ya. If she'll talk, which isn't often. Or you could ask Lokri. He wasn't there, but he knows all about it."

Brandon's eyes were still on Jaim. "Maybe I should cultivate your captain," he said. "I notice she's not unfamiliar with the Ulanshu kinesics. When does she practice?"

"Only with me," Jaim said. "She masses a lot—their bones are thicker than ours, and she's strong."

Marim shivered theatrically. "Don't spar with her—she'll break your arm without even trying. Jaim's the only one can manage with her."

" 'Their'?" Osri asked.

No one answered him; Marim stretched, then wandered over to dial something more to drink. Jaim got to his feet and walked out.

After a moment, Brandon also rose. Osri followed him out, and then said again, "Their?"

Brandon looked back, his eyes absent. "Dol'jharians," he said.

❋   ❋   ❋

Sebastian Omilov shifted position, trying without success to ease the discomfort of being wedged into a small fold-down seat in the galley. Montrose had given him tacit permission to wander where he willed on the ship, the only caveat being that he must return if he felt any symptoms of his angina.

Almost the moment he had taken his first steps outside the sick bay he'd met Osri hovering in a corridor. Looking continually this way and that, his son had brought him here. Silent until they were closed in, Osri then said, "I don't think Montrose will overhear us—he usually does his spying from here." He pointed to the console. "Father, the captain of this vessel is a Dol'jharian, and the Aerenarch knows it."

"So do I," Omilov murmured, and saw shock on his son's face. "I recognized her accent. Brandon probably did too; he had to spend a great deal of time with Eusabian's son Anaris, remember."

"I remember," Osri said in a flat voice.

"I have not discussed this with Brandon," Omilov said, his hand idly moving over Montrose's console keypad. "In fact, I've seen little of him, and those visits have only been in the presence of the doctor."

The imputation was oblique, but Osri's cheeks showed a ridge of color. "I confronted him," he admitted. "Demanded he do something—or let me lead." Osri looked up, his face earnest. "I can't forget he was abandoning his family—and everything we believe in—to join these very Rifters before the Dol'jharian attack even happened."

Thus making it impossible for him to speak alone to me, and unlikely he will confide in anyone now.

"He avoids me," Osri went on. "When I sleep he stays in the rec room and drinks. When I work, he plays with the computer in our cabin, or plays Phalanx with those Rifters."

"As good a way as any to find out information, that last."

Osri raised a hand in a tired gesture. "If I could be certain—if I could trust him." Omilov was about to speak, but Osri shook his head. "If you're about to defend him, spare your breath, Father."

To turn the subject, Omilov idly hit a series of keys on the console at his elbow, and at the display that came up on the screen, he sat back and grunted in surprise.

"That's a physician's cachet, isn't it?" Osri asked.

"And bears the seal of Timberwell," Omilov pointed out. "Certified as a neurosurgeon." He touched another pad, and another cachet appeared, this claiming that the bearer was a graduate of the Apanaush Gastronomie on Golgol. As in the physician's cachet, the name of the recipient had been blanked out.

"A surgeon and a chef," Omilov mused. "Montrose is a remarkable man. I do know he has a collection of opera chips, and he is one of the few people I have ever met who knows the game chess, though of course we have yet to play."

Osri grimaced. "Timberwell," he said with distaste.

Another symptom of the rot beneath the glory. Timberwell had expelled its Archon—Srivashti, he thought the name was—and instituted a popular reign of terror, earning a Class Two quarantine in the process.

"There can't be too many ex-Timberwell aristocrats with those qualifications," continued Osri, "for his accent and mode of speech identify him as coming from the Ranks of Service. My mother would know ... she would also know if there was some sort of scandal—" Osri stopped, shook his head wryly. "But you've always hated gossip, haven't you?"

Omilov cleared the screen with care, considering several things he might say. His son had, inadvertently perhaps, cut him off effectively from Brandon; he did not want to lose Osri as well.

But Osri went on. "Do you think this woman being Dol'-jharian endangers us the more?"

He does not want to lose me, either.

Omilov shifted again, fighting against the increased strain in his chest. "I do not believe her allegiance is to Dol'jhar," he said. "It's clear enough she's an exile, and from what I know of that planet, no one gets off without tremendous determination and effort. However, she is still Dol'jharian; my worry now is not so much what she will do with us, but what she might do with the Heart of Kronos."

Osri's face eased from anger to reflection.

Omilov confided further. "It's thought to be some kind of key to an Urian device of unprecedented power. We know no more than this. I am afraid that she might be able to find out how to use it."

"The Eya'a ..." Osri said, wincing. "They knew we had it when we crash-landed on their asteroid. First thing she did was take it away from me—" He frowned. "And Brandon just sat by."

"What should he have done?" Omilov asked.

Osri shook his head. "I don't know. But why is her being a Dol'jharian worse than her being one of these lawless Rifters?"

"Don't you remember Anaris? Not later, when he'd learned something of restraint from the Panarch, but when he first came to us?"

"You said that before," Osri said sourly. "But you seem to

forget—or maybe you didn't notice—that Brandon, and Galen, before he was sent off to school, did their best to make sure I scarcely saw him. I think I exchanged a sum total of five words with Anaris during all my visits to the Mandala."

Omilov leaned back tiredly, his mind ranging back through the years to a memory: Galen, a tall and weedy teen, with a smashed wrist in a cast, and Brandon, younger and smaller, lying in quarter-gee with a broken collarbone.

Don't tell Father, Galen said. *He'll send him back, and it will wreck the treaty.*

We all learned something, Brandon added, his laughter wheezing. *We learned that he's as strong as a Tikeris—*

Weighs as much, too, Galen put in humorously.

And he learned, or will, that to be civilized you have to know how to laugh. We're going to make sure he learns how to laugh.

Galen's sleepy smile had turned uncharacteristically grim. *Threatening to kill people every time you see them strains the conversation.*

Not to mention trying to carry it out, Brandon had added.

Omilov heard himself saying, *But this sounds serious. Please release me from the bond of silence; I really think I ought to speak to your father.*

Both of the Panarch's younger sons had shaken their heads. *We've said enough, and he'll get adult tutors in manners. What we'll teach him is a sense of humor,* Galen had promised. *From a distance.*

But if he goes for you whenever you're alone—

So we make sure that he never catches us alone, Brandon had promised.

Omilov looked up at his son. "With Dol'jharians, every confrontation becomes a contest of power. The captain seems civilized, but try not to make her angry." He hesitated, thinking of Vi'ya's straight body, its contours hidden beneath the anonymous dark cloth of the jumpsuit made tight to throat, wrists, and boot-tops. "And if you do succeed in enraging her . . ." He sighed, echoing Brandon's words of long ago, "Don't let her get you alone."

Six

*

TREYMONTAIGNE SYSTEM

"Enough!"

Captain Ng's voice brought silence to the plot room.

Commanders Krajno and Totokili sat back, radiating tension. A viewscreen displayed the frozen image of the action between the *Talon of God* and the *Prabhu Shiva* that had occasioned their disagreement.

Lieutenant Commander Navaz, the armorer of the *Grozniy*, exchanged a pained glance with Rom-Sanchez.

Rifters with FTL communications? Rom-Sanchez thrust the thought from his mind—he did not want to deal with the implications, especially with Eichelly's stomach-turning excesses on Treymontaigne so recently viewed.

So he turned back to the captain.

"Commander Totokili, your objections are noted," Ng said calmly. "Unless you can explain the action we witnessed without reference to superluminal communication, that is the assumption we will be working on."

Commander Krajno nodded in agreement. Now Rom-Sanchez was certain that Ng had let the argument go on as long as she had in part just to give Krajno an outlet for his emotions. There would be no time for authentic grief over the death of his mate, no time for the grief all of them felt at the loss of the *Prabhu Shiva*, until the killers had been dealt with.

"AyKay, Captain." Totokili stared at the viewscreen with a sour look. His jaw worked, as if he were chewing on something unpalatable.

Accepting that their Rifter foe was armed with some unprecedented ability to communicate faster than light without a five-skip—some sort of superluminal EM analog—was difficult for all of them, but especially for one whose entire education and experience was grounded in the science of energetics.

Ng turned to Rom-Sanchez. "We'll need to reprogram the Tenno as quickly as possible. Who's your best semiotician?"

Anticipating this request, he'd already run a search through the ship's personnel records. He tapped his compad, and two names appeared. He looked up at the captain.

"Ordinarily I'd say Lieutenant Methuen, but ship's records turned up something interesting. Ensign Warrigal got her doctorate in tactical semiotics with a thesis on first-order relativistic semantics in Tenno structures—it was quite unconventional and cost her some rank-points." He smiled. "After what we've seen, she'll be able to rub some noses in it at the Academy if she wants."

Ng raised an eyebrow, then nodded. "Get her up here." She turned back to Totokili.

Hearing the urgency in Ng's voice, Rom-Sanchez reached reflexively for his boswell, then stopped. It wasn't an emergency, and so didn't justify breaching Warrigal's privacy that way. He keyed his compad instead and then turned his attention back to the discussion.

※   ※   ※

Ensign Warrigal yanked down the hem of her tunic and tried once more to blink the sleep out of her eyes as she tabbed open the plot-room hatch.

The other officers in the room looked up, and Commander Totokili paused in speech.

Warrigal scanned them, noting the body tension of controlled anger in all of the officers present. *What has happened?* "Ensign Warrigal reporting as ordered, sir."

The captain acknowledged her and motioned the chief engineer to continue.

". . . so we can rebalance the ship's power distribution to give the shields all they will take, and make them faster to respond, although against that power level there's no guarantee that will do any good."

The com beeped and Ng slapped the accept pad.

"Wychyrski reporting. The reconnaissance results are in; I can give you the first pass of the discriminators."

"Do so." Ng looked back at Totokili, who continued as a faint twittering from the com indicated incoming data.

"But what should we sacrifice? Maneuverability or weapons?" he said. "I'd recommend sacrificing weapons power—the conformation of a destroyer makes it unlikely that they've been able to strengthen their shields much. In fact, I'd almost guarantee that the only weapons improvement they've got is the skipmissile. Other weapons systems just can't be boosted like that, but the skipmissile is limited by discharge rate, which they may have found a way around."

Ng remained silent for a time.

Rom-Sanchez caught Warrigal's eye and tapped his boswell, offering a private communication. She tapped acceptance. *(Do you know what's happened?)* he asked.

She shook her head. *(Z-watch.)*

(Prabhu Shiva. Look at this,) he replied, and tabbed a key. The viewscreen switched from an energetics graph to the grainy image of a long-range scan. The ensuing action, and the Tenno glyphs accompanying it, told the whole story.

Warrigal sat stiffly until it was done. Strong emotions burned away the last of sleep-need from her mind: first shock, then anger, fear, and sorrow at the loss of life on *Prabhu Shiva*.

Then the implications of what she had seen penetrated her consciousness, and excitement supplanted all. *(Superluminal communications!)* She looked away from the viewscreen to see Rom-Sanchez grimace, bringing home to her how hard it must be for a tactician to accept that. But now she knew why she'd been summoned to the plotroom.

Warrigal looked up to find Captain Ng watching her.

"Ensign Warrigal, I'm told you got your doctorate with a rather unconventional thesis," Ng said. "How does that relate to what we've seen here?"

Warrigal brought her thoughts to the problem at hand, finding balance in the subject she knew best. "I was investigating the assumptions behind the Tenno programming, sir. As I suspected, since they are so old, and based on the ideographic languages of Lost Earth, their inventors still thought in Newtonian terms, so that the relativistic linkages in the Tenno are for the most part first-order only."

Totokili made a gesture of impatience, so she hurried on. "As part of my proof I constructed a nonrelativistic semantics for the Tenno; the proctors criticized the result as interesting but not useful."

Now Warrigal permitted herself a smile as she noted the amusement in Ng's eyes. "That thesis is in the ship's records as part of my personal bank. However, even with that part of the work done, the integration of new semiotics into the Tenno is not something that can be done quickly. But," she added, sensing tension from the senior officers, "Lieutenant Rom-Sanchez and I can add the new symbolism and strip out the relativistic linkages where appropriate. Tracing all of the changes as they propagate through the Tenno glyphs, which are basically a semiotic computational system, is something else again."

"Speed is of prime importance right now," Ng said neutrally. "What is your recommendation?"

"I would recommend that you schedule us all for as much time in the simulator as possible before we go into action—as much for the benefit of the Tenno as for our own familiarity with the new glyphs."

"Excellent suggestion," Ng said. "The Rifters already know we're out here. There's no point in trying for a surprise attack."

She turned to Lieutenant Rom-Sanchez, who had uploaded the reconnaissance data and displayed it on the viewscreen. "What's the tactical situation?"

The young man, who had been watching the captain throughout, answered promptly. "The resonance field is down, and so far they've got a destroyer and a frigate in high Treymontaigne orbit—probably responsible for that atrocity at the Enclave. The reconnaissance shows nothing else, but the discriminators on the comscan you ordered imply perhaps three other Alphas and two or three more frigates in-system, plus some small stuff."

"Another ambush," Rom-Sanchez said, his eyes once more straying toward the captain. "Not much imagination, there."

"That's not surprising," Navaz put in.

"Rifters." Krajno's comment was almost a snarl.

"No," said Navaz. "What I mean is that they're not likely to have had FTL communications very long. How long do you suppose the Brotherhood could keep a secret like that? So they're not likely yet to fully understand its tactical implications."

"I concur," Ng said. "We'll use that against them." She looked around the room. "There's got to be more tactical imagination in this plotroom than in that whole Rifter squadron." She paused momentarily. "For a start, I'd conjecture that they're probably watching the standard naval emergence points, ten light-minutes normal to Treymontaigne, hoping to signal ahead to those targets they've left in high orbit."

"Then we'll avoid those points like the Thismian Thunder-Bloat," Totokili cracked.

"On the contrary," Ng said, grinning, "we'll do exactly what they expect us to—that is, the *Grosniy* will. What our corvettes will be doing is something else again."

The com beeped. "Ensign Ammant, Captain. The second pass of the discriminators turned up something I think you need to know. It's apparently part of a communication between the two ships in high orbit."

"Put it on."

The com crackled to life. ". . . don't care what you think. If you break position I'll hunt you down and pull your guts out through your nose—or better yet, send you to the Avatar. You won't like how he treats the chatzers who run out on his orders."

The com fell silent. The older officers' reactions to the name "Avatar" made stress grab at Warrigal's neck muscles.

Rom-Sanchez caught Warrigal's gaze and tapped his boswell again, offering a privacy. When she accepted she heard *(Avatar?)*.

"Dol'jhar." Ng's pronunciation was precise, and the ugly sound resonated in the quiet of the plot room. "It would appear that Eusabian of Dol'jhar has found a way around the treaty."

Warrigal felt a sense of unreality brush her mind. She'd been just a child during the Dol'jharian War; what little she'd heard then had given her nightmares that she still remembered. Now she was living it in reality; just a light-hour away burned the funeral pyre of five thousand new victims of Dol'jhar's barbarity.

". . . of a Shiidran brood-fouler." Krajno's curses died to a mutter.

"Thank you, Ensign." Ng tabbed off the com and looked around at each of the officers around the table. "This time we'll finish it."

Warrigal felt cold inside. The Dol'jharians were famous for their savagery, but she doubted that any of them could match the quiet, confident ferocity of that simple statement—a ferocity she could see echoed in the faces of the two commanders, the only others in the room who had experienced the first war against Dol'jhar.

There was silence for a time.

Then Ng seemed to shake off the memories that had gripped her. "Lieutenant Commander Navaz. We'll need a large quantity of antiship weapons for dispersal by the corvettes and even cutters, as well as heavier devices that we'll discharge. Do you concur?"

"Yes, sir." Navaz' voice was soft, almost hesitant. Rom-Sanchez didn't know her well, but sensed she was less comfortable with people than with her cims, the machines that created expendable weapons as needed, making a battlecruiser largely independent of its base. "My sense of the tactical situation is that we'd be best tooling up a large number of gee-mines and leeches, since I assume you'll be trying to lure them into cislunar space for the first phase of battle."

Ng smiled agreement. "Correct. How long?"

"That's all standard ordnance: we have a large inventory already. The cims won't require more than about half a day for any reasonable number more."

"Good. Then here's how we'll begin."

Swiftly she outlined the tasks she expected of her officers. Rom-Sanchez made notes of his own and watched appreciatively as she dealt with the others. If he ever made it to post rank, he knew who his model would be; in his opinion, there was none better.

Finally Ng stood. "Thank you, genz. Dismissed."

"Drones' reconnaissance complete and uploaded," reported SigInt.

The tactical screen rippled as the god's-eye view of the system adjusted, the Tenno flickering into a new, unfamiliar configuration.

Feels like I'm back in the Academy again, trying to learn the Tenno, Ng thought. The new, nonrelativistic glyphs Warrigal and Rom-Sanchez had devised were still strange, despite the intensive practice in the simulator. From the corner of her vision she noted Ensign Warrigal at a console reconfigured to tactical support, watching as the tactical data flooded in.

As she had surmised, the Rifters had posted sentry ships to watch both the standard emergence points ten light-minutes normal to Treymontaigne. Now they had only a minute or so before the Rifters detected the skip-pulses of the drones and the ships that had launched them. Even with the information from the drones, they couldn't be sure of emerging within range of any of the targets, since any competent captain, Rifter or not, would be flea-hopping to avoid just that.

"Launch corvette squadrons."

Commander Krajno tabbed his console, announcing moments later, "Corvettes away."

On the viewscreen Ng saw two of the squadrons—two corvettes each—come into view as they left the bays of the *Grozniy,* their radiants flaring. She smiled, admiring their lean beauty; adapted for atmospheric flight, the fairings and swept-back thorns of their weapons pods lent them the aspect of predatory sea creatures, sleek and deadly. Then they vanished in red bursts of light as they leapt out of fourspace toward Treymontaigne.

In her mind's eye, she saw them as they would be shortly, emerging and scattering their crop of dragon's teeth in cis-lunar space before vanishing back into fivespace. Tacponders to monitor the action, gee-mines to cripple fiveskips, and leeches—sneak-missiles armed with shaped charges—to stab through shields and hull metal with fingers of nuclear flame. With any luck, the targets in high orbit would already be crippled when the *Grozniy* emerged after its apparently standard approach. And if not, the dragon's teeth would be waiting for any enemy who emerged in cis-lunar space during the ensuing battle.

Ng's fingers, poised over her console, tingled as battle-readiness gripped her.

"Ruptor turrets ready, skipmissile charged," said Krajno.

"Very well. Take us in," she said.

"Ten light-minutes out and over Treymontaigne," announced the navigator when the fiveskip disengaged.

"Targets bearing 144 mark 32, plus 13 light-seconds, frigate; 186 mark 61, plus 80 light-seconds, destroyer, Alpha!" shouted Hjivarno at Fire Control, her voice overriding the emergence bells. The bridge trembled faintly as the ruptor turrets bearing on the targets discharged a spread barrage. They were unlikely to connect, but the discharge didn't cost them much, and if the targets followed the tactical rule of staying close to avoid losing contact, they might run into the spread.

"Target the first and shoot skipmissile," said Ng, keeping her voice calm. Telos was with them: against all odds they'd emerged—barely—within range. It was too good an opportunity to pass up.

The starfield on the screen slewed as the ship came about. Then the reddish chain wake of the skipmissile filled the image and faded. "Skipmissile charging," Hjivarno sang out.

"... eight, seven, six, five ..." The navigator counted down the thirteen seconds since emergence, by the end of which they had to skip to avoid being targeted by a destroyer in FTL contact with the closest target.

"Tactical skip executed," said Lieutenant Mzinga.

"Targets bearing 145 mark 32, plus 15 light-seconds, frigate; 187 mark 61, plus 83 light-seconds, destroyer." A few seconds later: "Hit! Target destroyed!"

The viewscreen flickered to a closer view, revealing a sharp-edged sphere of plasma with the intricate internal structure characteristic of an exploding ship.

"If they were in FTL contact, the others know we're here now," Rom-Sanchez commented as the crew cheered. Ng let them; the release of anger would calm them for the more difficult action ahead.

"But not where," Ng responded. "Better and better." She glanced at the tactical countdown indicating the status of the corvette squadrons assigned to cis-lunar space. It reached zero as she watched.

"Commander, take us to Treymontaigne."

Krajno tabbed his console. "Fiveskip to tac-level five. Engaging." The burr of the fiveskip was harsh, almost teeth-aching. With a lower frequency, they would emerge near Treymontaigne at a tremendous real velocity—they needed every advantage they could grasp against the Rifters' superior communications. *Which is like internal lines of command.*

"Cis-lunar Treymontaigne, planetary plus 100,000 kilometers, estimated velocity on emergence 25,000 kps." Ng fought a reflexive shiver: close to a tenth cee within planetary space was a risk in itself, even without an enemy. But they would be headed through the ecliptic, and their retuned shields would count for something, if they encountered any ship or solid object unlucky enough to be in their path.

"Emergence."

"Major targets bearing 13 mark 62, plus 95,000 kilometers, destroyer; 349 mark 279, plus 115,000 kilometers, frigate; minor targets . . ."

The voice of Fire Control faded from her mind as Ng concentrated on the Tenno.

"Negative on major targets," she snapped. They were too close to the Highdwellings, and the destroyer would be between them and the planet, making it impossibly dangerous to use a skipmissile on it—a miss would kill a billion-plus people on the planet. "Ruptors shoot on minor targets three, four, seven at will. Pulse the dragon's teeth for reorientation on major targets." Fire Control's console keened as the EM pulse retargeted the various weapons, sown by the corvettes on their first pass, against the destroyer and frigate they were passing up.

The bridge shuddered gently as the ruptors discharged. Bright coins of light marked the results moments later.

"Destroyer's coming about. Coincident in three seconds, two, one . . ." SigInt chanted.

"Tactical skip, now."

The fiveskip burped.

"Take us out for the second run."

"Some tacponder pulses received. Emergence pulse, one of ours, signal incoming."

The next thirty minutes remained a blur in Ng's mind afterward, even after she reviewed the auto-log the bridge computers had recorded. The Rifters were better than any of them had expected, using the vulnerability of the planet and the Highdwellings to protect themselves against the heavy weapons of the *Grozniy*. But she knew it was only by giving the Rifters that advantage that she could hold them to the battle.

Gradually the various dragon's teeth accounted for some of the enemy, but her crew paid a high cost as well. It was on their third run through cis-lunar space that the highest price was paid.

✳   ✳   ✳

Warrigal's console beeped at her. The Tenno response was ragged: some unanticipated second- and third-order semantic obligations had surfaced. She fought them back into stability, conferring rapidly with Rom-Sanchez via boswell to avoid adding to the confusion on the bridge.

The activity on the bridge had reached a frantic level as tactical information flooded in, with varying degrees of timeliness. The *Grozniy* was still untouched, but the fear of a smashing blow from one of the Rifter destroyers' apparently unstoppable skipmissiles hung over all of them, intensifying as the action wore on. Only the dogged harassment of the corvettes had preserved them thus far, but those were slowly being scattered by individual duels, and time was running out.

But through it all Margot O'Reilly Ng's voice never wavered, never rose above the quiet level of authority it always possessed. The only sign of stress that Warrigal could see was in her posture—leaning forward slightly, her shoulders tensed slightly—and in the sheen of sweat on her forehead.

"On emergence come about and target the destroyer . . ."

The *Grozniy* shuddered out of skip; stars skewed across the screen, stopped.

"Coming about. Five, four, three . . ." Mzinga's voice was ragged and hoarse.

"Skipmissile away. Skipmissile charging."

"Tactical skip, five light-seconds, now."

Their skip took them in toward their target. Seconds after emergence, a gout of light signaled success. "Hit! Scratch one Alpha."

Warrigal felt a tingle of delight; as the Tenno probabilities had indicated, that target had felt the sting of a gee-mine: its fiveskip dead, it had been unable to leap to safety.

"That leaves two more," Krajno growled. "Don't get happy just yet."

On the viewscreen Warrigal could see one of the *Grozniy*'s corvettes—the *Hevtana*—engaged with some small craft she didn't recognize. The Rifter jinked toward the planet—his fiveskip, too, had evidently fallen prey to the sharp gravitational pulse of one of Navaz' gee-mines.

"Emergence, Alpha-class, bearing 68 mark 22, plus 80,000 kilometers, vectoring on Raven *Hevtana*."

"Fire bearing ruptors. Target skipmissile and fire on acquisition."

The starfield slewed rapidly. A targeting cross swung into view. The red-pulse of a skipmissile arrowed away even as a skip-pulse bloomed where the enemy had been.

"Ruptors missed. Skipmissile missed. Target emergence, bearing 79 mark 45, plus 0.9 light-seconds, vectoring on Raven *Hevtana*."

"Fire bearing ruptors, target skip . . ."

A giant hand gripped Warrigal and squeezed. She felt her ribs creak; her ears rang. At the next station, Ensign Noyetra screamed as a gout of flame erupted from his console and washed over his upper body. The bridge tilted as the gravitors hiccuped and the lights went out, coming back in the red of emergency power. A galaxy of trouble lights illuminated the bridge from practically every console.

"Skipmissile impact, aft beta ruptor turret not reporting, skip-missile aborted, aft beta bay not reporting, engine two destabilized."

"Emergence pulse, 267 mark 183, plus 1.5 light-seconds, Alpha-class, skipmissile charging, estimate seven seconds to discharge . . ."

Totokili did it, the shields held! But Warrigal knew they couldn't handle another shot like that.

Ng vaulted back into her pod from the deck where the impact had sent her sprawling. "Damage Control, aft ruptor status."

"Alpha and gamma still on-line. Insufficient power for more than one turret at this time." The shields had drawn so much power that the reactors were slow to come back to full-load status.

Ng didn't hesitate, and Warrigal realized that even in the midst of confusion and disaster the captain had a clear image of the geometry of the battle. "Aft gamma ruptor, fire on acquisition, full power."

The viewscreen flickered to a close-up view of the deadly wasp-shape of a destroyer, foreshortened by its vector directly at them. Three seconds later it disintegrated, the missile tube spinning away end over end as the rest of the ship flared into a coin of brilliant light.

The viewscreen flickered back to the other destroyer, now nearly vectored on the *Hevtana*. Horror seized Warrigal as the Tenno revealed the situation: the corvette's battle had taken it into radius, between the planet and the destroyer. Its radiants flared as its geeplane accelerated it toward radius, where it could safely engage its fiveskip, and Warrigal scanned the glyphs, looking for a loophole. There was none. The corvette would reach radius exactly as the destroyer fired. At that point, if the corvette skipped to safety, out of the path of the skipmissile, the near-lightspeed plasma would impact Treymontaigne, killing most of the planet's population as the shock wave propagated through the atmosphere like a wall of steel.

"For'rd alpha turret, fire on that destroyer."

"For'rd turret not powered, seven seconds to ready status." said Fire Control, her voice hopeless. There were less than four seconds left.

Silence fell on the bridge as the corvette came about, abandoning its smaller enemy to face its executioner.

"Signal incoming, *Hevtana*."

Without waiting for acknowledgment, the com officer windowed up the signal, revealing the sweaty face of Lieutenant Methuen. Warrigal started; she hadn't known he'd volunteered for corvette duty. She wasn't surprised—he was a rare combination of semiotic knowledge and tactical expertise. But the fog of battle had betrayed him. Sorrow gripped her as she saw the knowledge of death on his face.

Then he smiled. "Raise a glass for us at the wake, we'll toast you back from Murphy's Hall."

Warrigal saw sudden understanding in Ng's face.

The captain saluted wordlessly, then Methuen turned away and spoke a single word. "Engage."

The window blinked out as the corvette vanished in a burst of bluish light and simultaneously the destroyer exploded in a glaring burst of radiation that blanked out the viewscreen for a long moment. Warrigal gasped. The *Hevtana* had become a missile, skipping into its enemy, taking it with it in a sparkling rosette of plasma which faded slowly to reveal the uncaring stars above the blue-white limb of a planet reprieved from death.

A long silence followed. Then the captain spoke quietly, bringing them back to the aftermath of battle.

"Stand down to yellow. Damage Control, report. Medical, report casualties . . ."

Warrigal let out her breath as Ng's voice continued, still calm, still quiet. With the last destroyer dispatched, there was nothing left in the Treymontaigne system to threaten them. Now they owed the living and the dying their duties; then they would discharge their obligations to the dead.

". . . and the Void shall yield up its dead, from light to light transformed, journeying in the company of the Light-bearer to the fullness of Telos at the end of Time."

On the viewscreen the hulk of the *Prabhu Shiva* still blazed, its nuclear fires little diminished by the day that had passed. Ng turned to Commander Krajno, resplendent in his dress uniform.

"Commander." She gestured toward Fire Control, the only console operating.

Krajno stared at the viewscreen for a long beat, then spoke in a quiet voice: "Fire."

Lieutenant Rom-Sanchez pressed a key, and the reddish pulse-wake of a skipmissile speared out, transforming the shattered battlecruiser into a glory of light that slowly faded from view, furnishing the final catharsis for their memories of lost comrades.

"The Light-bearer receive them," said Ng.

As the crew filed off the bridge, replaced by the new watch, Ng sighed. The news from Treymontaigne was bad, if what the Rifters had told their victims during their brief occupation was true. She wondered how many of the crew realized that their anguish was just beginning.

Seven

✻

ARTHELION

As the lock of the shuttle hissed open, the familiar sight and scent of the palace grounds caught at Anaris rahal'Jerrodi's throat with a complex of emotions that his Dol'jharian side forced him to repress. But something must have shown in his demeanor, for Morrighon, his new Bori secretary, looked up sidelong at him.

Filthy scuttler, Anaris thought, glaring down at Morrighon, and the Bori flinched away.

Anaris lengthened his strides as they entered the approaches to the Palace Minor, where he had grown up as a hostage, and whence his father now ruled the Thousand Suns. He could hear Morrighon's breath rasping in his throat as the pale, soft Bori struggled to match his pace. The Bori's lumpy body looked ridiculous in an ill-fitting tunic, the gray of service personnel; around his waist was clipped not one but three communicators. *And I thought, useful as he was, that there was no creature more loathsome than Barrodagh.* But the flow of information from Barrodagh had fallen off when his father's paliach succeeded; and now, just as he was summoned downside to

Arthelion, he'd been assigned this creature. *A spy for my father, of course.*

The meeting will be interesting, at the very least. His father had the advantage of established power, Anaris had the advantage of being the last heir—he was not expendable.

He felt a touch at his elbow. "The Avatar awaits you this way." Anaris suppressed a wince. Truly, his father, or Barrodagh, must have looked long to find such an unwholesome slug. Morrighon's voice had a resonance reminiscent of the mindripper, an insinuating whine that turned everything he said into a complaint against the universe at large.

But he has reason to complain. The Bori was short, dumpy, with an asymmetric, pockmarked face and squinty eyes so well hidden by the puffy flesh around them that he could never be sure just what the man was looking at. Anaris wondered how Morrighon had escaped culling.

Their boots echoed on the marble floor, two steps from Morrighon to every one of Anaris', as they entered the Palace Minor. Their Tarkan escort led the Bori and Anaris through a series of doors and down a long corridor lined with the busts of former Panarchs and Kyriarchs, set in alcoves. Amusement flared in Anaris again as he realized that their route had been designed to take them through the antechamber to the Phoenix Hall, despite the fact that it was out of the way. *My father's touch, part of purging the Panarchist poison.* As they passed the bust of the Faceless One he wondered what the Avatar had made of that refined symbol of Panarchist revenge.

As they left the antechamber, something shimmered silently across their path and melted into the opposite wall. The leading Tarkan grunted and jerked his weapon up.

"Ni-Dolchu karra bi-stest j'cha!" exclaimed another of their escorts—"Dol-forsaken lurking demon-spawn"—in tones that combined superstitious fear and long-suffering acceptance of a condition that couldn't be helped.

Controlling his own reaction, Anaris continued on his way, forcing the Tarkans to scramble to keep ahead of him. He'd recognized immediately what that flicker was. Old resentments sent blood surging to his head, but puzzlement was equally strong: what had reactivated the Krysarch's trick?

A flicker of amusement dispelled his anger. *Brandon is dead, and the best his shade can contrive is a computer-generated haunting.* He laughed sardonically, which caught the Tarkans by surprise. They slowed and turned to look at him with fearful respect. Acting on impulse, Anaris smiled at them and rapped his hand on the wall from which the haunt had emerged. *"Kanimichh duuni ni-pelanj marhh,"* he said: The shade of my enemy holds no power over me.

One of the Tarkans blanched as they turned their gaze forward again; the rank-inflection Anaris had used for the word "enemy" made it obvious to whom he referred. Coming so soon after their passage through the Antechamber of the Panarchs, the effect was all he could have wished. Beside him he noted Morrighon silently watching, apparently unaffected by the haunting. *Does he see what I'm doing?* More important, what would he report? The Bori's ugly face gave no hint of his thoughts.

Finally their escort halted before a set of tall, carven doors guarded by another pair of Tarkans. The guards grasped the door handles and the doors swung open, releasing a waft of cool air against Anaris' face. Inside, the marble flooring gave way to a soft, high-napped carpet in burgundy and subtle greens, with dark wood paneling below a high, white ceiling. Anaris recognized the room as one that the Panarch had often used to receive minor officials, or to speak *in petto* with those he did not wish to expose to the glaring publicity of court. Near the windows, against a rich backdrop of drapery whose heavy folds admitted only a sliver of bright daylight against the mellow light within, a tall chair framed the straight-backed figure of the Avatar.

Near him, in smaller chairs set before a small table, sat others. First was the Avatar's secretary Barrodagh, whom Anaris had not seen for a very long time: their communications had been through labyrinthine channels. The Bori's short, slight figure seemed thinner than ever, his pale skin stretched over his bones as if tension had been his only companion for far too long. Barrodagh glanced up at him, his dark eyes betraying no recognition, though he nodded respectfully.

Anaris turned his attention to the others gathered there. Kyvernat Juvaszt, and two other men who Anaris at first didn't recognize. Then, as he approached his father, he realized that one of them was Lysanter, the Urian specialist. The other, a fat young man with a florid complexion and the demeanor of a technician, was unknown to him.

He stopped before his father and, after an appropriate pause, bowed to him. Eusabian acknowledged him with a nod, and he took a seat across from the table, on the other side of his father. Morrighon sat next to him.

There was silence for a time. Juvaszt sat as if carved from stone. Anaris wondered if the kyvernat's presence was related to the unexplained action in orbit less than a week ago, when the *Fist of Dol'jhar* had apparently pursued something escaping into space, destroying the Node in the process. Juvaszt had been summoned downside immediately thereafter, and no one else would tell him what had happened; this was the first time Anaris had seen the captain since.

Barrodagh's eyes ferreted back and forth between Anaris and the Avatar, and Anaris knew without looking that his secretary's were doing the same. He stifled a sudden snort of amusement at the thought, remembering Morrighon's squinty stare. *No one can tell where he's looking—definitely a survival trait on Dol'-jhar.*

Finally a subtle signal from the Avatar brought Barrodagh to his feet.

"All major centers of Panarchist resistance have fallen," the Bori said. "Our forces have begun the next phase of occupation, dealing with secondary centers, while administrators have been dispatched from Dol'jhar to the octant capitals. Operating through the Syndics of Rifthaven, we have encouraged raids by nonallied Rifters to confuse the strategic picture, with excellent results."

The Bori's words confirmed Anaris' hopes: taken with Morrighon's appearance, his inclusion in this meeting was an unmistakable signal from his father that their inevitable duel for the succession was beginning. In the normal course of affairs it would take years, but they were no longer on Dol'jhar. *Whether he realizes it or not, the Panarchy is far more dangerous and subtle than Jhar D'ocha. There is much room for error.*

He felt a frisson of challenge as he realized that applied fully as much to him as to his father; then returned his attention to the Bori's report.

". . . so there is nothing standing between us and complete control of the Thousand Suns."

"Nothing except Ares, and the Fleet," Juvaszt said in a flat voice, with a glance at Eusabian.

"They can do nothing against the power of the Suneater, even without the full power we can expect once we have the Heart of Kronos," Barrodagh stated.

Heart of Kronos? Anaris knew of the Suneater, but what was this, and what did it have to do with the power of the ancient weapons of the Ur? He glanced over at Morrighon and was gratified, and a bit surprised, to see him industriously taking notes on his compad, keying them to a sonic record of the meeting. *Perhaps he will be of some use, after all.*

"Tell that to Eichelly." The lines in Juvaszt's scarred face deepened to a sneer. "There is at least one Panarchist captain who knows, as I do, that no weapon, however powerful, can compensate for tactical stupidity."

Barrodagh flushed with anger. "Is that how you explain the escape of the Krysarch Brandon nyr-Arkad three days ago? For a lesson in tactical stupidity, you might tell us why the *Fist of Dol'jhar* was unable to stop a ship less than one hundred meters long with no weapons even worth mentioning?" The Bori glared triumphantly at Juvaszt.

The news brought Anaris a strange mélange of delight and anger. Delight at the thwarting of his father's will; anger that that fool of an Arkad was alive, and free. But the symmetry of the situation appealed to his aesthetic sense. *My father is free, and I imprisoned; while Brandon's father is imprisoned, and he is free.*

Morrighon leaned over and held up his compad for Anaris to read. Now he knew how the haunt had been reactivated. *He looted the palace, stole an important prisoner, in effect wrecked the Node, and thumbed his ear at the* Fist. *The Avatar's wrath must have been impressive.* He looked over at Juvaszt with new respect—he must be even better than Anaris had assumed, for his father to have spared him after such a spectacular failure. But most of his surprise was that Brandon could achieve any of that and live.

Juvaszt remained impassive, while the Avatar watched with a strange glint in his eyes that Anaris could not interpret. "If you mean the Aerenarch Brandon vlith-Arkad," the kyvernat replied, emphasizing the correct title and inheritance sur-prefix, "I was ordered to intercept too late."

The fat technician yanked his finger away from an in-depth exploration of his nose and jerked upright. "It wasn't my fault. Serach Barrodagh's secretary wouldn't listen to me, and the palace computer misled me when I tried to reach him in person to report the Arkad's presence."

Barrodagh glared at the technician. *Bad move*, thought Anaris. *Now you've made an enemy.* The fat youth was evidently the top computer technician in his father's entourage, but that might not be enough to save him from Barrodagh's hatred. Anaris knew the Bori would not forgive this attack—as he would interpret it—in front of the Avatar. But the technician probably didn't even realize what he had just done—that type rarely understood human interactions. *Perhaps I should protect him; he might be useful.*

"You might report on your progress in expunging the . . ." Barrodagh hesitated, searching for a neutral word.

"Apparition," Morrighon whined, his countenance respectful. At the same time he held up his compad for Anaris to see: FERRASIN, HEAD COMPUTER TECHNICIAN, confirming Anaris' guess. He put the pad back in his lap and dropped his gaze to it, while Anaris looked at him thoughtfully.

Barrodagh glared at Ferrasin. "Well?"

The Avatar just then made a slight movement. Anaris looked up and their eyes met. Anaris suddenly realized that the glint in the Avatar's eyes was humor, of a sort his father had never evidenced on Dol'jhar. The trace of amusement was still there as Eusabian's eyes rested momentarily on Morrighon, inviting Anaris to share his amusement, and Anaris permitted a faint response to reach his face before he turned his attention back to the computer tech, whose florid features were now shiny with sweat as his lips struggled to form a reply.

"Why can't you just cut out the circuits responsible for the apparition and get this under control?" Barrodagh demanded. "Just yesterday, because of your incompetence and delay in dealing with this, two of the Tarkans posted in the Ivory Antechamber shot each other when the apparition suddenly appeared between them."

But Barrodagh had gone too far. By making his accusation so specific, within the realm of the other man's profession, he'd given him an out, and Ferrasin leapt at the chance.

"C-c-c-c-ut out the circuits?" The tech's voice squeaked with nervousness as he forced his way past a painful stammer, but the sarcasm came through clearly nonetheless. "Do you think the palace computer is like your communicator, a little chip on a substrate? This system is almost a thousand years old, distributed across thousands—perhaps millions—of nodes throughout the Mandala, or even the planet, self-maintaining . . ." He paused, swallowed as a strange expression crossed his face and his voice dropped to a tone of almost superstitious awe. ". . . almost self-aware."

Anaris listened carefully, trying to ignore the tech's irritating stammer. He could sense, behind the tech's words, a faint fear that the apparitions were more than just computer artifacts—or perhaps that was just Ferrasin's Panarchist terror of trespassing the Ban. But certainly the majority of Dol'jharians in the palace would interpret the specters as supernatural, no matter what explanations were offered.

That could make the haunting an integral part of Anaris' campaign, if he could understand its powers and limitations. *And I am the only one here who's had any experience with it— who is really sure what it is.*

"So find the node with the ghost in it and cut it out!" Barrodagh now had a tic occupying his right eye, and it fluttered furiously as the Bori apparently realized his error in using the word "ghost." The Avatar frowned, and Juvaszt's face lost a little of its impassivity.

"Of course, serach Barrodagh," said Ferrasin with snarling courtesy, his anger expunging his caution along with his stutter. "As well tell your surgeon, 'Find that neuron with the memory of getting caught with my *tuszpi* in my hand and cut it out so I don't have to suffer the embarrassment of remembering it.' " The tech's use of the Dol'jharian diminutive for penis—and the reference to masturbation, an abomination to Dol'jharians—was a deliberate affront; Anaris hoped that Ferrasin wouldn't go too far, for he could only do so much to protect him against Barrodagh.

But then the Avatar snorted with amusement, accelerating Barrodagh's tic and emboldening the tech. "No information in this system has any location, as we understand it, any more than memory has a location in your brain. The secrets of a millennium of Arkadic rule are here, and if we go about snipping and cutting to expunge a basically harmless holographic projection, we could lose it all. As it is, we're trying to remove the projectors from critical areas, as in here, but the computer keeps regrowing them—and that ability most definitely cannot be destroyed without crashing the whole system."

"Enough," said the Avatar. "We will endure the apparitions, as long as you continue to extract information from the computer. When the information ceases, destroy the system."

Ferrasin bowed and sat back, sweat dripping from his untidy hair. Barrodagh looked around for a moment, then turned his attention back to Juvaszt. His tic subsided slightly; apparently he hoped to overcome his setback by attacking a different victim.

"When we were interrupted, Kyvernat, you were explaining about tactics," the Bori said silkily. "Perhaps you would favor us with an explanation of why you fear the Panarchist Fleet, despite our command of the Suneater?"

Anaris saw that Barrodagh was trying to place Juvaszt in opposition to the Avatar by forcing him to, in effect, denigrate the power of the Suneater, and thus, by association, the potency of the Avatar's paliach. But Juvaszt had the courage of his convictions and accepted the challenge.

"Certainly. Eichelly is a perfect example, one I fear we will see more of, despite my best efforts. Eichelly did well enough from ambush, against an unsuspecting foe, but putting him up against a real tactician was like expecting *arrachi* to defeat a *chuqath* in the game pits. We can force our Rifter allies to fight, with the threat of disconnection from the Suneater to enforce our will, but we cannot make them good fighters. Unless we find and destroy Ares, the Panarchists will eventually rally against us. In my opinion, this is even more important than finding the Heart of Kronos."

As was proper, Juvaszt did not look at the Avatar as he spoke, but Anaris could tell that the man was watching his father nonetheless. A well-developed peripheral vision was a necessity in the Dol'jharian circles of power.

Eusabian frowned very slightly, emboldening Barrodagh to reply: "The Avatar has spoken clearly on this matter. The recovery of the Heart of Kronos is our primary goal. The estate of the gnostor Omilov and the university on Charvann are now being dismantled piece by piece. Unfortunately that idiot Tallis Y'Marmor shot Omilov's majordomo when he refused to cooperate, so we do not even know if Omilov actually received the Heart—the other servants could tell us nothing, even under a mindripper. Since the DataNet on Charvann was crashed by the Aegios at the Node there when the planet surrendered, it will take some time to trace all the byways of the ParcelNet.

"In addition, the Syndics of Rifthaven have been notified, as well as all fleet units, that a large reward will be paid for any Urian artifact, and a general description of the Heart has been supplied—without, of course, any indication of its true nature. Lysanter"—the Urian specialist looked up as his name was spoken—"is standing by to authenticate it when it is found."

Juvaszt inclined his head. "As the Avatar speaks it is done. But now at least one Panarchist knows of the hyperwave, or suspects it strongly. As that secret spreads, we lose even more of our advantage. And what of Rifthaven? It is a hotbed of Panarchist counterintelligence—have the Syndics successfully concealed the existence of their hyperwave? You will remember I recommended against their getting one, for once it is known there, the Panarchists will know of it."

"All communications through Rifthaven are released there with an appropriate delay, to ensure that no one deduces the existence of the hyperwave," Barrodagh said.

Anaris saw Morrighon make another note on his compad, and smiled faintly.

"And when the first Urian-equipped vessel puts into Rifthaven, as will inevitably happen, what then?"

"When that does finally happen it will no longer matter," Barrodagh replied.

"Very well. I accept your assurances. But there is one more thing. The volume of messages on the hyperwave is increasing steadily, much of it nonessential traffic. You must make stronger efforts to control this before it grows to the point where it impacts our tactical capabilities. The discriminators can handle only so much."

Before Barrodagh could reply, Juvaszt waved his hand, dismissing the subject.

"In the meantime, I wish to send Hreem the Faithless"—the captain's lips curled in disdain as he pronounced the Rifter's name—"from Charvann to Malachronte. Our agent on the Ways reports that the battlecruiser under construction there is very nearly completed. I have already dispatched a crew for it from Dol'jhar. They should arrive at almost the same time."

Barrodagh hesitated. "I have assigned Charterly to that task as soon as he completes . . ."

"Charterly is too far away," interrupted Juvaszt. "There is no time to waste, lest the cruiser power up and escape us. We do not have realtime communications with Malachronte, so our agent's information is already dangerously dated. But extrapolating from his last report, Hreem is the only ally close enough to reach it in time.

"As well, it would be best to detach some units from some of the less strategically important fleets and recall them here," continued the captain. "There is no doubt in my mind that the Panarchists will attempt a counterattack at some point, and we must be prepared. I intend to assign the *Satansclaw* to patrol duty as the first step."

Juvaszt paused just long enough to induce Barrodagh to begin a reply, and then overrode him. "I trust this meets with your approval?"

Barrodagh's discomfiture became complete when the Avatar spoke for the second time, forcing him to abort his reply even as his lips formed it. "Let it be done as you have said. This meeting is at an end. Henceforth you are to share your information freely with my son"—Anaris noted here the use of the Dol'jharian conditional noun form for son—"that he may participate in the continuing destruction and transfiguration of the Thousand Suns."

The Avatar stood and strode from the room, followed by Barrodagh.

Anaris felt a flare of pride that he had gauged his father correctly, but at the same time, the other side of him, the side that the Panarchists had trained, caught scornfully at the word "strategically." What none of the other Dol'jharians or their servants saw, despite their careful plans, was how strategically stupid it was for them to be mired here on Arthelion—which had absolutely nothing to offer to the war effort—when, if the Suneater was the base of their power as Barrodagh hinted, they should be securing that.

But they don't see it; the entire offensive is built around my father's obedience to the dictates of ritual. But while he is reveling in the possession of his enemy's home and treasures, are the Panarchists figuring out where the real power lies?

The others had remained where they were, watching him with strained expectancy. Ferrasin seemed poised on the edge of flight.

He restrained them with a motion of his hand. "There is much to discuss."

Eight

FIVESPACE: ARTHELION TO DIS

Ivard was happy.

For the first time Montrose had let him get up. Ignoring the pain in his shoulder as he walked out of his cubicle and into the normal gravity of the rest of the ship, he made his way to the rec room.

He rubbed at his wrist where the Kelly ribbon had bonded to his skin, hating to look at it—it made him sick to see the band of green round his arm. At least it didn't hurt. Mostly numb, once in a while it tingled. Almost a tickle. Strange.

Ivard hadn't told Montrose about the weird dreams he'd had since the ribbon bonded to him. He'd told Marim, but she'd said it was just the medication Montrose was giving him for the burn.

Except I wish I didn't have to take stuff that makes me dream about Greywing being lost someplace big and cold and dark.

Reminded of his sister, he felt the familiar ache inside. If only he hadn't lost the coin she'd taken from the Mandala, with the greywing image on it! *She was going back to Natsu to fight for freedom,* he thought, and felt a fresh pang. Losing her coin hurt even worse than losing Markham's flight ribbon.

He'd told Marim about all these things, and she hadn't laughed. Instead she said seriously, "Remember, Greywing didn't feel anything, and I bet she didn't even have time to get scared. I hope I get that kind of death when my turn comes. And as for that coin—if it's on board, I'll find it. Your flight ribbon too."

That made him feel a little better, at least when the lights were on and he was awake.

He lowered himself into a padded chair. Thinking about Marim reminded him that he was supposed to be happy. He was rich and the woman he loved seemed to love him.

He felt his face heat up, remembering with enthusiasm the fun they'd had he day before. She'd said she would show him that you could have great sex without moving a shoulder and he thought his answer had been fairly offhand. He hadn't wanted her to know that he'd never had sex with another person, except in his own imagination, ever.

"Don't tell Montrose," she'd said afterward, kissing him with a loud smack. "I'm not supposed to get you excited. But I can't help it! You're an exciting little blit."

"Hey, I'm as tall as you are," he'd protested. "And I'll be taller soon, too." He didn't add that his clothes were getting cramped in pits and crotch, a sure sign he needed to get some more. That didn't seem very sophisticated somehow.

"All right, I'll take you on," a voice interrupted his thoughts. It was a mild, mellow voice whose tone reminded him a little of a song—the Krysarch. No, Aerenarch now. His older brothers were dead, Marim had told him. "Let's set it up."

Brandon walked in, with Lokri right behind him. Lokri's pale eyes flickered round the room, and one of his hands half lifted, acknowledging Ivard.

Brandon also saw him, and changed his direction. Coming directly to Ivard, he said, "Good to see you out of the dispensary. How's that arm?"

Ivard hesitated, but Brandon did not turn away. He stood there smiling, his blue eyes direct, waiting for an answer.

"Fine," Ivard lied. He wondered if he should say anything else, and then he remembered that they had something in common, after all. "I'm sorry about your brothers."

Brandon's face altered, from concern to something a little more serious. Though Brandon did not move, Ivard felt as if had stepped closer. A vague sense of vertigo rippled through Ivard's mind, but it was not unpleasant.

Brandon said, "I am very sorry about Greywing," He spoke so softly Ivard just barely heard it. He sounded sorry, and for a moment it made Ivard's pain a lot worse. He could see in Brandon's face that he shared it too, which changed it somehow—lessened it—took the *aloneness* out of it.

"So you want to play more games?" Lokri asked, looking lazily back over his shoulder at Brandon. Lokri's question had an ambiguity to it that pulled Ivard's thoughts away from himself and made him feel uncomfortable.

Brandon smiled and touched Ivard's good shoulder before turning to Lokri.

"No, I want to win the price of this ship off you so I can start building me a fleet."

Lokri laughed. "Don't start the timer yet." He lounged over to the dispenser and got something cold and dark to drink.

Ivard licked his lips, realizing that he was thirsty. But by then Lokri was already at his console sitting down. Ivard's eyes went to the Aerenarch. Could he ask him? Brandon's back was to him, and Ivard could not see his face. The Aerenarch was polite—but he was a nick. Ivard scrunched down a bit in his chair: if Brandon said no, Lokri might laugh and he'd feel like blunge on a wall.

Do for yourself. You're supposed to be a man now.

Ivard shifted, wincing as a pang shot through his shoulder. The pain seemed to echo in his head, and the Kelly ribbon tingled, making his hand feel cold. Deciding he could drink later, he forced himself incrementally to relax again.

For a time he stayed thus, breathing softly so his shoulder would not move and ache anew. The coldness from his hand seeped over the rest of his body, numbing the pain. His thoughts were clear but curiously detached, almost as if he watched a vid.

Light and shadow shifted in Lokri's dark face, the only constant being his careless smile. Ivard's gaze moved downward, drawn by shaded contours in Lokri's shirt. He noted, was bemused by, the tension in the set of Lokri's shoulders, and in his hands.

"*It's only a game they play.*" Who said that? But thinking about it too hard made his head ache.

Was Brandon tense as well? The Aerenarch sat relaxed in his chair, no strain in his demeanor. His expression altered between humor and reflection as his fingers moved fast on his keypads.

They did not talk, but as Ivard looked from one to the other, he felt their concentration. Felt? No . . . he almost *saw* something. Or heard it, or tasted it. No, not that.

He squinted at the air between them, trying to still his breath. The numbness had turned to a comfortable kind of coldness so that his body almost floated, like in a low-grav dispensary cubicle. But here his mind seemed detached from his body, and his focus was drawn to the two men, trying to identify the charge between them.

But before he could, the increasing coldness of his body made him shiver, forcing his thoughts back on himself. *I've stayed too long,* he thought. *I've got to get back to the dispensary.*

His hands pushed at the seat, which woke up the pain again. Fire from his shoulder sent agony through him. He shut his eyes, sinking back.

". . . now?" A voice cut into his thoughts. "You have to come back to the dispensary," the voice sharpened. "Montrose sent me."

Ivard opened his eyes, stared for a few moments without comprehension at an unfamiliar face: square, short dark hair, dark eyes, big ears. Angry mouth.

"I'm to bring you," the man said.

Ivard remembered him then, the nick astrogator that the other crew members called Schoolboy. Vi'ya had put him under Montrose, doing Ivard's old galley jobs. *Osri Omilov. An astrogator—like I am.*

"I can't get up," he said—or tried to. Somehow his voice was gone.

Osri's lips pressed into a thin line of impatience, and he leaned forward and pulled Ivard to his feet.

Ivard gasped as the new flesh over his burn stretched.

"Need some help?" Brandon asked, rising to his feet.

"No," Osri snapped. "Thank you, Aerenarch."

Brandon withdrew, making one of those little hand motions that Ivard couldn't decipher, but he heard Osri's breath hiss.

Ivard hated being helpless, but the pain from his shoulder was eating his entire body, making it impossible to get any of his limbs to work.

Osri grunted, shifting his grip until he had taken all of Ivard's weight. Ivard counted the steps as they reverberated up his aching body until he smelled the familiar faintly antiseptic air of the dispensary.

When they reached his cubicle the relief of low-gee was sweet anguish. The fire dulled and died, leaving only the tingle in his wrist, which felt warm now instead of cold. Ivard closed his eyes as Omilov helped him get arranged.

"Here," Osri spoke. "I'm to—"

Ivard opened his eyes. "You're not going to touch it," He shielded his shoulder with his good hand.

"No," the astrogator said impatiently. "You have to eat, and he insisted I make it fresh. And drink. You have to drink two glasses of water while I'm here."

"Where is Montrose?"

Osri frowned, not in anger this time. "With my father. Some kind of treatment."

"Your father? Oh. Is he the old man we found in that torture room?" Ivard asked, and not waiting for an answer, "Marim didn't tell me he's your father."

Omilov adjusted the gees just enough to keep food from floating, then brought a tray from the warmer.

"Here. Eat. I cannot leave until you do," Osri said.

Ivard obediently maneuvered himself so that he could pick up a spoon.

As he ate, Ivard considered the man before him. Osri looked and acted like Ivard had always pictured Panarchist naval officers, his posture so stiff he ought to be in full-dress uniform instead of a pair of Jaim's old work coveralls. "This *noktu lesl* is quite good today," he said finally. "Did you prepare it?"

The question brought the annoyance back into Osri's face. "Yes," he said.

"It's the first thing I learned to prepare," Ivard said. "When I was in the galley. They learn it at the chef school, Montrose told me."

"Drink" was the only answer. Then, "More."

Ivard tried to obey, took too big a swallow, then choked, the fluid burning his nose. He coughed, sending pain racking down his arm. His spoon went flying, but Osri caught it, and the tray, righting things with hasty movements.

"Not so fast," he said, his voice much milder.

Ivard leaned back, trying to catch his breath. The Kelly ribbon tingled around his arm again.

"Eat when you're ready," Osri said, sitting back. "I'll wait."

Ivard sighed, rubbing at his green wrist. "I wish he could get that thing off."

"How did it occur?"

As he ate, Ivard gave Osri a brief description of the encounter in the Panarch's palace, and more questions led to a retelling of the firefight that had killed his sister and caused his wound.

When Ivard had finished, Osri said, "How frequently does this happen?"

"You mean the Kelly ribbon, or someone in the crew getting zapped?"

"The fights. And deaths."

Ivard shrugged. "Depends on what kind of action we see—and how often. Other than Jakarr's try to take over on Dis, when you came, we haven't lost many since . . . oh, since Markham died. Few burns the last brush we had with Hreem, the one at Red-Five Booster Field on Morigi II."

"The reward must be considerable for you to take such risks."

Ivard nodded, waving his spoon with enthusiasm. "Is! When we pull one. Been a long while, though, which is one of the reasons Jakarr acted like he did. Wanted to go raiding, Vi'ya said we had to stick to raiding slavers, Hreem being number one choice."

"Stick to slavers . . ." Osri repeated. "I believe I heard someone in Merryn refer to this Hreem madman as a slave-runner, but—" He frowned. "Surely this takes place outside the established boundaries of the Thousand Suns!"

"Most. Not all, though. And of course, there's Dol'jhar, hard up against the Rift right in the center. They got slaves, though no one much goes there or leaves. Or did," he amended soberly.

"So that is the connection between Eusabian of Dol'jhar and Hreem? Buying slaves?" Osri looked skeptical.

Ivard grinned. "Don't know; maybe, though they'd have to be special ones since most of the population on that place is slaves. Vi'ya said the cheapest commodities on Dol'jhar are people and ash."

Interest lightened Osri's expression. "You've been to Dol'-jhar?"

"Not me. Some of the others raided it a few times." Ivard shrugged with his one good shoulder.

"So you steal Hreem's, ah, cargoes of slaves, and resell them?"

"No, we sell the cargoes. Slave-runners almost always carry other illegal stuff, worth a lot on Rifthaven. Let the slaves go on a colony world, usually."

Osri's black brows rose faintly. "Finish your food," he said. "And drink this."

* * *

". . . and when I asked the boy if this woman jacks slaveships for revenge or for profit, he said, 'Both.' "

Omilov sipped at the hot drink his son had brought and observed him over the rim of his cup.

Osri frowned, his dark eyes distant for a few moments, then he looked up. "Not that I believe that they let the slaves go. He'd have to say that, knowing how stiff is the penalty for getting caught in such a trade. 'Slaves.' Distasteful word."

Distasteful. "Evil, I should say. Tragic." Omilov spoke in an undertone, and as always his son scarcely listened.

Not that he ignored his father, or cut in—he was too polite for that. But he paused for him to speak, and then went on in a musing tone, exactly as if Omilov had been silent, "He probably said it hoping that I would not report to the authorities the names of the individuals on this ship. But I shall." He touched his bare wrist. "Though I cannot record their crimes as evidence, I will remember."

Omilov repressed a sigh, studying Osri's face, so familiar, so odd a blend of his own features and his mother's.

And so readable.

Osri's emotions played across his features, moving the black brows so like Sebastian's own, and lengthening the long upper lip that Risiena's Ghettierus genes had given him. Risiena was just the same way—but unlike her son, she could hide her thoughts when she chose. It was just that she seldom chose to. She didn't have to, being an absolute ruler descended from thirty generations of absolute rulers on their terraformed moon.

Sebastian heard a pause and looked up. Osri's eyes were narrowed in exasperation. "You were not listening to me, Father."

I could not love his mother, but I do love him. But I don't seem to be able to protect him anymore.

"I apologize, Osri. I must be more tired than I'd thought."

Quick concern narrowed the dense black eyes. "What did that old monster do to you?"

"Eased my recovery considerably," Omilov murmured. "Whatever else he has done, Montrose is a superb surgeon."

"You do not seek to excuse these criminals?"

Omilov shook his head, feeling the weight of a very real fatigue. "We are here, under their control. Our duty is to aid the Aerenarch—"

"But he does *nothing*." Osri gritted his teeth. "And when he did take action, it was to lead them—not just to permit them, but to *lead* them—on a raid in the Ivory Antechamber. This ship, according to that fool of a boy, is packed with the artifacts they stole. And Brandon watched them do it, saying it was better they had the things than the Dol'jharians use them for target practice."

Omilov repressed a smile. "You must remember that those artifacts are part of the Arkad inheritance; I believe the law would dictate that they belong to Brandon—and of course, his father—to dispose of as they will."

Osri's lips pressed in a thin line, and for the first time, his gaze dropped. "I thought it was our duty to recover them."

"That is for the Panarch to say." Omilov watched his son accept this in silence, and then a new thought occurred to him, for the first time ever: *He's hiding something from me.*

Then Osri stood, running his thumb absently along the edge of the bed. "We will be emerging in a matter of hours. At their base." Osri closed his fingers into a fist. "This talk of slaves. They might sell us, and I believe Brandon will stand by and watch."

"You forget that of all of us, he is the main target," Omilov murmured. "I counsel you to wait, and watch, and learn."

ARTHELION ORBIT

Luri's huge, luminous eyes blinked slowly, and her full, curved lips parted. "You're the only one who understands Luri," she breathed, leaning forward in a cloud of subtle scents.

Warmth coursed through Kira Lennart.

"Luri wants to stay here . . . with you." The filmy gown strained over full breasts. Luri stepped closer, pressing her soft hands on Kira's shoulders, kneading the muscles there.

Kira sighed, feeling the warmth kindle into desire.

"A little shakrian from Luri?"

"Oh, yes," Kira said, her voice squeaking.

As the fingers massaged slowly down Kira's neck and arms, Kira sank gratefully into the whirlpool of sensual pleasure. It didn't matter that she knew Luri was probably gennated for pheromone production—that she would never be constant, any more than she had been for the old captain, Tallis Y'Marmor, or was for the new.

Luri leaned down, her silky hair brushing Kira's cheek. She kissed her ear softly, her tongue making a delicate exploration around its curve, then suddenly darting into the center. Kira groaned, pleasure sparking the urgency of passion deep inside her.

Luri nibbled her lobe, and then breathed: "Anderic watches. You know that?"

A faint sense of alarm steadied Kira. "Mmm," she said, partly pleasure and partly assent.

Luri laughed softly. Her fingers worked the muscles down the front of Kira's spare body, then with a sudden movement unfastened her jumpsuit.

Kira wriggled free and reached to slap the grav-control. Both women floated in the air, Luri, with a grace born of long practice, removing her diaphanous robe.

Flinging the robe expertly around them both, Luri bent close.

"I know he's reprogrammed the comp," Kira whispered. "He's got spy-eyes all over the ship now."

Luri's robe had settled over them. She pulled it across Kira's back, its silky gossamer folds sending shivers through her. Their heads were shrouded in the slippery robe.

"You are happy with Anderic as captain?" Luri murmured.

"No," Kira responded. "Tallis was a fool, but he was fair enough. Anderic's getting worse every day . . ."

Luri's eyes glittered. "He feels his power."

Kira grunted softly. "If I wanted to serve under such as Hreem the Faithless, I'd be on the *Lith*."

Luri's eyes flickered, and she bent forward and kissed Kira lingeringly.

"Luri feels sorry for Tallis," she murmured into Kira's other ear.

"Me too," Kira breathed.

"Perhaps Tallis can be helped . . ." Luri suggested.

Kira struggled to clear her mind as Luri's hands kneaded slowly down her body. What Luri was hinting at was mutiny—something the Karroo Syndicate was harsh about. They liked to protect their investments, and they had a chatzing long arm. But Tallis was Karroo's appointee. It was that Dol'jharian monster who'd yanked him without warning, forced them all to witness that disgusting vid when his eye was removed, and put Anderic in his place—with Tallis' missing eye replacing one of his own.

What is that with the eyes? Kira wondered. She'd done some exploring in the comp before Anderic had put log-watches all over: as far as she could ascertain, there was no Dol'jharian custom about ship captains and eyes. But there had to be something.

Luri's hands worked lower, splintering her focus. Kira's breath quickened.

"You'll help?" she whispered shakily.

"Luri will help you," came the soft murmur.

Well, it wouldn't be mutiny, would it, if we just restore the rightful captain? Kira thought hazily.

Luri smiled, her perfect little teeth just showing. "Now Luri and Kira-love give Anderic something to watch . . ." And she pulled forth from a hereto-hidden fold of her gown a long dilenja the likes of which Kira had never seen before.

"What the Shiidran Hell is that?" asked Kira, halfway between alarm and excitement.

"It's whatever you want it to be." Luri flicked a control on its handle with a long fingernail. The device seemed to shimmer, then, as Luri manipulated its handle with complex movements of her fingers, it rippled through an amazing evolution of shapes and sizes, various protrusions writhing in and out of its surface as it vibrated with a quiet hum. "It's a proteus, and it's all for you."

Kira stared for a moment, suddenly realizing that Luri was as much a master of the sensual arts as she herself was of the ship's communications. Then she threw back her head, laughing with abandon as she ran her hands lingeringly over Luri's generous curves.

They'd give him something to watch, all right.

❋   ❋   ❋

Anderic heard the crunch before he felt the pain.

Cursing in a rising voice, he spat out the tooth fragment he'd just ground off a molar. Working his aching jaw, he looked away from the spyvid, but almost immediately his eyes were drawn back.

What did Luri see in that toad of a Lennart? *She's doing it just to tease me,* he told himself—except the acrobatics in Lennart's cabin made it abundantly clear that both women were mutually, and repeatedly, satisfied.

He clenched his teeth again, feeling a warning twinge in one of his molars. This caused his—Tallis'—eye to throb.

He slapped the com off, pressing his thumbs carefully to his eyelids. He should be grateful, he thought bitterly; at least the pain took his mind off his straining nacker. *But Telos! Those legs, wrapped around Lennart ... That dilenja!* He groaned, grabbing at his crotch.

The movement reminded him of Tallis, down in the bilge, the Emasculizer hanging between his legs. Anderic wondered viciously if he ought to pipe this com down there for Tallis to watch.

Then his com flickered, and a moment later he forgot his eye, Luri, and her damned device. His frustration withered when Barrodagh's pale face appeared on the console.

"Anderic," the Bori said.

"Senz-lo Barrodagh," Anderic muttered, working his dry tongue.

The Bori smiled thinly at the Dol'jharian honorific. Anderic had learned that he liked such things.

"Have you adjusted to your captaincy yet?" Barrodagh touched his eye.

Anderic felt the pang again, echoed by fear. *He means the logos.* "Y-yes, Senz-lo."

Barrodagh gave a short nod. "You are to be posted to patrol duty in the middle system. Your orders will be uploaded shortly."

Anderic had just enough time to acknowledge, and then the console blanked.

Patrol duty. Here? A shiver of unease trembled down his spine, leaching away his lust. Of course the Panarchists would counterattack, once they figured out what was going on. And now he was in the middle of it.

He looked again at the screen relaying the two women's passion. Then he snickered. *Uploaded shortly. And Lennart is comtech . . .*

He tabbed the com to her cabin. She'd soon be too busy to even look at Luri. Too bad.

NINE

✳

CHARVANN ORBIT: THE NODE

The name on the door had been effaced by a low-power jac-blast, but the title was still legible: Aegios, Node Charvann.

Hreem tabbed the annunciator. As the door whispered open, he could hear the occupant within snarling, ". . . so get a tech and get it open, blunge-breath. I want my view back."

Hreem motioned the two burly crewman ahead of him. Inside, enfolded in an intricately stitched *griila*-leather chair, with his feet up on the vast, polished *paak*-wood desk, Naigluf looked up lazily, his hand hovering over the com control in one arm of the chair.

His expression turned to one of alarm as the two crewmen made their way around the desk without a word and plucked him out of the chair. As Hreem took his place behind the desk, the two slammed Naigluf down in an elegant, armless chair in front of it.

Hreem leaned back and looked around at the luxurious office that had once belonged to the manager of the Charvann Node. The exterior viewport behind him was blanked, on Hreem's override—from the overheard scrap of conversation, Naigluf hadn't known that—not giving a hint of the office's location forty thousand kilometers above the surface of Charvann.

The Rifter captain swung his feet up onto the polished surface of the desk and flexed his ankles rhythmically; the heel-claws in his boots slid in and out with a subdued click.

Across the desk from him Naigluf hunched inward on himself, his asymmetric mustache suddenly looking even more bedraggled than usual, and his pockmarked face turned the color of old cheese. Hreem enjoyed the way the man's eyes fixed on the shiny heel-claws—in and out, in and out. The ring of white around his dilated irises was even broader than the last time Hreem had seen him. *Hopper eyes. Probably hasn't touched ground since the attack.*

As though to confirm Hreem's thought, Naigluf's hand strayed toward one of the pockets in his wrinkled, grimy jumpsuit, then jerked away.

Finally Naigluf couldn't stand the silence anymore. "You want me to take another office? I can take another one, I didn't mean to . . ."

At a slight nod from Hreem one of the guards stepped forward and slammed his cupped palm into the side of Naigluf's head. The Rifter screamed, and blood ran out of his ear from his shattered eardrum. Hreem felt a pulse of delight lance through him.

"Naigy, Naigy." Hreem shook his head sadly. "You couldn't be satisfied with your twenty points, could you?"

The miserable Rifter's eyes widened even more, something Hreem hadn't thought was possible. He opened his mouth to protest, then shrank away as the crewman beside him raised his hand again.

"All the hopper you could pop, any prettyboy or girl you fancied, a nice office," Hreem continued. "Ran the entire Node. But it wasn't enough. What were you going to do with the rake-off?"

Hreem reached for a control in the chair arm. "No, I don't need this office, any more than you do now, or any more than she does." He jerked his head backward as the viewport dilated, revealing the vacuum-ravaged body of a woman splayed across the monocrystal port like a bloated spider, backlit by the bright, cloud-dappled limb of Charvann behind her. Her pop-eyed expression of agony contrasted violently with the elegance of her Douloi attire.

Naigluf gasped.

"Actually," said Hreem as he got to his feet, "I don't think this office is a very healthy place—practically everybody who sits here lately ends up dead."

The two crewmen plucked Naigluf up out of the chair; Hreem snorted as the skinny runt's legs made abortive running movements.

"Telos, Hreem, we've been working together too long for this." Naigluf's fear scaled his voice up to a near falsetto.

Laughing, Hreem directed the men toward the nearest airlock.

"Hreem, at least make it quick, use your jac, don't just shove me out there."

The Rifter's pleas grew in volume and vehemence as they reached the lock. Naigluf flung out his arms and legs in a vain attempt to prevent his escort from jamming him through the opening.

Hreem held up his hand. The two men released Naigluf so suddenly that his frantic flailings propelled him backward against the opposite bulkhead. As he slumped to the floor, looking up at Hreem, the Rifter captain grinned at him.

"You're right, Naigy, it's been too long to end it this way." As the shivering Rifter relaxed and essayed a trembling smile, Hreem continued, "This"—he jerked a thumb at the lock—"is too good for you."

"Hreeee-eeeeeeeem!" Naigluf howled.

"Take him to Norio, he knows what to do."

A shriek of terror accompanied by a waft of fetor from the miserable huddle on the deck made Hreem bellow with laughter.

The crewmen dragged the blubbering Rifter roughly to his feet and away, and Hreem strolled back to the office of the former Aegios, looking around with proprietary satisfaction. The Node was his—the Syncs were his. Almost a billion lives, all his. He'd let his crew do what they wanted on the ground, but the Node citizens were off limits: they were Hreem's to dispose of.

Hreem dropped into the big chair and stretched his hands over his head, contemplating his next move. *Maybe it's time for my hostages to see one of my entertainments.* He'd separated out the upper echelon of the Node and the temenarchs of the dominant Highdwellings, and had them incarcerated under guard, as insurance for the behavior of the rest of the Syncs. He didn't want any trouble.

A tremor of uneasiness made him glance at the viewport, at the dead Aegios. *Trouble. Who'd think the old bitch had that much fight in her?* He could still remember the way she'd laughed as she crashed the DataNet right in front of him, even as he held a jac pointed straight at her.

Hreem hated surprises. *What will scare all the fight out of 'em? I know. Let's give 'em Naigy's farewell performance.*

His thoughts spiraled out, to the unfinished business awaiting him on one of the moons of Warlock, the system's inmost gas giant. That had been a good surprise, finding out from an informant that Rifters were based on the moon—Rifters that the Archon had known about, and even communicated with.

That blungesucking chatzer Markham. Hreem closed his eyes, reliving the exquisite pleasure he'd had a year ago, firing a jac right into the man's laughing face, and watching him burn, and die.

But with the memory came uncertainty: behind him, he knew, though he never talked about it to anyone except Norio, behind him ever since was that black-eyed Dol'jharian tempath Markham'd had as a second. She and her pet psi-killers. He knew she'd come after him, and though he'd been public in his scorn, he'd been paying big money to get their base located so he could get her first.

And her base turned up here!

He'd had a good time with the *Sunflame*, but that was their second ship. He hadn't seen the *Telvarna*, and rather than land on the moon base and risk running into traps or those white-furred killers, he'd skipmissiled the moon, knowing she could not survive that. Nothing like being thorough.

But then had come another little surprise.

Hreem tabbed the viewport closed again and got up restlessly. Barrodagh's communication a few days ago was quite a shock: a Rifter raid on Arthelion, right under Jerrode Eusabian's nose. It had made Hreem laugh—until Barrodagh came through with the details: *The raiders were on a small ship, a Columbiad, and with them is the gnostor Omilov, wanted by the Avatar for questioning. Also with them is the Aerenarch Brandon vlith-Arkad, last reported in the Charvann system. The reward is . . .*

That had given Hreem a jolt: putting the Arkad together with the Columbiad meant the *Telvarna*, and it also meant Vi'ya was still alive.

He hit his boswell: *(Dyasil.)*

(Cap'n?) came the prompt response.

Hreem hesitated. Asking if any signal had come from the tell-tale they'd planted outside the ruined moon would give away his anxiety. As soon as anyone emerged from skip the telltale would report. And of course Dyasil would boz him the moment they got the signal—and then Hreem could skip in and flame the last of Markham's chatzing crew out of existence.

But he hoped they'd show up soon—Barrodagh was getting impatient with him for taking so long to search through every contact that Omilov blit had had, for some artifact that Eusabian was hot-nackered after.

Even before Hreem had found out about Markham's base, he'd decided to take his time with this search, and if possible find out just what this thing was that Eusabian wanted, and if he could get an edge by grabbing it first. But it was puzzling: something so valuable that Eusabian sent him to a planet with no strategic importance to recover it, and it was in the Parcel-Net?

Hreem shook his head. Better tell Barrodagh that the DataNet was blunged up in the attack, and searching back through all the shipment records will take time. Markham's tempath and her ship ought to be here by then.

(Cap'n?) Dyasil's voice broke into his thoughts.

Hreem drummed his fingers on the desk. *(Tell any crew not on watch to get up here. Norio's gonna give us a little show.)*

(Right, cap'n.)

Hreem disconnected and stood up. Norio should have finished with Naigluf by now, his tempathic sensitivities laying bare the man's deepest fears. All that remained was deciding the most entertaining way to exploit them.

After a final look around the elegant office, Hreem tabbed the door open and hurried out.

DESRIEN

Night had fallen, and Eloatri was lost. The realization brought her to a halt in the middle of the trail, just short of a clearing illuminated by the magenta glimmer of the rising moon. She stood among the shadows of the trees, their white trunks ghostly in the half-light. Around her the forest was silent, save for the whisper of a mild breeze and the occasional call of a nightbird. As she inhaled, the cloying sweetness of *nerisa* wafted to her from the clearing.

All day a certain weight had been descending on her, a formless dread with no object. She had let the feeling have its way, knowing that grasping at it would only perpetuate it. But now her back crawled with the diffuse fear of the dark that she had not experienced since childhood.

"The goal of a hejir is to go where the Hand of Telos guides one." True, but I thought that . . .

Her mind stopped. Shock flooded her as she heard the chattering inner voice that discipline and meditation had stilled threescore years before. What was happening to her?

Eloatri felt adrift: as if she had stepped off the Eightfold Path into spiritual chaos. She grasped vainly at the centering mandala she learned from her master so long ago, but her mind chattered on.

In the seeing there should be just the seeing, in the hearing just the hearing, in the thinking just the thought . . .

Then the weight descended on her in its fullness, the Hand of Telos sundering her from the moment. Eloatri groaned wordlessly and crumpled into the lotus position, a measureless sense of loss welling up in her.

"I take refuge in the Buddha, I take refuge in the Law, I take refuge in the Community," she said aloud, but the crowded trunks of the trees around her returned her words in mocking echoes, fragments of the beliefs being stripped from her: refuge, Law, Community, take, take, take.

She scrambled to her feet and hurried down the trail, and her third step took her out of the world into the Dreamtime.

* * *

"Here," said Tomiko, touching her elbow and indicating a table next to the street. The High Phanist smiled as they sat down and motioned to a waiter. The young man hurried over, and Eloatri tried not to stare at his atavistically pale skin and blazing red hair. On his hand she noted a large emerald ring.

Eloatri leaned her staff against a vine-entwined roof support next to them and placed her begging bowl on the table. Its battered brass clanked against the glass surface. At a nearby table a strong-shouldered, dark-visaged man stared at her for a moment before turning back to the woman with him, whose physiognomy echoed his. With them were two white-haired children.

Eloatri didn't hear what Tomiko ordered for them, but the waiter returned only moments later with two goblets and placed them carefully before them. Eloatri felt vaguely disappointed. Would they not eat?

Tomiko picked his goblet up and rotated it meditatively in one hand. Its metallic surface gleamed with condensation, the tiny droplets scattering rainbow flickers of light across his broad face and high cheekbones.

He raised the goblet to her and drank. She picked hers up and drank also, suddenly conscious of a tremendous thirst. A moment later she choked, slamming the goblet back on the table with a discordant crash: the taste was appalling, a compound of thick metallic heat and something so bitter that for a moment she couldn't speak. From the goblet now came the odor of blood.

"That's horrible!" she exclaimed, barely able to enunciate the words past the terrible constriction imposed by the bitter flavor.

The High Phanist raised an eyebrow. "The beings of the world are numberless; I vow to save them all."

His quotation of the first of her bodhisattva vows was like a slap in the face.

He smiled gently, and she noticed now that he, too, was speaking with difficulty, forcing the word through a bitterness almost too great to be borne. "Surely you did not suppose you drank that for yourself?"

He reached across the table and took her begging bowl. "You won't be needing this anymore."

She lunged across the table, grasping desperately at the battered brass bowl . . .

* * *

"No!" shouted Eloatri, and she awoke, standing in the moon-lit clearing, clutching her begging bowl with a terrible strength. After a moment, she forced her fingers to open, and the bowl dropped into the dust of the trail with a muted clank.

TEN

*

CHARVANN ORBIT: THE NODE

Hreem looked around the crowded null-gym with satisfaction.
The cavernous space echoed with the coarse jests of the Rifters
gathered at his behest. Nearby, set apart as much by their grim
silence as by their more uniform attire, were Hreem's hostages,
a mixture of Douloi and Polloi.

The gym was arranged as if for two-player nullball, with the
seating drawn in close around a ten-meter sphere where the
gravitors had been balanced out, surrounded by a nearly invisible netting. A number of air vortexers had been installed in
ports in the netting; the Rifters were already jostling for command of them. Near a larger opening stood Norio, holding a
black box about a third-meter in size; next to him two men held
the trembling Naigluf, who wore only a loincloth.

"Pilgrim Naigluf got greedy," Norio began as the crowd noise
died away, "and he got caught. Because he took more than his
share, there was less for the rest of you." An ugly murmur
drifted up from the crowd.

Norio held up his hand and the murmur died. "We shall re-
joice in our pilgrim-brother's journey along the path of enlight-

enment," he continued. "But Naigluf is a strange one among the Brotherhood. Oh, not in his greed." Norio smiled. "We're all greedy. But have you ever heard of a Rifter who's afraid of falling?"

Raucous laughter swelled from Hreem's crew. The High-dwellers sat in stony silence.

"Afraid of falling, and afraid of spiders too. That's why Naigluf's agreement to expiate his sin against the Brotherhood today is so special. For your pleasure and delight, Pilgrim Naigluf's going to engage in null-gee battle against one of the deadliest denizens of the Thousand Suns."

Hreem grinned at the cadence of Norio's voice. The tempath was really enjoying himself.

Norio unlatched a black box and reached carefully into it, pulling out a dull black spheroid about the size of his fist, holding it delicately with a peculiar grip. The Rifters nearby backed away, two of them with fear-spurred haste; Hreem shuddered when the spheroid sprouted jointed, hairy legs that waved wildly and sturdy, iridescent wings rattled against the tempath's fingers as the creature struggled to escape.

Norio held the creature out for the crowd's inspection. "The medusoid of Empalla IV." He smiled. "So named for its unique ability to turn human flesh to something close to stone."

Norio placed the creature carefully back in the box, held it up against the hatch, and tripped the mechanism. A swarm of the black arachnids burst out into the playing area, buzzing and fluttering wildly as they tried to adapt to the unfamiliar lack of gravity. Some tried to cling to the netting that enclosed them, but it was too fine and offered no purchase to their legs.

At a curt motion from Hreem the two men holding Naigluf dragged him over to the large hatch and thrust him through. As the hatch puckered closed, Hreem walked over and pushed two small nullball paddles through at Naigluf.

"Here's your weapons, Naigy. Give 'em hell."

The other Rifters roared with laughter as the skinny Rifter flailed wildly with the paddles, looking like one of the silly speculations about human-powered flight from the pretech age of Lost Earth. The hollow popping of the vortexers began echoing through the gym, their blasts of air setting Naigluf spinning.

Hreem glanced at Norio. The tempath was trembling under

the impact of the crowd's emotions, his eyes dilated. Then the Rifter captain felt the summons of his boswell. Alarm flared: *Telvarna's emergence—couldn't be worse timing.* He abandoned his own vortexer, which was immediately grabbed by another Rifter, and got out of his seat. *(Yeah?)*

Dyasil's voice whispered urgently: *(Message from Arthelion. Eusabian wants you to proceed to Malachronte, to assist in securing the battlecruiser under construction in the Ways.)*

The yelling of the crowd and Naigluf's frenzied screams seemed suddenly to subside to a low murmur as the blood mounted in Hreem's head. Malachronte!

For a moment he wavered. He wanted to be the one to blast that hell-cursed Vi'ya into atoms, but he had no idea when the *Telvarna* would return. It could be today—it could be months. He knew they had at least one other base. Then the image of himself on the bridge of a battlecruiser possessed him once again with an indescribable sense of well-being.

I'll assign Lignis and the Hellrose *to listen for the telltale.*

(Dyasil, get the crew on board and run through a status check. We leave in an hour.)

Then Hreem felt Norio's trembling hands upon his shoulders. "Ahhh," he said, wordless. "Ahhh, Jala." Hreem turned around; the tempath's eyes had rolled up into their sockets—only the whites were visible.

Hreem helped Norio toward the exit, but the tempath could hardly walk. The trembling of his body followed exactly the waves of sound from the crowd of excited Rifters, punctuated by sudden jerks that matched the shrieks of agony from the slowly dissolving Naigluf.

As they reached the exit, Hreem looked back. Naigluf was still screaming, but only twitching ineffectually, for both his arms and most of one leg had disintegrated as the bites of the medusoids turned them brittle, and black pools of fester were spreading across his torso as the creatures fed in arachnoid frenzy. The Highdwellers—those who hadn't been dragged off by Rifters for personal sport—huddled in abject terror, some watching in horrified fascination, others tightly curled on the deck, their eyes squinched closed and fingers in their ears.

Hreem laughed, feeling his pleasure resonate in the shivering tempath, and turned to leave. Life was good.

❊   ❊   ❊

FIVESPACE: ARTHELION TO DIS

Montrose closed the storage bin and straightened up. "Excellent timing," he rumbled. "We've completely run out of fresh vegetables, and we are nearly out of herbs."

Osri absently kneed the prowling Lucifur aside and glanced at the chrono in the galley, feeling a tightening at the back of his neck. According to the timer, this accursed Rifter vessel would be emerging outside its moon-based lair very soon. *And what becomes of us then?*

"You're shortly to see the very best hydroponics in this octant," Montrose went on. "Do you know anything about vegetables? How to pick an herb?" He laughed. "Have you ever even seen an herb outside of your food? Well, you will soon be an expert, for the captain wants you to continue under my tutelage."

His laughter was interrupted by the urgent tone of the emergence bell, cutting through the taped opera playing softly in the background.

"We'll watch things from here," Montrose said, slapping his console on and killing the music in the same motion. His big hands keyed a short combination and a view of the bridge flickered into being, with the viewscreens at the top.

Vi'ya was already at her post, absorbed in her work. Suddenly her chin jerked up, her mouth thinning. Her hand slapped a key and a harsh klaxon blared through the ship.

Montrose cursed softly.

Maybe five seconds passed and then the bridge crew ran in, Ivard pale and awkward in his traction bandage. Brandon appeared a moment later, tousled and heavy-eyed; his sleep period had just begun.

Vi'ya tabbed the intercom. "Montrose, confine the Schoolboy—belay that." She glanced over at Ivard, who hunched at his console. "Bring him forward and stand by with Jaim."

Osri turned to Montrose, who studied him appraisingly. "Be very careful in the next few minutes." He paused, apparently noting Osri's tightened mouth, then signed. "The lens of your prejudice blinds you to Rifter realities. This is not the Panarchy.

In particular, do not look behind the captain's words—she says what she means."

He pushed Osri out, and in silence they moved to the bridge.

Lokri was standing before Vi'ya, one hand resting on her console. Montrose paused only long enough to push Osri onto the bridge, then he disappeared, moving faster than one would expect of a man of his bulk.

"Norton's gone," said Lokri.

"We do not know that," Vi'ya responded, her eyes on her console.

"They're gone or they're dead," Lokri said. "Or there would have been a message at the telltale."

"We are going in." Vi'ya's hands did not pause in their keying.

Lokri struck his hand lightly against the dyplast. "And eat a chatzing skipmissile?"

Osri moved silently to stand near the Aerenarch, who was leaning against a bulkhead, arms crossed. "What is it?" he whispered.

Brandon spoke without moving his eyes away from the two at the commander's pod: "Something tripped a warning transponder. We scanned the Rifter channels. Com leakage from Node Charvann referred to Hreem going to Malachronte."

"Hreem is gone," Vi'ya said. "His fleet is all Rifters. No Rifter would wait around Dis on the chance we might show up, when everyone else is getting loot on the planet, especially with Hreem gone." She hit a control. "We have . . . just over forty-eight minutes until the signal from the telltale they undoubtedly left reaches the inner system, and someone comes after us. Let us not waste time."

"Agreed," Lokri said, turning away and then back. "We make for Rifthaven with our loot. Fast, before any of Eusabian's blungesuckers get there and talk about us."

"We go in," Vi'ya said.

"We *leave*." Lokri struck her pod again, this time with his fist. "No one is worth risking my life for."

"Lokri's right," Marim said. "*Sunflame*'s got to be long gone. That was your orders, wasn't it? And maybe we have forty minutes, but what if it's a destroyer that shows up?"

Osri watched with sour satisfaction. No one in the Navy ever argued with a superior officer. He hoped that ice-faced woman was enjoying having her authority flouted. But the little Rifter was right: a skipmissile would hit them before the emergence pulse from the destroyer that fired it arrived to warn them.

"I do not think we need worry about destroyers," Vi'ya said. "We know Tallis is at Arthelion, and Hreem seems to be gone. Those were the only two left in his fleet. Anything else we can deal with."

A faint chittering made the hairs on Osri's neck rise. The Eya'a were somewhere near by; he heard their twiggy feet scratching the deckplates.

Lokri's face blanched. "Threat?" he said softly.

Prickles of danger tightened Osri's neck. Next to him, the Aerenarch was very still.

Anything can happen, he realized. *These chatzers could start shooting—those psi-monsters could blast our skulls—and no one would stop them.* He scanned Lokri's body, looking for hidden weapons.

Vi'ya got to her feet, facing the comtech, who did not back away. She was very nearly eye-to-eye with Lokri. "It is my crew," she said, her accent very strong as she spoke each phoneme. "If there is one person there waiting for us, I must know."

Lokri tensed, then took one step back, and another. Crimson ridged his cheekbones. "You can't always use the Eya'a as a threat," he said, just barely audible. "Someday they will be gone."

Vi'ya's white teeth showed in a sudden laugh. "I did not summon them. They come when they hear death." She touched her forehead. "And time is passing."

Lokri dropped into his pod and Vi'ya sat down again, scanning her own console. Then she looked up and appeared to notice Brandon for the first time. "You will accept orders?"

"Yes."

"Take Fire Control," Vi'ya said. "Be ready for anything."

Osri stayed where he was, his nerves thrumming, as Brandon sank into the seat at Fire Control and brought his console to life.

"Ivard, take us to Dis." A moment later the vibration indicating skip hummed in Osri's back teeth. The vibrations were rougher than usual; Osri guessed that the captain had adjusted the fiveskip to a lower frequency tactical setting.

I know why I am here, he thought. *If Ivard fails at his task, this woman will demand that I take his place.* What would happen if he refused to obey a Rifter?

His eyes were drawn to the Aerenarch, whose face was not visible to him. *"You will accept orders?" "Yes."*

"Lokri, set up a full scan for emergence," the captain said, her voice unstressed, as if nothing had happened between them. "Relay to me for skip on detection of any activity."

His posture indolent, Lokri waited just a moment too long, and then tapped one-handed at his console. Vi'ya took no apparent notice.

Osri watched Brandon set up his console, linking it to Lokri's for the scan. The echo to the main screen revealed the Tenno grid pulsing in the uncertain pattern of insufficient tactical input.

There were no further words until the emergence bell rang again and the screen cleared from skip. Then no words were sufficient.

At first Osri thought the viewscreen showed a small asteroid that had somehow wandered into orbit around Warlock; it was a lopsided sphere with a crack down the middle and a fused crater near one limb.

Then, suddenly, his eyes adjusted as Brandon's Tenno grid rippled to a new configuration, declaring the scale of the view, and he gasped. It was—had been—Dis. Lao Shang's Wager was gone. In its place was a crater—at least two hundred kilometers across and inestimably deep—with rays splashing out across the moon and wrapping around to the far side. From two sides of the crater a massive chasm gaped, near to splitting the moon in two.

No, it did split it, Osri thought as the lopsided shape of the shattered moon registered on him; and now he saw a dull red glow deep within the crack. The fragments of the moon were attempting to reunite under the pull of gravity, heating the rock to a temperature it had not known since the coalescence of the Charvann system billions of years before.

"Telos—" breathed Lokri, shock widening his eyes. Then his console beeped. "No traces—wait—" He stabbed at the keys. "Something metallic at ambient, about a thousand klicks out, 274 mark 33. To you."

Vi'ya's console flashed as she accepted the coordinates. The starfield slewed across the screen, taking the horror out of view. The echo from Vi'ya's console on the main screen revealed they were under maximum acceleration. Moments later the screen flickered to maximum magnification, and new horror confronted them.

A terrible moan issued from the intercom; Osri recognized Jaim's voice.

It was a ship, as shattered as the moon, seared by plasma fire, its bow ruptured by a missile strike. It was rotating slowly end around end; there was no sign of life.

"Sunflame?" Ivard squeaked.

No one answered. A moment later he started to sway in his seat.

"Ivard," said Vi'ya, "go to the dispensary."

As the boy turned to her, his face sick and one hand clutching convulsively at his banded wrist, she added, not unkindly, "Now."

"I won't go to the dispensary," he said, voice cracking. "I have to know, I *have* to know."

"We'll set up the com in your bunk," Marim said.

"I'll meet you there," came Montrose's voice over the com.

As Marim assisted Ivard out, the intercom clicked. Jaim's voice floated out, tight and hoarse: "Request permission to join the boarding crew."

Vi'ya pulled her hands away from her console and flexed them. After a long pause she said, "There will be no boarding crew. It may be rigged for just that." As Jaim began to protest she continued, "We have forty-two minutes. Prepare to launch the waldo. Jaim, you can con it from there. We'll stand off at one hundred kilometers."

It took the little machine a surprisingly short time to reach the wreck of the *Sunflame*. On the screen the picture from its imagers grew rapidly, then slowed as Jaim prepared to maneuver it through the gaping hole in the hull near the bridge.

Montrose loomed suddenly, seating himself at the empty nav console. He looked across at the captain and said, "I put Ivard to sleep."

Behind his back, Osri flexed his own hands, which were slimy with sweat. He gazed up at the viewscreen again.

The jagged edges of the wound in the flank of the *Sunflame* expanded past the sides of the screen, and harsh shadows leapt to life as the waldo's lights came on. The interior of the ship was a shambles; whatever had blown the hole in the hull had thoroughly wrecked the bridge. A body hung motionless above one console, its limbs horribly contorted, its features effaced by vacuum bloat and plasma burn. Over the heart pocket on the chest of its tattered black uniform was a gold ringed sun.

"Norton." Montrose's voice was harsh with shock.

The view rotated as the waldo turned toward the stern and made its way off the bridge. The rest of the ship was as thoroughly wrecked; it became increasingly obvious as the terrible remote tour continued that much of the damage had been done by boarders. Other bodies floated by; Osri recognized one or two of them from their brief stay at the Rifter hideout, but as he watched the horror unfold, there was no room in him for triumph.

The imager revealed obscene graffiti scrawled on some walls in a flaking, black substance that Osri finally realized was blood. His stomach twisted. He looked away from the viewscreens in the console and glanced at the others on the bridge: all except Vi'ya exhibited horror or rage. The captain's face revealed nothing, though Osri did not like looking at her unblinking dark eyes.

An occasional click or beep from the instruments was the only sound, along with the quiet whisper of the tianqi. Finally the little machine reached the engine room, which Osri now realized had been Jaim's goal all along. *"—and Jaim's bunking with Reth Silverknife on the* Sunflame." *Who had said that?*

The motion of the machine slowed, stopped. In the center of the image was another body, not floating but pinned to an injector module by a metal rod through its neck. The face was frozen in the distortion of extreme pain unmasked by the ravages of vacuum. Osri could tell only that it had been a woman, but he noted the little chimes woven into her hair, like Jaim's. She was naked; a pattern of strange wounds—each consisting of three parallel gashes—scarred her body, with clusters of blackened blood crystals blooming from them like evil flowers.

A howl of rage and sorrow echoed from the intercom. *"Dasura chatch-nafari tollim nar-Hreem—"* the last syllable drawn out into a keening that raised the hairs on Osri's neck.

Now Osri remembered the heel-claws on the image in the rec room, and he knew whose work this was.

"Lokri. Take over the waldo. Hold it there," said Vi'ya. "Jaim—*Jaim.*" The keening stopped. "Come to the bridge.

Arkad, ready a missile. Fusion, twenty megatons. Rig for impact detonation and target the *Sunflame*."

Brandon's hands moved swiftly over his keys.

Would they not attempt salvage? Then Osri recalled something Montrose had once said: "Jaim is a devout Serapisti."

They worship fire as a sacrament of Telos, and give the bodies of their dead to the flames to cleanse their soul for the long journey.

The bridge crew was silent as Jaim entered the bridge. He had a knife in one hand; in the other he clutched several braids of hair with the little bells still on them. The harmony of the remaining chimes woven in his hair was mournful now, the bright upper registers missing.

"Twenty-eight minutes. Is that missile ready?" Vi'ya's voice was cold, controlled.

Osri realized that for a tempath, perceiving Jaim's emotions right now—not to mention those of the rest of the crew—was probably akin to staring into the sun.

"Yes," said the Aerenarch. He moved aside as Jaim came up to his console, laying his knife and severed hair carefully on the inlay above the keypads. The lanky Rifter stood there, staring at the screen, which now showed the *Sunflame* from an imager on the *Telvarna*.

"Jaim," said Vi'ya, her voice low. The lanky Rifter looked at her, his face cold.

"We can commit her to the flames immediately and flee," she continued, "or, with your help, we can seek vengeance."

Lokri jerked upright at his console and opened his mouth, then subsided as Marim made a sudden movement. Osri guessed that she had kicked him. Marim watched Jaim and the captain with pursed lips.

"Vengeance." Jaim's voice was harsh, his repetition of the word midway between a question and acceptance.

At a look from Vi'ya Brandon tapped at his console, apparently taking the missile back off-line.

"Can you rig the *Sunflame*'s engines for a gee-burst overload? And do it in the next fifteen minutes? If we can cripple the fiveskip of whatever shows up, *Telvarna* can deal with it."

Jaim looked back at the viewscreen for a moment. "Don't know." He moved over to Lokri's console.

With a gesture of ironic invitation, Lokri yielded his place.

Watching Jaim's face as he reactivated the waldo's imager, revealing again the body of his lover, Osri decided that only a madman would get in the way of the Rifter's vengeance at this point.

The image on-screen rotated away from Reth's savaged body as the waldo drifted over to a bank of controls. The crew watched in silence as Jaim worked. Less than a minute later he announced, "I can do it."

"Good," said Vi'ya. "Then here's how it will go."

ELEVEN

The *Telvarna* hung over the ruined surface of Dis, amidst a reef of dust and fragments ripped from the moon by the impact of the skipmissile. Vi'ya had brought them to rest with respect to the moon, holding position with the geeplane; the wreck of the *Sunflame* was just visible over the horizon, so that Dis effectively hid them from whoever showed up to investigate.

The viewscreen showed a magnified image of the *Sunflame*, sparkling with imaging artifacts as the computers struggled with the effects of the moon fragments fogging up the space around them. The faint, actinic glare of a welding probe flared occasionally from the rents in the ship as the waldo followed its programmed course; the com emitted terse comments almost discernible through static as the recording prepared by the crew ran through its loop.

The bridge was silent except for the whisper of the tianqi, which were now emitting a scent Osri had never encountered before. It made him feel cold and stony, with a feral edge to his thoughts that he didn't like. The feeling matched the expressions of the Rifters around him; even the Aerenarch's face had hardened, unexpectedly calling his oldest brother to Osri's mind.

Osri shifted on his feet, still leaning against the bulkhead.

Jaim and Montrose were in the engine room, so the nav console was empty, but the captain had not invited him to sit there. There was no other place for him to sit, but he didn't want to be locked up in the dispensary, so he'd kept silent.

A pulse of bluish light bloomed in the viewscreen.

"Emergence," said Lokri. "Reads like a frigate. Two thousand klicks out from *Sunflame*."

Vi'ya tabbed her com. "Jaim, shut down the fiveskip, now."

Osri gritted his teeth, finding that his jaw already ached. This was the most dangerous part of the trap their Rifter captors had set. Cold-starting a fiveskip resonance was an iffy thing—and if it didn't catch they'd be helpless against the greater speed and firepower of the frigate. But there was no help for it: when the *Sunflame*'s engines blew, radiating a sharp-edged gee-pulse with all their remaining power, any fiveskip within a thousand kilometers would be crippled, knocked into an unstable resonance that could take up to an hour to quell.

"Fiveskip off."

"Target vectoring toward *Sunflame*. Minus eighteen hundred kilometers." Lokri's drawl tightened incrementally toward normal.

Osri felt a spurt of disdain. *Only a Rifter would fall for this trap.* A naval vessel would stand off at a safe distance and use a missile or its beam weapons—but not Rifters, with the propensity for savagery illustrated by what they'd found on board the wreck. *They want more of the same sadistic fun, and they'll pay for it.*

"Sixteen hundred kilometers. I've got an image."

A window swelled on the viewscreen, revealing the predatory form of a frigate, molded in the archaic, angular form of the Techno-Mannerism Revival of 550 years previous. Despite its age, its flourish of projecting weaponry looked lithe and deadly. On its hull was blazoned a white rose with an eye in its center, with red flames writhing from between the petals, and in stylized script its name.

Lokri tapped at his console. "*Hellrose*. Harl Lignis is captain."

Marim snorted. "So I guess old Terelli is breathing Void. Better for us. Lignis'll want to play before he kills. He's even more twisty than Hreem."

"Is he"—Lokri smiled suddenly—"a Dol'jharian?"

Marim jumped, nearly strangling on a laugh of surprise, and Osri caught his breath when Vi'ya's black, unblinking eyes turned Lokri's way, then back again.

"Fourteen hundred kilometers." Lokri's drawl was back.

He think he's won something. Osri looked away, his guts churning.

Brandon's hands tapped precisely at his console, which still had Jaim's knife and hair lying across the top, like a strange kind of offering. The Tenno glyphs echoed across the top of the main screen rippled through a series of configurations as more information built up about their enemy.

"Twelve hundred kilometers."

The tension on the bridge increased. No one made any unnecessary movements. All of their attention was bent on the frigate, willing it into the killing radius of the *Sunflame*'s trap.

"One thousand kilometers."

Vi'ya did not move.

"What are you waiting for?" Lokri snapped, his bravado gone. "Blast him before he gets wise."

"The closer he is, the more damage it will do," Vi'ya said, her eyes on the screen. "We wait."

Lokri's fingers drummed lightly on his console. "Nine hundred kilometers."

Osri's mouth felt dry, but his hands were sweaty. Even if the trap worked, the frigate bristled with weaponry far outclassing that of the *Telvarna*. What did the captain have in mind? He slid a glance at the Aerenarch, but he was impossible to read, armored behind the Douloi shield.

Suddenly Lokri tapped at his console, his breath hissing between his teeth. "Eight hundred kilometers and slowing. He's coming about."

"Then it is time," Vi'ya said, and tabbed a key on her console.

There was a faint sparkle from the wreckage of the *Sunflame* and the looped conversations suddenly fell silent. The ruined ship crumpled inward, as if in the grip of an invisible fist; a few hull plates spun away into space. Osri felt a wave of nausea grip him, passing so swiftly he wasn't sure it was the effect of the gravitational burst from the *Sunflame*'s engines or the sudden release of tension.

The effect on the *Hellrose* was more dramatic. The frigate's radiants suddenly flared into painful brightness as the ship abruptly accelerated, heading past the wreck.

"Got him!" Lokri laughed. "Accelerating at fifty gees, course 250 mark 32."

Vi'ya tabbed her com. "Jaim, bring the fiveskip back up."

Moments later Jaim reported, "Fiveskip up." Osri could almost see the wave of relief sweep the bridge.

"He's heading for Warlock," said Brandon. "If he gets deep enough into radius he'll negate the advantage our fiveskip gives us."

"We will deal with him before that," Vi'ya said as her fingers tapped rapidly at her console.

The starfield in the viewscreen slewed, Dis whirling overhead, as the *Telvarna* spun about and accelerated away in the opposite direction, to avoid exposing the little ship to the more powerful weapons of the *Hellrose*. A short time later the *Telvarna* leapt into skip briefly, came about, and skipped again. On the viewscreen a graphic windowed up, showing a god's-eye view of Warlock and its moons. The course of the *Telvarna* was taking it straight at the gas giant.

"Arkad, attack one coming up."

Brandon's hands barely moved on the keys. "Aft launcher ready, missile barrage, wide dispersion; aft cannon ready."

Moments later the *Telvarna* shuddered out of skip.

"*Hellrose* detected: 182 mark 3, plus 12 light-seconds."

The ship trembled as the Aerenarch loosed the missile barrage and Osri could hear the faint susurration of the cooling pumps as the aft cannon discharged a burst of plasma at maximum power: the *Telvarna* had skipped ahead of the enemy, emerging between it and Warlock.

The starfield slewed again. This time a flash of orange announced the nearness of the gas giant and its deadly gravitational well. The *Telvarna* leapt into skip again.

"Emergence minus nine seconds for attack two," said Vi'ya.

The seconds ticked by.

"Three, two, one, emergence." Lokri's voice overrode the emergence bells. "*Hellrose* at 92 mark 7, plus one light-second."

Brandon stabbed at his console and the aft cannon discharged at the extreme of its sideways travel even as the ship slewed about to bring the aft launcher into play. A frightful glare lit up the viewscreen and the ship bucked, then jarred back into fivespace.

"Chatz! They hit us," Marim squawked. "Just aft of the starboard freight hatch." Her fingers blurred on her console. "Teslas kept most of it out, minor damage, no penetration." She swiped her arm across her forehead. "Too close."

The *Telvarna* jarred into skip, then out, and shuddered to another missile discharge. Then back into skip for a moment and out.

"*Hellrose* at 168 mark 11, plus 9 light-seconds."

The starfield slewed again, bringing a magnified image of the frigate into view. Moments later a gout of light effaced the view for a moment.

"Missile impacts," Lokri said, dead-voiced. "Evidence of cannon hits." He sent one lethal glance over at Vi'ya, and Osri remembered his words: *"No one is worth risking my life for." If we live through this there's going to be trouble later.*

Osri forced his attention back to the screens. First the plasma beams and then the missile barrages of the *Telvarna* had hit the *Hellrose* simultaneously from two directions—an advantage conferred on the smaller ship by its still-functional fiveskip.

"He's leaking, aft portside," Marim reported.

The viewscreen flickered to a close-up of the frigate: a bright cloud of ionized gas billowed from one side. Unable to deal with the simultaneous attacks, the frigate had taken at least one hit.

It took many more as the smaller ship pursued it toward Warlock, stinging again and again from two and three directions at once. The *Telvarna*, too, took hits, and Marim vanished from the bridge. Osri could hear her cursing over the com as she crawled through the accessways, jury-rigging the circuitry and coolant-conduits to keep the ship running.

As the pursuit wore on, Lokri's console lit from time to time with incoming messages, but Vi'ya directed him to ignore them.

The two ships drew nearer and nearer to the gas giant, cutting down on Vi'ya's ability to skip ahead of their fleeing prey. Instead, she began to concentrate on the frigate's weakest spot: its radiants, where the venting gases that cooled its laboring engines created an area that the shields couldn't fully protect.

"We're getting close to radius," said Lokri. "Too close. We're in the Bulge now, and the line is fuzzy."

Osri looked closer at the tactical plot, noticing for the first time that several of the moons of Warlock, including the largest, Pestis, were lined up. Their course would take them into that alignment, where the radius of Warlock would bulge outward in response to the gravitational pull of the moons.

Osri swallowed in a wood-dry throat. It was difficult to predict just how far out radius would extend beyond its normal reach—he hoped their Dol'jharian captain would err on the side of caution.

Vi'ya didn't reply for a moment. Then: "One more attack. Arkad, I want a maximum effort on his radiants."

Brandon studied his console for a moment. "If we can get within a tenth light-second, I can weaken his shields with a lazplaz and follow up with missiles. It won't work from further out, his teslas respond too fast." He paused. "I don't know if our shields can handle his response at that range."

"Never mind," said Lokri, with an unsteady laugh. "He's skipped."

Vi'ya's eyes locked with the dark Rifter's.

Lokri looked away, then his shoulders tightened. "Emergence?" He tabbed his console. "He fell out of skip, just a light-second further on! Two oh eight mark 28, plus 3 light-seconds."

The ship slewed around and the viewscreen flickered to maximum magnification.

Osri choked. The frigate now resembled a sort of metallic wattle-in-the-hole: a vast pudding of now-smooth metal surfaces pocked with small holes from which sprouted obscenely bloated objects like pinkish mushrooms which slowly collapsed, emitting puffs of vapor and ice crystals that glittered in the light of the distant sun.

The Bulge had claimed the *Hellrose*, inverting the frigate and its crew through strange dimensions into a horrible communion of flesh and metal.

Vi'ya said nothing, nor did she move.

For a moment no one else said anything; even the normally irrepressible Marim merely stared at the screen, her expression midway between a gloat and a wince.

Finally Vi'ya tabbed her console and the ship came about. "Back to Dis," she said.

✳   ✳   ✳

"Is that missile ready, Arkad?"

"Ready." The Aerenarch moved aside as Jaim took his place. Above the console the knife still lay, but the braided hair was gone. The main screen showed the *Sunflame*, little changed from its original ruin by the destruction of its engines in the trap.

The Serapisti's lips moved silently for a time. Then, with a curiously gentle motion, he depressed the firing key.

Osri felt a mild jar in his viscera, and the screen showed the missile streaking away toward the devastated ship. Moments later a glare of light blacked out the screen for a moment, clearing to reveal a beautiful sharp-edged rosette of light that slowly faded into oblivion.

"The Light-bearer receive them," murmured Brandon.

Jaim looked over at him silently, then nodded in acknowledgment and left the bridge, this time taking his knife with him.

"Marim," commanded Vi'ya after he was gone, "set a course to the fuel cache."

A short time later Vi'ya engaged the skip for a short hop. When the ship emerged Lokri tapped his console, then looked up. "Cache responds empty." He grimaced. "I guess Norton didn't manage that before Hreem caught him."

"Then listen in on Charvann some more. We need all the information we can get." Vi'ya tabbed her console. "Marim, take the nav console and plot a minimum fuel course to Rifthaven. Use one of these intermediate destinations, or others if I've missed one."

There was silence for a time.

Osri noticed Marim's hands moving aimlessly across the console, apparently rechecking settings and readouts. Her lower lip was red from where she'd been biting it.

After a particularly long pause she looked over. "I'm sorry, Vi'ya—I can't find a course with a positive margin, though there are a couple where Finaygel might save us."

Vi'ya checked her courses, a hint of a line appearing between her eyes. "Lokri, anything more about Hreem or his gang?"

"The discriminators aren't picking up much. I listened in at random to some of the signals from the Syncs—they sound scared and angry. Hreem's chatzers are running wild, the Node and all the Syncs under their control."

Vi'ya shrugged. "Then we're committed."

Lokri hesitated. "There's one thing more. I can't be sure, but it looks like Hreem has gone to Malachronte to take over a battlecruiser nearing completion in the Ways there."

Marim whistled. "That's all we need: Hreem chasing us in a cruiser."

"Good," Lokri drawled, at his most hateful. "We'll need someone to come find us when we run out of fuel." His hand indicated the blackness of space beyond the system.

Vi'ya appeared to ignore him, merely checking Marim's settings through her console. Then she looked up at Osri.

"Take the nav console, Schoolboy. Your Arkad friend here says you are an excellent astrogator. I require you to plot a minimum fuel course to Rifthaven via one of the intermediate destinations I've entered."

Resentment washed through Osri. "And if I refuse?"

"There's an airlock less than fifty meters from here. Your life will last as long as it takes to drag you there." Vi'ya's tone was utterly matter-of-fact; so much so that at first Osri couldn't believe what she had said.

Marim and Lokri watched him, the woman curious, the man merely waiting. With a mixture of outrage and fear flooding him, he turned to the Aerenarch, who rose and came to face Osri directly. "Their enemies are your enemies, Osri, and mine. For the sake of your oath to my father, if nothing else, do as she asks."

It was a command, as direct as the captain's, and unlike hers, it could not be ignored unless Osri wished to be forsworn.

Osri moved reluctantly to the nav console. As he began studying the layout already set up, he felt a new thrill of fear. *There's almost no margin of error; their fuel supply is perilously low.*

He began setting up the search paths for the most efficient course, taking into account gravitational flux, radiation densities, fivespace anomalies, and every other conceivable influence on the potential courses presented to him. The familiar work soothed him, and he soon lost himself in the pleasure of a difficult task well fitted to his talents.

An unknown time later he came out of his labors to awareness of his surroundings. That was perhaps the hardest test of his talents as a navigator he had ever faced. He locked in the course and faced the captain.

The others had not changed their positions. Vi'ya studied the course for a time. "There is more margin here than I expected."

Osri felt a surprising flash of pleasure at this comment, which he recognized, from the little he knew of Vi'ya, as the equivalent of fulsome praise.

She tapped her console. The starfield on the screen wheeled about, then blanked as the ship engaged. "Four and a half days to Granny Chang's." She looked up at Osri, her face dead calm but her dark eyes wide and unblinking. "You are free to go now, Omilov."

Osri walked off the bridge, but the silence behind him made him linger in the accessway. Sensing danger, he looked back just in time to see Vi'ya get up from her console and cross the bridge toward Lokri.

Beyond her, Marim sat, tense and still. Nearby, the Aerenarch watched, as always unreadable.

"My friend," Vi'ya said softly, but her voice carried.

Lokri had risen, and backed a step or two, his lips parted in a silent laugh. He held up his hands to Vi'ya, palms open, fingers spread.

Was the entire ship taken by some kind of madness? Osri watched as Vi'ya backed Lokri up against a bulkhead.

"Friend," Vi'ya said. "Let us share the fires together." One hand gripped Lokri's shoulder, and he winced.

Her other hand stroked down his face, the nail on her little finger scoring him from temple to jaw. Beads of blood sprang out on Lokri's skin, but he didn't move, didn't even seem to breathe, his light eyes locked with Vi'ya's dark ones.

She slid her hand down his arm, then gripped. Lokri stumbled toward the doorway where Osri stood.

He did not stay to witness the rest of this interaction. Retreating to the galley, he sat and watched uncomprehendingly as Lucifur prowled, ears flicking, back and forth, back and forth.

You are free to go, Omilov.

It was the first time she had ever used his name.

❊   ❊   ❊

The clashing of brass cymbals summoned Ivard from the darkness.

His body yammered for succor: screaming yellow fire in his back; hissing violet tide pressing on his eyes; the mutter of a curious green scent filling his nostrils. He struggled to rise, but his hands had turned to stone, unfeeling except the blue pulse around one wrist.

He tried once more to open his eyes but the pressure on his lids permitted the barest slit, awash in fluid, through which he saw the flicker of candles on either side of a hooded figure.

Arms raised, something golden glinted: clash!

"Hear me, you whom my soul loves," said a familiar voice. *Jaim.*

Identifying the figure steadied Ivard, and he relaxed back in his bunk.

It's Jaim, and he's doing something religious.

Jaim did religious things most every day, though seldom with the candles and never before with a hood over his head. Or was something really over his head?

Ivard tried to look more closely, but something was wrong with his eyes. They itched when he tried to open them, so he subsided. He didn't care anyway.

For the third time the cymbals clashed, a sweet sound that Ivard found comforting. He listened with pleasure until the faint ringing had completely disappeared.

"See me, you whom my soul loves." And a brightness flickered against Ivard's eyelids, followed by the sharp tang of incense.

The green scent filled Ivard's lungs, sending runnels of tiny blue fire inside him.

It was good to be here like this, better than the dispensary. In there he was closed in, and it got boring, but here he felt a kind of current, and he floated somewhere.

"Where do you wander now, you whom my soul loves, in the light of paradise?" Jaim's voice seemed to come from everywhere.

Paradise . . . what was that? Lots of planets seemed to have that name. *Rifthaven,* Ivard thought hazily as he drifted upward. *We're rich now. We can buy anything. That's Paradise.*

Then a whisper somewhere just behind his head drew his attention. Was that Jaim?

No, he could hear Jaim: *"The cleansing flame did I give you, yet still I hear your voice and feel your gaze . . ."*

The whisper behind Ivard carried a feeling of urgency. Was something wrong with the ship?

Because he realized he could see the whole ship now, including the white heat of the engines driving them silently through the void. He could see inside the ship too, only it wasn't like watching a vid, it was like feeling flames. Pale ones, bright ones.

The whisperers were watching the brightest two flames.

When Ivard turned his attention that way, he became aware of the triple watchers from his dreams. All of them were drawn ineluctably toward the glow.

Chaos.

That was the double whisper. Ivard glimpsed a flickering image, repeated many times over. He fought to bring it into focus and for a moment he saw the captain's cabin, things strewn or smashed, bright red smears on walls and deck.

The vision disappeared and Ivard heard mingled harsh breathing, heard hearts pumping blood through two bodies locked in bone-wrenching struggle.

*Rage-without-*fi . . .

It was a question, but he couldn't answer, not with the sound of blood filling his ears, and the heat that radiated past him like the singe from the Tarkans' firejacs.

Ivard saw the flickering image again as the bodies sprang apart, one of them stumbling against the shadowy shape of a bulkhead.

Lokri—that's Lokri.

The comtech straightened up slowly, sweat-dripping hair hanging in his wide silver eyes, and in his hand was a dagger.

He's afraid for his life, Ivard thought. His own heartbeat hammered counterpoint.

Lokri pulled back his arm, struck. In a blur of movement the captain feinted bare-handed, blocked the forward stroke of the knife with a crack that Ivard felt like lightning through his brain.

Lokri gasped, dropping the knife and clutching his forearm. Vi'ya grabbed up the knife from the deck, then slashed it down Lokri's body in one swift movement. Ivard watched with helpless terror—but Lokri did not die. With the other hand the captain pulled Lokri's shirt away from his bruised and blood-smeared flesh.

Lokri's head jerked up and he tried to free himself, just to meet a powerful openhanded slap from Vi'ya's palm that sent him reeling back against a bulkhead.

"For love is stronger than death, and more enduring than flame," Jaim's voice intoned somewhere behind Ivard, and again the cymbals rang.

The captain backhandéd Lokri across the other side of his face, and he landed flat on the deck, his arms outflung. She jammed the knife into a wall, and then she was on him.

Ivard tried to move away, to go back to Jaim and his candles, but the watchers forced him to stay: the two whisperers giving him flickering multiple images, the silent three sending sounds, and beyond sounds, a sense of touch so vast and terrible that Ivard's mind was paralyzed.

Ivard felt the susurrus of flesh over flesh, the salty sting of a hot tongue as the captain licked slowly, slowly, the hollow of Lokri's throat, tasted blood and sweat.

She was brown skin over cat muscles, her long back scarred under the drift of silky black hair. Her fingers dug into Lokri's outflung arms. His hands went rigid, clutching at air, when the seeking mouth moved down over his chest, showed teeth. Blood rushed and sang, sweeping away Ivard's own terror in a cataract of rage-driven passion.

"For love is stronger than death, and more enduring than flame. The waters of Ending cannot drown it, nor the Void claim it," Jaim chanted far away in the background.

The scents of fear and desire mingled with the hot copper taste of blood. Vi'ya sank her teeth into his belly, just to the threshold point of pain. Lokri's eyes closed: his pain, and desire, lanced through the watchers like jac-fire.

No sound beyond the heartbeats and the harsh crescendo of mingled breathing as the bodies suddenly locked, bound all around by her long black hair.

The whisperers said: *Cessation in joining?*

Once again Ivard missed the meaning of the question. Blood pounded through his brain, then suddenly diminished into darkness. The watchers abruptly left, and Ivard cried out frantically after them.

He was alone, and something suffocated him. But who could help? Was Lokri dying? He struggled to find his body again, and almost had it, guided by a banner of fire round his wrist. But then the darkness shimmered even around that.

The last thing he was aware of was the sound of cymbals, and Jaim's voice, soft and steady:

For love is stronger than death, and more enduring than flame. Turn your eyes from me, beloved, and go hence in peace. Await me in Paradise, for surely I will come.

Ivard heard Lokri cry out in anguish, and then he took his last breath, spiraling down into the darkness.

TWELVE

*

Montrose waited as Sebastian Omilov considered his next move. They were playing chess in the dispensary. Montrose had been delighted when he discovered the Panarchist not only knew the game from Lost Earth but was an ardent devotee of opera, ancient and modern. *It's a little like finding myself,* he reflected in amusement. *Or myself in a favored universe.*

Finally Montrose realized Omilov had not seen his last move. He waited a little longer: the gnostor was indeed facing the chessboard, but his eyes were focused a thousand light-years beyond it.

"Tired?" he asked. "We can continue another time if you need more rest."

Omilov slowly folded back the edge of the exotic dressing gown Montrose had loaned him, his eyes distracted.

A quiet "tick" brought Montrose's attention back to the board. With exquisite tact, Omilov had leaned forward and adjusted his knight on its new square.

Montrose looked up. "Forgive me. My move?"

"You'll note the clever placement of my knight?"

"Laying siege to my bishop?" Montrose smiled, then mused half to himself, "Where are the kings?"

Omilov's brows went up—and Montrose realized that he'd begun to drum his fingers on the edge of the antique chessboard.

"If you wish to postpone our match," the gnostor said as Montrose pulled his hand away from the board.

Before Montrose could answer, the door hissed open and Jaim entered the dispensary, carrying Ivard. The boy's face was swollen and blue-tinged, and they could hear his breath wheezing from across the room. The pungent smell of incense wafted in with the two.

Montrose leapt to his feet, knowing immediately what had happened, and hit the control for an examination table to emerge from its storage place. As Jaim lowered the boy to the table, Montrose jabbed at his dispensary console, and a moment later sprayed an anti-anaphylactic into Ivard's arm.

Almost at once Ivard's struggle for breath became easier, and after a few seconds he opened his eyes as wide as the swelling would allow. "Voices," he croaked.

"Voices?" Montrose repeated.

Ivard nodded, swallowing with difficulty. "Voices . . . and Lokri—" He sighed, and his eyes fluttered closed.

"I happened to look over at him and he'd almost stopped breathing," Jaim said.

"Allergic reaction," Montrose murmured, his eyes on the readouts above the table. "Probably to your incense."

Jaim frowned. "This never happened before, and he's smelled my incenses, lots of times."

"It's the Kelly band." Montrose looked down at Ivard's pale face as the boy muttered something about voices again. "I'll have to keep him in here until we reach Rifthaven." He pursed his lips, then said, "Why did he mention Lokri?"

Jaim's long face closed over. "I haven't heard or seen anything."

"It's been a few years," Montrose mused. Then, aware of the Panarchist listening on the other side of the dispensary, he added "If she's done with him, you might see if anything is left. I'll prep here."

Jaim nodded and moved out.

※   ※   ※

Our period of withdrawal is nigh. We have new word-nexi to celebrate within the world-mind. We celebrate words: we cele-

brate we-and-you, *we celebrate* sleep, *we celebrate* entities-separate, *we celebrate*—

Celebrate them in the world-mind. I have no need to remember them with you. Have you heard new word-nexi while I slept?

While you slept we separated the patterns of the angry-one, the damaged-one-who-hears-music, the moth-one amended by Vi'ya, the one-who-gives-fire-stone. We cannot hear the one-with-three.

Word-nexi?

Word-nexi are again betrayal, loyalty *from the angry one;* cessation *from the moth-one,* Ilara-in-cessation *from the damaged-one-who-hears-music,* loyalty *and the image of the Markham entity-in-cessation from the one-who-gives-fire-stone. We must repeat our contemplation of the word-nexus* loyalty *as its images in the pattern of the angry-one are not compatible with the images in the pattern of the one-who-gives-fire-stone.*

Then let us begin . . .

❊   ❊   ❊

Marim slipped into the dispensary cubicle, laughing at the way Ivard promptly blushed.

Sanctus Hicura, you're an ugly little blit. "Firehead!" She leaned down to kiss him.

Ivard hunched his skinny shoulders. "Montrose said—"

"I know, you have to rest, or he won't let you get off *Telvarna* when we reach Granny Chang's. But he's in the galley counting over rations with Schoolboy so I thought I'd just sneak in. I missed you."

Ivard's stupid grin almost made her laugh in his face.

"Tell me: Jaim says you been going crazy."

Ivard blinked, his pale eyes going opaque for a moment. "Voices," he said. "I think it's this." He touched his freckled wrist just above the Kelly band, now completely melded with his flesh. "But when I'm in here I don't hear 'em," he added, looking hopeful.

"Good. Don't want anyone spying on us when we bunny." She leaned forward to kiss him again, and paused when he winced, his blush now going purple. "Here, what's this?" She touched his hot cheeks. "Don't tell me you're bunking me out—"

Ivard shook his head, his lips pressed together.

She could tell from the lack of humor in his eyes that whatever was in his mind bothered him deeply—and she was not going to hear anything about it.

He couldn't *have been there when Vi'ya duffed Lokri.* Marim bit her lip against a laugh. She'd been the one to find her bunkmate after Vi'ya was through with him, and he'd refused to go to the dispensary so she'd brought Montrose to him. Even sedated, Lokri had refused to talk about what had happened.

Marim grinned at Ivard. *I'll get that story out of him.* She patted his head and talked of inconsequentials. Just before she left, she brought up his loot again, and noted that he'd completely forgotten to mention his missing coin.

✳   ✳   ✳

Jaim moved swiftly through the kinesic form, blocking a blow, striking lightly with fist and then foot. The Arkad countered these smoothly; he was not a person so much as a part of the pattern, and his movement together with Jaim's was a unity of opposites—cause and form—which soothed Jaim.

"Keep focus on the pattern, move within the pattern, and you will see how it extends out through space and time." That was what Jaim's mother had told him long ago.

The pattern which Jaim had thought was the harmony the universe strove toward, the syncretic he had found with Serapisti and Ulanshu thought: *the joining, the unity.*

Bitterness stung. *There is not unity, and there can never be joining.* The bright inner path he had always found so comforting was gone, replaced by the image of Reth's claw-slashed body stiffened in death.

Jaim moved faster, trying to force thought and memory into oblivion. Whirling speed, unending movement, brought a kind of peace until he sensed a faltering in his partner. He shifted abruptly out of the fight trance to see the Arkad backed against a wall, his chest heaving, with Jaim's own fingers extended knife-stiff against his neck.

Jaim dropped his arm. The Arkad closed his eyes, wiping dripping hair out of his face with a hand that shook. Jaim glanced at the engine room chrono and was amazed at the time that had passed.

"That was too long," he said. "Should've stopped me."

Brandon smiled briefly. "Good test . . ." He fought for breath, his light voice hoarse. "In a real fight . . . I can't call time . . . if I'm tired."

Doing a rapid mental review, Jaim realized he'd not only gone long over the time for a practice bout, but he'd forgotten to pull some of his moves. Yet the Arkad had handled that as well. *He's fighting his own shades, I think.* Out loud he said, "You learn quickly."

"Not quickly enough . . ." Brandon said, dropping onto a chair. He smiled ruefully. "You killed me half a dozen times."

Jaim was about to say something when a noise that had been tugging at his consciousness since he broke the trance resolved into the dancing melodies of classical music. Memory smote him again, different memory this time.

"KetzenLach," Brandon said unerringly, his head tipped to one side. And then, "Who is that playing?"

"Montrose," Jaim said. "Keyboard." *He has not played that since Markham died. Why is he doing it now?*

Brandon leaned back against a bulkhead, eyes half-closed, sweat shining down his shirtless body. "He's good." The faint emphasis on the last word evinced surprise.

Jaim pulled on his tunic, then mopped his stinging eyes with his sleeve. He could have told the Arkad that the *Telvarna* carried a remarkable range of taped music of every kind, from every era, but always Markham had preferred music made by living hands and voices.

Jaim frowned, hearing the music not in memory, but in reality: Montrose was playing, as he used to, loud enough to drift down the corridors.

And now I'd rather have silence.

Jaim saw a slight movement and looked up. The Arkad was staring off into the distance, his face reflective. He noticed Jaim's regard then and said with a half-smile, "Markham used to play that cycle on tapes. All the time."

"He liked music. Reth said . . ." Jaim winced, tried to force away the memory, and because it wouldn't stay forced, he spoke it instead. "Reth said he was changing crew around so he could have music whenever we went into skip."

"Who else plays?"

The question was idle, the Arkad's gaze off in the distance. "We—Reth Silverknife and I—with sansa-drum and twelve-tone cymbals. Paysud with windpipes. Ah, but Paysud is dead now. Lokri, if he drinks enough, knows songs from across several systems. Sings. Well," he added.

"So Markham had a better conservatory than he had a crew." The light voice, gaining strength, carried an edge.

Jaim considered before answering, decided the edge was not meant to cut him. "Not all of 'em," he said. "Jakarr hated music."

"Jakarr . . . He was the one who tried the takeover when Osri and I arrived, right?"

Jaim nodded, mopping his face again, slinging back the mourning-short hair around his face. "Was Fire Control on *Telvarna* until Markham found out Vi'ya was faster. Trouble started then."

The Arkad smiled a little. "Vi'ya? Makes music too?"

"No." Jaim hesitated again, wondering how much to say, then decided there was nothing to say. "But she listened."

KetzenLach's fast melodies, talking, all brought back images from a year ago. Laughter, song . . . plans. *Markham, Reth, gone. And the harmony gone with them.* Jaim winced, shook his head.

Brandon's face had eased, showing interest, reflecting Jaim's own regrets. Now his smile turned polite, masking his thoughts. He got to his feet. "Thanks," he said, indicating the mats, and went out.

Jaim looked around the familiar engine room, his realm for so many years. *The flame wanders where it will . . .* What had seemed wisdom was now merely empty platitude.

He walked out, bathed round by music and the memories it evoked, and went straight to Vi'ya's cabin.

✳   ✳   ✳

Marim leaned against the wall, her foot propped behind her, watching. Had Jaim really kept the Arkad twice as long as usual, or was it just that she was waiting—and bored?

But at last he appeared, his breathing fast, sweat defining his bare torso above the old, borrowed work pants. She jabbed her teeth into her lower lip.

His face was distant, and he would have passed right by without noticing her had she not reached out and caught him by the arm.

The muscle under the smooth brown skin hardened and he

stopped. She saw for a very brief moment a watchfulness, almost a warning in his blue eyes, and then it was gone, replaced by the courtesy he used as a shield.

So born nicks don't touch each other, do they? Reckless, she had to test it: she grinned at him, then swooped a hand down to pinch his crotch.

The courtesy disappeared; his eyes widened in surprise and he stepped back, blocking her hand.

A totally human reaction. She laughed in delight. "You're nacky," she said. "Want to bunny?"

The direct approach seemed to unnerve him. "I'm dirty," he said, his hands out in a deprecating gesture.

"I like it."

Red ridged his cheeks, and she laughed again.

He smiled, a smile of irony as well as humor: his control was back. "Am I being baited? What would you say if I said yes?"

"I'd say my bunk is this way, except Lokri's there, and he'd try to steal you. So we can use yours."

Brandon turned and continued on his way to his cabin. "Are you always this direct?" he asked.

She shrugged. "Usually. I don't see the value in hinting: the answer is no, or yes, and if you chatz up the scanners too much, you might be askin' to bunny and they might hear an invite to view your collection of Divtish gumslugs."

Brandon laughed. "But it's not always that simple."

"Sure it is," she chirped, and waited for the informative lecture on Douloi indirection, and how every human interaction carried unending consequences. Thus underscoring all on his own the innocence of her intentions.

They reached the cabin and he leaned against the door. He was still smiling, but the irony was very much in evidence. "In any society," he observed, "disingenuousness makes an effective tactic."

Warning tingled in her, causing her to laugh in surprise and delight. *But of course he assumes Markham talked through nights about nick doings. Which he did.*

And because she really was reckless, she leaned past him and palmed the lock. The door slid open behind him, and she gave him a gentle push. "You think I don't want to bunny?"

"Maybe you do," he said, obligingly stepping inside, "but I

don't." It was said so lightly, and with a rare, wide smile, that she was charmed.

And she was also in.

Wandering the perimeter, she scanned here and there, then turned to grin over her shoulder at him. "What's the matter?" she challenged. "You just like nick women? Or is it men only?"

He sat down on his bunk, spreading his hands. "What matter either way?"

"Because the first, I can show you things I bet those nick ladies only watch on their secret vids, and as for the second— well, I never did like following a dead trace." She finished her circuit of the room: nothing in sight. She found herself hoping that she *wouldn't* find the coin too soon.

Brandon sat back. "Since we're being direct, won't it hit that boy hard if you rack up with someone else?"

She pursed her lips. "He's on the sick list."

Brandon nodded. "And it won't help him recover any faster if his first love bunks him out for someone else."

She opened her mouth to say that Ivard wouldn't notice, except he would, and they both knew it. The boy was as sensitive as something with antennae. Besides, she'd known since they walked in that she wasn't going to get into Brandon's bunk— this time—so she got back to business. "It would cheer him more," she said, "if the stuff he lost would find its way back into his pocket."

Brandon looked surprised. "You mean he lost Markham's flight ribbon?" His face went serious.

"*And* something Greywing gave him."

"He never mentioned that," Brandon said absently. "Where? When?"

He's still thinking about Markham's chatzing Academy thing. "Here," she said, pointing outside. "When you got back to the ship after the raid on your palace."

Brandon looked relieved. "Then it ought to turn up."

Dead trace indeed. "Hope so," she said cheerfully. "If you happen to find it, or them, I should say, let him know."

"What else am I looking for?"

She shrugged, moving toward the door. "Little metal object," she said carelessly. "Old. But that flight ribbon is real important to him." She waited for Brandon's nod of acknowledgment—he believed her. "So I'll try you later. When you're clean!" Grinning, she disappeared.

❊   ❊   ❊

The green light was on in the annunciator.

Jaim tabbed the door open. Seldom did anyone go to the captain's cabin, though it was the most spacious one on the ship. It had a second cabin off it, for servants or lovers in more sumptuous days. Now that housed the Eya'a in a refrigerated room that was bare except for complicated fluttering hangings that the Eya'a wove themselves.

The main cabin was large and seemed larger, so barren it was of furniture. A narrow bunk was set directly beneath a viewport. On the opposing wall hung an age-battered tapestry, full of dark fires and destruction. These things were familiar: what was new was a tear-shaped stone hanging just below the tapestry. As always, no personal items were in sight. Nor was there any sign of blood, or destruction.

As Jaim crossed the white-tiled, antiseptic floor, colors muttered deeply within the tear-shaped stone, distracting him for a moment. *That's the stone the Arkad gave her on the Mandala.* He was surprised she'd put it up, like some kind of trophy; then he realized that raiding the Mandala successfully was an event that required commemoration if ever there was one.

Vi'ya was seated at her console. She shut down her work and saved it with a gesture, then turned to face Jaim.

He studied her for a moment, realized that the cabin was silent: Montrose's music did not penetrate here.

"After we refit at Granny Chang's," Jaim said, "where do we go?"

She did not immediately reply. They regarded one another for an unmeasured time. Jaim thinking back to a memory he had almost obliterated. *"A culture which does not permit the concept of regret creates burdens in other ways,"* Reth Silverknife had said to him, afterward, as she anointed his bruises with pungent ointment. *"You can forgive, which helps you to understand, and understanding releases you from that burden."*

Reth's smooth round face gave way to the long oval face before him. Reth's compassionate gaze disappeared before Vi'ya's dark eyes, cold and dense as winter ice. She sat straight and still, her hands laid patiently across her console, her black suit, made high to her neck, concealing the strong body with its tell-tale scars.

The contrast made him blink; the harmony he had fought so hard to attain was gone, and with it his hold on the here and now. Echoes of past pain ripped at him with sharp claws.

Vi'ya spoke, inadvertently saving him. "Stay with us until Rifthaven."

It was a command, but it obviated the request and the explanation that he found he could not make. He nodded wordlessly.

"We'll stay at Chang's only long enough to refuel," she went on. "I want to get to Rifthaven quickly."

The problems facing them in the here and now steadied Jaim. He considered. "You think Eusabian's allies know who we are?"

Vi'ya shook her head. "I have given it much thought. Those on Arthelion know only that a vessel named *Maiden's Dream* broke atmosphere, landed near the palace, and later took off, escaping the *Fist*. Strictly speaking they have no way of identifying the ship with those who raided the palace—"

"Of course they'll assume it."

"That is correct. Which means they will assume that the gnostor is with that vessel."

"So you will confine him to quarters at Rifthaven?"

"All three," she said. "We have to assume that their fastest ships have been dispatched to all centers, and the price on the Arkad's head, should they discover that he is alive after all, will be high enough to buy anyone's loyalty."

"Lokri?"

Vi'ya's face did not change. "He will not sell us out."

A moment of thought brought the realization that Brandon, if sold to those who wanted him, only had to talk about his raid on Arthelion—and the real name of the ship—and they'd be dead meat. Lokri wouldn't sell the Arkad because all he'd get for his reward would be hooks through his ribs in some sulphur pit on Dol'jhar.

Jaim let his breath out. "Still, it's dangerous. What if someone puts the death of the gnostor's torturers together with the Eya'a? Enough people know they're with us . . ."

"They know that the Eya'a can kill, but the effect of their *fi* varies too much to identify them." She stopped and looked up sharply.

A moment later the light above the door indicated someone

outside. Vi'ya slowly reached over, reluctantly, it seemed to Jaim, and tabbed the passkey.

The door slid open and Brandon walked in, fresh from the shower, wearing the clean tunic and trousers Jaim had loaned him. His eyes went from one of them to the other. "Should I return?"

Jaim rose to leave, but Vi'ya moved her hand.

But it's obvious he wants an interview alone, Jaim thought.

A pause developed into silence. Brandon waited for Vi'ya to speak, but she sat where she was.

He said, "We're arriving somewhere soon?"

"Chang bubbloid," Vi'ya said.

"Would it be possible for the Omilovs and myself to disembark there?"

"Perhaps," Vi'ya said.

Brandon walked slowly along the perimeter of the room, then turned and smiled. "The question," he said, "was an attempt to get an idea of our status. Are we passengers or prisoners, or somewhere between?"

"There is nowhere safe in your Thousand Suns now," Vi'ya said.

"We can take our chances on that," Brandon countered.

She shook her head. "If you are found, your enemies, and ours, will not be long behind us."

Brandon's face did not change. He gave a slight nod, his face considering, and walked a few steps further, looking at the glittering stone. He turned then, smiling, and made a quick flourish, an airy gesture that managed to combine humor with elaborate ceremony.

Vi'ya said nothing.

"In any case," Brandon said then, glancing at the silver ball above Vi'ya's console, "Sebastian would not wish to leave without his artifact."

Vi'ya still said nothing.

Jaim felt a prickling of discomfort at her blank face and the unblinking gaze that stayed on the Arkad as he walked the length of the room and back. *She did not ask him to sit down, and he's too polite to just do it,* Jaim realized.

"What is this?" Brandon said, indicating the tapestry.

"Dhur'zhni Jharg'at Choreid," she said

And Brandon translated, "The Annihilation of the Isle of the Chorei."

Jaim was surprised into speech. "You know Dol'jharian!"

"Some," Brandon said. "In self-defense, when I was small, I tried to learn it. Anaris had a picture much like this, but he wouldn't tell us what it was."

Anaris rahal'Jerrodi, Eusabian's son, the hostage after Acheront, Jaim thought. *I wonder if he's still alive.*

Brandon leaned forward to examine the tapestry, without touching it. "Where did you get it?"

"Bought," Vi'ya said. "On Rifthaven. From a dealer in rare artifacts." Her voice had flattened.

Brandon crossed the room to the Eya'a door, then turned and walked back. The cold air of the room, comfortable for a Dol'jharian, stirred, and as the Arkad passed, Jaim caught a faint trace of soapscent.

"Have you ever seen Eusabian?" Brandon asked.

"No."

The question had included them both, so Jaim shook his head. Brandon's blue eyes brushed past his face, but his gaze was distracted: Jaim wondered if the Arkad even saw him. *He's trying to read her, and failing.*

Another silence built, and unexpectedly Vi'ya broke it. "The nobles on Dol'jhar seldom appear to any but their peers, and perhaps to an enemy, just before battle."

Which he must know, if he studied the language. He wants to know what her station was before she left.

Brandon crossed back again, then he stopped before Vi'ya. "Thank you," he said. And he turned and left.

When the door had closed behind him, Vi'ya tapped her console to life, a sharp, quick gesture.

Jaim said, "We all need some R&R."

Vi'ya looked up.

Jaim went on, "No one will want to stay here to guard those three. You have only to let Granny know that they're to return to the *Telvarna* and she'll see that they do."

She gave a slow nod. "True."

Jaim got to his feet. She did not detain him; if she'd had something further to discuss before Brandon's interruption, apparently she'd changed her mind.

He went out.

The music had stopped.

PART TWO

✳

THIRTEEN

ARTHELION

As they rounded a corner in the second sublevel of the Palace
Major, something shimmered out of the wall near the feet of
Anaris' Tarkan escort. The guard's grip tightened on his weapon, his eyes flicking toward Anaris, who tried to project amusement mixed with boredom. Reassured, the Tarkan marched
on—but his fingers were white on his jac. It undoubtedly didn't
help that the lights were set low for the nightwatch, leaving the
corridors indistinct and corners obscure with unquiet shadows.

Anaris glanced at the Bori stumping alongside him. The lighting had been Morrighon's suggestion; after he arranged to deflect Barrodagh's wrath from the computer tech, Ferrasin had
been only too willing to report that the lighting cycles were a
part of the palace computer's programming not safe to tamper
with. *My Bori scuttler was a terrible mistake on Barrodagh's
part.*

The report of his first encounter with the haunting had
spread rapidly. Now the Tarkans were beginning to treat him
as more than the conditional heir, although never in the pres-

ence of the Avatar. This encounter would merely strengthen the rumors.

The Tarkan paused before a scuffed wood-paneled door. Morrighon reached past him and tabbed the annunciator, and the door swung open.

"Wait here," Anaris said to the Tarkan. He entered Morrighon's quarters, followed by the Bori.

Inside, Anaris looked around. The small suite was almost painfully neat: a long, plain desk against one wall was piled with geometrically precise stacks of paper and carefully arranged datachips, the chair drawn up in the leg well at an exact angle. The other furniture in the room—a few chairs and a low table—were also placed with geometric accuracy.

Anaris looked through the opening into Morrighon's sleeping room. Arranged on a low shelf within easy reach of the bed was a row of at least ten communicators, each with a color-coded band of dyplast around it. They were all live, and the whisper of voices from them made the room seem crowded.

Something else caught his eye. The pillow on the bed was on the end jutting into the room, not against the wall, where two slightly shiny patches, faint greasy stains, confirmed that Morrighon slept with his feet against the wall, and his head facing the door.

Confidence, or mere eccentricity? Anaris knew he could never sleep in so exposed a position. He eyed Morrighon as he returned to the sitting room and seated himself in the best chair, near the low table. His assumptions about his secretary were undergoing another adjustment. *There is a depth to this one that he conceals very well.*

Morrighon stood respectfully opposite Anaris until the Dol'-jharian motioned him to sit.

"We can speak freely here, lord," said the Bori. "The words the listeners hear will not be those we speak. Indeed, what they hear will implicate Nyzherian, one of Barrodagh's close allies."

Anaris raised an eyebrow. "Ferrasin." It was not quite a question.

Morrighon smiled in acknowledgment. "Your protection of him has advanced us a great deal."

Anaris stared at the Bori until the man's eyes fell. The claim implicit in the word "us" was an astonishingly bold statement to make, even as true as it was. *You have made your decision, it seems, and I must make mine.*

"Indeed," said Anaris neutrally, after he judged enough time had passed. Morrighon's squinty eyes relaxed a trifle, and some of the fear leaked out of his posture.

There was a long pause. Anaris could see that the Bori was gathering himself to ask a question he feared might offend. The Dol'jharian uncrossed his arms and placed his hands on his thighs.

"My lord," began Morrighon formally, "it is needful that I inquire on a matter touching the ancestors. Have I your leave, free of pain and iron?"

Anaris snorted, and the Bori flinched. "You are well trained, Bori, but out of the hearing of others, you may dispense with formality."

Morrighon inclined his head. "It is about the apparitions. I do not understand why they seem to follow you. If . . ." He swallowed, still nervous. "If they were truly the shades of dead Panarchists, as the Tarkans think, then that would be reasonable, but as they are a computer artifact, why is that?"

Anaris merely looked at him for a time, impelling the Bori to continue. "I ask not from mere curiosity, lord, but so that I may better know how to exploit them to your benefit."

The Dol'jharian nodded. He couldn't do everything himself, and since the Tarkan would report this meeting—the listeners would know they were being gulled, but would not be able to prove it—Morrighon had committed himself to Anaris' service. If Anaris failed, Morrighon would die—painfully. *And you know that I know that, don't you, my scuttler?* The Bori's subtlety pleased him—he might indeed be a match for Barrodagh.

"That is correct," Anaris acknowledged, and proceeded to tell Morrighon the story of the Krysarch's practical joke and its consequences.

When he was finished, to Anaris' amazement, the Bori snickered, a strange, falsetto gurgle, as though he had a tree frog concealed in his throat. "It is indeed the Aerenarch's shade, then, even though he is still alive. How wonderful that your enemy should be helping you to the throne of the Avatar."

Anaris smiled, savoring irony.

* * *

Morrighon wiped his eyes and took a deep breath, energized and relieved by the heir's acceptance of his jest. He found Anaris an unsettling master. Most of his actions were those expected of his father's son, but at other times his behavior was unpredictable.

For one thing, Anaris seemed to accept him as a person, despite his ugliness—certainly no other Dol'jharian noble the Bori could think of would have so easily agreed to come to his quarters. That was demeaning in Dol'jharian terms; and it had taken all of Morrighon's courage to make the suggestion.

Anaris was looking at him now, expressionless, his dark eyes intelligent in the strong-boned face.

"According to Ferrasin, there may be even more to it than that," the Bori continued. "He insists that since our meeting with the Avatar, when he directed that the computer be spared so long as it continued to yield information, it has been easier to extract data from it."

Anaris' brows lifted in disbelief.

"He believes that the computer can distinguish between people, and deal with them according to their degree of threat to its well-being. He points out that the Avatar is not visited by apparitions, even though the Tarkans, when he is not with them, frequently report their appearance in the Palace Minor."

Now Anaris looked thoughtful. "Then he truly does believe it sentient?"

"Yes." Morrighon snickered again, remembering the mixture of fright and pride the fat technician exhibited when speaking of the palace computer—like the father of a changeling. "A wonderful twist, here at the heart of the government that imposed the Ban. And whether or not this is true, it could make a useful ally. Indeed, if he is right, it is probably listening now."

Anaris smiled at the ceiling. "Then, computer, I assure you that as long as you assist me, I will protect you from my father."

Morrighon stared, taken aback by the heir's easy acceptance of the computer's possible sentience. Not that Dol'jharians, any more than the Bori, shared any of the Panarchist abhorrence of machine intelligence. But there had been a veneer of—*well, politeness,* Morrighon thought, at a loss for a better word—in his speech to the machine. And since there was no guarantee that the machine was listening, or could understand, Anaris had revealed a most un-Dol'jharian willingness to appear ridiculous.

After a slight pause, as if waiting for a response, Anaris

looked back at Morrighon. "Has Ferrasin made any progress on the communications situation?"

Morrighon nodded, pleased. *That* was one of the most satisfying aspects of his duel with Barrodagh. "Oh, yes. He has established parallel, hidden channels via hyperwave with a number of our Rifter allies, most notably among the Syndicates of Rifthaven."

Anaris nodded, and Morrighon experienced a thrill at the heir's evident surprise and approval of his rapid success, in this most critical aspect of their efforts.

"Of course," the Bori continued, "we've not contacted any of the firsts among the Syndics, but as with all such organizations, many of the seconds are eager to succeed, and impatient of the normal course of events.

"Best of all, your father cannot really object, should our efforts come to light, since it is in the best interests of Dol'jhar that the Syndics be kept off balance."

Anaris nodded. "If the computer here is cooperative, I expect you could find evidence of similar arrangements by the Panarchists." His eyes were focused on distance, his smile faint.

Now it was the Bori's turn to be surprised, for that had indeed been the case. Without the information that had suddenly materialized on Ferrasin's console, while he and the computer tech were working up their plans for Rifthaven, they would be nowhere near as far along as they were. Truly, Morrighon thought, Anaris was a fascinating amalgam of Dol'jharian severity and Panarchist subtlety. Did Eusabian fully understand how dangerous an opponent this made his son? Morrighon devoutly hoped not.

He remembered the vidchip of the scene in the Throne Room, how the captive Panarch had virtually defeated the Avatar, and how at the end the Avatar's brooding figure had been dwarfed by the magnificence of the chamber, the center of Panarchist power. Looking at Anaris, who had been raised here, Morrighon suddenly realized that this Dol'jharian would fit that room, might even fit that throne. *And I can put him there.*

Barrodagh snapped off the recording with a vicious twist. "Of course, we can be sure that those are not the words actually spoken in that room."

Eusabian merely looked at him for a moment. His strong hands toyed restlessly with his dirazh'u; the shiny silken cord caught the light in faint glimmers as it twisted between his fingers.

"But I will have Nyzherian watched, nonetheless," the Bori continued, "in case that simulation was meant to serve a double purpose."

The Avatar nodded. The curse-weaving cord made a dry, whispering noise in his hands, like the progress of a snake across a bedsheet. "That Bori is more subtle than you expected."

The implied criticism stung, but Barrodagh could not answer without making it worse. And it was true. Had Nyzherian turned? Or was that simulation merely to sow distrust between them? Or was that what he was supposed to think? He cursed silently: he had seriously underestimated Morrighon, who, now that he was under the protection of Anaris, was no longer subordinate to Barrodagh.

The Bori picked up another paper, hoping to get the Avatar on to the next subject, but Eusabian continued in a musing tone, "It was a similar mistake by Ezrigar, my father's secretary, that led me to the throne." The Avatar smiled coldly, the glint of that strange humor in his eyes again. "But that was before your time."

The room felt chilly. Barrodagh had arranged the disgrace and death of his own predecessor, Terreligan, not five years after the Avatar assassinated his own father to assume the throne. Of course, Eusabian knew this—the Dol'jharian nobility even encouraged the internecine warfare among the Bori bureaucrats that ran the state, apparently believing it guaranteed that only the most able survived to serve. But why was he referring to it now?

Then, as the dirazh'u went through yet another evolution in his lord's hands, the Bori suddenly understood. The Avatar was bored. The Panarchy lay supine beneath his feet, his enemy lay imprisoned in his own palace, and there were no immediate challenges for him. Barrodagh knew, and knew that Eusabian did also, that that would change, once the Panarchists gathered their forces, but for now, it appeared, the Avatar was finding amusement in other ways.

The Bori waited. He could feel sweat trickling down his back.

The com chimed, and Barrodagh's relief at the interruption made him almost knock over a stack of datachips in his haste to respond. The screen lit with the face of the captain of the *Fist of Dol'jhar*, who was responsible for monitoring the increasingly complex tactical situation of their Rifter forces.

"Kyvernat Juvaszt here. We have lost contact with the Charvann system. The *Hellrose*, the last ship in-system with an Urian relay, has been destroyed in battle with another Rifter vessel."

"What!" Barrodagh could see the sudden anger in the Avatar's face. They still hadn't found the Heart of Kronos, nor any clues to its whereabouts, and now they no longer had realtime communications with the system. If the Heart was found, it would be five days before they knew.

"I have dispatched a frigate with a relay from Charterly's fleet. It will arrive in six days—I judged the situation at Malachronte to be too critical to further reduce Hreem's forces."

"But what happened? How do you know it was another Rifter, and not Panarchists?"

"We have a transmission from the ship's captain, Lignis, that was terminated by its destruction. It entered skip too close to radius."

"Put it on," Eusabian ordered.

The Bori thought he saw the ghost of a sneering smile directed at him as the captain's visage was replaced by a view of a fat man with a shiny bald head and heavy jowls. A jagged pink scar snaked across his forehead and down one cheek, lifting one eyelid into a permanent expression of surprise. Behind him Barrodagh could see frantic activity on what was evidently the bridge of the *Hellrose*: a bedlam of damage reports, shouts of rage, and an array of red lights that indicated a ship in trouble.

The fat man looked over his shoulder and shouted, "Keep trying Brotherhood channels. She's gotta respond."

A woman's voice shouted in the background, "Fiveskip's coming up! Ten seconds."

"Skip as soon as it's stable," said Lignis, his face breaking into a smile as he turned back to the screen. "And belay that last message. Tell her to kiss my nacker."

"We've got it under control now, we'll be outta here in a moment. But you'd better send some more ships here, if you want to get your hands on . . ."

"Fiveskip's up!"

The screen rippled and the fat man suddenly screamed. Barrodagh stared in horror, his gorge rising, as the man's mouth got wider and wider, his lips folding back over his cheeks, his teeth and gums following. The top of his head opened up and a fungoid growth of brain tissue flowed out across his skull as his face split down the middle and folded outward. Somehow, he kept screaming the whole time. Then, mercifully, the transmission terminated.

Barrodagh clamped his teeth together and held himself rigid, fighting the resurgent memory of his utter terror outside the kitchens when the pie-flinger had attacked. He'd thought this was what was happening to him. Juvaszt had known how this would affect him. Who had talked? Anger fought the nausea down.

"Fascinating," said the Avatar. "Play it again."

Barrodagh stifled a protest and restarted the recording. He didn't dare shut his eyes, so he defocused them, and tried hard not to listen. The attempt was not entirely successful.

"That is very like the Panarchist terror weapon employed against Evodh," said the Avatar. The Bori noted that his hands were still now, the dirazh'u quiescent. "Have the technicians search the computer for any record of such a weapon based on the fiveskip technology. It will be useful for quelling restless populations."

The Bori nodded jerkily. Reports were already surfacing of resistance, here and there, and the terror inspired by such a device would be necessary to give the upper hand to the small occupation forces that Dol'jhar could field.

But it was utterly unlike the Avatar to so involve himself with details—it was a measure of his boredom. Barrodagh would have to be especially careful now, for with Eusabian in this mood, it would be very difficult to slip anything past him. *Perhaps the Panarchists will counterattack as Juvaszt expects, and he'll have something to occupy him.*

Lacking that, Barrodagh did not look forward to the next few weeks.

❊ ❊ ❊

OORT CLOUD:
GLORREICKE SYSTEM

"Emergence pulse, battlecruiser, six light-seconds." SigInt's announcement brought a flash of tension to the bridge of the *Grozniy* until she continued, "ID confirmed: *Mbwa Kali*, Captain Mandros Nukiel, commanding."

Ng sighed in relief. They'd had to wait less time than she'd expected, once the *Mbwa Kali* had been identified as the ship whose posted itinerary, garnered from fleet tacponders during the *Grozniy*'s long patrol, made a quick rendezvous most likely. They'd arrived at the Glorreicke system, yet untouched by the war, two days ahead of *Mbwa Kali*'s ETA; but less than twelve hours had passed before Nukiel found their message in the tacponder directing him to a rendezvous in the Oort Cloud of the system.

"Navigation, take us in to ten thousand kilometers. Communications, open a channel and hail him on emergence."

A window ballooned on the main screen as the *Grozniy* shuddered gently back into fourspace, revealing the lean, dark-bearded visage of Captain Nukiel.

His somewhat forbidding expression eased as communication was established on his end. "Captain Ng. A pleasure. What brings you here, waiting with such an urgent summons in the tacponder?"

So he doesn't know yet. Ng was momentarily at a loss about how to tell him. She'd met him just once, and from reviewing his records while waiting for rendezvous, she'd obtained an impression of a somewhat rigid character, known for a by-the-book approach. Not surprising in the scion of one of the old Douloi families of the Tetrad Centrum. However, a brief conversation with an officer who'd served under him had revealed him to have a surprising streak of tolerance for off-the-axis officers and a willingness to consider new ideas if well presented. *Well, this certainly qualifies.*

Before she could reply, Nukiel looked aside at someone just

out of view of the imager. He listened, then turned back to the screen, now concerned.

"Excuse me, Captain Ng, our scan reveals some damage to your aft beta section. Do you need assistance?"

That made it easier. "Thank you, no, Captain Nukiel. It's worse than it looks, and a great deal better than it could have been." She took a deep breath. "I regret to be the one to inform you that Eusabian of Dol'jhar has abrogated the Treaty of Acheront, arming several fleets of Rifters with weapons of unprecedented power and striking at targets throughout the Thousand Suns." His disbelief was no more than a widening of his eyes. She continued, speaking just a shade faster. "We believe that Arthelion has fallen and the entire royal family, with the exception of the Panarch, is dead." She paused, then added the clincher: "I've already dispatched a courier to Ares with what we know."

He looked at her in silence for a long beat. She could see him struggling to come to terms with her information.

Finally he spoke. "I see. Request permission to come aboard for a discussion of strategy."

Ng smiled, relieved. "You're very welcome, Captain Nukiel." By offering to come aboard the *Grozniy*, Nukiel had tacitly admitted her superior rank.

After arranging a time, they signed off, and Ng left the bridge to prepare. She knew what she wanted to do, and despite her ranking Nukiel, it was always better to convince than to order—especially with fellow battlecruiser captains, whose independence was a byword in the Fleet.

      ❊   ❊   ❊

"It's still hard to believe," said Nukiel, gesturing at the viewscreen elevated from the table in the plot room, "despite the utterly convincing evidence you've shown me." He fingered his beard, frowning.

Rom-Sanchez watched, fascinated by the interplay between the older captain of the *Mbwa Kali* and Captain Ng. Even with the Navy's complex rank-point system that took into account not only seniority but experience and talent as well, it was often difficult for older officers to yield gracefully to younger ones of equal rank who outpointed them.

Nonetheless, although Nukiel's face was not that of a man accustomed to following—one would not expect such in the command pod of a battlecruiser—he appeared comfortable with the situation. His other officers, who had accompanied him to this meeting, appeared less comfortable. One in particular, Lieutenant Nardini, a husky man younger than Rom-Sanchez, radiated well-bred impatience.

"You say you've already evolved a Tenno set to deal with this new form of communications?"

"Yes," Ng replied. "Sub-lieutenant Warrigal here developed them."

Belatedly the new sublieutenant looked up. Rom-Sanchez stifled a grin: deep in a boswell privacy with her opposite number from the *Mbwa Kali*, a stout young woman, Warrigal had obviously experienced again the shock of recognition that was part of coming to terms with a sudden promotion. *But she certainly deserved it.*

"They're brilliant, Captain," said the tactical lieutenant from the *Mbwa Kali*. "And we should be able to bring them up in our system without much trouble." Rom-Sanchez struggled with his memory for a moment. *Lieutenant Rogan.*

"She's already prepared a download for your tactical officer," Ng continued as the two lieutenants returned to their discussion. "But as you can see, obtaining one of these FTL coms is of critical importance. Without it, we have no chance of anticipating their moves—it would be like trying to overhear a spread-spectrum burst with your ears."

"Even with one, there's no guarantee that we could use it." Nukiel held up his hand as Ng prepared to reply. "I'm sorry. It's taking some time to get used to this. You're right, we have to try. What do you suggest?"

"We need to force a large number of Eusabian's allied ships into conflict, so that in the fog of battle we can attain our primary goal: concentrate on one ship, board it, and capture the FTL device. In my opinion, there's only one way to do that—a counterattack on Arthelion, which is exactly what Eusabian, given his cultural background, will expect."

"Excuse me, Captains," burst out the young officer seated next to Nukiel. "If their weapons are as powerful as you say, we'd take tremendous losses, unless we made maximum use of ruptors and skipmissiles, which wouldn't leave enough of a ship to board."

"That's true," replied Ng, unruffled by his outburst. "We'll have to use a lazplaz to disable his drives, while other ships keep off any possible assistance. We will take losses, but such is war. The alternative is surely defeat."

"I agree," said Nukiel. "When do we leave?"

Ng hesitated. "Captain," she replied, "I would prefer that you proceed to Rifthaven to monitor ship activities there." She pushed a datachip across the table to Nukiel. "As you will see when you review the full record of our interrogation of the Rifters from Treymontaigne, the Syndics of Rifthaven are apparently deeply involved in this. There is as much chance of you obtaining an FTL com by intercepting traffic from Rifthaven as we have in the heat of battle, and at a far lower cost."

Nukiel was silent, a sour expression on his face. Rom-Sanchez guessed he was struggling with his desire to join battle with the Rifters who were tearing apart the Panarchy, aided very little by the realization that Ng's suggestions—which could easily be made an order—made perfect sense. Lieutenant Nardini, next to him, apparently liked it even less, but said nothing.

"In addition," Ng added, "you may find out a great deal more from interrogation of the Rifters you capture, and you will be closer to Ares there than we will be, if Ares is still where my records put it."

Nukiel finally nodded. "I agree." Rom-Sanchez saw him glance at the young lieutenant, who was biting his lip. "I'm no young firebrand, aching to close with the enemy, but I still don't particularly like it."

He grinned wryly, an expression that suddenly made him look less forbidding. "And there are some captains between here and Arthelion—like Armenhaut—who for the sake of the Fleet and Fealty have to be kept from command of such an effort. I'd surely like to be there to see you deal with them."

Rom-Sanchez saw no reaction from Ng at this comment.

"Very well, Captain Ng, Rifthaven it is." Nukiel stood up. "Thank you for your hospitality. We'd better both move on this immediately—the Avatar will certainly waste no time."

Just before he reached the door, he paused. "By the way, Captain, are you any closer to your port wriggles?"

Ng looked over at him, faint surprise on her face.

"We were recently in the Poseidonis system, where Captain Hayashi has his destroyer squadron on patrol. He said to remind you, if we ran across each other, that your twenty-five years are almost up." Nukiel smiled. "That's on the way to Arthelion from here. You'll need him to harass the *Fist of Dol'jhar* while the rest of your fleet goes after the FTL com."

Nukiel's bantering tone had not changed, but Ng reacted more to this last statement than to anything previously said.

"Thank you," she murmured. "That's an excellent suggestion."

Rom-Sanchez felt a sinking sensation in his stomach, certain, although he wasn't sure why, that the name "Hayashi" meant quite a lot to Ng.

FOURTEEN

✳

FIVESPACE: DIS TO GRANNY CHANG'S

Osri was alone in the cabin.

He touched the Tetradrachm's hiding place, then dropped his hand. *It's just a metal object,* he thought. *Proof that the Aerenarch willingly participated in a crime against his own home, his own people.*

Restless, he surveyed the tiny cabin, saw the console. He sank in the chair.

Dol'jhar . . .

Flashing over and over in his memory was the image of the skipmissile obliterating the cruiser over Charvann, and counterpoint to it Vi'ya's manic gaze and savage grip on Lokri just after the disaster at Dis.

He flicked the console into life and called up the *Starfarer's Handbook*. The screen promptly filled with words.

DOL'JHAR

TYPE: Class II (habitable, marginal resources)
PRIMARY: GB, S.I. 0.9 (subject to flares)
MEAN ORBIT: 2.05x10exp8 km, eccentricity 0.86
ORBITAL INCLINATION: 33 degrees
ORBITAL PERIOD: 375d22h (sidereal, standard)
DIAMETER: 15,379 km
GRAVITY: 1.5 SGU (standard gravitational unit)
ROTATIONAL PERIOD: 31h22m

Dol'jhar circles a fairly ordinary Population I star, with the distribution of industrial metals expected of a second-generation primary. Thus it is surprising that Dol'jhar has almost no surface metals, a fact that explains much about its social structures. There are traces, especially in the far north and south . . .

Osri scanned rapidly down the description of the planet, gaining an impression of a harsh environment with a very narrow band of geography that was actually habitable—and that area was far from what anyone sane or civilized would consider comfortable—rocked constantly by seismic activity, beaten by unending storms, with bleak soil which yielded few crops. Yet its people maintained that the planet was a gift of Dol, to make them strong.

What was it the boy told me? "Vi'ya says that the most common products are people and ash."

Osri scanned further. They had conquered a planet in a neighboring system, a temperate world banded by islands, called Bori. Forcing the Bori into a subsidiary position, the Dol'-jharians had obtained from them everything save metals. The Bori had fought unsuccessfully, and until Acheront, had run trade and bureaucracy for their Dol'jharian rulers.

Despite two centuries of domination, the Bori and Dol'-jharians had remained two distinct groups: Bori under the inescapable force of Dol'jhar's heavy gravity usually ended up sterile; few Bori lived to bear progeny to the much larger Dol'jharians. And Dol'jharians who did resort to sex with the Bori were universally scorned by their peers: as small and weak specimens of humanity, the Bori were regarded somewhere below children and animals.

Fascinated and repelled, Osri read on. The *Handbook* said little more about Dol'jharian social structures, except to point out the changes imposed by the Treaty of Acheront. Since Bori was now a Panarchist Protectorate, the Bori left on Dol'jhar were the last generation. Then it outlined the hierarchy, which began with the Avatar and worked down several levels.

> *The higher the nobles' rank, the less frequently they are seen by others. It is enough when their liege-servants give commands in their names; the inhabitants have little desire to view their overlords, as they customarily only appear when they are displeased and wish to see justice executed publicly.*

Each noble defended his or her house not only against encroachers but also against their own progeny.

It was here that Osri slowed the scan, feeling a strange mélange of foreboding and embarrassment as he read:

> *There is no concept of marriage on Dol'jhar. Several times a year are the Days of the Kharusch-na rahali, the "Star Tides of Progeny." During this time those who desire heirs ambush likely partners. Consent is seldom an issue, except in alliances for political purposes; though there is no word for rape in their language, by any other standards, this sums up normal sexual relations on Dol'jhar. It is assumed that a good fight will ensure strong offspring.*

Osri read rapidly ahead.

> *The nobles usually imprison their selected partners until either they prove barren or a child results, and then there is no further use for the partner. Relations between serfs and slaves are more complex; at times there are even what resembles long-term partnerships, though there is no legal status for this. Children of these classes are usually sold into service by their tenth year.*
>
> *Offspring of the nobility are raised to compete for place with their siblings. If they live to adulthood, they are ex-*

*pected to assume the place of the parent through rigorously
circumscribed warfare . . .*

The door slid open.

Osri quickly killed the console and looked up.

He was surprised to see the little blonde leaning in the doorway, her face merry with a dimpled grin, and one hip outthrust.

Regarding her with distrust, Osri wondered if he had locked the door. Of course he had. But she obviously knew a bypass code. She had ignored him except when they'd been required to work together; what did she want?

"We'll be arriving at Chang's soon," she said, coming in uninvited. "Vi'ya says you and the old man and the Arkad can come along with us."

Politeness required him to answer during a pause, but he knew that politeness did not dictate Rifter interactions. Grimly he maintained his silence.

She wandered the room, her gaze darting here and there, then back to his face. Once again she grinned. "Ever been to Chang's?" she asked, leaning against his console, her proximity breaking the invisible but nearly palpable boundary ingrained in the Douloi.

He felt crowded and tried not to stare at the small, rounded breasts molded by her sky-blue suit, or the generous curve of her hip as she swung a leg up and perched. He breathed in: her scent was a subtle blend of jumari and spice.

"No," he said, keeping his gaze on her face.

"You'll have a great time." Her light-colored eyes were sharply observant in their smiling lids; it jolted him, just a little. "Everyone always does—there's something for every taste."

She's too close. Unnerved by his heightened awareness, he moved his chair back a trifle.

"So I've a question," she went on.

What is she after? A nasty thought: *It couldn't be the coin or the ribbon—*

"What do you military nicks do for fun?"

Osri swallowed. "Discuss planetary defense emplacements. And if it's a real wild night, count stars on a projection field." He attempted a humorous deflection of Brandon's sort, and hoped it was successful.

Marim laughed, a delighted chuckle that brought a reluctant smile to his face. Then she reached forward and gently tugged one of his earlobes. "Your father, he's got those ears too. Know what my creche-mater told us about big ears?" Her gaze slid downward.

The tug on his ear had caused a not-unpleasant sensation, but her direct sexual invitation brought alarm.

"Probably something obscene," he said flatly.

Again she laughed. "You're so predictable," she said, still chuckling. "But that's probably part of what makes you the kind that people trust. They do, don't they, those high-end nicks? Trust you?"

Interest warred with foreboding. "I endeavor to be trustworthy," he said even more flatly.

"If he'd been lucky in where he was born, Ivard would've been like you," Marim said, her eyes sharp again. "He trusts people. I think it's crazy—you die sooner that way—but it was the way he was made." Once again she paused.

Osri took refuge again in silence.

"He lost something," she said. "Montrose thinks he won't recover till he gets it—was a pledge from his sister, who got burned down by those blunge-eating Tarkans on the Mandala. It's here, on *Telvarna*."

The Tetradrachm. He kept his face controlled, though his heart began banging painfully against his ribs.

"And though Lokri's my bond-brother," she continued, "I can't trust him. Your father I could, but he never comes out of the dispensary. And that Arkad is . . ." She made a large gesture which could have meant anything, but Osri took to mean untrustworthy. *You're correct,* he thought.

"And Jaim's in mourning," she went on. "So I'm trying to find it for young Firehead. And I can trust you, I think, so I'm asking you to help me look. Will you?"

Osri was silent, recognizing a masterly campaign. He made a vow never again to underestimate any of these criminals. Striving for indifference, he said: "Were I to find anything of your property, be sure that I would immediately restore it to you."

Outside the room, Marim gave herself up to laughter. *He's got it. Now comes the real fun.*

✳   ✳   ✳

CHANG HABITAT MINUS 1,000 KILOMETERS

Osri had just sunk into a deep sleep when a hard rapping on the cabin door forced his mind back to wakefulness.

"What is it?" Brandon muttered from the other bunk, sitting up. He'd come in while Osri was asleep.

Osri's gritty eyes found the clock: 04:07.

"Me!" Marim's cheerful voice piped, somewhat muffled, from the corridor.

Brandon sat up in his bed and shook his head violently. Osri caught a stale whiff of alcohol: the Aerenarch had been drinking. Osri pulled on his trousers and a tunic, and as the rapping sounded again, he slapped the doorpad.

Outside Marim stood, face bright with excitement.

"Marim," Brandon greeted her, rubbing his eyes, his voice husky. "It'd better be a flank attack from Eusabian—or a time bomb at the least—or I am going to murder you and sleep on the remains."

Marim grinned. "We're comin' into Granny Chang's, and Vi'ya says there's trouble."

"I thought her talents were strictly short-range."

"Are. But she 'n' Markham were made honorary members of Granny's tong and she says the welcome message has a tong emergency code hidden in it. Jackers."

"Tong?" Osri asked.

Marim's face swung toward him, but she turned back to Brandon before she answered. "Some sort of gang, generations old." Marim shrugged. "Anyway, she says we gotta help or we're stuck here for good—not enough fuel to go anywhere else safe. Montrose has to guard Firehead 'n' the old man, *and* hold the con! Get dressed, Arkad," she added, giving Brandon an appreciative up-down. "We've got caf waiting." She whisked herself out.

Osri stayed in the middle of the floor, uncertain.

Brandon got out of bed, rubbing his eyes. "We're being recruited to defend this place against jackers, not Panarchists."

"What difference between these Rifters and some other group?" Osri muttered under his breath.

Brandon did not answer as he reached for his clothes.

Osri did not pursue the issue. Instead, he said, "What I find difficult to comprehend is why I should be included at all, unless this is some sort of ruse to get me killed."

Brandon looked amused. "If they wanted you dead, you would have taken a walk out of a lock long ago. They're short-handed, and they know you're adequate at sim-fighting, so they are hoping you're as good in a real fight."

Osri felt a mixture of gratification and annoyance. "If she's right and the danger is jackers, then this ship is in jeopardy—"

"—and your father. If that will assuage your lacerated sense of duty," Brandon said, pulling on his boots, "regard it as true." He got to his feet, then paused. "And if you were considering pulling a serial-chip stunt like using your jac against the captain, remember that the Eya'a will know before you hit the firing stud."

Osri opened his mouth to protest, but Brandon was already out the door.

"Here's our nicks," Marim greeted them when the reached the rec room. She handed each of them a steaming cup.

Osri saw the somber-faced Jaim sitting at a table. Near them, a hateful smile on his lips, was Lokri. One of his arms was in a cast, and bruises marked his face.

Osri remembered what he had read in the *Starfarer's Handbook* and looked away quickly.

"Boz'ls for all," Marim said, handing out the wrist computers.

As Osri strapped his on, he noted that it was the very latest, most expensive kind: with neural induction. He fought the sense of relief he felt to have a boswell on again; the urge to start recording everything had to be ignored. He knew he would not be permitted to keep this one, and anything he loaded into it would probably be downloaded by the captain later.

"Jacs," came Montrose's voice from behind.

Osri was given a standard weapon, a worn Dogstar LVIII, which he checked the charge on and then clipped to his belt. Looking down at the weapon, he felt a strange sense of unreality: he had never in his life handled a weapon except in practice, back on the Academy at Minerva. *Which is probably radioactive slag by now.*

He noted that Marim had picked a jac of an unfamiliar design. Although it wasn't quite as bulky as the two-hander Montrose favored, its barrel was longer, there was a small canister just forward of the trigger, and there were two folding projections, hinged near the aperture, that he couldn't identify. She carried it on her back, barrel down. The others also had individualized weapons; he did not recognize the make of the stiletto-like jac that Lokri carried.

"I thought Chang's was a bubbloid," Brandon said. "Wouldn't these be a bad idea?" He pointed at his weapon, a twin to Osri's, which still lay on the table before him.

"Granny's is all up-to-date, so we can use jacs—not like Rifthaven," Marim said.

Osri drank gratefully from his cup, which contained real coffee. He breathed deeply, feeling the stimulant burn away the cobwebs from his head. As he lowered the cup he heard and felt a gentle scraping thump resonate through the ship. Then a louder clank from the direction of the nearby lock. They were docked.

Another thought occurred to him. "But how does she know they're not Panarchists?" he whispered to Brandon.

Marim laughed, splattering caf on the table. "At Granny Chang's? About half her gee-nth grandchildren are nicks! Changs have always had one foot on either side of the Rift."

Gee-nth? He suddenly realized that Granny Chang was a real person, and that she must be a nuller. Very few people ever adapted to permanent null-gee, but only those that did lived long enough to see many generations of their children.

Then he remembered the magister Roderik Chang at the Academy, who taught courses in the spiritual dimensions of warfare. *Is he one of Granny's children?*

"What's the matter, Arkad, caf not kickin' in?"

"It will," Brandon said. His expression was bemused.

Osri wondered if he, too, was contemplating with an equal lack of enthusiasm the possibility of violence—and then remembered with a jolt of anger that it was Brandon who had led these people on a raid against his own home on Arthelion.

But Dol'jharians were holding it, not our people, Osri re-

minded himself. This second jolt threw him off balance. Unable
to deal with it, he turned his thoughts to the future.

*I'll be off this ship, and I'll have a weapon. So where would
I go, if I decided to flee? I'm certainly not likely to join whoever's jacking Granny Chang's. They're not being stupidly trust-
ing to give us weapons—they're being expedient.* The sense of
unreality increased, and deep inside his mind, for the first time
in his life, he felt the urge to laugh at himself.

"What's the plan?" Lokri drawled, strapping his weapon on
one-handed with a dexterity that indicated he'd be able to handle himself, broken arm notwithstanding.

"This is it—" Marim began to talk fast.

She described the basic layout of Granny's bubbloid, a habitat
formed by injecting a metallic asteroid with volatiles and melt-
ing it to blow it into spherical form. There was slightly less than
standard gee inside at the equator and null-gee at the poles,
where ships docked, and in the center where Granny lived and
did her trading. They'd be using the boswells in covert mode,
walking in as if unaware of any problems—and then they'd
have to improvise.

Halfway through her outline Vi'ya joined them, her long tail
of space-black hair wound into a tight knot. When she turned
her head slightly as she tossed something onto the table before
Osri, he saw faint lines of tightness around her eyes, and a dark-
ish tinge to her lower eyelids.

Osri's gaze strayed to Lokri, to observe no reaction in his
face at her appearance.

As she strapped on her boswell, Vi'ya said to Osri, "You two
will wear these." She indicated the dark cloth items on the table.

Brandon picked one up and Osri was amazed to see a domino. With a quick gesture, Brandon pulled the gold-embroidered
black velvet over his head, adjusting it with tugs until it lay
smoothly, obscuring the top of his head. Only his square chin
was exposed, and his mouth, which quirked at the corners, ren-
dering him unrecognizable to anyone who did not know him
well.

Osri picked up the other domino, a blue one with scarlet
leaves sewn in a diagonal pattern across it. He had never seen
the sort of establishment which High Douloi preferred to visit
disguised; he knew it was a convention in some circles, but he
had known no one in them. He pulled the silk-lined cloth over

his head, feeling peculiar. It was expensively made; where had the Rifters gotten these?

And then he remembered Markham vlith-L'Ranja. Looking over at Brandon, who was looking down at his hands, he thought: *It seems we are destined to follow Markham's path through the Thousand Suns for a time.* Osri blinked, adjusting the eye slits to widen as much as possible his field of vision, and then he dropped his hands surreptitiously to his boswell.

Marim said, "Let's go!"

Vi'ya turned to lead the way out, and as the others followed, Osri quickly tapped his boswell, offering Brandon a privacy: *(Do they fear we'll find allies, after all?)*

(They fear someone wanting to collect the prices on our heads should Eusabian have distributed bonus chips to his fleet,) Brandon returned with acidic humor.

A price on their heads? At every step the sense of unreality increased. Osri found himself wishing he were back in the galley, stirring a twenty-spice *Hulann* delicacy and fending off Lucifur's attentions.

Brandon fell in step beside the captain. "What do the Eya'a make of all this?" he asked.

Vi'ya said, "They are fascinated by the concept of an inside-out world, and they seem to find Granny's age incomprehensible."

As they passed near the dispensary on the way to the lock, Osri heard an unlikely sound: the strongly marked triple beat of a waltz. It only added to the unreality of the situation, especially when Marim, who must have seen some of his reaction in his face, touched her finger to her wrist with a wry gesture.

Ivard's Kelly band. Somewhere he remembered having heard that the Kelly, not surprisingly, were indifferent to all human music save the waltz. The idea that Montrose had to play this music for the boy made Osri feel slightly queasy: what other effects was that band having on him?

They reached the lock then, where the Eya'a were already waiting. For the first time they were wearing something other than those translucent garments with the micro-fine patterns woven in. In fact, Osri could only recognize them because he knew there were no other sentients that small on board. The Eya'a were swallowed up in coarse robes of a dull gray color, with rumpled hoods pulled over their heads. The fronts of the hoods were held shut by a metal screen with an ornate swirling pattern in it. The outfits were vaguely familiar; he remembered once seeing something like it on a chip.

"Azuni Oblates from Pimenti IV," said Vi'ya, smiling faintly.

"A useful disguise for this kind of situation," Brandon countered with easy humor, "the Oblates being—as I recall—famed for their insistence on nonviolence." He regarded the swathed form nearest him with a mock-critical air. "Although he, or it, or she, seems a little tall for a Pimenti."

"She," Vi'ya corrected. "They're both females. Their mate never leaves their colony."

Discussing Eya'a biology somehow increased the unreality to the boundaries of farce. Osri fought against a sudden, irrational urge to laugh as he fingered his weapon's unfamiliar weight against his hip.

And then the inner door slid shut behind them.

FIFTEEN

✳

Outside the lock, they entered a long tunnel made of some flexible, ribbed material that glowed pearlescent with its own internal light. The air was redolent with a faint, spicy-sour scent that tickled his nose. Osri could feel his sinuses thickening. *Skipnose again. Do Rifters ever get used to the changes?* Neither Jaim, Marim, nor Vi'ya seemed to be affected, but Brandon winced, and Lokri sniffed, then pinched his nose. There was no telling with the Eya'a.

Since the lock tunnel was in null-gee, there were guide cables running along its length, which everyone but Marim used. She moved along with almost imperceptible flicks of her fingers and toes—she was barefoot as always—against the side of the tunnel where it curved, pausing frequently for the others to catch up.

Without warning they came up out of the tunnel into a large cylindrical vestibule, as though climbing out of a hole. The sudden shift in orientation dizzied Osri for a moment. The vestibule was large in radius but short in length, with other entrances piercing its walls all over. Running around it about halfway along its length was a bright yellow-and-black-striped line; beyond the line the walls were smooth, and rotating slowly with respect to where they stood.

Next to the opening they'd emerged from was a small dais with two holes in it. Marim drifted over to it, waiting as the others followed and one by one thrust their feet into the holes.

When Osri's turn came he found the sensation familiar—not sticky, not magnetic, but somewhere in between.

Affinity dyplast. It was a ubiquitous technology, but he'd never encountered this use of it before.

When everyone was done, Marim made a reluctant gesture and touched her feet to the deck—and they stuck. Some of Osri's disgust at the black mat of microfilaments on the bottoms of her feet dissipated at this evidence of their utility.

Vi'ya led the way, Jaim falling in behind. Marim and Lokri traveled side by side; he noted more than once one or the other of them tapping their boswells in a private communication. He fought against the affront this engendered; Rifters had no concept of appropriate etiquette.

As they approached the black and yellow line, Osri saw transparent letters of red flame hanging in midair above it; upside down at first, they dissolved and re-formed as sensors detected their orientation.

*WELCOME TO CHANG'S VARIGEE HOSTEL
AND WHOLESALE EXTRAVAGANZOO!*

A strange wailing, thumping music commenced.

Then a voice spoke out of the air. "What'll it be, genz and Captains? Buying, bunking, or both?"

"Buying." Marim laughed. "Go-juice and gutstuffing."

"Comestibles are available at every gee-level, and you may negotiate for fuel at the same time. Orientation is available at any time through Rift-3 on your boz'ls." The voice became formal. "Cross the line and accept house rules. Ignorance is no defense. Do you wish a summary, or printed list?"

"Nope," replied Marim.

"Enjoy your stay." The letters winked out.

"Anything about these rules we should know?" Brandon asked.

"No special rules," replied Marim. "Pretend you're in somebody's palace and you'll be fine."

"He'll probably need some help in null-gee courtesy," Vi'ya murmured. Her tone indicated experience, and Osri remembered Marim's words: "She and Markham were made honorary members of Granny's tong . . ."

"If you enter a room, you orient your head to match the people already there, unless they're all over—then they're nullers and don't care." Marim wrinkled her nose. "And since it sounds like you've got a nice case of skipnose comin' on, remember: don't ever sneeze—hold your nose and blow your eardrums out if you have to." As she continued, Marim rolled her eyes up in her head, apparently trying to recall to mind things that were second nature to her.

Osri remembered the visits he'd made to various Highdwellings. Remembering the facility with which Marim had maneuvered along the lock tunnel, he thought: *She must have spent a lot of time up at the spin axis.*

His eyes took in the quiet space, and he felt his body relax incrementally. With any luck, whatever problem had faced the proprietors of this establishment had already been dealt with.

As they crossed the line, Brandon asked, "It doesn't seem very busy here. Is this normal?"

"Might be at the other pole, or just slack time," Marim said in a careless tone.

And then fear doused Osri with a cold flood when Vi'ya's voice came to him through the boswell: (*No. This is too slow. Look relaxed but be alert. A little of the Panarchy-blit attitude will probably help.*)

"Panarchy-blit." Osri knew that as another Markham reference; he recalled one of his earliest memories of Brandon's friend, surprising them in an Academy cadet lounge while Markham was in the middle of an elaborate joke-tale. Osri had been irritated at his exaggerated impression of a certain Service scion—the goggle-eyed, unassailable air of superiority mixed with amusement at the antics of one's inferiors—but the cadets had obviously thought it hysterically funny.

And so must have these Rifters, he thought, carefully not subvocalizing.

(*That should be real easy,*) Brandon's reply came. (*I've had a lot of practice in the last ten years.*)

Suddenly they heard a hiss from the Eya'a, and Vi'ya winced. They were now standing on the other side of the line, in the bubbloid proper, and Osri noticed that the aliens were canted at a strange angle, as though subject to a different gravitational environment.

(What's the matter?) Brandon asked.

(I'm not sure—it may be the coriolis or the gee-delta. They've never been in a spin-habitat,) came Vi'ya's answer.

The rotation of Granny Chang's didn't create enough of a gee-differential to bother humans; perhaps the equilibrial sense of the Eya'a was diffused throughout their bodies, making them far more sensitive.

(They say they want to go on, but they are disoriented. We may not be able to rely on them.)

While this colloquy was going on, Marim kept up a constant chatter aimed at Brandon and Osri, as if introducing a not-too-bright acquaintance to Granny's.

Brandon's smile widened to a gape as they came to the end of the vestibule. Osri turned his head, fighting the urge to yank at his eye slits, and looked inside Granny Chang's.

To his Downsider eyes they stood at the edge of a dizzying precipice. The cylinder of the vestibule jutted out into space at one axis of an immense sphere—confused by null-gee he couldn't begin to estimate the size. Above his head a broad catwalk extended out to a smaller sphere in the exact center of the space; he noted with some discomfort that the catwalk was upside down with respect to them, and at some distance a figure was standing on it head-down.

The smaller sphere, which he guessed was where Granny herself lived, was entirely covered by brightly lit signs—everything from giant flat posters in the ancient fashion to holograms and lumensquiggles—advertising a bewildering array of goods and services.

YANDRA'S GREENZLS WILL
GRAB YOUR GULLET—LEVEL THREE

USE IT OR LOSE IT AT
NOZZIPAOUT'S HOUSE OF GOOD REPUTE

GULLET GAS? DON'T GET SPACED,
GET SACKBUT'S NULL-CARMINANT

There was no sound accompanying these displays, but he could hear faint snatches of music and other noises. He noticed that his boswell was flashing, indicating an incoming signal on public-access frequencies. He reached to accept out of curiosity, but Marim put a hand over his wrist.

"Don't bother, unless you want that"—she waved at the lightshow ahead—"inside your head."

But Osri was no longer looking at the advertisements; drawn by the faint sounds he'd noticed, his eyes had finally registered the rest of the habitat. He'd been in several Highdweller communities, but they were so large that one could almost forget they were in orbit—if you could ignore the landscape hanging kilometers overhead.

Here was very different. Granny Chang's was far smaller than the typical Sync, and the interior of the sphere was divided into a series of progressively larger ring-terraces from the spin axis to the equator. He realized that each ring represented a different gee-level, giving guests the choice of acceleration. There were people in all the rings, some strolling along brightly lit walkways, others riding in little open carriers in slots at the center of each ring. All their heads, of course, were oriented toward the spin axis of the sphere—once he realized that, Osri became more comfortable with the layout.

There was no central illumination, so the interior of the sphere was a mind-boggling confusion of lamps and strip lights; and he suddenly noticed that many of them formed enormous ideographs not unlike the Tenno glyphs that Brandon used so well.

The others began to pull themselves up a guide cable to the catwalk overhead, somersaulting onto its surface as they reached it. They were met about halfway across by a tall young man with slanted eyes and a smooth complexion the color of old parchment. He held a jac at ease as he stepped into their path.

"Your pardon, genz and Captains, this is a private residence. May I suggest instead the inestimable delights—" He stopped, apparently recognizing Vi'ya.

She bowed to him—the gesture looked odd in null-gee—and said something in a fluid, singsong language; all its vowels were at the back of the throat with the mouth open. Osri didn't recognize it. He thought he recognized some distorted versions of Uni words in it, but the tonalities defeated his ear.

The man's eyes lit and he bowed back. "Ancestors and honor," he replied formally. "Excuse me." His eyes slid away and his lips moved slightly for a time as evidently communicated via his boswell with someone inside.

(There's definitely something wrong,) came Vi'ya's voice. *(He should have replied in Han—somebody is monitoring him.)*

A few moments later the man's face closed into coldness and he bowed again to Vi'ya.

"Your humble sibling apologizes deeply, sister Captain, but the venerable Chang cannot receive you at this time."

Vi'ya reached into her pouch and pulled out a small figurine—some sort of dog-like beast with a gaping mouth and flowing mane—carved from greenish stone. With a jolt devoid of anger for the first time, Osri recognized it: part of the loot from the antechamber to the Hall of Ivory.

"This dutiful daughter wished merely to present a small gift to her venerable mother."

The man's eyes widened and he sucked in his breath between his teeth; clearly he recognized the piece. Again the silent conversation commenced; now he appeared to be arguing.

(He's one of Granny's family, out here under duress, judging from his emotions. I think she's being held hostage. He'll get us inside now—wait for my cue.)

Finally the man said, "Come with me."

(How will we know friend from foe?) asked Brandon as they followed the man.

(The Changs are purists—any that don't look like him, don't belong.)

At the end of the catwalk the young man opened a hatch and motioned them through. They entered the lock, and the door closed behind them. The inner one was already open, and Osri tensed himself for whatever might come next.

A greenish wisp of light resembling a Tenno glyph danced in the air beyond the inner hatch, and it preceded them down the corridor, beckoning them onward. Osri noticed that the hatches in the corridor were likely to be found in any of the four surfaces—there was no "down" at all. As they pulled themselves over one hatch, he glimpsed machinery in a darkened room.

At the end of the corridor they came to a larger hatch, bordered in some smooth, shiny reddish substance ornately carved with ideographs and mythical beasts. Some of them resembled the small figurine in Vi'ya's pouch.

The hatch swung open as they approached, and they stepped out onto a small balcony-like projection in the most confusing room Osri had ever seen.

It was a fairly large cube—perhaps fifty meters in each dimension, but the clutter of furnishings and bricbrac made it look smaller. Furniture stuck out of all six surfaces and floated in the air, while potted plants drifted about in apparently random orbits, and several large, sleek brown dogs with goggle-eyed faces not unlike the lion drawings, and polydactyl toes, lounged against various surfaces.

There was even what appeared to be an incense burner, a black lacework pot with a little fan attached and a red glow within; smoke drifted out of it as it moved about, diffusing into the air in a way quite foreign to Osri's Downsider expectations. The smell of the incense was sweet and resinous.

In the very center of the space floated something reminiscent of a sedan chair with a vaguely humanoid crumpled bundle of cloth and sticks in it. Next to it floated a huge, fat man who wore a enormous Hopfneriad Signeur wig.

Osri blinked, not believing his eyes. Those wigs were reputed to still be in fashion among the Downsiders of Hopfneri, though the Highdweller nobility families had dropped them soon after their induction among Douloi Service Families. Osri had seen them in vids and retained an impression of complicated rolls of white hair built high and tumbling down over shoulders, decorated over the entire structure by shifting lights, or blooming and closing flowers, or a myriad of other eye-pleasing variations.

This man's wig was so large it made him seem nearly double his size; looking more closely at his proportions, Osri noted that he was actually quite short. The wig itself was an astonishing concoction of curlicues, roleaux, and braids, and nestling, hovering, winking, and whirring among those was an agglomeration of lights, fantastical insects, and color-changing jewels. Osri wondered how large a powerpack was needed to animate this mess, and then he turned his eyes to the rest of the man, who sat in midair as one who commands, grizzled face sneering, his arms folded.

Despite the sneer, his piggish eyes squinted uneasily at them;

Osri thought he saw something in one of the man's hands. He did not at all resemble the young man who had greeted them on the catwalk.

There were a number of people in the room; after a moment Osri's eyes sorted them into two groups. One group was distinguished most immediately by the fact that their heads were oriented in the same direction. They were also armed, their gazes assessing the newcomers with narrow-eyed distrust and, with the exception of one woman, did not look like Changs. *Just your usual gang of jackers,* he thought.

(The Changs are unarmed,) came Vi'ya's warning.

The Changs—there were only four of them—floated at all different angles around the room. They were also positioned with their legs near a piece of furniture. *Is that a nuller instinct?* His hand reached to tap his boswell, but the eyes of one of the jackers raked over him, and he overrode the impulse.

Better to ape the stupid Panarchist tourist, he thought, fighting that same weird urge to laugh that he'd had at the *Telvarna*'s lock. He looked over, saw Lokri smiling at the nearest group, with his old insouciance, and he recognized the expression for the first time: bravado.

Suddenly the bundle of sticks on the sedan chair opened the biggest pair of shining black eyes Osri had ever seen, and the form resolved itself into an unbelievably aged woman. To Osri she looked like nothing so much as a doll made from some sort of dried fruit he'd received from some ambassador as a small child.

(Granny Chang,) came Vi'ya's voice in his head.

"Welcome, daughter," said the apparition in the chair in a surprisingly clear, strong voice. "You bring us guests?"

Vi'ya inclined her head. "Health and prosperity to you, venerable mother." She motioned to Marim, Jaim, and Lokri. "My crew you know." Pointing to the Eya'a and to the Panarchists, she said, "And these passengers paid us for a tour of the best entertainments in this octant. The Oblates are under Silence, but they still wished to sample the delights of the Extravaganzoo, as do these genz."

As if on a cue, Brandon chimed in, "An entirely astonishing pleasure, mezda Chang."

Osri saw sneers from some of the jackers at Brandon's ripe

plummy accent, emphasized by his growing inability to breathe through his nose.

Brandon executed a formal deference—equal-to-equal with the seniority-acknowledged overtone—but with a clumsiness bordering on parody that reminded Osri forcibly of Markham's joke that long-ago day on Minerva. "This is *most* sensational, I must say—" he began, waving a languid hand around at the room.

"May your daughter inquire of her mother an introduction?" interrupted Vi'ya.

Granny waved an arm at the man next to her. Osri felt a tingle of near disgust at the fragility of the limb: it looked like he could snap it between two fingers. The old woman appeared crippled; but he knew that in null-gee there was no need for muscle bulk.

"I have formed a new syndicate. This is Nokker, my new partner."

(That's got to be blunge. Granny's run this place alone for almost two hundred years, since her husband died,) came Marim's voice. Osri noticed her drifting slowly to one side, her boswell arm hidden by a piece of furniture.

Osri decided to stay put, knowing that his clumsiness in null-gee would make any movement on his part obvious. The Eya'a didn't move, but they still leaned at an angle. Several jackers watched them curiously, but more of them were looking at Brandon. Osri shifted slightly to see what the Aerenarch was doing, and suffered a small shock.

Brandon was only looking around, but at rest his posture unmistakably gave him away. That blend of grace and assurance stood out among the tight angles of the jackers and the helplessness of the Changs; it stirred a memory that he knew was important, but he could not think of that now. Danger threatened: *These jackers might not know High Douloi usage, but they can recognize an anomaly.*

"Health and prosperity to you, Nokker." Vi'ya nodded to the man, then addressed Granny Chang again. "May this one approach her mother?"

"You're doin' just fine where you are, dolly." The man's voice was a strangled hiss, as though something had damaged his vocal cords. "Granny tires easily these days; perhaps you'd better just give her that present and come back later."

Vi'ya reached slowly into her pouch; the eyes of the armed figures followed her. While everyone watched her, Osri watched from his domino eye slits how Jaim drifted back toward a wall, and Lokri, grunting with pain as he fiddled with the catch on the side of his cast, bounced from a piece of furniture toward a clump of people. He waggled his hands and feet, mouth open. One of the jackers snickered and shoved him with the butt of his jac toward a houseplant, where he got tangled in the leaves.

The fat man's eyes shot a warning at the jacker, then glittered as Vi'ya held up the little statue.

(Arkad, we need a distraction.) That was Marim. *(Schoolboy, you take those two nearest you.)*

Osri's heart thumped against his throat, and he fought to subdue an urge to wipe his sweaty hands down his clothes. Near Granny one of the dogs slowly stirred his tail. Osri noted just then that the Eya'a were both facing the animal.

Meanwhile, the fat man leaned forward to take the statue. Several jackers looked up at Brandon, who sniffed and rubbed at his nose, uttering a series of strangled snorts gradually increasing in volume.

"Excuse me." He coughed, sniffing repulsively. "But the incense—"

Out of the corner of his eye Osri saw Vi'ya face the Eya'a. Marim was some distance away now, and the attention of the jackers was divided between Brandon and Vi'ya.

Then Brandon sneezed rackingly, expelling a copious cloud of snot globules into the air. "Your pardon," he gasped in his best Panarchy-blit tones, "but I'm not accustomed to—"

KERFLOOSH!

Another blast splatted out. One of the armed men near him practically turned a somersault trying to get out of the way of the snot cloud.

At that same moment, the brown dog just behind Granny moved lithely through the air at an angle over Nokker's wig, and lifted his leg.

A clear stream of urine splashed directly into the wig, which emitted a sudden explosion of sparks and smoke. Several of the fantastical insect-constructions abruptly zoomed away at high speed, emitting shrill squeals, as if in pain.

"Gyyyyaaaaagh!" Nokker screamed, his cry echoed by another jacker whose face had intercepted one of the insects, and

Vi'ya's crew swung into action microseconds before the jackers: Lokri launching his houseplant directly at a knot of jackers, and Jaim, cool and expressionless, picking two off with deadly precision. Jac-bolts sizzled this way and that as everyone scrambled for cover.

Osri also took refuge, his legs and arms swimming desperately, behind a group of wicker chairs; he pulled his jac, but by then the two Marim had directed him to "get" had launched themselves in different directions, firing as they went.

Osri looked around, trying to make sense of the battle. His attention was caught by another, bigger explosion from the wig. Several of the rolls of hair began to flap wildly, impelling the writhing Nokker upward. The smoke swirling from his head made him look like one of the flying warships in an ancient flatvid Osri had once seen, falling out of the sky after losing a midair duel. He flung his arms wide and the control he'd been clutching in his hand flew across the room, directly toward Osri.

Without a thought he lunged out and caught it in his hand.

And that was apparently what Granny and her children had been waiting for. Suddenly the lights went out, leaving only the glow of the incense burner. Osri ducked as a jac-bolt sizzled past, shouts and screams echoed through the room. A globe of light suddenly bloomed around Granny's chair—*That's got to be the smallest tesla shield I've ever seen,* Osri thought distractedly—and a bolt of plasma lanced out of it and fried the fat man, silencing his screams.

Dull fires on some of the furniture provided enough light to see by as a lull in the action gave everyone a moment to take stock. The dogs had disappeared entirely, and crew, Changs, and jackers alike had taken cover around the room—save one of Nokker's gang whose inexperience in null-gee betrayed her. As a jac-bolt from Vi'ya sizzled past her she tried to duck, and instead pulled her feet off the deck. Trying to defend herself, she made the mistake of firing her jac in midair, which threw her into a tight spin. She vomited noisily, throwing off a wheel of foulness, and began to choke.

This is becoming a real festival of excretions, thought Osri with a sort of desperate hilarity just before a jac-bolt ignited his wicker shield. He used it to launch himself toward a wall behind an ornate cabinet. Heat singed past his ankle and one shoulder, but he arrived safely. Peering around a corner, he scanned for al-

lies: he couldn't see the Eya'a anywhere, and he'd lost track of
Brandon.

Suddenly something like a comet streaked across the room,
screeching imprecations in a familiar voice. It was Marim; she
had unfolded the hinged projections on her jac and put her feet
on them, and was using it as a combined weapon and propulsion
system. *That canister must be reaction mass,* he thought.

Marim twisted expertly and fired; the jac-bolt emerged at an
angle and spun her around. She landed on a wall, jumped off in
another direction, fried one of their opponents with a jac-bolt,
and used the momentum from that blast to jet off in another direction, caroming off a potted plant and sending it into the face
of another of the jackers, who whirled away with blood splattering from his nose.

For a few moments more the room was awhirl with action lit
only by jac-bolts and smoldering furniture. Marim jetted past
again, jac-bolts reaching for her but missing by a wide margin
as she fired, spun, and fired again.

Then, suddenly, it was over. The lights came on; Granny's
chair hung in the center of the room as before, but now the other
Changs were armed with their foes' weapons and were moving
purposefully around the room, towing corpses toward hatches
and dealing with the wounded with brusque efficiency.

Osri winced as one of them casually plunged a dagger into
the back of a wounded jacker's neck; the victim convulsed and
went limp.

Marim drifted up next to him, breathless and merry. "They'd
just space 'em anyway—this is quicker." She grabbed his arm
and beckoned to Brandon. "C'mon, Granny wants to meet you
two."

She launched them across the room to the sedan chair, brak-
ing them with bent legs on its base; they ended up floating only
a couple of meters from the ancient proprietor. Around her neck
Osri noted the gleam of a shock collar.

Silently Osri offered the control still clutched in one hand,
and the bird-claw fingers took it. The huge black eyes regarded
Osri and Brandon unblinking for a moment, than a smile split
Granny Chang's face, adding not a whit to the mass of wrinkles.

She sketched a gesture that Osri recognized as a deference in
a style that nowadays was only seen in historical serial chips.

"The House of Chang is honored, young Phoenix," she said

in a whisper just barely audible. "How is it that a scion of the Mandala finds himself at the back end of nowhere?"

Brandon's face in its domino was blank, but Osri read surprise in the sudden stiffness of his shoulders. Then he bowed, the innate grace confirming her guess even as he pulled the domino from his tousled head. "I've come to meet you, of course," he said with outrageous flirtatiousness. "What better pilgrimage is there?"

Granny Chang gave a sharp crack of laughter: "Be easy, O Arkad. Nothing said here today will go beyond these walls. You have a story to tell: you must give it to us when we celebrate. First you will clean up, while we prepare a feast. It is a special day indeed that brings an honored daughter and a Krysarch to us, and it is doubly blessed when the honored guests gift us with our lives."

Sixteen

✳

DESRIEN

Eloatri came to the top of the grassy hill, then stopped, horrified, as she saw the spires of New Glastonbury thrusting arrogantly into the sky before her. The last light of day gilded them with ruddy health, emphasizing their heaven-storming reach, drawing earth and sky together in confident embrace. Faintly she heard the sound of chanting, and then, in a clangorous summons that the last dregs of her spirit cried out against, a peal of bells.

It was too much. She turned her back on the cathedral and sat down, weeping. Of all the faiths of Desrien, of all the faces of Telos, why had this one been chosen for her? It was everything her heart had always denied, even as she granted it the tolerance demanded of every inhabitant of Desrien for every faith there planted. The world not as illusion to be surmounted, but a story to be lived; the celebration of attachment, even unto bloody suffering and death. *No way out. No way out.*

It is too much. She stood up and without a backward glance, made her way down the hill again, away from her hejir.

❋   ❋   ❋

Night came, and with it a dense fog, rising up out of the earth like the breath of some vast beast. Eloatri felt the potentialities trembling around her, and she trembled in response. It was the *pekeri*, the dream fog of Desrien, and it had swallowed her.

Now she was truly lost, but every time she tried to rest, an irresistible restlessness, a spinning sensation in her breast like an engine out of control, shook her tired frame and impelled her forward. Some time back she had lost her staff, her cloak, and her sandals; she clutched her begging bowl with grim intensity. Her yellow robe was damp with dew; it clung to her in a clammy embrace, like the shroud of a drowned corpse.

From time to time she saw eyes in the mist, some lambent yellow, others glowing green, but they looked past her—they were not part of her story. She would have welcomed the sudden leap of some beast of prey, to save her from her fate, but the predator that followed her had neither parts nor passions, nor would It ever tire. She stumbled onward, exhausted beyond thought, a hunted creature in the forests of the night.

Now she could hear a breathing behind her, a diapason of power, rising from the stony bones of the planet under her feet. Soon, she felt sure, It would form her name, and she would turn . . .

Eloatri began to run, at eighty years of age a frightened child lost in the dark. Her fear-sharpened senses brought vivid impressions: the cool earth under her feet, her hoarse panting, the ear-deadening blanket of the fog. The damp air carried a sweet scent, a gentle perfume that intensified inexorably.

Then, suddenly, she blundered into a thorny hedge. Its clawed embrace enfolded her as she tried to fight her way through it, panicked by the sound of her pursuer. A clearing loomed ahead; she pushed frantically toward it, heedless of the ripping of her robe. The thorns caught at her flesh.

Then she stopped. Before her stood Tomiko, his features shadowed in his cowl. As she stood panting, the High Phanist pushed back his hood. Eloatri gasped. His face was terribly disfigured, seared and blistered. His eyes were milky white and blind, and yet she knew he saw her. Wordlessly he held out his hands, one palm up, beseeching, one palm down with fingers curled, concealing some small object.

She stood still for a timeless moment. He said nothing, but she could feel his entreaty. Slowly she stepped toward him. The reek of burned flesh filled her nostrils. She placed the begging bowl in his upturned hand.

He smiled, a ravaged grimace full of painful joy. "The gates of the teaching are many; I vow to enter them all," he whispered: the third bodhisattva vow. She held out her hand, and he opened his. The Digrammaton, symbol of his office, fell into her hand.

It was searing hot! Eloatri shrieked, curling up around the pain, and fell senseless to the ground.

The sound of chanting awoke her. She sat up. Dappled sunlight played across her through the leaves of the massive flowering thorn tree against whose trunk she sat. Her hand throbbed and burned; she opened it and looked at the Digrammaton, Aleph-Null, its metallic gleam echoed in the flesh of her palm in the seared white puffiness of a third-degree burn.

Eloatri looked up. Across a little valley loomed the joyful exuberance of New Glastonbury Cathedral, its spires and buttresses leaping toward heaven in celebration of the goodness of Creation and the transforming power of descending love. Eloatri blinked.

Across the grassy sward a procession wended slowly toward her, men and women, some in glorious robes and some in stark black and white. She could smell sweet resinous incense and see its smoke rising among them, and their words came faintly to her: "... *Fons vivus, ignis, caritas, et spiritalis unctio* ..."

She smiled; the sound was beautiful, meaning would come later.

"You didn't think you drank that for yourself?" Eloatri laughed. Was it the redheaded boy who needed this? Or some part of herself not yet revealed? Or both? Then the shadow of sadness swept across her soul. Tomiko was dead by violence, and he had been on Arthelion, among the High Douloi. There might be many now who needed the message of a faith that saw history as a story with a purpose.

But that was in the Hand of Telos.

She looked back at the approaching group. Now that they were closer she could see that one of the processors carried a tall, pointed hat, strangely divided, another a folded garment more glorious than any of the others, and another a tall staff whose top was bent in a graceful crook. The procession made straight for her.

She stood up, and the last tatters of her yellow robe fell away from her. A gentle breeze caressed her body and the sun shone warm on her flesh as she advanced down the hill to meet her new life and await those who would come.

❊ ❊ ❊

GRANNY CHANG'S

Osri sat back, replete after a feast of myriad exotic dishes. Next to him his father was deep in conversation with Montrose, his face more relaxed than Osri had seen it since the long-ago days on his verandah on Charvann. The Eya'a had returned to the *Telvarna*, and Jaim was with them, ostensibly to supervise their refueling and to hold the con. But the others were all present, even Ivard.

His mood hovering between celebration and grief, Osri studied his hands. He had drunk the light, expensive wines presented to them, his first drink in what seemed eons: he remembered, with a twinge of shock, toasting a fellow officer on Merryn just before he'd gone on leave. *How long did Qu'isran live beyond his promotion?* The memory brought a quick sorrow: whatever happened to them now, there was no returning to the old ways, for Tanri Faseult, the enlightened Archon of Charvann, was dead, and jackals much worse than Nokker and his gang ran wild in once-peaceful Merryn.

Forcing his mind away from the past, Osri scanned the room as a group of musicians played an unending selection of complicated music from many worlds.

It is not just the drink, Osri realized as his gaze went from one person to another. The range of emotions he had experienced that day had taken their toll, and what he suffered now was reaction. He needed time to think through what had happened, to assess.

Across the room Lokri lounged amid a group of ornamental young Changs of both sexes, their laughter frequent. Ivard sat between Vi'ya and Montrose, his thin face flushed and his eyes brilliant with either fever or some other reaction; Osri saw Montrose glance his way quite often. Ivard seemed happy as he watched the free-fall dancers performing a short distance away, gyrating with lascivious agility in the center of the spherical room, reaction modules at wrists and ankles emitting puffs of sweet-smelling smoke. At their center Marim performed with skylark grace, her blond hair swirling about her laughing face, and her nearly naked body decorated with a crisscrossing of bells and beads.

In the center of the gathering, though, was Brandon, dressed in a splendid tunic that someone had produced from somewhere. It fitted his slim body to admiration, as did the tight black trousers and the high glossy boots. The Aerenarch was at his very best in the social arena; his attention divided equally among all his hosts, he kept them amused and entertained. Osri watched him lean toward Granny, whose old eyes gleamed with humor.

Osri considered his earlier observation, wondering why it had struck him as important. He knew now what the discrepancy between Brandon's parodic aping of Douloi movement and his unconscious elegance later had reminded him of: it was that same incident with Markham, who, when he had finished his story, moved back across the room with that very same elegance born of control and command.

But why was it important? Osri tried to blink away the muzziness threatening his skull from the unaccustomed alcohol.

"You are silent, son," Sebastian Omilov said on his right, breaking into his thoughts. "Is something amiss?" Above the polite smile, his father's eyes betrayed anxiousness.

He sees me as a wayward child to be humored. The observation came from that same part of his brain that urged him to make the connection in his observations, that insisted on their significance.

"I am merely tired, Father," he said. "Remember, it was just at the start of our Z-watch when we docked."

"I think we are nearly finished here," Omilov said. "Though I must say, I am reluctant to leave."

"Enjoy it," Osri said, forcing a smile. "I am."

Just then Granny Chang touched a control on her chair, and a ringing chime cut through music and talk. "It is time," she said, lifting her voice only slightly, "to hear what our honored guest has to say about events outside."

And Brandon moved his floating pillow into the center of the gathering with a smooth movement; then he began to talk.

"Arthelion has fallen," he said in a clear voice, mild but not indifferent. Absolute silence greeted these words. "My brothers are dead, and my father lies secreted somewhere, awaiting transfer to Gehenna. In my father's place is Eusabian of Dol'jhar, and these deeds are part of his vengeance for his defeat at Acheront twenty years ago."

Again, silence. Brandon looked around, his expression now hidden behind the deceptive shield of mildness that Osri had always equated with weakness.

And suddenly the observation was there: Markham vlith-L'Ranja, standing in a group telling a story with just such sureness, except his face had always reflected his thoughts.

"Adopted into the L'Ranjas from an obscure background . . ." His own sneering words came back to him.

Markham was a perfect mimic.

Osri remembered the mocking pantomime in the cadet lounge, the slight exaggerations that had still managed to convey a clear portrait of an unloved instructor whose social ambitions much outranked his station. Afterward Markham had returned to the others with just the grace that Brandon moved with now: *Markham was always a mimic. He learned to move from watching Brandon,* Osri realized as the alcohol fumes blurred Brandon's outlines. For a moment he could have been Markham, except Markham was blond, and his laughing face had never—

He learned the moves, but never the shield. That was it. Osri knew himself how he had raged ineffectually as a youth against the blank-faced Krysarchs, whose control had seemed so innate. *Even when they were punished, they hid their thoughts, just as they always read mine.* But Markham had recognized that he could never learn it, and so he had never tried.

Why was this important? *Because . . .*

But his mind refused to think, splintering into a collage of memories overlaid with angers past and present, and sorrow, and plain human exhaustion.

And through it all came Brandon's voice, outlining with graphic imagery the destruction of the *Korion* above Charvann, and the race in the little courier to escape a Rifter destroyer; he described vividly the crashlanding on the moon Dis, and how the *Telvarna* had gone to Arthelion. Then he told them about the raid against the Mandala; horror infused the smooth narrative, but not his tone, as he described what he had found in the Hall of Ivory, something Osri had not heard word of hitherto. More horror when he told them of Eusabian's torture room, and Omilov imprisoned there. Compassion blended with the head-long narrative as he gave them the flight through the palace, chased by Eusabian's deadly Tarkans, and how Greywing, Ivard's sister, was killed and Ivard wounded; and when it seemed almost unbearable he gave them a humorous release as he described the fight in the kitchens with the little mechwaiters as weapons.

His voice took on color at last, and Osri's guts tightened as he relived the terror of the *Telvarna*'s race up the Node cable toward radius and escape. One by one Brandon touched on heroic actions of the *Telvarna*'s crew: Lokri, who carried Ivard to safety, Montrose in his rescue of Omilov. Jaim ʌıd Marim working against time to recondition the ship's engines.

No one moved as he told of the appearance of Eusabian's *Fist of Dol'jhar*, though several people gasped when he told of its last attempt, the ruptor beam that had to have ripped apart the Node and killed everyone living on it.

Then he told them what they found at Dis, and how Vi'ya had driven Hreem's watchdog into Warlock. He finished with Osri's own part, how he gave them a margin of safety despite dangerously low fuel as they came directly to Chang's. Osri felt an unaccustomed glow make his face heat up, but then another thought occurred: *He has not mentioned my father's artifact.* And then: *He has not talked about his part at all.*

Osri lifted a bulb of wine, watching a moiré pattern shift across its surface. Touching the control, he waited for the thin tube to extrude. He knew he should not drink any more, but clear thought was beyond him now, and he sought escape from the shadows of the past that were catching up with him now that he had the time to think.

Out in the center of the room, Brandon was bombarded with all the questions his auditors had saved up. For a time he fielded some of these, and at last he held up a hand. Presently silence fell, and he said as his eyes moved from one face to another, all around the circle: "I don't know what Eusabain plans for the future. My own plan I will tell you: I want to find myself a fleet of daring ships and make a raid against Gehenna to rescue my father." And his eyes came at last to rest on Vi'ya.

He smiled at her, a laughing challenge, and she returned his gaze with unwinking coolness as around them pandemonium broke out; the Changs cheered, laughed, and several drunkenly swore to join any expedition that Brandon cared to lead. Granny Chang sat quietly until the furor had died down some, and then the old woman leaned toward Brandon, involving him in earnest conversation.

Vi'ya leaned forward to spear a piece of food, as though nothing had happened. But beyond her, on the other side of the room, Osri caught a glimpse of Lokri amid his decorative young audience. As they chattered and laughed unaware, Lokri's pale eyes watched Brandon, his mouth thinned in a trace of a smile.

"Here. Catch this!" Someone called to Lokri, and he spun away, lost in his group as they brought out a smoke-pot and started some pungent incense.

After this, what? Osri thought. *He can make theatrical statements, but that doesn't mean he intends to lead a fleet anywhere, any more than these people will remember their vows past the hour their livers have processed what they've drunk.*

He still had no idea what Vi'ya's intentions were toward any of her Panarchist passengers; she seemed impervious to Brandon's words.

Granny leaned back and made a signal. Hard-beating music started up, and several people scrambled to join the dancers.

Osri sat where he was, sipping his bulb of wine as around him moods metamorphosed into a different kind of appetite.

Osri saw Marim pull Ivard toward one of the shadowy alcoves; Lokri had already disappeared with two or three of the Changs. He was surprised to see that Montrose, too, had disappeared; next to him, his father, still recovering from what he had endured on Arthelion, had fallen gently asleep.

Only Brandon and Vi'ya remained, Brandon talking to a cluster of Changs, and Vi'ya watching, silent and cool. As Brandon gestured, a glint on his hand brought Osri's attention to the ring he still wore: Tanri Faseult's ring.

"How can I raise a fleet to rescue him? Who would follow

me?" Brandon had said that, or something like that, during the argument in their cabin.

He is forsworn . . . Osri shook his head.

A mistake to drink so much—

"Would you like anything more, genz?" a mellow voice murmured near Osri's ear.

He looked up through swimming vision to see a young woman with the slanted Chang eyes smiling at him. Her wide, attractive mouth curved invitingly.

"No," he said, struggling to make his numb tongue work. He felt a tug of attraction, followed promptly by alarm.

"Some shakrian to release tension?" she offered.

He tried to decline, but she was already behind him, her fingers kneading his shoulders. Little zings of release sang along his nerves.

He shut his eyes, wavering between what he perceived as his duty to keep his distance from Vi'ya's riffraff allies, and an enticement that grew increasingly persistent.

Under her steady ministrations the worrisome questions went away. And so, at last, did his inhibitions, the anger-forged iron control he had put between himself and the universe since childhood.

So when she tugged him from his seat and slid her fingers down the front of his tunic, he forgot where he was, and among what kind of people, and buried his face gratefully in her scented cloud of hair.

❋   ❋   ❋

POSEIDONIS SYSTEM

Rom-Sanchez' face sometimes reminded Ng of her favorite hound when she was small. "I'm a little worried about the couriers, sir," he said. "One of them should have reported back by now."

Ng nodded but didn't reply immediately. The bridge of the *Grozniy* was quiet, a subdued murmur of status reports the only sound. From under one console a pair of legs protruded; there was a flare of light and a muffled curse, then sudden silence as, Ng guessed, the technician recollected where she was. Ng repressed an impulse to laugh; the crew was adapting well to their new wartime status.

The more things change—

The SigInt console bleeped. "Emergence pulses, three of them, destroyers." Ensign Wychyrski's clipped tone betrayed excitement.

Rom-Sanchez twisted back to his console and started slapping keys.

Alarm burned momentarily through Ng as the navigator's voice broke in. "Bearing one, 90 mark zero, plus 6 light-seconds; bearing two, 90 mark 120, plus 5 light-seconds; bearing three, 90 mark 270—"

"They've got us bracketed," said Rom-Sanchez.

Ng suddenly laughed as the significance of the destroyers' positions became clear.

Trust Metellus to make an effective entrance . . .

SigInt and Communications spoke simultaneously.

"ID established, they're ours—"

"Beam incoming—"

"Put him on-screen. I know who it is, Mr. Wychyrski."

She relaxed in her command pod as a window blossomed on the main screen, revealing the broad, high-boned face of Metellus Hayashi. His grin below the hawk-nose was piratical.

"Captain Ng! Welcome to Poseidonis system."

As he spoke, the SigInt console bleeped once more, and a moment later the communications console twittered. Ng guessed that the courier that had found Metellus was reporting in. She tabbed her console without looking away from the screen, notifying Ensign Ammant to relay the report to her via boswell.

"Thank you, Captain Hayashi. That was quite a greeting."

He laughed. "I never pass up an opportunity to undermine that stubborn Fleet bias toward battleblimps."

Ng noted her tactical officer's head snap up toward the screen in a motion of protest. She felt her mouth twitch. In her inner ear the courier reported that Hayashi had mentioned dealing with some Rifter activity in the inner system, but had given no details. There had been no mention of war.

"But I'm afraid that, welcome as your presence is, Captain," Metellus continued, "you're on the Blister Patrol—"

Ng burst out laughing, the tension of the past days finding sudden release. *How I've missed you, beloved!*

"Showing up after the work is done," she said, aware of the stares of her crew. Behind her the aft hatch hissed open. "How I wish it were so, Captain," she continued, suddenly serious. "But I believe our work is just beginning."

His smile hardened, and he nodded once. "I was hoping the rumors were the usual exaggerations, even with the interruption in the DataNet—there've been almost no couriers into Poseidonis for a week." He paused—*his boswell*, Ng thought. *Report on our damage?*

"And the Rifters—I thought they must've been crazy, storming into the inner system like they'd never heard of the Navy."

"Any losses?" asked Ng, as Commander Krajno slipped into his pod next to Rom-Sanchez.

Hayashi snorted. "Against Rifters?" Then he stopped and looked directly out of the screen at her, his eyes narrowing. *He did get our damage stats.* "That wasn't a joke, was it?"

Before she could reply he straightened up in his pod and spoke formally. "Request permission to come on board, Captain."

"Please," she replied. "We have much to discuss."

❋   ❋   ❋

Metellus Hayashi strode to the wall with his hands clasped behind his back, then turned around. "This is making my head reel. Do you realize, we're sitting here planning an attack on Arthelion?"

"I know," Ng replied. "I keep expecting lightning to come out of a bulkhead or something." She had shifted in her pod so she could watch Hayashi's peregrinations.

Lieutenant Rom-Sanchez watched the interplay between the heavily muscled destroyer captain and Margot Ng, struggling with the sourness in his stomach. *This is stupid, Sergen,* he told himself. *Did you really think you could have gotten anywhere?* He tore his mind away from the senseless feeling of regret and listened.

"But the real planning will have to wait until we reach the Arthelion system," she continued. "I just want to have a general tactical and strategic structure in place when the others join us."

Hayashi's mouth tightened. "Armenhaut," he said, not hiding his distaste. Then he gave Ng a sudden grin. "He's never forgiven you—and he's never caught up, either."

Ng returned his smile. It was a secret shared—no, it was more than a secret shared, Rom-Sanchez thought, with another surge of jealousy.

Then his captain's eyes turned to him, and Rom-Sanchez fought back a sudden flush of embarrassment. Had she noticed anything? But Ng's manner was easy as she spoke: "Mr. Rom-Sanchez, how many couriers do you estimate we need to guarantee contacting the *Flammarion*, the *Joyeaux*, and the *Babur Khan* for a rendezvous at Arthelion in the time allotted?"

"The closer a ship was stationed to Arthelion, the more likely it will have heard of the war and have moved on," replied Rom-Sanchez. "The problem soon becomes indeterminate; but my best estimate is that more than twenty-four couriers will just give us diminishing returns."

"Very well. Please draw up the orders." Rom-Sanchez heard the dismissal in her voice and stood, gathering up his papers as Ng turned back to Hayashi. "I'd like you to bring together your commanders and tactical officers for a presentation by Lieutenant Warrigal on the new Tenno. They'll be critical to our success; we'll need to spend as much time as possible training on them."

As Rom-Sanchez reached the door, Ng addressed him once more. "And, Lieutenant, please post a meeting for ten hundred hours tomorrow in the plot room, department heads in Armory, Weapons, Communications, SigInt, yourself, Lieutenant Warrigal, and Commander Krajno."

"AyKay, sir," replied Rom-Sanchez, and tabbed the hatch open. As he stepped through, Ng turned back to Metellus Hayashi.

"And I request the pleasure of your company at dinner tonight, Metellus, twenty-one-hundred . . ."

The hatch hissed shut across the remainder of her words, and Rom-Sanchez clenched his teeth, mixed frustration and amusement swirling in his mind at his captain's subtlety. *She saw, all right. She knew—and she let me down easy.* Then he shrugged and walked away.

He had work to do—and then he needed a drink.

❊   ❊   ❊

Margot Ng woke up first, and rejoiced.

Metellus lay asleep beside her, his breathing deep and slow.

Her eyes memorized the contours of his face, noting new lines, new gray in his temples. The signs of age made him that much dearer, and she fought an almost overwhelming urge to kiss him awake again.

How long had it been? Almost two years? It had been pure luck that had placed them on maneuvers in the same system then, giving them a chance to grab thirty-six hours together.

Sleep, my love, she thought. *Telos knows how much rest we'll get when we reach Arthelion system.* A darker thought—of the sleep eternal—shadowed her thoughts, but she pushed it away. It was the risk they lived with in the life they'd chosen.

But the thought didn't stay banished, for her hand reached convulsively to touch his bare chest above the sheet, to feel the warmth of his flesh and the steady *lump-lump* of his heart beneath the smooth muscles.

His eyes opened, instantly alert. The lines at the corners of his mouth deepened. "What's this? Want more? You'd think we haven't had any for two years."

She smothered her laughter in the hollow of his throat, and then trailed her fingers down and down through the soft curls of hair on his chest.

After a time she opened her eyes again, turning her head quickly to check the chrono. An instant later she felt his muscles tighten; he was doing the same thing.

She sat up, laughing softly as she clasped her hands around her knees. He crossed his hands behind his head. "Ready to start some real planning?" he asked.

Ng shook her tousled hair back. "Yes, but I was thinking about Armenhaut. He'll be hard to deal with, but even so I feel sorry for him," she said. "It's his kind that will take it the hardest."

"You mean the loss of automatic patronage now that Semion is dead?" Antipathy narrowed Metellus' eyes. "I can't find it in me to pity him for that."

The faintest trace of hauteur in the verb made Ng think that it was not just Armenhaut's general unfitness for high command that irked Metellus, there was also the Douloi resentment of the Aerenarch's noted preference for the High Douloi scions of Downsider Tetrad Centrum Families. *No matter where human beings go they rank themselves,* she thought. *And within those ranks there are yet more ranks.*

"If we do win, what's going to happen to us? Will there even be a government for us to protect?" she asked.

Metellus stared at the ceiling, his forehead creased. "I don't know," he admitted. "If those Rifters were right and the Panarch lives, then change might not run deep. People embrace the old systems, historically, if enough of it exists after a war. Better the tame demon you know than the wild demons of chaos."

"If he's gone?"

Metellus shrugged. "Chaos, then. People will probably look to whatever remains of us ..."

"Including Armenhaut," Ng said with a wince. "But there is the third son, if those Rifters are correct."

Metellus shook his head. "If he's even alive, I've never heard anything about him indicating any ability to lead. If he does turn up somewhere, he'll probably be surrounded by high-cost drinking companions and toadies. He'll be a focus for factions scrambling for a toehold in the power vacuum who'll want the clout of his name. I almost hope he doesn't turn up."

"Grim," Ng said, sliding her fingers into his.

He toyed with her hand, his eyes going abstract.

"Have you heard from Alys?" she asked carefully.

He smiled. "You mean, do I know if she's alive? No, I don't."

She sighed. Time was when she'd felt ambivalent about the smooth-faced women Metellus had had to marry eighteen years before. A decade older than they were, Alys ban-Kerrimac had been philosophical about accepting his relationship with Ng as part of her marriage with the Hayashi dynasty. At that time Ng was still struggling to understand the Douloi attitudes toward marriage, love, and family; there had been moments when it had seemed she would make more sense out of the Shiidra than these old families with their singsong voices and poised bodies.

But she'd come to know Alys over the years, to understand her as much as their backgrounds, and their interests, allowed, and even to like her.

"I hope she's safe," Ng said, her fingers tightening on Metellus'.

"Alys is a canny one," he said. "She has ears with ears; my guess is she would have had enough warning to get out. And the

Shiidra hits are still recent enough in memory that evacuation plans were kept up-to-date."

"This war is going to hurt business," she said, tracing patterns on his palms.

"It will hurt everything," he said. Adding fiercely, "I'm glad it is us who will be fighting over the Mandala. Though I know we can't win."

"We will win," she said, smiling. "Even if we all get blown to hell, so long as one of our couriers gets that hyperwave to Ares, we win." She glanced again at the chrono and sighed. "Ten minutes. Hadn't we better—"

Instead of freeing her hand he gripped it and brought his mouth down on hers.

She reveled in sensory fireworks and then reluctantly pulled away. "We have to meet them in ten minutes . . ."

"Margot," he breathed, his palms on either side of her face, his eyes steady and smiling. "We have ten minutes."

She laughed.

SEVENTEEN

TELVARNA: *GRANNY CHANG'S TO RIFTHAVEN*

Marim leaned her chin on the back of her chair and watched Vi'ya lock in the course. A moment later the shudder of the fiveskip engaging shivered in her viscera, and she turned her cheek, hiding a grin.

Rifthaven. She had just a few days to find that coin. The challenge merely added to the fun.

Montrose and Ivard came in then, the surgeon's hand on Ivard's good shoulder. Ivard's eyes homed straight for Marim. She smothered a sigh and beckoned. *Never again am I going to be anyone's first.* Fighting a spurt of impatience, she remembered how long it had taken to calm him down after he woke up at Granny's, did a locate on his boswell, and found her at Red Mik's joyhouse. *Damn boz'l*, she thought, glancing in relief at her arm, bare now that they were back on the ship. *Lucky thing Red Mik also sells vids.*

Ivard sat down at the nav pod and she kissed him loudly. He hunched up, scanning the others to see who might react.

Of course no one did. Lokri was busy at his console, and Jaim stood, arms folded, at the back of the bridge.

Vi'ya nodded and Montrose stationed himself at the door.

"We go to Rifthaven," Vi'ya said. "The fiveskip needs re-tooling, and we can have it done better and faster at Furn's Refit than if we must do it ourselves."

Lokri looked up right then. "Search on gossip from docking vessels while we were at Chang's turns up no references on Hreem, *Satansclaw*, Heart of Kronos, Eya'a, or anything having to do with us."

"Store it," Vi'ya said.

Lokri swept his hand over his board and sat back, the fingers of his good arm drumming on the pod. "Rifthaven?" he said, looking up. "But what if those chatzing Dol'jharians have fig-ured out the Arkad is still alive? Hreem was at Charvann, he'd be able to put him together with us. And the first place he's gonna look for us since he blew our base away is Rifthaven."

"Hreem can't be coming after us anyway," Marim interjected, looking from Lokri to Vi'ya. "He went to Malachronte, right?"

"Hreem won't go to Rifthaven." Jaim looked up from con-templation of the deckplates. "Sodality Adjudicates have some business waiting for him."

Marim laughed at the understatement, and Lokri shrugged his agreement.

"We will stand off and contact Jucan first," Vi'ya said, indi-cating Jaim, who looked up again briefly when his brother's name was mentioned. "We might be a few days behind Eusabian's fastest ships, if he posted word of Omilov's escape from Arthelion. If we lock up the nicks for the duration of our stay, I believe our anonymity is protected."

No one reacted. Marim, watching Lokri from the corner of her eye, thought: *She's been through this with him.*

"Also this: you will want to go to the vendors to sell your share of the loot from the palace. You must be careful to sell only what is not so rare it can be recognized as from that col-lection. Those items will have to wait until another time. Montrose will identify what is safe to sell now." When no one spoke, Vi'ya went on, "What we must now consider is our next destination."

"We got to go to the other base," Ivard said. "And hide."

"We can't hide out at the other base," Marim said, considering the future beyond Rifthaven—and her fortune—for the first time. "It was Hreem that duffed *Sunflame*. What you want to bet he scanned the comp first?"

"We will have to assume that he did this," Vi'ya said. "The other base is as nothing to us now."

A chill went through Marim. *Rich at last—and nowhere to go!*

Lokri smiled grimly. "Who says," he drawled, "that *we* have to do anything?"

Marim sighed to signify publicly her regret that the crew was breaking up at last, and was surprised to feel a real twinge of regret. *It's always been this way,* she thought. *Ever since the creche. You get used to one gang, you work to the place you want, and then boom! All gone, and it's to be done all over again somewhere else.*

Ivard's thin, feverish fingers stole into hers, clinging.

Lokri said, "What about the Panarchists?"

"They are mine," Vi'ya said. "I will dispose of them as I deem proper, a way that will not lead our enemies to us."

Marim squeezed Ivard's hand, but her attention was on Lokri and Vi'ya. *I wonder if Lokri hears the warning in that?*

Montrose grunted. "Then you'll have to kill them. Anything else, anything at all, will lead our enemies right back to us: if you sell them to the Panarchists, they'll talk willingly, and if you sell them to our enemies on the other side, they'll talk even more."

"There is another alternative," Vi'ya said calmly. "You will be safe enough."

Lokri was silent. *He hears the warning, all right.*

Vi'ya went on, "I will leave as soon as the engines are refitted."

So we'll have maybe a week to find another bunkhole and get our stuff off this ship, Marim thought. *Means I got a week to get the gilt I want, then ditch my red-topped parasite here.* She squeezed Ivard's hand again and smiled at his freckled, weak-eyed face.

❋　　　❋　　　❋

Osri leaned back on the seat.

"That's it," his father said, grunting with effort as he rose. "I suppose I had better get back to the dispensary so we can avoid awkward questions."

The three Panarchists were crowded into the galley, with Lucifur winding in and around their legs, making his racheting purring noise. Osri had activated Montrose's spy and they had listened in silence to the discussion on the bridge.

Sebastian left. Brandon leaned on his forearms, staring into the console as if reading a hidden message there.

Irritated by his silence, Osri reached past and flicked the console off, then he returned to the chopping block and began to slice the vegetables that Montrose had laid out.

Perhaps the knife thudded more sharply than he'd meant it to; Brandon suddenly blinked, his eyes distracted. "She knew we were there," he said.

"How do you know that?" Osri asked, and at the flat-toned rudeness he heard in his voice, he added quickly, "But you're probably right."

"By what she didn't say," Brandon murmured.

"You think she would have told them what she intends to do next if we hadn't been listening?"

"No." Brandon picked up an onion and hefted it absently in his hand. "Not if they're disbanding. Protect everyone that way. In any case I think what happens next depends on what she finds out on Rifthaven."

Osri looked from Brandon's meditative smile to the onion bouncing gently on his palm, then he remembered: "The Heart of Kronos."

Brandon nodded. He stood up, stretched, then leaned back just slightly and glanced out the door. "She didn't mention the Eya'a," he said.

Osri frowned, ready to dismiss this as irrelevant. But he swallowed the urge, and turned to scrape his chopped vegetables into the simmering sauce.

Brandon seemed to notice what he was doing for the first time. "That smells good," he said.

Osri snorted a wry laugh. "Unwilling and untalented, I seem to have acquired an amazing amount of Golgol chef skills—"

"Worthless," a big voice grated. Montrose loomed, his teeth gleaming in his beard, his wide-spaced eyes amused. "You know nothing at all. It takes years, *years*, to make an adequate chef."

"But what he's making smells as good as anything we got at home," Brandon said.

Montrose sighed theatrically, his shoulders slumping. "Must you say it in front of him?" He jerked a huge thumb in Osri's direction. "How will I keep him appropriately humble?"

Brandon laughed, and Osri shook his head, turning back to his chore. Brandon leaned over, dropped his onion, and expertly snagged a chocolate square. "All right. Come on, Lucifur, we're not wanted."

Osri fought back his impatience and returned to the chores at hand.

"This meal," Montrose said, "is for my guests in the dispensary, but you are also invited."

Osri nodded. "Very well," he said. *She didn't mention the Eya'a?" What does that mean?*

Montrose shot him a squinty look from under his bristling brows. But he confined his comments to the cooking lessons, and Osri forced himself to be patient until at last the meal was finished enough for him to slip away. He found Brandon in their cabin, busy at the console.

"I have to ask you a question," Osri said.

Brandon looked up, his hand hovering over the kill-pad. "Montrose?" he murmured.

"Preparing a dinner for my father. And I found his spy-eye for this cabin and disabled it."

"Wiped it?" Brandon asked, frowning slightly .

"No. Merely reset the date for it to be activated for ten years from now. I hope," Osri added trenchantly, "we will be gone from here by then."

Brandon gave a soundless laugh.

"What did you mean by the captain not mentioning the Eya'a?" Osri went on. "I don't see the connection between them and where she might go after Rifthaven."

"I think . . ." Brandon leaned back, waving at the console. "Take a look for yourself."

Osri stepped closer, and saw that Brandon had windowed up the *Starfarer's Handbook* entry on Ysqven V. The warning code for a quarantined planet was the first designation, and the brief information that followed made the place seem grim beyond human toleration. Puzzled, Osri scanned quickly past the listings of the seasons (deep winter and deeper winter) and of the many horrific plant and animal predators.

At the end of the entry was the header for indigenous sentients, and Osri was only partially enlightened with what he saw: a brief physical description of the Eya'a, followed by a listing of ships that had landed there and not lifted off again.

Brandon was still waiting when Osri looked up.

A sudden nasty idea occurred to him. "You don't think she'll force us to go *there*, do you?"

Brandon smiled. "I think she wants us—and them"—he tipped his head toward the rest of the ship—"to think so."

"But you don't?"

For answer, Brandon got up and hit the door lock. Then he sat back down at the console. "Watch," he said.

Osri leaned against the console inset, just inches from where he had secreted the Tetradrachm and the flight ribbon, and waited while Brandon quickly navigated the ship's system. He hit several areas that required codes, and each time, Brandon went past, typing in the code with a speed that revealed what he had been doing with much of his free time.

Then they were in a hidden area, where Brandon had stored chunks of info. In surprise, Osri saw that the entire *Starfarer's Handbook* entry on Dol'jhar was listed there, along with the ship's log for the past several years.

"You broke into the system," Osri said.

Brandon didn't answer directly. "Markham designed the present system," he said. "And Vi'ya seems to have left it mostly intact. Knowing Markham as well as I had, it did not take me long to figure out his codes. I've found most of what I wanted—"

Osri almost let that get by, waiting for Brandon to reach his point, but this time he saw the point ahead of time, and pounced on a side issue that seemed more interesting: "Most?"

And it turned out to be the point, after all.

Brandon gave a wry smile. "She has apparently redesigned certain portions of the system and I can't crack it."

Osri opened his mouth to observe that this was standard operating procedure, but Brandon was waiting expectantly. So Osri returned to the previous track. "What have you not found that you wanted?"

"Captain's log," Brandon said. "I found Markham's; I even found a file he'd started for me—" He broke off and shrugged.

"What was in it?"

"Observations he thought I might enjoy. Some proof of Semion's culpability in his father's ruin—none of it matters now."

"But you can't find the present captain's log."

"No."

"Are you sure there is one? Maybe Dol'jharians don't keep logs."

Brandon shrugged again. "I'm not sure. Except there are other things I can't access." He flicked a hand dismissively. "Now look at this."

He punched up the captain's log, scrolling it back to the beginning of Markham's career as the *Telvarna*'s captain. Osri watched as Brandon flicked through screen after screen of cryptic entries.

"Rifthaven again ... Dis. Rifthaven—" Osri looked up. "They seem to have ranged through different octants without any discernible pattern. Including systems I've never heard of. What am I supposed to be seeing?"

"Any anomalies here?"

"Anomalies? For Rifters?" Osri said, but even as he said it, a third reference to Dol'jhar made him stop. "That?" He tapped the screen. A horrifying thought occurred. "But you *don't* think Markham—"

"No. Eusabian seems to have hired his Rifter allies just around the time Hreem killed Markham. And who knows, that could have been some of Hreem's motivation in cutting down competition." Brandon's mouth twisted. "These are raids, pure and simple."

"I still don't see the connection."

Brandon tapped his fingers against the console, then saved and stored the system. "Let's go find out if there is one."

Osri had never seen the captain's cabin. He followed Brandon the short distance around to the other side of the ship, expecting anything from sybaritic ostentation to savage displays of skulls and arcane weaponry.

When they entered, it was Brandon who stopped dead as if he'd walked into a force field, staring with manic eyes at the eerily real holographic display of the sequoia park on the Mandala. Osri felt his head buzz; through it came the familiar trill of birdsong, birds Osri had only heard on Arthelion.

"Have I made any egregious errors?"

The cool voice belonged to the captain. Amusement blended with the Dol'jharian twist to the consonants, and amusement matching her tone exactly was in Brandon's reply:

"It's too cold in here, the air should smell like loam and pine, and have the tianqi jack up the oxygen content." Brandon gestured. "Then you'll be close enough."

Instead, the captain hit a control and the familiar beauty of the forest vanished, to be replaced by the starkly plain walls of a cabin whose only decoration was a tapestry and a gemstone that Osri belatedly (and with an echo of the rage that hovered never far away) recognized as one from the Ivory Hall.

"You wanted to see me?"

The woman was sitting at the console, which had been obscured by shadows in the holo.

Osri waited where he was by the door, but Brandon advanced into the cabin. "After Rifthaven," Brandon said.

Vi'ya said nothing.

He's right—she knew we were listening. Brandon crossed the room, touched a dark tapestry whose subject was obscure, and from this distance unpleasant. "Sebastian won't last a day there," he commented.

Vi'ya's chin jerked up.

Osri missed her answer because the meaning of Brandon's words impacted his brain like a missile. *Dol'jhar? She wouldn't take us there!*

Brandon smiled, crossing his arms and leaning against a bulkhead. "Might it be a test? Might it be"—he touched the discreet inlay above the console—"the same test he faced?"

He? Osri looked at the inlay, which was a tasteful evocation of the Archaeo-Moderne mode of 150 years ago. *The ship was restored by Markham vlith-L'Ranja.*

Markham. Tested? A pang of headache shot through Osri's temple, compounded by the frigid air, and he rubbed his head, but it did not dissipate the tension radiating from the two across the room.

Vi'ya stood up slowly and clasped her hands behind her back. "Eusabian of Dol'jhar is gone from the planet, and with him the worst of his nobles," she said. "I know places to hide where you will never be found."

"But you haven't answered my question," Brandon said lightly.

"It is an absurd question."

"Then you did test Markham," the Aerenarch said, smiling. "Because you've been testing me."

A pause. Osri felt the pang again. "A game," Vi'ya said. "Like this."

She hit the control behind her, and they were pitched into a holo of space, with asteroids hurtling toward them. Osri barely had time to react from the shock when the scene altered, this time to the breathtaking beauty of a snow-topped peak on a mountain of black stone. A red dwarf sun was setting on the horizon, bathing the scene with a glory of reddish colors. The scene was followed by several in succession, each vastly different.

They were inside a gloomy, high-ceilinged cathedral vaguely familiar to Osri when Brandon reached across and tabbed the kill-pad. "I also know places where my enemies will never find us."

A faint chittering noise reached Osri then, scraping along his nerves: the Eya'a. Brandon glanced aside, his eyes distracted. Vi'ya did not turn her head.

"Let us go," Brandon said, so softly it was scarcely audible above the quiet hiss of the tianqi.

Vi'ya did not answer. Instead, she reached back and tabbed another key, and the room was replaced by a bleak landscape, with smoldering volcanoes in the distance, and overhead a storm-torn sky.

Brandon walked out.

Osri followed, glad to turn his back on Vi'ya and her grim landscape, which he guessed was Dol'jhar.

Back in their cabin Brandon slammed his fist lightly on the console again, bringing it to life. Tapping rapidly, he straightened up, then stood looking down the display, rubbing his thumb along his jawline.

Osri, looking past him, saw that the hidden files were gone. Nausea gripped at his insides, until Brandon dropped into the chair and laughed.

The com beeped. Osri touched it with sweaty fingers.

"We're waiting for you, Schoolboy," came Montrose's familiar grating voice. "You don't want your father to eat congealed *chzchz*, do you?"

"Never," Osri said hoarsely. And with another look at Brandon, who sat with his head in his hands, still laughing, he went out.

✳   ✳   ✳

Omilov leaned back, appraising his son's face. Montrose and Ivard were talking about wine.

The supper that Montrose had presented to them was superlative, and the man had exerted himself to keep the conversation light and general. But he'd only been partially successful: Osri sat mostly in silence. Not an angry silence, but reflective.

He sighed, wondering what to do. Meanwhile, the others talked on as the courses appeared and vanished. And the conversation, though three-way, was merry. Though he'd been retired for ten years from court life, Omilov resumed with ease his skill at conversing on any number of topics while thinking about something else. Ivard's thin face was flushed with fever and high spirits, and he participated willingly enough—when he did not fall into reveries. Omilov would not have thought anything of these sudden quiet moments, except for the frown on Montrose's face when he observed them.

Omilov left worries concerning the boy to the surgeon, who understood them; his own concern was with his son, who seemed to have left his anger back at the asteroid—and replaced with a much more serious turn of mind, indicated by the little gesture Osri had used to betray inner turmoil ever since he was a boy, an absent running of the inside of his index finger along the knuckles of his other hand. This gesture when Osri was small had presaged a gnawing of those same knuckles, often until they were raw. When Lady Risiena had discovered this she had somehow ruthlessly eradicated the noxious habit; the nervous rubbing remained.

At last the meal was over, and Omilov wondered how he could get Osri alone.

"What shall it be, Sebastian?" Montrose asked as he stacked his plates into the cleanser. "A play, or perhaps a duel to the death?" Montrose offered, waving at the chessboard and smiling.

"Neither, thank you. While I was going through your catalog

the other day, I chanced upon an opera I haven't heard for years: *The Tragic History of Macclom Singh*."

Montrose gave a thin, humorless smile. "I'm not surprised that it had fallen from favor—the late Aerenarch could hardly have found its message comforting."

Omilov felt a wash of sadness. *Even Rifters recognized the danger, but Gelasaar refused to see.*

"Very well, Sebastian, the *Tragic History* it shall be. There may be a lesson in it for these times. Osri, does that suit you?"

"Thank you," he replied with slightly absent politeness, "but I think I'll retire."

"My son has never developed a taste for opera," Omilov said. "Perhaps we can save it for another time—"

"No, Father. I really do want to retire," Osri said, and he went out.

Omilov repressed a sigh as Montrose tapped at the console. The lights dimmed as the far wall of the dispensary wavered and vanished, dissolving to a panoramic starfield. The view panned down, and a planet in flames rolled into view as the massive, sorrowful grandeur of Tamilski's overture filled the room. *Vellicor,* thought Omilov, *still a dead world after six hundred years. How many have joined it in the past weeks?*

Then he lost himself in the story of the Praerogate Singh, who, in contravention of his oath, delivered the Anathema of the High Phanist Gabriel to the Faceless One following the Vellicor Atrocity. Singh's dramatic renunciation of fealty and suicide immediately thereafter isolated that Panarch from his supporters and led directly to his deposition and death.

Shortly into the first act, the trumpets blazed forth with a fanfare based on the Singh leitmotif.

Suddenly Ivard made a noise, and Montrose stilled the chip with a wave of his hand.

"Are you all right, Ivard?"

He really is worried, Omilov thought.

"Uh, yes. Sorry. I guess I got to dreaming, and then I heard this music, and I thought—" Ivard blinked up at the holo. "That's the Praerogate Singh!"

Now it was Omilov's turn to be surprised. "You know Tamilski's *Tragic History*?" Except for the interminable waltzes that Montrose played when the boy thrashed through sleep periods with nightmares, Ivard had never seemed to evince any interest in the music in Montrose's library.

"Tamilski? No, but Singh was one of the most famous Invisibles, and I really like—" He stopped and hunched up.

Montrose laughed, evidently understanding what was going on. "Talk, Firehead."

Ivard looked askance at Omilov, as if expecting mockery or disdain. "I really like *The Invisibles*. I've collected almost a hundred volumes." He grinned. "With the loot from the palace I might even be able to get an original Volume One. It was made in 248 A.A., over seven hundred years ago."

So Osri was right, they really did loot the palace, thought Omilov. *Well, under the circumstances, there's certainly no one to denounce them.*

Aloud, he said, "I'm afraid I'm not familiar with this 'Invisibles.' What is it?"

"A serial chip," Ivard said, exhibiting muted surprise. He motioned at the screen. "That music is just like the music on the chips."

Omilov did not hide his surprise. "A serial chip that's been going for over seven hundred years? It must have something to recommend it, then. Certainly their choice of music couldn't be bettered."

"Sgatshi, it's good!" Ivard exclaimed. "The others laugh at me about it, sometimes, but Greywing, she said—" He broke off, his eyes going wide and shocked.

To distract the boy, Omilov said, "I would certainly like to see some of your serial chips someday soon, Ivard. I've never developed a taste for them, but that is more likely a flaw in my character than a flaw in the art form."

Ivard winced, and rubbed his eyes as though trying to banish a memory. Then he looked up doubtfully. "Really?"

The gnostor suddenly realized that he must present a fairly fearsome aura to the boy, freighted with the complex associations inculcated by Archetype and Ritual into the popular view of the Ranks of Service.

"Really. You have one about Singh?"

"Oh, yes, that's one of the best."

"Perhaps you'd enjoy seeing part of this opera, then. Then I could view your chip, and we could see how the two types of art treat the story."

"Uh, sure. D'ya mind if I ask questions?"

"Not at all."

Montrose, smiling at this exchange, moved to start the playback again, then paused as Ivard spoke again.

"Well, I've got a question, but not about the opera." He leaned forward, all knotty elbows and knees. "Brandon told me you're a Chival, so that means you did the nickstrut in the Mandala."

Omilov smiled. *"Strut." An apt description for many at Court.*

"Yes, I did, for a time."

"Did you ever meet a Praerogate?"

He stifled a laugh. *Every day, in the mirror.* Then he felt a sense of melancholy. *But does it have any meaning now?* He realized that the knowledge that he could, if confronted with real evil, speak with the full authority of the absolute ruler of the Thousand Suns, wielding the high and low justice alike with none to gainsay him, had been a deep, if rarely considered, comfort to him. Now it was gone.

"Well, Ivard, there's a problem with answering that—you never really know until afterward. Of course, I've known some Praerogates Overt, after they revealed themselves to put right a malignant situation, but I had never known any of those while they were still Occult. So, to answer what I think is perhaps your real question, there doesn't seem to be anything to distinguish a Praerogate Occult from any other person."

"So, it's just like *The Invisibles*. The evil blits can't tell until it's too late!"

"Exactly. So, shall we proceed?"

Receiving Ivard's assent, he settled back in his chair as Montrose resumed the playback. From time to time during the opera he stole a glance at the young Rifter. At first Ivard was restless. Then the music gradually drew the boy in, and during the soaring Aria of Renunciation near the climax, he was astonished, and pleased, to see the luminosity of unshed tears in Ivard's eyes. He felt an answering sting in his own. He remembered what Osri had told him about Ivard's background.

There was no place for this ardent spirit in the ordered world of the Panarchy, save in unskilled labor. Here, at least, he has room to grow—there is no one to force him into a mold.

For the first time Omilov began to really understand the large and unacknowledged part the Rifter overculture played in the life of the Thousand Suns.

But now it is too late. We rejected them, and they have become a tool in the hands of our worst enemy.

In the holo Macclom Singh lay dying before the Emerald Throne. On the throne, the Faceless One—played, as always, by an actor in a shimmermask, that nothing might lend that abhorred figure even the semblance of a face and therefore anamnesis—slumped hopelessly as the realization of defeat gripped him. Ivard was leaning forward in his seat, completely lost in the action, his face shining with the mix of exaltation and sorrow that good tragedy brings.

Not all of them, decided Omilov. *This boy's spirit would not have survived association with anyone who would join Eusabian.* For the first time, despite his unfortunate interview with the captain, he began to hope that they might yet win through to safety with the Heart of Kronos.

EIGHTEEN

We fear, we fear.

I do not understand your fear.

We fear the dissolution of Telvarna-hive, for to Eya'a dissolution of a hive is cessation.

Again I repeat, cessation-of-a-hive for Eya'a is emendation for humans, just as emendation for Eya'a is cessation for humans. Each one from this polity you call a hive will go on to join other polities, and this we see as emendation. Again I repeat, Telvarna *is not a true hive.*

But Vi'ya is its world-mind, and the ones inside the metal hive with him are his hivemates.

I hear as Eya'a hear, but I am not a world-mind. Humans have no world-minds.

We fear.

Again I do not understand your fear.

The words we have celebrated carry images that change. And we fear, because we are approaching a great chaos that has no center.

We come to a human polity called Rifthaven. I hear your fear, and tell you to withdraw to your world-mind. Celebrate again

*the words you have learned, but also celebrate my own confu-
sion. I ask again: is the world mind one hive or many?*

Vi'ya felt the withdrawal of the Eya'a; they had already begun the
process of hibernation. She closed her eyes, breathing deeply: the
contacts were easier every time she made them, but still they
ended with a sense of vertigo if she was not careful.

She opened her eyes, saw Lucifur lying across her bunk,
watching. She touched him, checking his mind. He was hungry.

She hit the doorswitch and he leapt down and ran out, disap-
pearing with a flick of his tail.

Then she passed into the Eya'a chamber. Already the temperature was dropping toward the frigid approximation of their
upper-level caves where the hivemates hibernated.

She found them, each curled up and wrapped in a silken co-
coon made of fine-spun metals. Staring at the small, still bodies,
she wondered why they had not answered her question about
their world-mind. Hereto they had always referred to it as a single entity, as if there were only one.

She had envisioned this world-mind as being a type of sentient DataNet, connecting everyone across their world. What she
had not been clear on was the precise function of the male of
each hive, outside of the obvious procreative one: she knew that
they did not move, did not speak, and were cared for by the females.

In fact, it was the reverse of the hive patterns familiar to
Earth-descended biologies, the queens and drones. But they had
been definite about the pronouns: they themselves were females,
would bear females in time, except maybe one of them would
be selected to bear a male, an experience—as much as she could
gather—much valued, though apparently the female did not live
beyond the birth.

She frowned down at the curled forms, remembering how
they had given her a male pronoun—the first time they had ever
done so. They defined her function as captain in terms of directing the fates of the others, and listening to them on the mental
plane. That argued a similar function for their males.

Were the Eya'a males, then, the center of each hive world-
mind? This would mean . . .

Competition between hives. Which would suggest that the

mission of my two is to carry back information meant to give them some kind of edge.

Interesting. This would bear further examination.

She checked the bank of mosses that they grew for sustenance, saw that all was well. The ship's computer now ran the bio-tank she'd designed for them. She reflected on their inability to interface with the computer on their own. As one would expect from a race of telepaths, they had no written language. *And the humans confound them yet again with their quasi-religious ban on machines with artificial intelligence.*

Amusement at the dichotomies which made each race incomprehensible to the other flickered through her mind as she ran her fingers over one of the gossamer-thin weavings they were making. She recognized the stylized shape of the *Telvarna* in it, and intertwined figures that might be humans, but the fires and other symbols she saw were impossible to figure.

She looked around, feeling her skin thickening as the temperature dropped. She could already see her breath, a white cloud that froze in tiny droplets and fell before dissolving.

Time to go.

Time.

She left, looking at her chrono. Emergence soon, at which time she had the sequence of events planned out. Until then, she just had—time.

She looked up at the Heart of Kronos, then grasped it firmly, ignoring the nauseating side effects of its inertialessness. She'd thought to occupy this time with the Eya'a in a last attempt to unlock the mystery of the thing, but they were now beyond communication. She could call them out of hibernation, but it would take time for them to be functional.

Anyway, the exercise would be useless: they had established as much as they were able that this weapon was missing an integral part. She dropped it into her pouch, where it rested against her hip as an unfamiliar weight.

Another glance at the chrono.

Now would have been the time to be planning the next run with the crew, but the next run was going to be solo, except for the Eya'a and her three prisoners: the astrogator, whom she could force to work, the old man who knew something about the Heart of Kronos that he would not tell her, and Brandon nyr-

Arkad—no, he was vlith-Arkad now, wasn't he? Markham had said those words so often: Brandon nyr-Arkad.

For a moment she allowed her thoughts to sort through memories. *"Brandy said . . ." ". . . Brandon nyr-Arkad and I planned a . . ." I thought the Arkad was the satellite to Markham's sun, and I believe Markham thought so as well.*

She smiled a little. *If I am right I will use this Arkad star to torch my homeland.*

It was a plan, which was better than no plan, or— *Regret is an illusion.*

Regret was also one of the emotions she called the hiltless knives. She'd never seen it before she met Markham, and she'd been fascinated at how it shadowed his mind in unexpected moments of repose. They had talked much about human reactions and emotions, Vi'ya trying so hard to understand them that she sometimes felt some of them coloring her own thoughts.

But to desire that an action had never taken place—it seemed merely a futile line of thought.

So she killed it, and went to wait on the bridge for emergence from fiveskip. She had told Lokri that she would handle the communication with Jaim's brother herself.

BLOODCLOT SYSTEM:
RIFTHAVEN MINUS TWO
LIGHT-SECONDS

He didn't know the woman: perhaps eighty years of age, short, stout, with an open, intelligent face. She was dressed in a costume he didn't recognize, comprised of a long-sleeved black robe with a stiff, upstanding white collar, buttoned from her neck to the hem. He wondered momentarily how long it took her to put it on.

He did know he was dreaming, and so, with a sort of good-humored superiority born of that knowledge, he said to the dream woman, "So where am I, and who are you?"

"This is Desrien," she replied, "and you are summoned."

* * *

Mandros Nukiel opened his eyes and sat up. After a moment he laughed, a short, humorless bark, and swung his feet out of bed onto the deck. A dim light sprang into being in response to his movement, leaving most of his cabin obscured in shadow. The only sound was a quiet murmur from the tianqi; the faintest ghost of a breeze caressed his forehead.

He sat motionless for a moment. Perhaps the dream was not so surprising. Certainly the duty he'd drawn would make virtually any change a welcome one. The *Mbwa Kali* was stationed just outside the resonance field generated by Rifthaven, poised to intercept ships leaving the Rifter habitat. So far they'd pulled in nothing but riffraff, as ignorant of Eusabian's plans as any servant of the Panarch. And none of them had any inkling of the FTL com. The only common thread was the gossip they all had picked up on Rifthaven—all of it ship-carried—about the ongoing disintegration of the Panarchy under the lash of Eusabian's revenge and the greed of his Rifter allies.

Mandros Nukiel groaned and ran his hands through his hair. It was agonizing, stuck out here in the middle of the Rift while everything that made his career meaningful was being destroyed. He'd dispatched a courier to Ares as soon as they'd taken up station here—assuming the Fleet center hadn't already been located and vaporized by Eusabian's forces. But it would be many days before an answer came back—and that answer might well be to continue what he was already doing. Ng's orders—phrased with exquisite tact as a request—had been entirely sensible, but that didn't make them any easier to follow.

He padded over to the console, bringing up the tianqi settings. Just as he thought, the Telos-damned thing had slipped into a Downsider mode again: it was in the spring rain cycle, with increasing ionization, falling barometric pressure, and variable breezes, but everything was exaggerated compared to the gentler cycles enforced on a Highdwelling. He slapped at the keys and reset the tianqi to Highdweller mode.

Then he tapped another few keys, calling up the duty roster for the Environmental Section. *Chemiltut, eh? Well, we'll swing him over the radiants tomorrow; for now, back to the Z-watch.*

And no more dream nonsense.

He was asleep as soon as his head hit the pillow.

* * *

It was a spring afternoon on Sync Ferenzi. Up near the spin axis the sun-glow had nearly reached the southern extreme of its track along the diffuser. From his vantage point in Criana triant, Nukiel could see the far north of the Laeteria triant, arching into the sky 120 degrees spinwise from where he stood, dimming into evening. Mellifera triant was masked by clouds, their tops bent into the familiar hook-shape imposed by the rotation of the habitat.

With him were some other people. He didn't recognize them. One was a slim young man whose back was turned, but whose stance marked him out as High Douloi; another was an atavism, with pale skin and blazing red hair. Two were aliens whose appearance disturbed him deeply, but he didn't know why. The others were unremarkable. They stood at the edge of the Commons, the vast expanse of grass and wildflowers that every three years hosted the Great Hum. No one said anything: each seemed absorbed in thought.

Nukiel stretched, reveling in the heady scent from the orange grove at the nearest edge of the grassy sward. It was good to be home. He looked south, where the mists of the Arctiel rain forest billowed at the base of the rainbow-feathered waterfall spiraling down the face of the end-cap from its source near the spin axis. He smiled. Downsiders could never understand why Highdwellers thought planetary waterfalls so boring, until they saw what the rotation of a sync did to water.

There was a faint rumble. Nukiel frowned. Then, as he looked around, an impossibly loud blast of sound, melodious and yet agonizing, knocked him to his knees. He clamped his hands over his ears, but it didn't help. The sound went on and on, battering at him until he thought it would burst his ribs and strip the flesh from his bones. Then it stopped, without an echo.

Nausea seized him, disorientation, and then terror as he realized that he was in free-fall. He clutched at the tough grasses, but his grip failed and his flailing fear propelled him into the air. His gaze swept across the southern end-cap. The waterfall was straight! Impossibly, the rotation of Ferenzi had stopped in an instant, yet the sync was intact.

Then the sun-glow flared and guttered to extinction, leaving the habitat in gloomy darkness, illuminated only by a sourceless light too dim for colors. Nukiel stared, his breath catching in his throat, as the fog along the edge of the Commons mutated into glowing human forms, forms he recognized: his dead father, his tutor from first-school, crushed in a transit accident, and others. Many he did not know, but from their expressions, the other, living people with him seemed to.

The dead paid him and the others no attention, gazing instead intently into the darkened sky, toward the spin axis invisible four and a half kilometers overhead.

". . . from light to light transformed . . ." Where had he heard that? *Light burst in on him and the dead rising through the air, as the surface of Ferenzi peeled back and unrolled like a scroll in the hands of an angry god. A violent wind sprang up, hurrying them along like the leaves of a dying tree toward the bright limb of an immense planet looming too near. It was not Ferenzi's primary, Munenzera, but another, and Nukiel thought to recognize it just as it melted into the face of a woman, her eyes flaring with internal light, her gray hair standing straight out from her head in a lightning-laced corona. She held up her hand and a searing red light blazed from its palm.*

Nukiel shrieked. It was the Goddess, come in Her aspect of the Destroyer!

"This is Desrien, and you are summoned," she said.

Nukiel fell out of bed and awoke tangled in his bedclothes, his terrified shout still echoing in his cabin. The lights sprang on, but he lay still, trying to get his breathing under control. He had the dizzying sense of having awakened to a world less real than the one he had just experienced, a feeling that, try as he might, he could not shake.

He pulled himself to his feet and sat down on the edge of the bed, his head in his hands. He remembered, from long ago, a gnostor at the Academy, lecturing on the spiritual aspects of warfare. What had he said?

"One of the worst mistakes of the ancients was their belief that the subjective is the unreal, that only the objective has true existence. Do not make this mistake—it will destroy you as surely as it destroyed them . . ."

Nukiel shook his head. How easy to hear that in the comfort of a lecture hall, and how hard now. How could he justify making a hejir, in the midst of war? He shuddered. How could he avoid it? If he refused, what would the next dream entail? Whatever the answer, he wasn't sure he could face it. A court-martial would be a day at the spin axis by comparison.

He had a sudden image of himself, suspended in space, caught midway between the irresistible collision of two planetary masses: Duty and Desrien. The shape of each was palpable and immediate to his imagination: the shape of his entire life in the Navy, its traditions and its pride, and the looming mystery of the Magisterium, which once had even reached out to destroy a reigning Panarch.

And abruptly the masses balanced and canceled out, leaving only his will and the simple knowledge of an oath sworn and a life lived in loyalty.

Mandros Nukiel sighed and lay back on his bed, and the lights went out. After an unmeasured time his mind quieted, and sleep returned at last.

❉   ❉   ❉

BLOODCLOT SYSTEM: RIFTHAVEN MINUS 100 KILOMETERS

"I believe we're about to dock," Montrose said, turning to Omilov just behind him. "Would you like to take a glance at Rifthaven, as seen from its best vantage?"

Now everyone was on the bridge; everyone human, anyway. Marim did not see the Eya'a anywhere, and Luce was prowling around down below. She laughed at the range of expressions on the nicks' faces as they stared through the viewscreen.

"If this is its best vantage, what must it be like inside?" Omilov murmured.

"More confusing, of course," Marim said cheerfully. Her eyes went to Osri, who stood close behind his father. His gaze met hers and then slid away.

Annoyance made it hard to keep smiling, but she managed. That stupid stiff-ass nick was not going to rizz her out of what was rightfully hers, but she'd have to be careful.

He's got it on him, she thought. He'd taken care to be with either Brandon or his father ever since she'd searched his cabin, which made her think the sneaky blit had planted some kind of telltale that she'd missed.

Well, there was still time. She stole another look at him, eyeing the close-fitting jumpsuit he wore. No pockets at all on the outside—he'd probably sewn the stuff against an inseam. Maybe his armpit. *Couldn't pickpocket that even if my fingers were still hot.*

She repressed a laugh, thinking how bad her skills had gotten since the old days. *Being around Markham and Vi'ya was a rotten influence—nothing makes you as slow as honesty.*

She turned back to the viewscreen, trying to remember her first view of Rifthaven. What was it like for the nicks? To her, Rifthaven had looked like nothing so much as the result of the worst multiship collision in the history of the Thousand Suns, a jumble of constructs of even wilder variety than the spacecraft they served.

She remembered her delight when she realized that some of its component parts *were* ships, haphazardly bolted, welded, webbed, and otherwise constrained together in a mishmash of metal and dyplast. Light shone from numerous viewports; radiants venting heat glowed dully here and there. A forest of antennae and what looked like weaponry jutted from every surface.

Beyond the station loomed the red dwarf star—dubbed Bloodclot—that formed one third of the celestial triad that was Rifthaven. The other component, Bruise, was not visible. It was a brown dwarf: a gas giant nearly big enough to be a star, radiating in the low infrared. Rifthaven orbited in one of the trojan positions of the system, protected from skipmissile attack by an internal resonance generator that created one of the largest skip barriers in the Thousand Suns. *Almost as safe as their secret base Ares, so Markham said, if less neat in appearance.*

Omilov was frowning out at the bewildering swirl of arriving and departing vessels of every imaginable size, shape, design, and function. Tiny tech craft drifted in and around the bigger ships, adding to the chaos. "Why are we approaching so slowly?" he asked.

Montrose spoke up. "Rigid speed limits imposed by the Defense Caucus. Closer you get, the slower you have to go," he said. "No warning shots, either."

Omilov nodded and squinted, as if trying to force some sort

of order on the visual confusion. Marim's eyes went to the silent observers beside him.

Brandon appeared to be enjoying the sights, turning his head this way and that, the better to observe details. His eyes narrowed once or twice as he scanned passing ships. He said nothing.

Osri had forgotten her, and looked fascinated. Interesting: she had expected his sniff-nose nick face. She figured he had probably never seen anything even remotely like this place; he was a perfect example of the type of nick whose life hitherto had been confined to the orderly, pleasingly designed spaces accessible only to those of the highest rank.

"Oooh, look! Zhazrit's Instantiations is still there. So they didn't get flamed, after all, huh?" Ivard spoke up on Marim's other side. "Oh! I see a new subdeck, right in there where they used to have the free-fall kiting ..."

Marim ignored him, knowing he'd never notice. Half the time now he talked back to weird voices that no one else heard anyway. She shivered, glad he wasn't touching her. Just as well he seemed to have nosed in on Vi'ya's fun with Lokri: it seemed to have killed his desire for bunny, which saved her from having to bunk him out. He acted too much like he had a nasty disease.

Jaim stood at the back, his face blank. A trace of incense clung to his clothing.

Marim stole a look at Vi'ya, who was watching the screen dispassionately, alternating her attention between the stream of information on her console and the low-pitched chatter on the approach frequency.

Lokri also seemed largely uninterested in the promising sights through the viewport. He lounged at his ease at his console, hands cradled loosely around a stimdrink, his lazy, pale blue gaze on Brandon. Marim recognized in the stillness of his posture and the slightly narrowed focus of Lokri's eyes the focus of the predator on prey. *He hasn't talked to me at all since Dis. What's he planning?* Again she tried not to laugh. *Nothing good.*

"What'll you carry?" Marim ended the silence, looking around at them all. "I'll go break out the weapons."

"Nothing." Jaim's voice was almost inaudible as he strapped on his boz'l.

Marim saw Brandon give him a quick glance of concern. Marim could have told him not to worry: Jaim's mood wasn't suicidal, it was lethal. She fought a laugh. "Lokri?" Turning to the comtech, "You got your springblade, right? Anything else?"

Lokri shrugged slightly. "Wristknife."

"Montrose, can I borrow your stenchgun?" Marim asked. "I'll bring it back before I bunk my stuff out."

"Be my guest," Montrose responded. "I have a number of things to do here before I seek another post."

Brandon looked from one to the next. "Something wrong with taking energy weapons?"

"One law on Rifthaven nobody crosses—no matter what," Marim said. "You can carry a firejac, but if you use it, you win a one-way trip out the nearest lock. Neurojacs are legal but they make people rasty when they jam everyone's boz'l for ten meters around, and people have been spaced for less."

Brandon nodded slowly. "I see the reason for the law—one puncture and half this place would vent to space. But I thought there was no law enforcement of any kind on Rifthaven."

"Depends on where you are. Some of the mercantile pods are as safe as anyplace in the Panarchy, patrolled regularly by enforcers hired from Public Order. Crime's bad for business." Montrose said. "Others—" He shrugged.

"But anywhere, someone tabs their energy weapon and everybody around will help execute the rule," Marim put in. "Some people wear their hardware anyway, but I don't carry anything I can't use."

A gentle thud resonated through the ship and Vi'ya pulled her hands away from her console. "We're in."

The engines spun down into silence.

Lokri got up and said. "Arkad, you ever seen Rifthaven?"

Vi'ya said coolly, "He won't this time." She started shutting down systems, adding, "He'll be safe enough here, with the Eya'a to guard him."

Lokri got to his feet. "I think I could keep one renegade Arkad safe from the bites and the gouges." He leaned one arm against the wall, looking down at Vi'ya with an expression difficult to interpret. His voice was exactly as lazy and pleasant as always, but Marim felt the prickling of danger and again smothered the urge to snicker. "A last gift."

Vi'ya said simply: "No."

Lokri was silent for a long moment, then he straightened up

and shrugged, giving Brandon a humorous look. "Have fun with the vidchips."

Omilov started asking questions about docking rules, and Marim went out to the weapons locker. There, she found what she'd half expected: Vi'ya had taken away most of the weapons, except what had already belonged to the crew, and a few utilitarian ones.

I guess this is the end, then, Marim thought. *She really does expect us to vanish.*

Marim grabbed what she needed and skipped back to the bridge. There she handed out the armload of weaponry, noticing the nicks looking at the huge, ornately decorated and brightly colored projectile weapon thrust through her belt.

"What's that?" Brandon asked, pointing. "Looks vicious."

"It's supposed to," Marim said. "It won't kill anybody, but you'll wish you were dead if one of the stench capsules bursts on you. Not many argue with the prospect of twelve hours of retching."

Lokri saluted them silently with his knife and sauntered out, adjusting the wrist sheath under his loose sleeve.

Jaim turned to Vi'ya. "I will return at seventeen hundred to oversee the work on the engines."

Montrose said, "Come along, Firehead. Let's get you along to al-Ibran's Chirurgicon. You can sample the fleshpots after we get this thing off you." He touched the Kelly band on Ivard's wrist.

The boy turned fever-bright eyes to Marim. She kissed the air near his head. "See you later," she said. *In another lifetime.* Once Ivard had given the captain her cut, Marim had snagged the best of Ivard's treasures, now all packed carefully in her carry gear, waiting for her to sell. Ivard never noticed.

As Montrose and Ivard left, Vi'ya said to Omilov, "The rest of you must stay in the dispensary until Montrose returns; then your movements will be restricted to your cabins and the galley in addition. Use whatever you wish from the library for entertainment."

"Thank you," Omilov said.

Marim stole a look at the Arkad, wishing there'd been the chance to win her bet. *Oh well. Let Lokri win one. I've gotten everything else.*

NINETEEN

✳

RIFTHAVEN

Montrose guided Ivard into the Chirurgicon, which was crammed, as always, with a variety of raffish individuals, most of whom had suffered recent wounds, and here and there a soberly dressed trader whose distant travels advertised themselves in more exotic conditions. Montrose saw one man obviously suffering from Dyrjwarsian Nose-fungus, whose eyes kept crossing at the colorful parasite squirming on his face. He caught a nasty tang in the air and decided that the woman sitting alone in a corner with the empty seats around her must have come down with Mirkwudi Stenchrot. These were two of the more common symptoms of human interface with totally alien biology, and he smiled as he thought of the equally exotic cures.

He looked down at Ivard's shivering body. He'd counseled the boy to keep his sleeve over the Kelly band. Ivard had acquiesced without argument, something that disturbed Montrose. Usually Ivard queried everything, showing what Montrose considered a healthy interest in what was going on around him (as well as an adolescent distrust of anyone's skills besides his own). Lately, though, he seemed more interested in whatever crazy fumes the damned Kelly band was pumping through his brain, behaving with such docility it worried him even more than the continual light fever he ran now.

"May I help you, genz?" the melodious voice of the Szefteli healer who worked with the Chirurgicon's doctors interrupted him.

Montrose pointed at Ivard's shoulder cast. "Burn. Want Atropos-Clotho-Lakisus to look at it."

The Szefteli blinked her golden eyes. "Threy are in the midst of a long gene-repair process. Perhaps you would like to have a burn specialist on al-Ibran's staff see it?"

Montrose knew that mere burns did not warrant the attention of the Kelly trinity, who usually worked with more exotic problems.

"He was exposed to some type of, ah, parasite, before we were able to get to him," Montrose said quickly. "I brought such a case to Atropos-Clotho-Lakisus before, and threy said to consult threm first if it ever came up again."

She nodded. "There will be a wait," she warned. "What is the parasite? And your name?"

Montrose hesitated. Here was where he had to be careful. He and the Kelly physician did know one another, but there had been no such interaction between them.

"Tell threm Hendyln," Montrose said, naming a very obscure Kelly disease he had once read about. "And Montrose."

"Hendyln," the Szefteli murmured, looking puzzled. "I've never heard of a human with it."

"Now you have. But I hope Ivard won't for long."

She bowed, accepting the hint with a slightly pained air, and withdrew.

Within a very short space of time another staff member appeared. "Montrose?" he called. "Montrose."

Montrose touched Ivard, who had fallen into a reverie while slumped against his side. Rising, he staggered, wincing as though dizzy. One of his hands fluttered spasmodically.

Supporting the boy's light body, Montrose followed the man through a narrow warren of corridors in what had once been a luxury yacht and a prefab naval medical lab now welded together.

They reached a huge cabin partitioned into cubicles. The tianqi spread a cool, slightly astringent scent through the air.

Montrose saw Ivard sniff and straighten up, his eyes as wide as if he'd received a stimshot.

"Who's there?" Ivard said. "I smell—" He broke off, blinking in confusion. Montrose felt queasy.

A moment later a green Kelly trinity danced into the wide chamber, fluting and blatting. "Montrose, what is this? Hendyln is impossible for humans to—"

Montrose had wondered how Atropos-Clotho-Lakisus would react to Ivard's band, but he never expected what he saw. The two tall Kelly, Clotho and Lakisus, stiffened, their headstalks writhing wildly. Atropos, the Intermittor of the trinity, emitted a low, weird hum, and then all three swarmed toward Ivard, who quivered, his nose twitching. He swallowed convulsively, then licked his lips again and again as the Intermittor ran its headstalk up and down his body while the other two patted his head and shoulders and moaned in polyphonic discord.

Montrose watched, silent.

As the Intermittor's headstalk reached his wrist Ivard's eyes closed and without warning he crumpled, but the two tall Kelly bore him up gently, carrying him into one of their cubicles.

Atropos blatted reedily, "The Archon. We thought threir phratry dead forever, but threy live, in this Ivard."

The Archon of the Kelly? Montrose whistled, long and low. No wonder the Kelly were so excited: according to his datachip on the Kelly, the Archon's ribbons carried racial memories reaching back to the very beginnings of Kelly sentience.

"Threy live, but for how long?" Montrose grated. "His body is trying to adapt, and it's killing him."

The Intermittor bowed, tapping Montrose lightly on face and arm. "So it is, so it is, and we can do nothing without killing the Archon's phratry. But there is somethree who can help you."

"Here?" Montrose felt a surge of hope—which surprised him.

"No." Clotho and Lakisus returned and the Kelly twittered and blatted, then Atropos said, "Who have you told of this?"

"Only my shipmates know about the band, and no one knows whose it was."

"It is a charge," the Kelly said. "A sacred charge. We will help him as far as we can, and we will protect you as far as we can, if you will convey him to Portus-Dartinus-Atos, whose subphratry can incubate the Archon's genomes."

"If I can," Montrose warned. "Where?"

"We do not know, but we will find out. Leave him here. He will be safe with us."

Montrose sighed, relieved despite his conviction that Vi'ya would not change her plans just to accommodate the boy. *Her mind is running on death and revenge, not on saving Kelly phratries.*

But he'd try.

First to sell some of these artifacts, his and also those of Ivard, who would need money to pay his medical bill. And later—when he'd done everything Vi'ya asked—he would find the most expensive joyhouse in Rifthaven and sink mind and body into oblivion.

✻   ✻   ✻

Most of the Syndics and their seconds had seated themselves when the door slid open and a short bald man entered. Lyska-si felt her stomach churn.

His age was impossible to guess, he favored long dangling earrings, and was robed like a devotionist Oblate: Giffus Snurkel. He nodded greetings at the other Syndic chiefs and their seconds as he passed to the empty seat at Lyska's side.

Lyska-si knew that her mother detested Snurkel almost as much as she did, but disgust gave way to a faint sense of foreboding when Lyska-si glimpsed Snurkel's primly folded lips as he smoothed his robes fussily and sat down. She knew the little slimecrawler well, for that had been her mother's first order to her shortly after she'd pulled her from the rat-wars and informed her that her training in Karroo was about to begin.

Always find out your rivals' vices, her mother had said to her. *And you will have made the first hit past their defense.* Giffus Snurkel, so it happened, had a taste for youth, boys or girls didn't matter: the younger, smaller, and more reluctant the better. So Lyska-si's job was to keep him entertained, and she had, until a sudden growth spurt had made her weedy body longer than Snurkel's. Since then she'd taken care to supply him with volunteers from her own rat-pack, usually disguised: he never recognized any of them, convinced as he was that they came to him fresh and innocent.

Lyska-si's lip curled as she stared down at his bald head, shiny with a sheen of oil and sweat. Being new to Rifthaven, he had yet to realize that no rat left the nest innocent—and eventually you had to pay for your fun.

But he sure didn't see any of that now. He was gloating over something, she knew from those pursed lips. About what? There was no news in Karroo, and nothing of any import in Rifthaven—she would have heard.

She turned her attention to the meeting.

"So we're agreed, then?" Xibl Banth said, grinning around the table at the other chiefs, his Draco smile feral with those nasty pointed teeth. "As soon as the first of Dol'jhar's allies show up, we invoke the new approach laws—"

"That covers Defense," Pormagat of the Yim said in her snivelly whine. "But Defense ends at the lock doors, or have you forgotten, Xibl? What about Public Order?"

"And Trade?" the Houmanopoulis' old chief, Jep, put in with his fierce frown.

Xibl sneered at fat Pormagat at his left; the two most powerful Syndics on Rifthaven, controlling Defense and Public Order—outside security and inside respectively—hated each other with deadly passion, from the two chiefs right down to their rats and runners.

Lyska-si tuned them out, knowing they'd brangle for the next few minutes, about who had insulted whom. Instead, she went back to watching Snurkel, and was just in time to catch his pudgy fingers worming over his other wrist: a privacy on his boz'l. She scanned the room. Someone in here? Although at least half the chiefs had their hands below the table, none of their throat muscles moved. Then she saw it: Nuub, second to Jep in Trade. Why was Snurkel talking to Trade, one of Karroo's bitterest rivals?

She shifted her stance behind her mother's chair to afford her a better vantage. She felt the eyes of some of the other runners note her change in posture, and she let her hands show, indicating no threat.

Everyone was edgy; the meeting had been called to decide how to handle the onslaught of Dol'jhar's allies, who at any time might be skipping in, full of loot and triumph, their ships armed with some kind of superweapon. Their squabbles could be planned for; what remained to be hashed out was the sudden influx of wealth they'd bring, which could throw the entire economy of Rifthaven, which was a painfully achieved, precarious balance at the best of times, into chaos. Everyone present knew from experience if they were old enough, or had heard, how vicious trade wars could be: Draco and Yim controlled the two top positions on council, but that could change—would, if the other Syndicates had their way.

Lyska-si studied Snurkel again, feeling a trickle of cold warning. Karroo was at the bottom—their department was Recycling—which meant they tried extra hard, her mother had explained. And Karroo had been enormously successful in recent years, enough to scare the others a little.

Mostly because of that disgusting worm, Lyska-si acknowledged.

"Has the Dol'jharian's second issued any further instructions that can be shared?" Willem spoke up, his rheumy eyes keen. Lyska-si had a great deal of respect for the old wart's staying power; in a place where things changed quickly, he'd ruled over the Kug—who controlled Engineering—for nearly five decades.

Several glances were sent toward the next room, where the ugly Urian communications device was installed.

"Not since the word came in about the raid on Arthelion by the missing heir," Corolaris Rouf said in her mellow voice.

They all knew Barrodagh did his best to keep the tensions high; Dol'jhar needed Rifthaven's goodwill, at least while his forces—most of whom were Rifters—were stretched so thin. He needed them especially now, while what little trade still existed in the Thousand Suns was conducted through Rifthaven. But everyone knew the alliance would last just as long as the balance of need was more or less equal.

Lyska-si listened with a small portion of her attention as the Syndic chiefs argued over what protocols they would adopt, and how they would be safeguarded, when the Rift fleet did appear. Most of her attention stayed on Snurkel, who watched through hooded eyes, his pursy smile never fading. He never spoke once, and when at last the meeting broke up, Lyska-si maneuvered herself behind her mother, hiding her hand so she could send a private:

(Snurkel was gloating about something. And he had a privacy with Nuub.)

(I saw. I'll handle it. But first we have to talk, and rapidly too—you and Nistan have been drawn to take the com for the next watch.)

Lyska-si felt her heart accelerate. The lines of power were shifting indeed—Karroo had only been drawn once so far in the "fair lots" to take turns at Eusabian's com. She looked across the room at tall, bony, slant-eyed Nistan, the runner for the Y'Mered, who controlled Atmospherics, and caught a speculative glance from him.

Things were going to get interesting.

❋   ❋   ❋

It better be now, Marim thought, and reached one-handed for her clothes beside the bed. Digging under them, she located her boz'l and tapped out a private code to Lokri.

"Hey." A long, muscular arm reached lazily for her.

Marim smacked the hand away. "Gotta pee."

"Well, hurry up."

"You ready again, sneezewit?" She reached over and rumpled her fingers through Rex's chest fur. "Don't move!"

Marim hopped out of the bed, grabbing up her boz'l. In the disposer, she made sure the door was locked and then hit the light. She slapped the boz'l against her wrist and hit the receive, looking at the door while she waited for a response. She still couldn't quite believe what Rex had told her. *Not just skip-missiles like to bust a moon wide open, but FTL coms. There's no place safe.* She wondered briefly why the knowledge wasn't widespread yet on Rifthaven—likely the Syndics found that advantageous somehow. They still had time

But she couldn't tell anyone yet, not even Lokri. As soon as Vi'ya found out, and she would, they'd be off Rifthaven instantly. *And I haven't cashed in yet on the Mandala loot.*

Lokri's response splintered her thoughts. *(What is it?)* came his voice. *(I'm in the middle of a game.)*

(I think you better know. I was at—I met Rex, you know, off the Tantayon *... They skipped into Treymontaigne system a while back, and skipped right back out 'cause Eichelly and his gang had taken the planet.)*

(Bad for Treymontaigne,) Lokri's sarcasm came clearly through the neural induction. *(But what—)*

(Eichelly works for Eusabian now, who sent out orders about the Arkad. They know he's alive, and there's a price worth ten planets on his head. And a price almost as high for anyone crewing a Columbiad called Maiden's Dream.*)*

There was a long silence. Marim tapped her boz'l. *(Still there?)*

(Yes.)

. *(So we lay low, right?)* she went on. *(You know what would happen to you if you tried anything on with those Dol'jharian blungesuckers.)*

(I'll keep my mouth shut.)

She breathed in relief. Lokri had a way of hearing things, and she was afraid he'd find out about that damn reward and not stop to consider what would happen to anyone who tried to collect it.

She killed the connection and the light and went back to slide into bed. Rex was waiting impatiently, and she pounced on him with enthusiasm.

When he was asleep again, she thought through her moves with satisfaction. If she could just hustle Rex into finding her a berth on *Tantayon*, she'd be set up fine; *Tantayon*'s captain had a rotten temper, but the ship was fast and powerful and their runs were always successful.

So I'm safe. As long as Lokri does keep his mouth shut, and doesn't—

She sat up suddenly. Beside her, Rex mumbled a protest. She realized just what it was that Lokri had promised—and what he hadn't.

Cursing, she whipped out of bed and began scrambling into her clothes.

Rex rolled over, blinking. "What? Where you going?"

. Marim tapped her boz'l. "Vi'ya sent out a code yellow. I gotta go supervise the rebuilding of that chatzing aft undercannon," she improvised.

"Can't it wait?" Rex asked, smiling sleepily. "Been too long since we saw one another." He sat up in the bed, and Marim looked at his big dark eyes, and the curling hair on his chest, and her knees weakened. Another moment and she'd be right back in that bed.

"True thing, Rex," she said, hastily fastening her tunic.

"Free-fall bunny," Rex said, grinning. "Meet at the gym when you get free."

Dashing through the bewildering maze of corridors, halls, and tubes, she didn't stop until she reached the *Telvarna*'s docking bay. The guards nodded her through, and she started to run toward the ship's ramp.

A lazy voice behind stopped her. "What's the call?"

Marim whirled around. Lokri stepped out of the shadows, where he had obviously been waiting for the right moment to slip back on board.

She sagged against the ramp. "You're going after the Arkad," she accused. "Why, when I told you the danger?"

Lokri came toward her at an unhurried pace. "You told me," he said, "because you want me to do something about it and you don't dare." He smiled. "I being the gambler, and you just a thief."

His irony did not escape Marim, but she ignored the accusation. What he threatened was more dangerous than her plans for the nick treasures. *Vi'ya gave him a truce—and now he wants to break it, over the pretty face of a vault-bred Panarchist nick.* Giving a sigh of exasperation, she said, "Can't you leave her alone? Can't you"—she took a deep breath—"leave *him* alone?"

"Why should I?"

She frowned at him, struggling with reactions she'd scarcely bothered to define before. As always, she opted for the immediate. "Because if you sell him to anyone we're all going to die. You know they won't stop with just you."

Lokri shook his head. "I don't intend to sell anyone."

"So why are you here?"

"I thought," Lokri said, "that the Arkad might enjoy a game of Phalanx."

Marim tipped her head back, studying his face. He smiled down at her with that not-quite humor in his light eyes.

She bit her lip. *It's not just sex he wants from the Arkad, it's more than that. He ran this one on Markham too, and nearly got us all killed. Why? I know Lokri better than anybody in the crew, and I don't know him at all.* She said: "I don't want to end up on some Dol'jharian torture rack, mumbling through broken teeth about our Arthelion run."

Lokri smiled. "All I have in mind is some fun, and at the same time a reminder to Vi'ya of the limits of her reach."

Marim sighed. *He won't dare do anything while Vi'ya's still on board. With any luck she won't leave the ship. And they aren't likely to talk about Eusabian's FTL com where he'll be playing. I hope.* She flicked up a hand. "If you need me, I'll keep this thing open." She tapped her boz'l and then left, punching up Rex's bozcode as she went.

❊   ❊   ❊

Vi'ya breathed in the air, sorting carefully. It was almost right—but not quite.

Opening her eyes, she considered the sequoia forest around her. One could almost be convinced it was real; certainly it had given both the Panarchists a jolt when they walked into it. But the air ... she'd spent some time playing with the tianqi but so far was not successful. It was an intellectual challenge: all her other environments were disturbingly real in sight, sound, and smell. It was important to get this one defined in precise terms and translate it to code.

It was a game she played, to take a place that dealt in strong affect and break that affect down into reproducible components. But this one was proving difficult.

Her annunciator light flashed, and she killed the holo.

Montrose came in. "Ivard's got the Kelly Archon's gene imprint," he said. "The Kelly surgeon can't do anything about it, swears protection and aid if we'll get the boy to someone who can."

"We?"

Montrose's bushy brows went up. "Said I'd stay with you—if you don't go off to that damn ice planet." He gave her a fierce look, his voice a low rumble. "Or—it's the Schoolboy that suggested this, and maybe he's raving—that hellhole you were born on."

Vi'ya laughed. "Time limit?"

"The Kelly didn't say."

Vi'ya studied him, sorting rapidly through her options. "We can accommodate Ivard and these Kelly only if it is safe enough to do so," she said at last. "My plans beyond that are my own."

Montrose's eyes narrowed. "You're going to haul those damn Panarchists wherever you go?"

"Maybe."

Montrose grunted. "I'll let you know what I find out." He turned to leave, then turned back. "Why are you letting our people go?" he asked abruptly. "They're a good crew, or as good as any you'll find these days."

"They want to leave," she said.

He made an impatient gesture. "You could pull them together again. All of them. You did it after Markham was killed." He frowned. "Unless you *want* them gone."

Vi'ya cursed mentally, then felt a bleak flicker of laughter at the futility of calling down karra-fire. All those devouring demons and vengeful ghosts were fantasies, another link in the chain the lords of Dol'jhar used to leash a difficult people.

Reality was this man standing before her now, asking what to him was an honest question. To put personal discussion into words was to bare one's back to the flaying knife, but Montrose had been a loyal crew member. By her own code this required an answer, though perhaps not the whole answer.

Montrose waited, huge and patient as a rock.

She said, "I see little profit in a run to Gehenna."

Montrose's indrawn breath indicated surprise.

She was about to remind him of Brandon's stirring speech at the Chang banquet, but Montrose spoke first. "Yet he's done nothing to suborn your crew. Nothing at all. And he has had the time."

Vi'ya felt a stab of self-mockery at the realization that Montrose was not surprised, after all, at the possibility—he was surprised that she'd seen it.

She said, "He has spent his time with *Telvarna*'s computer."

It was a harmless enough statement on the surface. But they both had been there at the Panarch's palace, when the Arkad had cheerfully shown them how as a boy he'd broken into the oldest system in the Thousand Suns, just to write in practical-joke worms.

Vi'ya watched carefully for the delayed reaction, gauging from the perceptibility of it how much Montrose judged he had revealed of himself in the files he'd buried in the ship's system.

She knew he had secret files—they all did. She'd set herself to master the systems they designed, if not necessarily the contents (which smacked of Bori skulkery, something she scorned), just because it was her ship, and it was cheap defensive insurance. So she knew just how quickly the Arkad had successfully breached the system.

"I see," Montrose said, flexing his hands. "Well." He stared fixedly at a wall for a time and then shook his head. "Well," he said again. "I'll be in the galley, guarding your nicks."

"Be watchful for only one more shift," she said. "I must oversee things from the outside for a time."

He nodded and she followed him out, her mind already racing ahead to the work she had set for herself. The preliminary diagnostics showed a lot more minor things that needed fixing than she and Jaim had counted on. Impatience warred with prudence; she had to supervise the work, and she had to get away to visit the vendor, but all of it had to be done swiftly. The longer the *Telvarna* was on Rifthaven, the greater the chance of someone linking them with their enemies.

Montrose turned to enter the dispensary and Vi'ya walked on toward the engine room. As she passed the dispensary door, Brandon came out and they nearly collided.

Behind him Montrose loomed, his face speculative. Vi'ya's attention flickered his way, then back to the Arkad, who gave way before her with a gesture of deference.

Her orders had confined the nicks to the dispensary only until Montrose returned. The Arkad's gesture was just elaborate enough to convey challenge, diffused by the humorous expectation in the tilt of his head. He was trying to provoke her to speak.

She moved around him and continued on her way.

TWENTY

✳

Sebastian Omilov was startled out of a deep sleep by bangings and thumpings elsewhere in the ship. Disoriented at first, he remembered where he was, and waited with painfully accelerated heart rate for the sounds of an attack. Nothing happened, except for the rhythmic tappings, clanks, and clunks: he realized at last that what he heard were the repair people hired by the captain.

After the fourth time he was jerked out of sleep he arose, donned his robe, and moved out into the treatment room. Montrose was seated at his console, the light flickering on features lined with tension. He look up, his expression altering to the familiar one of the assessing physician.

"I cannot sleep," Omilov said, just as a metallic banging reverberated through the deckplates below their feet.

Montrose smiled. "A good excuse," he said, "to break. Shall I brew up some real coffee?"

Omilov sat down with a sigh, not trying to hide how gravity and age and stress dragged at his limbs. It was almost a relief not to be asleep, dreaming yet again of the Heart of Kronos, of getting it back within his governance—and waking up to the truth.

"What do you know of the Kelly?" Montrose asked over his shoulder as he went about his preparations.

Omilov shut his eyes, breathing in the aroma of fresh-ground coffee beans. "A little," he said.

"Did you know the Archon?"

"We were acquainted." At the reminder of the terrible deaths suffered by those gathered in the Ivory Hall for Brandon's Enkainion, Omilov felt a stirring of never-quite-dormant sorrow.

Montrose sat back. "The Archon is not quite dead, it seems."

Omilov looked up, startled, as his mind finally made the connection. *The Kelly band on Ivard! It seems my preoccupation with the Heart of Kronos has dulled me to the obvious.*

"Death, sometimes, is relative," Montrose went on musingly. "That ribbon round Ivard's arm carries the Archon's gene pattern, and therefore memories. It has invaded the boy's own DNA. A Kelly physician I'm acquainted with knew as soon as we walked into the examining room. But if we don't get them separated soon, both will die."

Omilov tugged his earlobe. "This . . . creates a complicated situation," he said slowly. "What can be done?"

Montrose looked grim. "That depends on the captain."

The door slid open then, surprising them both.

Lokri entered, smiling. He wore a silky black tunic, tight black trousers and high boots, and jewels woven into his hair, the effect of which brought into the sterile atmosphere of the dispensary an air of polyphonic music and exotic appetites, of danger and passion. Omilov felt suddenly old beyond his years, for it had been long since he'd been in the company of those who sought such pursuits. Even while young, knowledge of these things appeared to have passed him by; he had yet to figure out whether he was to be pitied or envied.

"Lokri," Montrose said. "What brings you back here?"

The comtech lounged over to the service console, taking a deep, appreciative sniff of the aromatic coffee. "It seems I came just in time," he murmured.

"Want some?" Montrose offered.

Lokri waved a hand.

"Captain know you're on board?" Montrose asked, reaching to pour a cup.

"No," Lokri said. And before Omilov's horrified eyes, the

fingers of Lokri's good hand swiftly produced a knife, reversed it, and efficiently struck Montrose across the back of the head.

He moved back as the physician fell heavily to the deck. Lokri smiled across at Omilov. "Either you join him here, or you retire." He gestured toward the cubicle. "Take your coffee." With an air of humor he gestured to the cup Montrose had just poured.

Omilov did, trying to buy time, to think, but his brain refused to work: this was not a situation that called for words, but action, and he had always been a man of words.

He did pause in the doorway of his cubicle. "Where is the captain?" he asked, his mind on the Heart of Kronos.

"Probably still in the office wrangling with the techs over the redesign of that aft cannon," Lokri answered, pleasantly enough.

"So why—"

"Good night, gnostor," Lokri said.

Omilov stepped into his cubicle. He saw Lokri's fingers hit the control and the door closed, and locked from the outside.

Omilov set the cup down, dropped onto the bed, and rubbed his eyes.

✳   ✳   ✳

Anticipation made Lokri's hand tremble. He flexed his fingers, then keyed the Arkad's cabin door open.

On his long wait for Vi'ya to leave he'd entertained himself wondering what the Arkad's reaction would be to his appearance as liberator. Gratitude or haughtiness? Anger? Fear?

Despite the time being late in the shift Vi'ya had put the Panarchists on, the Arkad was not asleep. Lokri saw him sitting before the console, his face intent. As Lokri entered he turned around quickly, his light blue eyes tired.

Lokri lounged against the doorway, smiling. "You're free."

He hadn't expected humor in return.

Brandon lifted his hands from the console and sat back. "Is that a philosophical observation," he asked, "or an invitation?"

Lokri gestured toward the door. "Go," he said. "Vi'ya left the ship, and I believe her psi-killers hide out when we first hit a port, which is why we haven't seen them, either."

Brandon tapped the keypads with an abstracted air, then looked up again. "Sebastian and Osri?"

Lokri gestured with his good hand. "Asleep," he said, wondering what was on Brandon's console.

"How long would Sebastian last in this place?"

Lokri was about to say, *What does it matter?* but he knew it did matter: he realized that the Arkad wouldn't leave without those Omilovs.

"Let him sleep," Lokri said, stepping casually to one side. "I'll give you a tour, and you can always come back for them."

Brandon appeared to consider it, and with a sudden smile he tapped something out on the console, saved and cleared it with a gesture, just before Lokri walked into range. "Very well," he said. "What do I need to take?"

"Nothing," Lokri said. "Unless you have some spare AU."

"Not a token," Brandon said cheerfully.

"I thought that might be the case, and I am, unfortunately, down to my last hundred—" He laughed at the look of surprise on Brandon's face. "I haven't sold all my share of the loot; most of it is stashed in a safe place against the possibility of a less unstable future. For now, I arranged a little diversion."

Brandon looked his inquiry, but Lokri said nothing. He backed out and scanned quickly up and down the short corridor.

"Do the Eya'a ever sleep?" Brandon asked.

"I don't know," Lokri admitted.

Vi'ya did not appear, nor did they hear the scraping of twiggy feet on deckplates, or the high weird voices of the Eya'a; no one came out as they made their way to the hatch.

Just as they reached it, Lokri put out a hand and the Arkad stopped, his eyes curious. Silently Lokri handed him a strip of dark blue velvet material with pale blue jewels across the top, then pulled a black mask over his own face. A moment later Brandon had his mask on, his ice-blue eyes glinting out from under sapphire gemstones. The mask covered him down to his cheekbones, effectively blurring his countenance. Lokri waited, but the Arkad did not question Lokri's wearing a mask or the symbolism of the jewel patterns.

So Lokri led the way out, his focus shifting away from the ship, and the threatening shade of its captain and her psychic guardians, as they walked down the softly booming ramp. He glanced sidelong at his companion, straight and slim in old clothes borrowed from Jaim: though Granny Chang had given him an elaborate outfit of the sort one expected to see on high-ranking nicks, Brandon had never worn it since the banquet at the asteroid.

He walked with a swinging, easy stride that brought Markham forcibly to mind, as many of his movements did. Watching the body and not the face, Lokri could almost believe it was Markham at his side again, just the two of them alone, embarking on one of their twenty-hour Rifthaven runs punctuated by laughter and games of risk.

Anger, and something not quite anger, twisted inside him. *Vi'ya's a fool.*

Brandon said nothing, nor did he appear to notice the gazes of the refit techs raking him as he looked around the tidy hangar with a mildly curious air.

It wasn't Markham, after all—Markham, whose face had always been easy to read. This was Markham's highborn sidekick, apparently willing enough to be entertained.

Lokri would entertain him.

He hit the door control and watched in appreciation as Brandon recoiled from the almost physical barrage of noise, colors, and smells beyond.

The narrow corridor, lined with a confusing array of shops, branched frequently. The crowd thronging the passage comprised every imaginable variation on human genes, dressed—or not dressed—in an even more staggering array of fashions, augmented more often than not by a formidable display of weaponry.

"This way," Lokri said, his voice nearly lost in the roar of shouts, whistles, and jangling, thumping music pouring out from all sides

But Brandon heard, dodging quickly around a group of five tall, thin humans who wore nothing but fantastical tattoos. His arm came close to brushing against the last of them, and she turned, baring filed, red-dyed teeth. Brandon lifted his hands in a gesture of deference and the Draco moved on.

The next moment he stopped, brought up short by a rare sight indeed. Pirouetting down the corridor was a Kelly trinity. Lokri was ready to move past; he'd seen Kelly once or twice, and outside of speculation about their sexual habits had never had any interest in the short, rotund tripeds with their dense lacework of fluttering, green tape-like ribbons.

But as the Kelly walked past in a waltz-like movement, the

long eye-crowned proboscis springing from their torsos twisting in a constant helical motion, Brandon made finger signals, causing a sudden outburst of hooting and blatting from the Kelly. They bobbed and writhed with renewed energy, the gaudy, bejeweled boswells on their headstalks glittering as their "fingers" patted and stroked the Arkad's head, arms, and torso.

Several passersby gave them curious glances, and Lokri gestured quickly, getting Brandon's attention. "Let's go."

Brandon came willingly enough, the Kelly dancing on their way, soon swallowed in the crowd.

Lokri felt a twinge of alarm. "What was that about?" he said, jerking his head behind him.

"Greeting," Brandon said, with a slight air of surprise.

Lokri swallowed the warnings he felt like uttering: what he really wanted to say was, *Don't do anything unexpected again.*

"This way," he said instead. "My diversion won't wait forever."

For a long time Lokri and Brandon did not talk at all.

Lokri led him through a bewildering maze of emporia whose wares, and styles of promotion, had utterly nothing in common, unless it was the compounded assault on the senses. Music not so much heard as felt through the soles of the feet and the back teeth blended dizzyingly with the light, breathy sounds of bizarre wind instruments; a few meters further on, the clash and tang of brass cymbals accompanied a weird voice singing in some ancient tongue, evoking the mysteries of the bazaars of Lost Earth.

Light pounded, pulsed, flashed, and dazzled; scents swirled, stung, and singed. Lokri had long ago learned not to discriminate, instead permitting the sensory buffeting to flow over him and then pass on. He glanced at his companion, but could read nothing from the Arkad's face.

They moved aside as a procession of Kyresian Devotes in their polychromatic robes passed, hopping first on one leg, then on the other, pounding resonators on their heads and heels and singing monotonously in voices made shrill by the strange drugs of their cult.

A young woman grabbed his arm, taking advantage of their momentary pause. "Map to th' Founder's Ship? Guarantees you find the treasure—"

"Get lost," Lokri said pleasantly.

The Rifter vanished in the crowd; a moment later she re-emerged, grabbing someone else by the arm.

"Founder's Ship?" Brandon looked interested.

"Legend. Maybe truth—who knows?" Lokri said. "Somewhere, buried in the total chaos of accretions we call Rifthaven, is the original ship. No one knows where or how old it is. I've never believed in the treasure."

They were only approached once or twice more, and always Brandon responded with a quick shake of the head and a half-raised palm in one of those revealing Douloi gestures.

Lokri watched for reactions from the vendors working the crowd, but no one seemed interested in Brandon; the mate-masks merely indicated a pair of slumming nicks.

Once Brandon turned sharply, and a moment later Lokri felt a fragile hand touch his side where a belt pouch might have rested; he paused, looking down into a small face. Lokri laughed at the feral snarl the child gave them before it darted away.

" 'Ware the rats," Lokri warned.

"Rats?"

"Brats. They're lethal. They start playing wargames with each other as soon as they can walk—no adult takes the packs on and wins. Jaim grew up that way," Lokri added with a laugh. "Never mind. We're here."

They ducked through a low door. They felt the subtle sonic tingle of a scan, and the burly guard at the console held out his hand. Lokri dropped his neurojac into it and the door slid open, inviting them into cool, clean air.

Soft music greeted them as they went down a fast lift to a lower level, then entered a wide room with terraces built around a central waterfall. Greenery hung over the terrace walls.

On each of the levels people milled about, involved in games of chance from an astonishing number of worlds. Lokri led the way to the highest level, having to give another code before they gained entrance.

Here, the men and women were nearly all young, or as young-looking as expensive medtech could make them. Handsome bodies were enhanced, if not hidden, by expensive clothing.

"There you are," an arrogant male voice spoke suddenly. "I'd begun to fear for your courage."

"A concern I salute you for, sho-Glessin," Lokri answered blithely, moving toward a tall, hard-faced man who lounged against the low terrace wall.

The man raise a glass in answer, seemingly unaware of the fifty-meter drop just beyond him.

"We're all here," the man said. "And ready."

Another man and a woman moved out from the shadows of a booth, dropping silently into the padded seats around an octagonal bank of consoles. One man already sat there, a silent man who wore a full-face mask. He raised his arm and stripped off his boswell, placing it in full view on the top of his console. The others followed his example.

"Thousand suns per round," this individual said.

Lokri shrugged.

"Boring," the woman said, her voice hard. "Let's add some fun to it: hundred sun per ship, and five for supply centers."

Again Lokri shrugged, smiling as he lounged over to a console. Brandon sank slowly into the chair next to him, his expression pleasantly bland, but his eyes watchful as he punched himself into the game.

"Level?" the masked man asked.

"Three," Lokri said.

Brandon gave Lokri a muted glance, and Lokri realized he'd dropped the Rifter tonalities in his speech. Inwardly he cursed, resolving to keep Douloi patterns from marking his words.

Then the consoles before them lit up, and Lokri's entries flowed across Brandon's screen, indicating for the first time what was about to happen: the two of them were going to play Level Three Phalanx against all these others, for astronomical sums of money.

And now he's wondering why I didn't warn him.

A moment later Brandon looked up in muted question, to receive a challenging grin in return.

The Arkad said nothing, running his hands over the keyboard to imprint its feel.

"Ready," the man in black said. "Begin."

Lokri had played often enough against Brandon to guess where he would lead; still, it was all he could do for the first desperate minute or two to provide a solid backup.

The first minutes of the game were the most crucial, as all players raced to discover, conquer, and hold as many supply areas as possible. Lokri felt his throat dry at the thought of the chance he'd taken, but it was not in his nature to regret it. A hunt was nothing unless you took some risks.

This first step in his campaign was meant to shake the Arkad out of that affable but relentless control, and to do it he had to jam up the stakes. If they lost they'd both be dead, or worse, but he didn't think they'd lose.

The Arkad dropped the mask of vacuous amiability just long enough to cast him one slightly pained look, which Lokri only laughed at, then Brandon's gaze went back to his console.

Lokri divided his attention between his board and Brandon, whose fingers danced rapidly across the keypads.

Brandon pulled a coup, fell back, Lokri provided backup, and once again Brandon launched to the attack. Across from them, the fat man gave a short cry of dismay, and Lokri saw his board go dim.

One down.

Piriag took her lip between her teeth. Lokri moved to block her himself, hoping Brandon would not waste the time doubling his efforts. *Perhaps I should have discussed a basic strategy with him,* he thought, feeling his own control slip for a moment. Piriag was not a pleasant loser, but she was a worse winner. She dealt almost entirely in the slave trade and Lokri guessed where she would send them if she could . . .

The console beeped softly, and once again Brandon made a desperate maneuver that netted a big win.

Lokri saw Piriag exchange a fast look with sho-Glessin. Lokri had been worried that sho-Glessin might recognize Brandon; the man had made and lost a fortune running gambling halls for the Douloi until he'd been caught cheating a few years back.

Lucky, this new fashion for mate-masks. Lokri wondered how Brandon would react if he figured this out, and he smiled inadvertently. Looking up, he caught a flickering glance from Piriag, and he hoped the smile had worked to his advantage.

Another attack: a win. The first round ended, and Brandon sat back, flexing his long hands.

"Do we get anything to drink, or do we just dance in the arena?" he asked.

Dance in the arena? Preoccupied, Lokri ignored this inanity, lifting a finger to signal one of the hovering waiters. Nothing but human servants in this place; Lokri wondered if the Arkad took this rarity for granted. Brandon showed only mild interest as he surveyed the company. Brandon had no money, no weaponry, no boswell, and he was wearing Jaim's cast-off clothing, yet it never seemed to occur to him he might not have been permitted entrance.

He knows he's better than anyone in this entire hellhole. He knows it so well it's probably never been a conscious thought, and if I were to point it out to him he'd deny it, and mean it as well.

The waiter approached and asked their desire. Lokri ordered drinks and threw his last remaining hundred AU onto the gleaming obsidian of the table.

Their opponents moved away, ostensibly to order, but Lokri knew it was to confer.

Brandon leaned toward him. "I thought you didn't have anything but a hundred."

"I don't," Lokri murmured. "In fact, less." He swept up the few remaining tokens and pocketed them.

Brandon's brows lifted. "What if we lose?"

"Then we belong to the winners."

The drinks came then. Brandon whistled softly. Lokri sipped with care, aware how quickly the alcohol dimmed his speed, but Brandon drank one cup straight off, setting the crystal down with a musical *ching*.

Lokri saw their opponents take this in, and smile.

Round two . . .

❋   ❋   ❋

Montrose opened pain-blurred eyes and gaze up in uncomprehending silence at the two faces above him.

"Eh?" he grunted. His protesting brain reluctantly provided identities: the two Omilovs.

"Drink this," Sebastian murmured, handing something down.

Montrose sipped, tasted one of his own pain-reduction concoctions, laced with good brandy. The resulting fire seemed to cleanse out the pain and restore enough brain function for him to sit up. And memory.

"I turned my back on Lokri," Montrose said, wincing in self-disgust. "No less than I deserved."

"You were tired," Omilov murmured, his face tight with concern. "And a fellow crew member, presumably trustworthy—"

"I don't trust anybody," Montrose said, wincing as he felt over the back of his head. "Damn! Broke the skin. Telos knows I have a hard head." His feeble attempt at humor brought no answering smile from the Omilovs. "We were making coffee. . . . He drop you too?"

Sebastian shook his head, as Osri said, "Locked him in there." A jerk of his head toward the sleeping cubicle. "I woke up, found you, let my father out." They exchanged glances.

"What is it?" Montrose demanded, recognizing that the concern on Omilov's face had, if anything, increased. "Where's Lokri?"

"Gone," Osri said curtly. "And so is the Aerenarch."

❧ ❧ ❧

"Round three, game to the challenged."

Lokri kept his face bland as they rose from the chairs. Brandon gave him a quick look, his expression a tolerable mirror.

Sho-Glessin handed Brandon a small chip and said, "If you ever leave this chatzing cheat, you can name your salary with me." He laid down his share of the money and stalked off.

Piriag gave them a murderous glare but she said nothing as she paid up. The man in black noted the money, utterly impassive.

"What now?" Brandon breathed, looking amused.

"We get out of here as fast as we can, because they'll both have friends watching," Lokri muttered.

The laughter in Brandon's eyes became more pronounced.

"Let me show you the Xi games," Lokri said loudly.

After he retrieved his neurojac, they went down one lift, then he shoved Brandon into the next lift and they went up one level. They stepped out, Lokri motioned downward, and Brandon laughed as they saw a man and woman wearing green, with shiny green eye implants, move close to the lift. Both of them held some sort of weapon in their right hands.

"Piriag's hired flash," Lokri said.

Brandon shook his head. His eyes were bright, but he did not seem unduly worried—as if none of this were real to him. "So what now?"

"We buy our way out the back, of course," Lokri said. "Say nothing, just follow me."

TWENTY-ONE

"Here she is," Montrose said, his voice sounding husky with relief to Omilov.

The door slid open and the captain appeared, tall and composed. "Lokri has disabled his locator," Vi'ya said, her accent very marked.

"There's worse," Montrose said. "Listen."

He touched a control and a recording of his recent conversation with Marim played back:

"Have you seen Lokri? He's gone and so is the Arkad."

"What?" The shriek made the console crackle. "And I told him that was dangerous—"

"Told him what?" Montrose's voice sharpened.

"I got it from Rex off the *Tantayon*—Eusabian knows that the Arkad is alive, and he's got the biggest reward ever posted hanging over his head. But I *told* Lokri not to do anything, because you *know* what will happen if anyone tries to collect—"

"Where do you think Lokri would be?" Montrose cut in.

"Galadium, of course. I'll go myself," came Marim's voice. "And when I'm through with him, you'll have to put him back together with specimen tongs. Him *and* that chatzing nick!"

Montrose ended the tape and looked up at Vi'ya. She turned her black eyes Omilov's way. "Did you know about this?"

"No," he said.

"Marim told Lokri about the reward," Montrose rumbled, his ugly face fierce with anger. "He could be doing anything—"

But Vi'ya made a slight, impatient gesture, cutting Montrose off: she didn't care about Lokri. "Arkad being alive is not general news," she said. "We need to find out who else knows, and why it has not been released." Her eyes narrowed as she stared down at the deck. Omilov studied her, trying to see if she had the Heart on her. Frustration kindled a helpless anger in him. There was nothing he could do.

Osri crossed the room, sitting down next to his father. "If Brandon left," Osri said softly, "we may very well never see him again."

"I don't believe it," Omilov murmured. "I think he will return, and I think—" He let the sentence die out when Vi'ya looked up.

She went to Montrose's console and hit some keys. Her face did not change, but her stance altered slightly, from tense to still, and then she hit more keys.

No one spoke. She suddenly killed the console and murmured something in Dol'jharian, then turned and left.

Osri leaned toward his father. "What was that?"

"'So it begins,'" Omilov said.

Montrose rose with an effort and crossed to the kitchen annex. "Shall we have a second try on the coffee?" he suggested.

✳   ✳   ✳

The Urian communicator was even weirder than Lyska-si had expected. She walked over to the red-glowing melted-looking machine and gingerly laid a hand on it, then snatched her hand back: it felt like flesh, blood-warm, slightly yielding. "Ugh!"

Nistan just grinned at her as she sat down. He was her age, and though the adults in their respective Syndics were currently in the midst of a silent struggle, unbeknownst to them Nistan's rat-pack and Lyska-si's had been allies in one of the worst wars.

They spent the first hour or so just watching the feed. The uncoded chatter—bragging sessions, really—between Rifter ships and the images that came over the hyperwave were entertaining, and sometimes chilling.

Nistan grinned at her, his slanty face looking wicked. "Shall we record this slag? I want to try to pick it apart later."

"Good," Lyska-si said.

Several streams of coded messages came through, and then nothing; Barrodagh, the unseen Bori slug who handed out Eusabian's orders, was busy this day. For fun, they tried to crack the codes, but of course they couldn't. Lyska-si did make a copy of the message-distribution log, which noted which mail drops they went to. That was one of the primary reasons for the rotating watch on the com: to monitor this traffic. Any Syndicate that received more than its share of coded messages from Dol'jhar, even though their content couldn't be known, would fall under suspicion of having cut a deal.

As time wore on, the interest wore off, and several times Lyska-si almost suggested cutting the recording. They'd get into big trouble if any of the chiefs came in and caught them. But then another brief code-burst came through, and when it ended she gasped, hitting the playback. "That's Snurkel's mail code."

"Who's the message from?" Nistan said, squinting down at the console.

"I can't tell. Could be from anywhere."

"Let's make a chip," Nistan suggested. "I can take it to Korbis later—he's the best I know at codebusting. In fact," he said, tapping at the console jury-rigged to the Urian device, "let's dump everything and have him run statistics on it. Might be some interesting patterns."

"We'll owe you," Lyska-si said formally. It was a risk—she knew her mother was mad at the Y'Mereds now, and might not want to back her up. But Lyska-si couldn't quite make it personal, for reasons she didn't really understand.

Nistan flushed. "Accept," he said. He turned back to the console and wiped his long hair back from his face. But Lyska-si could see that he was smiling.

❉   ❉   ❉

We do not hear the one-who-hides or the one-who-gives-fire-stone.

You will have to come out of the great sleep, and walk among the single entities.

We will walk among the single entities. The world-mind says this is instructive for Eya'a. We will locate the one-who-hides and the one-who-gives-fire-stone.

Vi'ya opened her eyes, rubbing her hand impatiently across her temple to banish the vertigo. She went out into her own cabin.

That was it, then: if anyone could find Lokri and Brandon Arkad, it would be the Eya'a. And then . . .

And then the wisest thing would be to get out of Rifthaven, fast. Much of the repair and enhancement work could wait; that which had been ordered was now paid for, thanks to the sale of one of the artifacts Vi'ya had taken from the Arthelion palace. And the two which were very rare were safely stored. But—

She pulled the silver ball from her pouch and hefted it in her hand. She'd almost gotten used to its inertialessness.

Without warning the Eya'a were in her head again: *The world-mind wishes to understand the eye-of-the-distant-sleeper. The world-mind celebrates Vi'ya joining the sleeper to the eye-of-the-distant-sleeper.*

And they were gone. Vi'ya stood there a moment longer, holding the Heart of Kronos. Could she bear to wait until some future date to find out how to use this thing? It seemed to enable the Eya'a to reach her at a distance, rather than only face-to-face. What other powers might it have?

Decision reached, she slipped it back into her pouch. The orders concerning the ship could be done quickly. The Eya'a would soon be searching; as soon as Lokri and the Arkad were found, and on their way back to the ship—with the Eya'a as guards—she would make a fast visit to the one person on Rifthaven who could possibly tell her more about the Heart of Kronos.

And then they'd leave.

She opened the com and asked to talk to the head tech.

❉   ❉   ❉

Brandon followed Lokri down a dim corridor.

A short time later the doors slid open and they entered a plain foyer.

"Signe's Garden, this is called. You'll like this place. If we have anything to celebrate we usually come here; this is where we held Markham's wake." He touched the lift console.

They spurted down a short distance, the lift opened, and they were met by a young woman in discreet gray clothing. "Welcome, genz. Would you like to join the company?"

"Private," Lokri said. "But with access to the performance."

She bowed and led them up some shallow, curving stairs over a spectacular garden. Breathtaking mosaics lined one wall. The other looked out on brilliant stars—or the semblance of same. They could have been deep within the structure of the station, but the place gave the illusion of vast space.

She stopped before a door, palmed it open, and they entered a tiny room with low couches and a gleaming black table.

"The furnishings are controlled here," she said, touching a small console on the side of the table. "You can be served by one of us, or you can use the monneplat."

She bowed and disappeared.

Brandon sat down on one of the couches, looking around in open appreciation. Tianqi units vented air subtly scented to remind one of verdant gardens. The lighting was indirect, the walls painted with highly stylized figures in shades of gray, black, and bronze.

Lokri flicked one of the controls on the table and one wall slid away silently, affording a view of a stage. Several musicians played soft music, their costumes artfully designed to blend with the decor.

"Drink?" Lokri asked.

Brandon stripped off his mask and dropped it on the table. "Vilarian Negus," he said with a sudden smile.

Lokri took off his mask and played with it in his hands. "Expensive tastes. Luckily we can afford it."

Brandon grinned. "I've only heard of it. Its use is not encouraged where I've been living."

"Well, I've had it once. Here. Markham found the place, not long after he took over *Telvárna*. I'd never heard of Vilaria or their dream-dealing Negus until he and Vi'ya had it brought out: apparently they release very little of it each year, but the owner here has a standing order."

Lokri tapped out an order code, and a few moments later a cabinet door slid aside just below the window to the stage, and on a tray sat two tall, gently steaming drinks.

"It's better if it warms up a little," Lokri said, taking them out and handing one to Brandon.

Brandon took his, but made no attempt to drink. "Its dreams

are reputed to be addictive," he said, staring down into the milky liquid.

Lokri could not quite place his tone. "It's highly addictive. And if you've had any of a long list of drugs within the last standard day, it'll kill you, though it is supposed to be a pleasant death. They use it for religion on Vilaria, for ritual suicides—and for executions."

"What shall I expect?" Brandon asked, looking up suddenly.

"The effect is supposed to be different for everyone. But you'll dream well," Lokri said, "when you do go to sleep. And don't try to put off sleep too long—the Negus won't be denied."

Brandon said, "I wouldn't have thought this kind of thing something Vi'ya would drink."

"She told us the Negus mutes the psi-waves here."

"Rifthaven?"

Lokri nodded. "She hates the place."

Brandon did not hide his surprise.

Lokri grinned. Closing his eyes halfway, he said with a fair imitation of her austere voice, "So many people crowded in so small a space, broadcasting hatred, greed, murder, anger."

Brandon said, "If she doesn't like those things, why is she a Rifter?"

Lokri laughed in delight. "Just the question I asked her."

"And she said—?"

Lokri leaned forward to tip his glass against Brandon's. The crystal rang, and Lokri sipped deeply of the creamy, very cold liquid. "Like clouds . . . herbs and clouds."

Brandon took a sip, his head canted. "Spices I can't name," he said at last.

Lokri set his glass down. "She just laughed at me. Markham answered for her: said it was the only job going for an ex-Dol'jharian slave."

"She was a slave?" Brandon repeated, one brow aslant as he idly turned the signet ring on his hand.

"Her mother found out she was a tempath, so she was sold well before the customary age of ten—she was a valuable liability. Could be her mother even bought her own freedom with Vi'ya's price. Anyway, she was sold to a rock-quarry owner, and she spent the rest of her childhood managing the huge rock-lifting saurians. Humans did the digging."

Lokri smiled at the effect these words had on Brandon. He

went on, "It was Markham who got it all out of her and one night he told me. She'd never told us anything about her background. Oh, maybe Jaim, a little. But he's worse than she for closed jaws."

Lokri paused. Brandon glanced up briefly, his expression enigmatic as he continued to twist the ring. Lokri's eyes were drawn to it, catching a brief glimpse of the face. Not the expected Phoenix, but an ebony-faced charioteer.

Brandon did not speak, but Lokri read interest into his attitude. So he went on. "Life is cheap on Dol'jhar, and infractions usually earn instant retribution. She couldn't get into trouble—she was too valuable—but her friends could be used against her, so she learned not to have any. When she was in her teens someone organized a slave revolt. She escaped along with the others, but her talent for 'hearing' pursuit kept her from being caught and tortured to death. She learned to stay alive in the city and eventually found her way to a spaceport, stowed away on a mining tramp, and luckily for her it went to one of the asteroids rich in platinum. Not long after, it was raided—"

"Rifter raid against Dol'jhar?" Brandon said. "Eusabian could use the *Fist* for defense, couldn't he?"

"Yeah, but the RiftNet carries a lot of information on Dol'jhar—probably some of it placed there by Panarchist sources," Lokri said. "They don't mind having Rifters do their dirty work for them and were probably happy to see Eusabian harassed. But not many have the balls to run a raid on Dol'jhar, even with lots of info. As it happened, one of the few exceptions was Markham."

"Ah." Brandon smiled humorlessly, his eyes staring through his drink. "Go on."

"Little else to tell. It was Markham's first big raid as a captain. By the time Eusabian's forces scrambled, Markham got away with a cargo big enough to hire on Norton and the *Sunflame*, and he also got a tempath who was fast with her hands and a dead shot."

Brandon sat very still during the relation, his eyes on the performers below. Now he looked up at Lokri, his face bland but his eyes very direct. "Why did Hreem want Markham's death?"

The question was strange, especially uttered in that tone of indifference.

"He had seven reasons, all of them having to do with us jacking him when he carried slaves," Lokri said.

"Slaves?"

"There's a thriving market out in the Fringes where your nicks can't, or won't, patrol. One thing about slavers: they rarely carry just one illegal cargo. Markham made plenty selling the subsidiary cargoes."

"What did he do with the slaves?"

"Turned them loose, usually on some fringe world. Jakarr and others were getting tired of the cost of his ethics. You saw the end of that particular argument when you first arrived on Dis."

Brandon sat back, looking down on the stage. Then up again. "But you approved?"

Lokri shrugged. "As long as the take is good, I don't care where it comes from."

The shift to the present went by unremarked. Brandon's next question, still uttered in that soft, indifferent voice, hit Lokri by surprise. "You were at the other base?"

How did he know that? "I was."

The musicians on the stage below had been replaced by masked players who mimed a highly stylistic play. Lokri waited, old anger invoked, for Brandon to contemplate these events outside his control. *Your Panarchy is dead, Aerenarch,* Lokri thought. *As dead as Markham and his ideals. Do you see it yet?*

When Brandon finally spoke, it was again a sidestep. "So is this a wake, or a performance?"

Lokri glanced at the stage and then at the Arkad, whose mouth had taken on the twist of irony. "Meaning?"

Brandon finished off the Negus and set the cup in the exact center of the table. "Meaning what else do you do for fun?"

Lokri sipped slowly at the last of his own Negus, his mind working rapidly despite the dream images at the edge of his thoughts. He realized, too late, that the Negus had been a mistake; this time the dreams would not deaden old memories, but reawaken them.

His expectations changed from moment to moment, which made this run interesting, but his intention remained: he wanted to see the Arkad's mask shatter, just as his Panarchist world had shattered. Nick morality and mercy were gone, ripped apart by weakness, greed, lust, and revenge. Markham was gone—and everything he'd believed in.

I want a fleet to take to Gehenna to rescue my father ...

Hatred twisted Lokri, for a system that didn't work, and for this handsome scion of wealth and power who persisted in believing the illusion.

Lokri would demonstrate to him his powerlessness. And then ... And then ...

Memory-desire merged unsettlingly with the immediate. His thoughts, drive by the Negus, spiraled.

But catching something concrete steadied him: a tactical error.

His mistake had been in choosing the finest places, the ones that compared with nick establishments. To the Arkad this was just home.

It was time for something different.

He smiled. "There's a lot more to see."

Brandon said, "Lead on."

Lokri threw a stack of AU into the hopper, which closed up and disappeared. "Put that mask back on: if Vi'ya does catch up with us, that'll keep me alive. Maybe." He laughed.

No one hindered them when they walked out.

❋   ❋   ❋

"Look here," Nistan said.

Lyska-si abandoned her own work and glanced at his terminal.

"I've broken some of it out. The sender code for Snurkel's message is almost the same as these other messages. And some of the other Syndics are getting messages from the same source."

Lyska-si whistled. "Arthelion."

"Weird thing is, the only ones getting these new messages are seconds."

Lyska-si felt a shock of memory. "Is Nuub one of them?"

"Yeah. And Zafid Rouf—"

"Water," Lyska-si whispered.

"And Gurpahee—"

"Weird! The Kug *hate* the Rouf. I thought."

"*And* Tir down in Hydroponics." Nistan looked thoughtful. "Who else on Arthelion is working for Eusabian?"

Lyska-si shook her head. "Far as I know, Barrodagh is the only one speaks for him." They looked at each other.

"Then there's someone there working against him," Nistan said.

"And they might be allied with old Giffus and those other seconds," Lyska-si said. "Maybe a cross-Syndicate coup by those impatient to succeed their firsts. That's it. Trouble or no, I've got to tell my mother." She tapped the copy code on her boz'l and loaded Snurkel's and the other messages in. "I won't tell your part," she said. Then she signaled her mother; no answer.

Nistan's grin was twisted. "Trouble on Rifthaven," he predicted.

✳ ✳ ✳

Both Eya'a paused, and Vi'ya cast a swift look around. The crowd following them in the corridor broke and flowed around them, eyes turned away and voices silent.

Noting this, Vi'ya was tempted to laugh, but the reminder of her errand brought back anger. She damped it from her thoughts immediately; the Eya'a were close enough to protective action already. Furious as she was with Lokri, she did not want them to fry his brain as soon as they located him.

She started walking again, the Eya'a following. They continued to scan and sort the myriad mental energies surrounding them, their nearly incomprehensible emotions a strange hybrid of joy and terror that seared Vi'ya's nerves.

We hear the one-who-gives-fire-stone, the Eya'a said again.

They moved suddenly in one direction, and she ran ahead, guiding them toward a lift. They ran into it—and an assortment of hard-faced spacers stampeded hastily out.

The Eya'a moved along the next level.

✳ ✳ ✳

"There's something going on," Lyska-si said. "I know it. The way Snurkel was gloating at the caucus today, and now these messages. And some of the others were hinxy too. Chatz! It could be starting now. Why won't Lyska answer?" She tapped her boz'l again, but her mother did not respond.

"Do a locate?" Nistan murmured, his eyes intent on the console before him.

"She always has that disabled," Lyska-si answered. "Ever since that bomb plot against old Willem—"

"Here, look at this," Nistan said. "I knew Korbis was the one to ask. So happens he's on the Defense desk right now, so he can do stuff for us."

Lyska-si moved over to his console and sat down on the edge, leaning forward. Her mind was distracted between the console under his fingers and the boy himself. Eyes the color of Yolen nightbirds, those straight shoulders, and he *smelled* good.

But he was a Y'Mered, and anyway, there was biznai at hand.

What she saw made her forget everything else. "Korbis wired the shop!" she gasped.

Nistan grinned up at her. "Snurkel took over an old Sybarad luxury yacht, had it welded right onto Falkowitz Street. Korbis built a model back in our pack days, and he knows 'em down to the bolts. He's gonna activate us a spy-eye, right in Snurkel's back room, and pipe it over to us. We'll owe him big, since Snurkel's next security sweep'll catch it and blow Korbis' setup on Falkowitz for good, but for now we can watch Snurkel right here for the rest of this shift."

Lyska-si grinned. "Then move over."

He shifted in his pod, but not too far away.

"This is Marim's favorite place," Lokri said. "Or one of them."

He blinked, trying to clear his eyes of the halos around every light. He was very drunk. The screams of an excited crowd smote their ears when they entered the stands high above a bright-lit platform. On it two Tikeris androids—man-sized creatures dressed in swirling, brightly decorated robes—postured with eerie grace, their stylized movements belying the keen edges of the long, curved swords they wielded in each hand.

On each side of the platform stood their Barcan handlers, swathed in shanta-silk, wearing red-tinged glasses even in this dim light, their absurdly large codpieces waggling as they stumped about excitedly, waving their arms and wailing hoarsely. Two players labored at consoles, modifying the emotions and response patterns of the Tikeris in an attempt to overcome their opponent's android. The air was heavy with a mixture of sweat, drug haze, and an unfamiliar spicy scent.

There was a sudden flurry of movement, a shriek of mixed delight and frustration from the crowd, as the swords flashed and one of the figures spun away, blue fluid splattering from a deep slice across its chest. Its expression did not change; but a piping howl of agony keened from its lips. After a moment it returned to the attack.

Lokri could see in some of the faces of the crowd the look of mixed guilt and pleasure that was part of the attraction of the Tikeris and their obscene near trespass on the Ban. He heard a noise from his companion and stared in surprise as an expression of nausea crossed Brandon's face. At last the mask was broken, and Lokri dissolved in laughter.

Brandon turned to face him, his blue eyes suddenly lambent.

Lokri's mind was hazy with the fumes of liquor and triumph. He said, "So you've recognized a campaign at last."

"I thought the tour was to be instructive." Brandon's light voice was almost drowned by the howls of the crowd. "But you haven't finished telling me: who set Markham up?"

He thinks I did it. Pain shot through Lokri's head. Memory almost overwhelmed the immediate; he struggled to speak, until a dark shadow appeared at his side.

"This fool wanted Markham to himself, not dead," said Vi'ya.

Lokri looked up into Vi'ya's cold dark eyes. She looked past him, though, to Brandon.

"And you?" said the Arkad.

Vi'ya's teeth showed in a not-quite smile. "I had him to myself."

Brandon, for once, was not smiling. For a long moment they stood there on either side of Lokri, neither of them moving, and he realized belatedly that his campaign had failed: that Brandon had had an intent all along, and it was this, to force a duel with Vi'ya, on neutral territory.

He looked from one to the other, feeling suddenly as if he'd been cast into the midst of a river and there was nothing to hold onto, a sensation augmented by the Negus and alcohol haze. "She didn't kill him," he croaked, his voice coming from somewhere outside his head. "It wasn't that at all—"

Vi'ya glanced at him once. "Two crew members sold us out," she said. "Both are dead. Lokri's only mistake was to try to supplant me with Markham."

"So you weren't just Markham's lieutenant," Brandon said. "You were—"

"Mates," Vi'ya said, eyes cold and voice like ice.

Brandon didn't move or speak, but suddenly it became possible to look elsewhere; Lokri felt it as a physical release, and so must have Vi'ya, for she turned to grip his shoulder. "Back to *Telvarna*. Now. The Eya'a will take you there."

She turned and walked out.

One of the Eya'a brushed a twiggy finger over Lokri's arm. He got up fast, lurching outside.

When he reached the causeway he paused, and was thoroughly and unequivocally sick.

TWENTY-TWO

Vi'ya breathed deeply, endeavoring to dispel her fury.

What was it Markham said about Lokri? *"A smile here, a word dropped there, then he stands back and watches the firefight. A deadly hobby; he reminds me of the Masaud family, who are known for such high-stakes games in Court circles."* He'd taken her hands and said, *"Shall we try to win him over? That kind, if they ever do give their loyalty, it's forever."*

You won his loyalty, Markham, but to your person, not to your group. And when you died, he could not forgive you for dying. She fought the sudden urge to sink into a killer rage; it was Markham who had taught her that release did not truly come that way. Instead she walked faster, as if to leave the memories behind, threading her way through the noisy crowd. *Now Dis is gone, the* Sunflame *with it, and I am losing the rest of my crew. All because of Markham's Arkad—who thought I had killed Markham.*

She balled her fist and struck it against a lumensquiggle, feeling a zing of satisfaction as it cracked, sending sparks shooting off.

Violence: it is the way of the ghosts and demons. She forced herself to respond rationally, to review the scene in the Barcan

Tikeri Dome. Both men reeking with liquor. Lokri's witless gloating at the effect the Tikeris made—and how the Arkad shifted from passive to attack so fast Lokri had been caught with his shields down. *And then I broke my own pattern and spoke the unspoken.*

What was done was done.

She drove the matter from her mind. They were found, and miraculously no one was the wiser. Now to address the matter of the Heart and then get on with her plans.

A lift brought her before the row of discreet shops controlled by the Karroo Syndicate. Here few troublemakers dared to come; armed guards in fantastic uniforms from ancient times stood before each door. The costumes did little to hinder these men and women from doing their duty promptly when necessary.

The last shop was the smallest, and it contained the most fabulous wares of the row. This was the showcase of the Syndicate's prime broker, Giffus Snurkel. The *Telvarna* had done good business with him; his specialty was ancient art objects. Markham had had a good eye, and Snurkel had been deeply appreciative—which meant he paid well.

He was also an unctuous, sniveling liar with the persistence of a ship-bred cockroach. The one time Vi'ya had met him away from his shop, the contradictions between what he said and the driving emotions had nearly driven her mad. It was almost a relief to have those emotions damped by the mindblur device he regularly used in his shop; since last year, she had handled their negotiations.

She paused for a moment, eyeing that door. When she'd first set out to do this errand, her plan was to bring the Eya'a as backup. But on the search for Lokri and the Arkad they'd come within meters of Snurkel's shop, and the beings had reacted with such distress Vi'ya was afraid they'd use their deadly *fi* on the entire row of merchants. She could not understand the flow of imagery they sent, but she figured the mindblur was exponentially worse for them: they sensed it clear outside the shop, while standing on the concourse.

Now she faced the most important negotiation she'd ever had with the fork-tongued rocklurker Snurkel, and she would have to run it on her own.

As well we're blasting out of here within hours. At least I'm not without defense, she thought, conscious of the sere-edged knife in the top of her boot, and of her face, which she'd learned since she left Dol'jhar was considered as warm and expressive as that on a corpse.

She stepped up to the guards before Snurkel's shop. They ran their eyes down her, scanned her for energy weapons, and one of them gave a short nod.

The shop was small, but it conveyed an almost heady aura of great wealth, even to the live carpet underfoot, a rare, fragrant, thick blue-green moss. Art objects from a number of worlds, each breathtakingly beautiful, and totally different from anything else in the room, were set carefully in framing nooks of rare fine-grained woods. The overall arrangement was pleasing to the eye.

She passed further inside, seeing the glimmer of light along a worked-gold neck torc of unimaginable age, and winking on a strange, U-shaped metal-faceted artifact from a distant world. A wooden cask, carved with ferocious demons, gave off a sharp scent of incense that evoked ancient mysteries. The air stirred as she walked, and she heard the faint, melodic tinkle of an unseen wind chime.

A woman came out and bowed. "How may I serve the genz?"

"Selling, not buying," Vi'ya said.

"If the genz would be so good as to display the items in question?" the woman said incuriously.

"I think Giffus Snurkel will want to see these."

The woman bowed and retreated. A moment later, Snurkel himself stepped out, licking his lips, his soft, fat hands pressed together in a pose meant to convey peace and goodwill. His rubbery face split into a smile of delight when he saw Vi'ya.

"Ah! It is the captain of the *Telvarna,* come back from far places to visit our humble abode. I bid you welcome." He bowed elaborately.

Vi'ya merely waited, unable to furnish any reply. Silence, when one was unsure, was the best answer; among her people on Dol'jhar, there had never been anything remotely like what Montrose and Lokri called small talk.

Snurkel hesitated, his eyes flickering over her. He radiated anticipation, and covetousness, stronger than he ever had. She repressed a surge of revulsion when he licked his lips again.

He bowed even more deeply, then said, "Please, *Telvarna's*

captain . . . Vi'ya, is it? It is so cold, so formal out here. Do come within my little shop, where we can sit comfortably."

She thought about saying no, for she knew that his mindblur was on in the back—she could feel its tickle inside the back of her skull, like a knife blade just scraping the hairs on her skin. She thought about insisting on staying out front, but she figured he probably had a mindblur hidden somewhere there as well.

If I show hesitation he will see that as an advantage. She shrugged, and followed him into the back.

Here was a room crowded with shelves and a wild array of art objects, many in the process of meticulous reconstruction or repair. They passed through that to a tiny cubicle with a desk. The mindblur buzzed supersonically, and Vi'ya felt her thoughts muffling, as if a soft blanket had dropped over her consciousness.

"Would you care for some refreshment, perhaps? I can offer you some hot spiced barleywine, which I understand is preferred among Dol'jharians."

"No," Vi'ya said, hiding a flash of surprise. *So he's been doing some research on* Telvarna's *new captain, has he?* "Thanks anyway."

"No? Very well, very well," the man said, his wet lips creasing. "Now, then. What have you to show the eager Snurkel?"

"There's this." She reached into her pouch and carefully removed a small object. Unwrapping it, she displayed one of the least rare of the treasures from the Mandala, carefully set aside for this interview.

Snurkel's eyes widened. He reached out, then pulled his hand back. Vi'ya set the tiny butterfly down, and Snurkel pulled a magnifying lens from behind the desk and emitted a pleased "Ahhhh!" as he examined the fragile gold framework inlaid with stylized shaped jewels.

"I do believe this is a genuine Lallic," he said softly. Then he looked up, his watery eyes suddenly acute. "I know of scarcely a dozen, the best of which was housed on the Mandala itself. This item compares with the best."

Vi'ya shrugged.

Snurkel smiled tolerantly. "Well, well," he said. "Many of our best collectors would unclip their purses if they but knew that artifacts were to appear that hitherto were seen only by the eyes of one family."

Once again Vi'ya shrugged. Her thoughts wormed their way as if from a great distance. *That's got to be a guess; the comp showed dozens of these in existence. Anyway, even if he recognizes this piece he can't know that was us. The ship was never identified, save by its old registry. He wants to know who we jacked* ... Pressure was building in the back of her skull. She forced herself to breathe slowly, trying to release it without revealing her distress.

"How much?" she said abruptly, poised to take her stuff and run.

"Without a certificate of ownership, you know these things are more difficult," he said, opening negotiations.

They dickered a bit, which steadied her: this was like normal.

"Times are very unsettled now, and with all this nasty talk of war and fighting," Snurkel said at last with a mendacious sigh. "It does not seem a good time for art, does it?"

He'd named a price much lower than she'd counted on. But she nodded, accepting his offer.

"What else have you?" Snurkel asked, his eyes gleaming with hope.

"How about this?" She pulled out a little book and carefully opened it.

"It appears to be another pre-Exilic artifact," he said.

"See. It's handwritten," Vi'ya pointed out. "It has to be old."

"Perhaps ... perhaps ... There was a fashion for handwritten copies of old materials just before the Exile. This is definitely not the original binding, you can clearly see. These copies are really classed as curios—but it is not without value. Note the clever illustrations." He chuckled fatly. "This one here—'The Waif of Bath' (you see I have some knowledge of Pre-Exilic scripts). This drawing is quite amusing for someone who has, ah, a taste for the, er, vigorous crudities of a bygone era."

As if worse things aren't going on right above us now, you old thief. Vi'ya nodded. "If it's worthless, I'll keep it."

"Worthless? Did I say worthless, my dear Captain? I did not! No indeed, not for such a good supplier ... You know, we might really speak again about the possibilities of your joining our Karroo Family. In these times especially, the protection would be most invaluable ..."

A warning pang shot through her temple. "How much for the book?"

"Well, now, let me think . . . I will have to take a quick peek at my records here . . ." His fingers tapped at his console, and a screen lit up, scrolling rapidly down encoded lists.

He's excited, I can read that much. But then, this stuff has to be good—the Arkad can be trusted that far. She just hoped the old cheat would get on with it. This was already taking longer than she'd planned, and she knew she'd no longer be able to avoid a massive headache.

". . . though if you sell me both, we might both like a rounder sum?"

"All right. They are yours."

"Anything more?" he asked, making a show of keying open a drawer. He pulled forth a sheaf of AU scrip.

"Just a question." She stopped, hearing a harsh edge to her breathing. "About Urian artifacts."

"What sort of Urian artifacts?"

"Any kind. Where does one go to find information?"

"It depends largely upon what you seek," Snurkel said, licking his lips again. "I would not hesitate under ordinary circumstances to direct you to the excellent learning establishment housed upon the planet called Charvann, but I have received most lamentable news indicating that their operations have been interrupted. Have you found something you think might have been left behind by those mysterious folk we term the Ur?"

His words were blurring, sounding to her as if he spoke through a mouthful of meal. Forcing her mind to concentrate, she touched her pouch, hesitated, then she decided. *If I don't try, I find out nothing at all.*

She pulled the sphere free.

"Ah. It seems an ordinary metallic object, Captain," Snurkel said in disappointment. "Who led you to believe it was an Urian artifact?"

His disappointment relieved her. Enough so that she turned her hand and dropped the sphere to the table. The speed with which it fell, stopping with no bounce whatever, caused the man to blink. He tipped his head, and without warning the mindblur whined into a high setting.

Lightning stabbed through her brain. Vi'ya gritted her teeth, giving her head a hard shake. When she forced her stinging eyes open, Giffus Snurkel had picked up the sphere and was thoughtfully moving it from hand to hand.

"I'll take it back," she said, no longer able to hide her ragged breathing. "Do you have to have that fire-cursed mindblur on force nine?"

"Please pardon me. The mechanism is faulty. As it happens, I do have a buyer who will pay enormous sums for these baubles . . . enormous sums, and with them comes the gratitude of a powerfully emplaced individual."

"I'll take it back," she said, holding out her hand. "I just want information—"

"Almost nothing is known of these things, my good Captain," Snurkel said. "If you will entrust it to me, I can seek out information. I will give you a great sum as insurance—"

"No. I want it back." She stood up, ignoring the pain every movement caused.

"But I do have a buyer . . . A very eager buyer . . ."

She snatched at the sphere, and Snurkel dropped it behind his desk.

His voice sharpened. "And sadly to say, my life would be forfeit if my buyer knew I had let such an object pass through my fingers. There is also a price on the head of the bearer, but as we've done good business in the past, if you'll accept my price and leave, no one will know of our dealings here."

I'm a fool, she thought, *but I'm not lost yet.* And lunged across the table.

Snurkel emitted a squeak of fear and slammed his hand on a pad at the edge of his desk. Vi'ya subvocalized the emergency code on her boz'l, then leaned down to whip out her knife. *I just hope one of them hears that . . .*

The little man cowered in his chair. "Guards!" he screamed. "Stop her—get her!"

A clatter at the door interrupted him, and the two guards appeared, pulling free their weapons. From the look of them, they fired low-velocity pellets of some sort. *Probably nerve poison.* Vi'ya vaulted over the desk and yanked Snurkel up against her as a shield, while she surveyed the back of the desk. He had a hundred tiny drawers there, all of them closed.

"Get me free! Now, or I'll have you gutted and hamstrung!" Snurkel's shrieking voice sent waves of pain through Vi'ya's head.

When he stopped, she became aware of pain on her arm; too

late she saw that he'd freed her boswell. He dropped it and stomped on it, still screaming for his guards to kill her.

So much for the homing signal. Let's just see how fond they are of their master ... She kept the blade at his throat, and the guards edged apart, taking one step forward at a time, their weapons trained steadily on Vi'ya and her wildly struggling hostage.

❋　　　❋　　　❋

Lokri was sick again twice more. Brandon steered him into a pissoir. Lokri was dimly grateful for the presence of the tiny Eya'a, the mere sight of whom fended off two pickpockets and a file-toothed Draco hopperpopper seeking companionship, while he voided his system of its unwanted toxins.

At last he leaned against the wall, shaking, drenched in sweat, his eyes closed.

Brandon said, "You probably won't welcome this news, but you'll live. I even know an effective treatment, but I'll need to raid Montrose's stores for the ingredients. Come on."

Lokri opened his eyes. His head still ached, but his vision was a lot less bleary. A faint gleam of humor flickered in his thoughts. "I guess I will live." He drew in a shaky breath, then said accusingly, "You've got some kind of built-in alcohol neutralizer?"

"Nothing but forty-odd generations of hard heads, plus ten years of little else to do but drink," Brandon said with a laugh. "If I do manage to stay alive another ten years, I'll probably need a new liver. Let's get out of here before those two start a flood."

Lokri looked over at where the Eya'a were intently examining a plumbing fixture. Their multi-faceted eyes swung toward him at once, and one of the round blue mouths opened.

Lokri pushed himself away from the wall and they left. A knot of people waited, oddly subdued, at the door—and as soon as the Eya'a had glided past, they rushed inside the facility and the door hissed shut.

Lokri moved into the crowded corridor with its ever-present flashing signs and booming music, then stopped, feeling a tingle from his boswell; a flash of red light bloomed momentarily behind his eyes. He thrust back his sleeve with shaking fingers. His boswell showed a single blue light.

"Vi'ya," he said. "Trouble."

"Does it have a locator?"

"Yes. I'll—"

A few seconds later the light winked out, and stayed dead.

"Emergency over?" Brandon asked.

Lokri shook his head slightly, then winced. "She should have flashed the green." He frowned. "But ... I know where she is ... I think."

"Let's go," Brandon said.

"To the rescue?" Lokri laughed again, leaning against a wall to catch his breath. "Life ... is a farce," he gasped. "What about them?"

One of the Eya'a emitted a high, keening noise, and then without warning both of them disappeared in the crowd.

Meanwhile, Lokri hit his boswell, spoke, then looked up. "Marim's on her way," Lokri said. "And so is Jaim."

"Then let us endeavor," Brandon said grandly, and Lokri laughed.

They ran to a lift, and while they waited Lokri bent, his hands on his knees, sucking in slow breaths of air. "A great time for a fight," he muttered.

They jammed into the crowded lift, emerging into the merchants' corridor. The front door to the last shop was closed, and no guards stood there.

"That's Snurkel's," Lokri said. "Shut door means trouble."

"Force the door?" Brandon said.

"No—it'll be wired for that. Back way."

"Tell me this," Brandon said as they ran through another shop, ignored a protesting clerk, and skidded into a narrow service alley. "Do you always know a back way?"

Lokri choked on a laugh. "Always."

They ran up the corridor and found the last door shut. A small console gleamed at the side. Lokri grimaced, dug in a pocket, and pulled out his neurojac. Lokri glanced around, then jammed it up against the console and triggered it. There was a shower of sparks; he cursed and dropped the weapon, shaking his hand. The door clicked and swung ajar as an alarm screeched.

"Another reason they don't like neurojacs on Rifthaven—they're hell on electronics," said Lokri as he pushed the door open and they rushed in.

Inside, they heard a hoarse, angry scream, and burst into a
room to see Vi'ya backed into a corner near shelves and shelves
of art objects. A small man was gripped tightly against her, a
thin trickle of blood at his neck. Two guards stood poised at either side of the room, looking for an opening.

Just as Brandon and Lokri arrived, a side door slid open and
four burly men in coveralls appeared, truncheons in their hands.

"Nice timing," Vi'ya greeted them in her cool Dol'jharian
voice. "Clear the way back to the office—"

That was the last chance any of them had for talking.

✻   ✻   ✻

"Lys!" Nistan yelped. "Look at this!"

Lyska-si had been monitoring another long series of coded
messages. She dropped the flimsies printing out and ducked
over to Nistan's console.

"What's going on?"

Nistan looked down at his boz'l with a distracted air, then
said, "Korb says he got audio before visual. The woman—
captains a ship called *Telvarna*—came in trying to sell some
stuff, and the old blungesniffer was hinting around that it came
from Arthelion—"

Lyska-si gasped. "You *don't* think that's the ship that raided
the Mandala?"

"I don't know," Nistan muttered. "But if it is, Snurkel is in
for big credit."

"That's probably what he logged onto this for earlier, you
think? When he sent his message to whoever his contact is at
Arthelion? That's got to be it," Lyska-si said, tapping the red-
glowing casing of the Urian hyperwave.

"So one of these blits here might be the missing Arkad."
Nistan looked over at her. "Should we—"

She shook her head. "We're not doing this, remember," she
said. "Anyway, we don't know if any of them are anybody the
Dol'jharians want."

Nistan nodded in agreement. "Then let's watch."

Lyska-si scanned eagerly. She spotted Snurkel, being held
hostage against several of his hired flash by a tall woman with
long, swinging black hair. Two men, both tall and lean, and both
masked, came to her aid.

Lyska-si watched a hired thug swing a truncheon at one

man's head. He ducked, his foot lashing out, catching the man in the crotch.

The other, a rakish fellow dressed all in black, had his wristknife out, and lunged at one of the others, who backed away hastily, knocking into a crystal 3-D chess set on a stand.

"Nooo!" Snurkel screamed. "Stop them! Kill them! Don't touch the merchandise!"

Lyska-si stuffed her wrist into her mouth to keep from laughing. *I always believed you'd pay.*

One of the guards tossed Snurkel his weapon, and the woman thrust the man violently away. By the time Snurkel had brought his shaking hands up to take aim, she was crouched behind a display case full of porcelain. She rammed the butt of her knife through the back of the case and grabbed objects. She began potting them at Snurkel, who shrieked on a high note of escalating rage as each one smashed, but he did not dare to move away from his cover.

The first man, a slim fellow dressed very plainly, but wearing a dark blue nick-mask, was beset by two fighters who knew what they were doing. But so did he; she watched with growing appreciation the grace and surety of his moves as he ducked another blow, feinting toward one so that the second one lunged, missed, and nearly hit the first. The second one bumped against a wooden case, which creaked warningly.

Snurkel screamed imprecations at the guards as well as commands, which distracted them. The guard still armed with a poison gun looked on helplessly, unable to find an opening. Finally he holstered the gun and pulled out a long knife, moving in on the fight.

The man in black took the opportunity to toss his boot knife hilt-first to the other, who caught it, flashing a smile before he dodged a concerted attack by his two assailants. His head turned; Lyska-si could tell by the angle that he was checking on the woman, who looked over at him the same moment. She made a carry-on signal; he laughed and gestured, no more than a turn of his wrist, but the intent—humor and deference—was clear to Lyska-si. "He's the nick," she said. "The Arkad."

Nistan watched as the man grabbed a long candlestick and whopped one man across the back of his neck.

"Nah," Nistan said. "Other one, if anyone—he's dressed flash—like you'd expect a Krysarch to dress."

Lyska-si looked from one man to the other, but her eyes were drawn back to the one in the plain clothes. It wasn't his looks, it was the way he moved that caught at her interest. *Like a dance, and he's laughing. It* is *a dance.*

His blow with the candlestick was not enough to do more than stagger the man, but it deflected him long enough for Blue-mask to leap over a counter to a better defensive position. Here, he had an array of fantastic mosaic vases to grab and fling at the men, which he did, quoting some kind of poetry at each throw. The hired flash backed hastily away from the barrage, their faces turning in growing annoyance from him to their shouting employer.

The captain popped up suddenly and clipped one behind the ear, and he fell heavily against the creaking case, which toppled with slow and dignified inevitability. The musical sounds of tiny smashings came from inside, then it hit the ground with a crash.

The man in black whooped, thrusting a huge statue over onto one fellow, who did not duck in time. The statue crashed into a million shards—and over it a female guard leapt, grappling Black-shirt to the floor.

The captain rounded a corner, but Snurkel moved at the same time, closer to the office door. "Keep him away!" the captain shouted.

Blue-mask obligingly lobbed a huge vase at the little merchant, who scuttled away, then tried convulsively to catch the vase. It smashed, flinging shards over him. Snurkel screamed in rage.

Black-shirt and his attacker rolled over, rose halfway, then lurched into a side alcove. The sounds of tinkling and clangs came from there, punctuated by Snurkel gibbering threats in a constant babble.

One of the guards pulled free the sword at his side, lunging at the captain. She ducked back, and the man pulled his arm back for another lunge—in time to take a full hit on his gaudy helmet from Blue-mask's candlestick. The bonging sound seemed to shake him for a moment; then Blue-mask saw a rapier lying in a smashed case, grabbed it up, and he and the guard began an energetic sword battle, right there in the middle of a sea of smashed crockery.

"That's got to be the Arkad," Lyska-si said. "Look how he handles that blade—*just* like a vid."

"I thought those nicks were too stupid to do anything besides sit around." Nistan whistled. "But scan Snurkel."

The merchant was watching the fight with narrowed eyes, distracted only when the woman edged around, then dived through the office door.

Snurkel jumped up and ran after, in time to meet a kick from Blue-mask's boot. He slipped in the broken porcelain and fell, rolling.

Blue-mask backed away, fighting to hold his position. Snurkel began crawling along the perimeter of the room, and then Blue-mask yelled, " 'Ware, Vi'ya!"

The captain glanced up once, then ducked behind the desk as pellets from two weapons crossed where her head had been.

Meanwhile the sounds of drawers opening and slamming came clearly from the office.

Snurkel reached the doorway and viciously jabbed at something on a little console hidden in the wall next to him.

Vi'ya straightened up as if she'd been shot, her hands going to her head. Lyska-si was vaguely aware of a high, thin whine.

The merchant took aim—and Blue-mask dropped his sword, flinging his candlestick through the doorway. *Whap!* It hit the merchant across the back of his head, and he dropped the weapon.

Then a guard dropped on Blue-mask from behind, and they went rolling through the wreckage. Blue-mask struggled desperately, trying to free his arms, as the man's hand clawed down his face. Suddenly the man jerked, then his weight fell away.

Blue-mask rolled to his feet, yanking the mask free. He shook his head, and Snurkel pointed, his mouth open and his face the color of ripe cheese.

"Arkad," the man squeaked, and he lunged at his desk.

Lyska-si had seen that face often enough, but only on vids. Yet here he was, the third son of the legendary Panarch, right here on Rifthaven, smashing up Giffus Snurkel's shop. An overwhelming sense of justice having been done made her almost giddy. "It *is* the Arkad," Lyska-si breathed.

A moment later Nistan jerked, tapped his boz'l. When he looked up at Lyska-si, his eyes were huge. "He wants a squad of enforcers. Not saying why. What do we do?"

Lyska-si thought rapidly. She remembered cheering when the news first came out that the Panarchists had fallen. But since then the news was of atrocities and wholesale killings enough to turn the stomach of the lowest Shiidra-loving deviant.

A reward big enough to buy an octant for grabbing that man, and Snurkel to claim it?

"Can we jam it for a time?"

Nistan wordlessly tapped his boswell, and a moment later said, "Korb did it, though it'll last maybe a minute. At this rate we'll never pay him off."

"So we'll owe him big," Lyska-si said decidedly. "I don't care about the reward or anything—if we tried to claim it Eusabian would probably just have us killed. Snurkel *deserves* to lose."

Nistan nodded, a grim set to his jaw that made Lyska-si realize just how far the old vendor's reach had extended. "We give the Arkad a chance to get clear, him 'n' his pack. Then it's up to them."

Just then Lyska-si's boz'l tingled in the pattern that meant her mother. She thought quickly. She couldn't tell her about the Arkad—she wouldn't understand. But she could tell her about Snurkel and the other seconds. She smiled, evoking a puzzled look from Nistan. If she made it sound urgent enough, the resulting uproar might give the Arkad and the others the edge they needed.

She subvocalized rapidly, grinning as her mother's outrage made it clear her impromptu plan would succeed. Then she tapped off the boswell and turned back to watch the rest of the fight.

TWENTY-THREE

✳

Marim arrived just ahead of Jaim. She stopped, staring in amazement at the smashed front door of Snurkel's shop. Inside was a riot of bobbing heads; a quick glance showed that Vi'ya, Lokri, and the Arkad were vastly outnumbered—but then Snurkel didn't have Jaim, who launched himself straight into the action.

Looking back out, Marim saw a crowd gathering. Always a bad sign. Stepping in the lee of a carved pillar, she loosed her stenchgun in three directions, and watched in satisfaction as the corridor outside the shop cleared fast, people kicking and clawing to get away from the terrific stench and the projectile vomiting of those too close to escape. As the air currents spread the gas, an edge of the smell caught at the back of her throat and she plunged back inside the shop.

Vi'ya dived through a door from the other side just moments before a cross-hatching of lethal rays in the doorway activated. She came back with a stack of AU scrip in her hand, which she shoved at Lokri. The black eyes caught sight of her. "Montrose. Get Ivard, *whitecode*," Vi'ya ordered.

Whitecode: start up the ship for a fast getaway. Marim swiftly bozzed Montrose and passed on the message.

As she did, the fight ended abruptly, and for a moment everyone stood or leaned, breathing hard and looking at one another over the fallen guards.

Lokri was the first to move. He stepped over two of his assailants, who lay on the ground, one of them moaning, and the other quite still with the knife in his back. He pulled free his knife, and with a wince, cleaned it on the man's gaudy shirt.

Around him cases glittered with fragments of crystal and glass; Lokri lurched against one as he straightened up, holding his bad arm against him. Steadying himself, he poked his head inside the case, then grabbed a beautiful golden torc from the single remaining shelf where, miraculously, it lay undisturbed. Then he ripped off his mask and swiped his hair out of his face with shaking hands. The side of his head was dark with dust and blood mixed. He grinned rakishly as he handed the golden ornament to Vi'ya. "Truce?"

She took it with red-streaked fingers and laughed softly. "Now we must run," she said, jamming the torc over her arm.

As if to concur, an alarm whooped, seeming to come from everywhere at once.

"Lockdown," Jaim said. "He'll have to tell them who we are."

"He will show a vid of us." Vi'ya looked grim.

Brandon swooped down and grabbed up a fantastic swath of embroidered shanta-silk. "Here." He pitched it at Vi'ya, who swathed her body and head in it.

"Put this on," Lokri said to Brandon, holding out his mask. "I'll take this." He reached down and pulled the jacket from one of the unconscious guards. "Not much of a disguise, but maybe it'll get us a little further."

They started out, Lokri shrugging the jacket on.

The corridor was suspiciously deserted. Jaim smiled briefly, then said, "It's time to find some of my old ratways. Come."

❋   ❋   ❋

Montrose arrived at the Chirurgicon breathing heavily. He had thought out a story on the run through the twisting corridors, and had it ready.

But when he arrived at the surgeon's, one of the aides pulled him through a door as soon as he walked in—as if they'd been watching for him.

Alarm seized him and he groped for the knife he'd grabbed at the last moment.

But then Atropos-Clotho-Lakisus waltzed in, their headstalks twirling rapidly.

"You must take Ivard/Archon to safety," the Intermittor fluted.

"You know—"

"Lockdown," Atropos continued, its voice reedy. "We shall aid you, and the vlith-Arkad, but you must—"

"Vlith—everyone knows he's here?" Montrose cut in, alarm turning into fear.

"We met him in the corridor a short time ago—the Arkad genome is known to us. Otherwise, just one vendor, and the Caucus for Public Order," the Intermittor said. "You must promise to get Ivard to Ares."

"Ares!" Montrose repeated. "Nobody knows where it is—"

"The Archon's subphratry is there. Portus-Dartinus-Atos. You must get Ivard there."

Montrose thought of Omilov and nodded slowly. "There may be a way."

"It is well. But you must do more, or surely fail."

Alarm kindled in Montrose. "What do you mean?"

"Dissension burns in Rifthaven; Dol'jhar has overreached. But we must add fear to the mixture, to break the locks that hold you and yours within."

A sharp scent burst from the Intermittor, and a small portion of its ribbons near its headstalk changed color, shading into a purplish tone. Atropos' headstalk looped down in a sinuous motion and plucked a small portion of ribbon, holding it out to Montrose.

"No harm will come to you, Montrose," sang the Intermittor. "You will understand when the time comes."

There was no time for questions, and he knew the Kelly would do nothing to imperil the safety of the Archon's genome. He nodded. The Intermittor slapped the ribbon against his throat, then Lakisus and Clotho swathed his neck in a silk scarf as a fierce itching commenced.

"None will stop you now," said the Intermittor, its headstalk looping in the curve that Montrose knew indicated amusement.

It turned and waltzed away in step with Clotho and Lakisus, its headstalk turning back to address him one more time. "We go to help you. Move quickly: we move quickly as well."

Montrose heard a step behind him and saw Ivard there, looking thin and pale but his smile was cocky and his eyes bright.

"We gotta run, huh?" the boy said. "I'm ready."

Montrose bowed silently to the departing Kelly, then put his hand on Ivard's good shoulder to guide him out.

The trip was quick but nerve-racking; despite his intentions, it became obvious very quickly that Ivard had not much stamina. His breath was coming in wheezing gasps long before they reached the refit shop where the *Telvarna* was docked. And Montrose himself didn't feel entirely normal: his whole torso itched, and he felt bloated, like he'd eaten two or three normal meals in one sitting. He hoped the Kelly had rightly judged his biology.

Then Montrose came to a halt, ramming the boy into a narrow doorway between two shops. At that very moment a group of tough, dangerous-looking Syndicate enforcers wearing Draco colors, with their red-stained filed teeth bared, took up a station before the doors of the dock, armed with pellet-jacs. Nearby, a smaller group of Yim, wearing the brassards of Public Order, stood glaring at the larger Draco contingent, fingering their weapons.

"What now?" Ivard muttered. Montrose noticed distractedly that the boy was shivering. "Oh—wait. Here."

And a moment later Montrose saw something he'd never seen before—a single Kelly, the Intermittor of the surgeon triad, Atropos, undulated down the street, its headstalk quivering.

The heads of the Draco turned sharply; they knew what a rarity it was for a Kelly to be seen alone. Apparently some of them knew the surgeon, for one stuck out her weapon in front of the Kelly and said, "What's your hurry?"

"It is imperative to investigate the rumor," the Kelly twittered in a loud drone.

"Rumor?" Another Draco stepped forward, his gun at a threatening angle. The Public Order squad moved closer as well, keeping a wary eye on the Draco.

"The Thismian Bloat has broken out in this sublevel," the Kelly trilled. "We must investigate . . . and encourage all to wear oxygen masks, and not to touch any surface with any portion of skin . . ."

A crowd had gathered, but at this news, the listeners started backing away.

"Thismian Bloat!" someone yelled. "During a lockdown?"

"Here?" one of the Draco demanded. He looked at the hatch behind him, evidently weighing his orders against this new information.

"Yes," said Atropos. "Be alert for anyone with an unusual rash, or who is covered up. But do not, if you value your life, shoot them or otherwise break their skin. That will only spread it faster." The Intermittor moved on.

Montrose saw the Draco look at one another, the points of the guns lowering—then jerking up again as a third group of armed people arrived at a trot.

"Get out of here!" one of the Draco yelled.

"This is our sector," one of the newcomers yelled back. "We'll protect our own—"

"We are Public Order!" the Draco leader shouted.

"You Kug can go suck blunge," a Yim shrieked.

A riot seemed on the verge of breaking out—right in front of the refit shop where the *Telvarna* awaited its crew. Montrose shook his head.

"I think it's my turn," he breathed, now understanding what the Kelly had done to him.

"What's Thismian Bloat?" Ivard asked. "I never heard of that one."

"Then you're lucky," Montrose said. "Shiidra used it against humans early in the war."

"What happens?"

"Starts with an itch, and then you start to belch and fart like a Nolifer Windsack. It's all downhill from there, until the virus converts your guts into gas all at once and blows you all over the landscape." He pushed the boy back into the shadows. "Stay put."

He walked out, scanning the Draco rapidly. None of them had seen him before, he was certain of that.

Their eyes went to his scarf, and the leader said, "What do you want?"

Montrose opened his mouth to reply, and the volume of the ensuing belch surprised even him. "Excuse me," he said as the echoes died away, sensing heads turning all up and down the corridor. "A bit of bad *yeelm*, I think."

The Draco glanced at his compatriots uneasily. "Well, you can't get through here."

Phweeeeeet-Pop! Montrose felt his pant legs flutter, and the smell was like nothing he'd ever experienced before. The Draco evidently agreed; two of them began backing away. The Yim and Kug also backed away, in different directions.

But their leader was made of sterner stuff. He stepped forward and pulled the scarf away from Montrose's neck with the point of his jac. His eyes widened.

Braaaaack-Kaboom! The Draco jumped back, his face drained of color. Montrose suppressed the urge to look down and see if his legs were still attached to his body—the Kelly command of their ribbon chemistry was truly awesome. He hoped there were no open flames nearby, or this part of Rifthaven would be blown right out of orbit.

"It's the Bloat!" screeched a bystander, and the corridor abruptly transformed into a riot scene as everyone, the Draco included, fled in terror.

"Come on, boy," he said, trying not to laugh. "Let's get the ship fired up." He only hoped the Kelly-induced symptoms were gone by the time the rest of the crew got back, or he might end up living in the airlock for the rest of their journey.

❊   ❊   ❊

The run for freedom was a revelation for Jaim.

He had realized within an hour of his arrival at Jucan's shop that a return to his family was a mistake. The reasons why he had left, which had seemed diminished to insignificance by Reth Silverknife's death, had returned, like carrion birds, to feed on his spirit.

Jucan was happy to see his twin again—too happy. His lifemate Tura made it clear he was less welcome now than he had been on his last visit.

They had carried out all the food rituals, but Tura with many dark looks in his direction, looks which made the drink bitter and the bread taste of ash.

When Jaim had tried to tell his brother he needed to talk, for his spirit was troubled, she had somehow overheard, and interrupted to request him not to poison the light in their home with his disharmony.

It had been in his mind to say that the disharmony was brought by her, but he was silent. He never answered her jibes, even though they surprised his brother, who insisted that she was mild as milk most times. Jaim would never tell his brother that it was he, and not Jucan, whom Tura had wanted first, and the poison had been her gift to him for his refusal.

Lokri's call for aid had been a relief; he had gone with only a word of peace to his brother, and no words at all to Tura. But he had felt her eyes watching him, long after the door was closed between them.

It had half been in his mind to lose this fight, to find peace only in death. But once he arrived, his training had taken over his body, and soon a kind of balance returned to his thoughts.

And what he observed brought to his awareness a new window, a new light. The window was Brandon Arkad in action.

The warrior whose feet stay on the Path does not become tangled in the jungles of anger. The leader of warriors keeps the Path clear for all who follow.

The spiritual truths had burned with the *Sunflame* but the martial ones had rekindled themselves. Vi'ya, and Jaim himself, could easily best Brandon in a fight, but none of them led so effortlessly.

Jaim had thought Vi'ya a good enough leader: she knew strategy well and issued clear orders. And she had, after her own fashion, considered the welfare of her crew, something she had learned from Markham.

But as the five of them ran through the tortuous byways of Rifthaven, encountering danger at nearly every intersection, it was Brandon who kept them laughing with a stream of absurd commentary on the passing sights, interspersed with snatches of song. Once, even, the nonsense rhymes of childhood, used to set a rhythm as they fought their way through a gang of angry Draco that set upon them without warning.

Lokri once joined in a song, his clear baritone marking a melodic counterpoint to the light tenor voice; somehow it was easy to disable, and not to kill, the gang of angry Yim who accosted them. And though the Arkad was not the best fighter, it was he who watched for the others, calling exhortations, encouragements, and warnings when a platoon of roving Kug met them, or some drunken spacers enjoying the sudden outbreaks of fighting all over Rifthaven did their best to join in; it was he who first detected the dissension among their enemies and exploited it, with adroit words, setting some of the prowling packs onto each other as they slipped by.

It was the Path. The light.

Even Vi'ya was smiling as they ran down the last street toward the refit shop. Her smile disappeared, though, when they saw the *Telvarna*. Jaim noted the utter absence of people in the street. Alarm burned in him. What was going on in Rifthaven?

As they ran up the ramp, he felt under his feet the unmistakable thrumming of the engines firing up, and he homed straight for them.

They were a long way from safe.

❋   ❋   ❋

Marim was swung off her feet when a strong arm suddenly snaked out from a dark doorway and snagged her. A mouth pressed hard on hers, and a hand ran down her body.

"You forgot me—you left me waiting for you at Ebo's," a thick voice mumbled. "You won't forget me now."

Furious at herself for lagging behind the others so she could boz Rex undetected, she twisted her head and stared up at this new problem. The sweet/sour scent of drug-laced tabac was on his breath, and his eyes were red-rimmed. She didn't recognize him at all.

"This time'll be better, Marim," he mumbled.

She exhaled in relief; he didn't want a fight, he wanted bunny. She wouldn't have to try to kill him.

"Captain wants me now," she breathed, kissing the working lips. "Boz me."

"Not long . . ."

He freed her arms and she ran flat out for the refit, skidding through the door to the sound of accelerating thunder. *They almost didn't wait for me.* She was surprised at the spurt of anger she felt. As if they owed her—as if anyone really owed anyone.

Relief washed through her when she saw the ramp still down. Racing up to it, she heard Vi'ya's voice through her boz'l: *(Marim, close it up.)*

Uh-oh. She's rasty. She was smiling on the run—what's happened now?

Getting the ramp locked down in record time, she caromed around a corner and flung herself into her pod just as Vi'ya smacked her palm down on *Telvarna*'s go-pad.

For a time no one spoke as the ship maneuvered with deceptive slowness out of the jungle of tubes and constructs. Marim used this time to scan the other faces. Vi'ya was filthy and bloodstained, a bruise darkening on the side of her head.

A quick glance showed Lokri with blood caking his jaw, and his eyes were, for once, wary and somber.

In Fire Control the Arkad sat, safe and secure, but his face—which was barely recognizable for the scrapes and blooming bruises—wore that expression Marim had long ago privately dubbed Markham's Blastshield. Something had happened, all right. Just now? Or back at Snurkel's?

It's got to be Lokri. What's he done?

"We're out," Vi'ya said. "Lokri, monitor Brotherhood channel. Listen for anything remotely resembling Karroo codes."

Marim fought a sudden yawn, running her eyes over her console. Everything shone either blue or green. *So glad I didn't get my gear off ship—and Schoolboy and my coin are safely stowed in the dispensary.* Her heart sank when she saw Ivard at his post; some idiot had gone and gotten him out of the surgeon's.

A quiet voice spoke from the background: "I wish to know where we're being taken."

Marim saw the gnostor enter the bridge, his face polite. *Sanctus Hicura,* Marim thought. *Can't he feel the rads? He couldn't have come in at a worse time.*

Vi'ya said, her eyes on her board, "I do not yet know."

"Then I must request you tell me our status. If we are not actually prisoners, I would like to request we be set down as soon as possible at some location where no harm will come to either of us."

"There is no such place," Vi'ya said, her voice hard.

"That's true," Marim said, trying to ease the atmosphere. "Rex off the *Tantayon* told me a lot. Eusabian's let his allies go, no controls. Some of 'em are chasing Panarchists out to the Fringes, and others have gone on a sacking spree like no one's ever seen, not even in a wiredream."

"Captain," Omilov said. "My request—"

Vi'ya kept her eyes on her screen. "Denied."

Marim watched Omilov incline his head and go out.

Jaim's voice came over the com: "They know about the Arkad."

Then Marim said slowly, her eyes on the screens, "And they got some sort of FTL com—they can talk between systems just like being in the same room. That's how they get the news around so fast. I just found it out from Rex," she added hastily.

They believed the lie—but only, she sensed, because the news was such a shock.

Silence stretched out for an eternity, and then Vi'ya turned, her eyes narrowed to pinpoint beams of cold light: "You knew this, Lokri."

Lokri threw his hands up, wincing when he moved his bad arm. "Heard it in the Galadium, but I didn't believe it."

"Thirty minutes to radius," Ivard put in.

Brandon closed his board, stood looking thoughtfully down at it, then he went to Vi'ya's console. Marim strained her ears, but she could not hear his low murmur.

Vi'ya got up. "Ivard. Let me know when we're three minutes to radius." She walked out, Brandon following.

Marim whirled around and fixed Lokri with a glare. "All right, blit. What happened?"

Lokri sighed, twisting his neck slowly. "Outrun, outgunned, and unmanned."

Marim eyed him, then took a risk of her own. "I hate it when you talk like those chatzing nicks."

A flush of anger ridged Lokri's cheekbones, and for a moment his face went hard. Then he shrugged, giving his old, lopsided grin. "We won at the Galadium. And I tried to drink all our winnings. Lost it all over the corridor."

"We?"

"I took Brandon for a tour of Rifthaven. Masked, but for the end."

"You blungeloving scum. Why?"

Lokri sighed and shut his eyes. "You may as well hear it. Get me something to drink first."

"You can get it, you—"

Lokri's eyes opened briefly, blue and very, very tired. "If I could get out of this chair without passing out, I would. We also," he breathed shakily, "drank Negus."

"I'll get you something," Ivard said in a subdued voice. "Watch my console?"

"I will." Marim waited until the boy had gone out, clutching his shoulder as if it pained him. Then she said soberly, "No wonder she's mad at you. Snurkel's going to call out all Karroo after us."

Lokri opened his eyes. "Maybe. But I promise you this: she is more angry with herself."

❋   ❋   ❋

Osri waited in the dispensary for his father to return, biting back the ready anger when he saw how gray Sebastian's face was. Montrose, still taken by occasional hiccup fits, frowned in concern and started fussing over him, but Omilov suffered his ministrations without any lessening of the strain in his eyes.

Vi'ya and Brandon appeared right then, and Osri sustained another shock. The woman had two bleeding wounds, one on her arm and one on her temple, which she ignored. Her dark skin showed the shadow of a bruise at her jawline; a golden torc over one arm added a counterpoint of barbarity. Brandon looked far worse; Osri would not have recognized him but for the familiar clothes and the Faseult signet on his hand. He smiled, the swollen bruises on his face shifting.

Montrose moved to Vi'ya's side, extending a bandage. She held out her arm, but her attention was on Omilov.

She said abruptly, "I lost the Heart of Kronos."

A spasm of pain tightened Omilov's features.

All the control in the world could not have prevented Osri from saying with heartfelt bitterness, "I trust you got a good price."

Vi'ya ignored him. "I promised you I would try to find out its powers."

"It's not a weapon," Omilov said, his voice hoarse. He looked up, his eyes dark with strain. "How did you lose it?"

"I took it to an antique dealer I've done business with. He had mentioned Urian artifacts once before. Eusabian of Dol'jhar must have put the word out about this artifact. Snurkel was waiting for someone to come in with just that device."

She drew a short breath; Brandon realized that some of Omilov's pain must be echoing back on her. She said, "There was a fight."

"I was there, Sebastian," Brandon spoke up. "We did our best, and nearly lost ourselves in the process."

Omilov winced and put up a hand to shade his eyes.

Vi'ya said, "The Arkad was seen by this merchant, which is why we've departed Rifthaven."

Comprehension worked its way into Osri's brain, dousing all

the anger. Two thoughts occurred: *There is nowhere we can go.* And, *Brandon did not betray us.*

"Then we are all hunted creatures," Omilov murmured. " 'And they ran unto the borders of darkness, pursued by the Daemons of Hell.' " He pinched his fingers to his eyes, then looked up tiredly. "What do you intend to do with us?"

Vi'ya shook her head. "I don't know. The Eya'a seem to think we should go to their planet, but I'm not sure we'd live long there, supposing we aren't followed and slagged."

Osri saw Montrose signal Vi'ya with his eyes, then glance toward Omilov; Vi'ya nodded fractionally, then turned to go.

Osri said, "I wish you'd let us go back to our own people."

Vi'ya stopped and faced him. "Where?" she said. "Perhaps once, your Panarchy represented a kind of order. Now it is gone. Whatever you do, it is gone forever."

"We can rebuild," Osri said. "We will rebuild."

He saw Brandon nod slowly in agreement. "Dead or not, we have to try," he said softly.

The captain looked quickly across at him. She seemed on the verge of speaking, but then the com crackled.

"Vi'ya!" Ivard's panicky voice reached them clearly.

She whirled and ran to the bridge.

Brandon followed Vi'ya to the bridge, fighting the buzz of exhaustion settling over his brain like a blanket. The euphoria of their successful escape through the streets of Rifthaven had dissipated, leaving the old bleakness—purposelessness. It seemed to be his place in life to have a clear goal, but none of the wherewithal to carry it out.

Of course he had kept himself busy enough during the long days on the *Telvarna*. Self-irony pricked at him when he thought of his carefully built campaign to obtain justice for Markham by flushing his betrayer, except he'd been completely wrong.

And of course justice would not bring Markham back.

He looked over at Vi'ya. *Mates.* Another blow, from an unexpected direction: it seemed impossible, but Dol'jharians did not lie. He thought he had known Markham better than anyone; if any of this crew had shared his bed he'd assumed it would be Marim, or even Lokri, the ones who never looked back. For that was the kind of liaison both Markham and Brandon had sought, back in the days of their companionship.

Mates. It hinted at a side of his friend he had never seen, which served to push Markham further into the shadows of memory, to make him the more unreachable.

He blinked, fighting a moment of vertigo as he followed the silent woman onto the bridge. It was time to focus on the present.

Every muscle and bone in his body ached as he dropped into the fire-control pod, but his hands stayed miraculously steady as they brought up the Tenno glyphs. Awareness of impending danger, of action, steadied him as he scanned the screens.

There were several ships moving in on them as Rifthaven dwindled behind. The *Telvarna* moved at the exact same speed as the pursuers.

"Why are we moving so slowly?" he asked.

"Chase mines. There are rigid speed limits around Rifthaven. Here are the parameters," replied Vi'ya.

The Tenno grid rippled as the information flowed from Vi'ya's console. Brandon blinked and opened his eyes wide, fighting a wave of fatigue that suddenly washed over him. The Tenno glyphs took on an air of numinous clarity for a moment, reaching directly into his visual cortex as his mind blurred. The Vilarian Negus. . . . *the Negus won't be denied* . . .

He glanced over at Lokri, noticed a glaze to his eyes that he suspected was reflected in his own. *This should be interesting. It's a good thing that glyph-thinking is mostly visual and automatic* . . . Then there was no more time for conscious thought as missiles streaked toward them from the pursuing ships.

Brandon's fingers raced across his console, strike and counterstrike, thrust and parry. A random gleam of light reflected off the Faseult signet on his hand; for a moment it seemed to blind him. Images from the fight in Snurkel's shop mingled with memories of the booster flight. . . . *it is the Phoenix House that is honored* . . . The glyphs waxed large in his vision, but through them the reality of the screens was overlaid.

More ships appeared, some ahead of them, responding to the chatter of code emanating from Lokri's console. The slow pace imposed on them by the chase mines lent the battle the aspect of a nightmare.

. . . *the arid sands stretched to the horizon, flinty rocks punishing his feet, slowing him. Behind him the wrecked chariot lay on its side, one wheel spinning lazily in the shimmering heat* . . .

"Other Syndicates are joining Karroo," Lokri shouted. "I

can't read the codes, but if enough of them agree, they'll release the passcode to the mines, and then we're vapor!"

... entangled in its traces, two sphinx panted as their life-blood drained into the sand ...

A near miss buffeted the ship.

"With that damned hyperwave, they're probably talking to Eusabian right now—he'll promise them anything to get the Arkad." Marim's voice was strained.

... now the pungent scent of cinnamon rose up around him as the shredded bark of the nest crunched under his claws. Around it, the lean-haunched, hunch-shouldered predators closed in ... there was no safety here ...

"Arkad!" came Vi'ya's voice. "We're going to have to run for it. Can you keep off the mines?"

... his immature wings flapped uselessly, stirring up clouds of myrrh. He opened his beak, a harsh cry emerged and died away.

"I can." It was his own voice, but a distant voice.

"Marim! Give him control of the teslas."

... the beasts lunged at the nest, fell back, raked by his claws, then lunged again. Suddenly the shadow of immense wings fell across him; a beast howled as a vast claw broke its back ...

Marim let out a yell of triumph. "You got one of 'em. They're scattering! Kiss my radiants, blungesuckers!"

... and then he felt himself lifted into the air as the glory of the descending Phoenix burned around him ...

Vi'ya's voice cut in, sharp-edged: "That wasn't a missile strike! Ivard. How—"

Her words were drowned by the terrifying squeal-rumble of a ruptor beam. The glyphs dwindled back into the grid and Brandon awoke to the reality of the bridge as the ship began to vibrate, and he felt every bone and tooth vibrate with it. His hands gripped his console as the sound dropped toward the deadly subsonics that would break apart the ship. On the viewscreen the bright coin that marked the death of a ship was fading away. The radiants of the others dwindled as they fled, but not fast enough: one by one they flared into brightness and vanished.

TWENTY-FOUR

"Ruptor!" Montrose leapt forward and hit his console. The bridge appeared. Omilov gazed at the blurring picture.

"Who's out there?" Montrose yelled.

The captain didn't seem to hear them. "Karra-chatz nafar . . ." Vi'ya cursed, jabbing at her console with no success. The ship bucked but did not respond.

But the ruptor stabilized short of disruption, halting at a deep thrumming that made Omilov's eye sockets ache and his sinus begin to water.

"Point-five light-seconds and closing." Ivard's voice shook, his breathing harsh.

Marim said flatly into her com: "Never mind override, Jaim—drive cavity's gone."

Suddenly a harsh voice modulated out of the deep hum: *"HAILING FREQUENCY 417, HAILING FREQUENCY 417 . . ."*

The captain's teeth bared as she slammed her hand down on her console. "Acknowledge."

In grim silence Omilov and the others in the dispensary watched Lokri fight to get the vibrating ship to respond. The hum intensified, and trouble lights began to flash on Marim's board.

"Hurry, damn you, it's shaking us apart!" Marim yelled.

"I'm—trying—" Lokri muttered, his face green with nausea. A sudden sparking from his console made him swear and slap frantically at the keypads. "There," he said, wringing his hands. "But all I can give him back is audio, and if they don't release us, we'll lose even that."

Vi'ya slapped a key and they all looked up at the main screen.

A man's face appeared, a hard face with an iron-colored beard. The man was dressed in faultless blues. Omilov stared in blank amazement as he said, "This is His Majesty's battlecruiser *Mbwa Kali*, Captain Mandros Nukiel commanding. Power down and prepare for boarding."

"Acknowledged." Vi'ya's voice was flat and cold.

The screen blanked. Lokri shifted to a view of space. The bridge crew, and those inside the dispensary, looked up at the bright dot of light which rapidly resolved into a disc.

Vi'ya jabbed viciously at her console, and Omilov heard the sound of the engine die. As the screen showed the disc growing with frightening speed into the familiar silver egg-shape, Vi'ya looked up at the imager.

"Your wish has just been granted, gnostor," she said.

Beside Omilov, Osri gave a long sigh of relief. "*Now* we'll be safe."

The hum died away to a low level, and Omilov began to breathe again. The *Telvarna* jolted suddenly as a tractor beam took over from the ruptor.

"I hope they don't shoot before asking who we are," Lokri said.

Vi'ya turned on him. "They are not going to shoot, fool. Why do you think they're hanging around Rifthaven? They want information and they want it badly."

The cruiser filled the screens, its silvery hull redly reflecting the light of the distant sun. As hundreds of meters of silver, bristling with antennae and weapons nacelles, passed by, a splash of color quickly resolved into a blazon on the hull. A stylized painting of a fierce-eyed dog appeared, and above it the Sun and Phoenix of the Panarchy of the Thousand Suns.

Omilov transferred his gaze from the viewscreens to the

Aerenarch, whose profile was just visible from the angle of the spy-eye. His face, as much as one could read beyond the distortion of swellings and bruises, was utterly expressionless.

"Father, you'll want to get dressed," Osri said.

Omilov glanced distractedly at his robe, then turned back to the console.

I wish I could believe that his guaranteed safety, he thought. *But I'm beginning to think there can be no safety, no surety, ever again.*

His eyes strayed to the view of the bridge on the console.

Brandon was still staring up at the cruiser's blazon. What was he thinking?

He has made a full circle.

The thought brought with it a sense of grief for all those who had died since the holocaust in the Mandala's Ivory Hall.

Though the unexpected had happened and they were shortly to be repatriated with their own people, Omilov's mood was somber as he went to change into the tunic Montrose had given him.

✳   ✳   ✳

On the bridge of the *Mbwa Kali*, Captain Mandros Nukiel looked down at his weapons officer. "Cease fire." The subtle pulse of the ruptors ceased.

"Communications, tell them to shut down the reactors and disarm. All personnel to the lock."

The officer spoke quietly into his pinmike, and Nukiel sat back and sighed, trying to ease a neck stiff with tension. "Lieutenant Rogan."

The short, square woman at the tactical console looked up with faint inquiry. "Sir. Do you want me to oversee this interrogation?"

"I'd like a shot at this one," said Commander Efriq unexpectedly, turning to Nukiel from where he'd been conferring with the ensign on the environmental console. The dapper first officer's face showed the strain that was weighing on all of them, but his uniform's creases were as razor-sharp as ever. "That old Columbiad has some interesting modifications, and it's considerably better kept than most of the trash we've picked up lately."

Nukiel blinked, fighting off fatigue, looking back and forth between the two officers. Rogan gazed back at him, her eyes steady, though her face, too, was marked with exhaustion. He swept his gaze over the rows of bridge officers, each busy at his or her console. No one looked up or spoke, except softly, relaying information, yet he could feel their tension as well.

"Very well, Commander." Efriq saluted and left the bridge. Rogan turned back to her console; he sensed mild disappointment.

His mission had proved unexpectedly hard. It seemed Eusabian had a limited number of the mysterious hyperwaves and had chosen very carefully who should have them. They dared not attempt interception of incoming ships, for fear one escape would alert Rifthaven and make their task impossible, but though *Mbwa Kali* had successfully boarded several outgoing Rifter ships, they had found nothing. No doubt Efriq hoped that this interrogation would be different.

It had better be. Their mood had been grim before they came around the gas giant after an unsuccessful chase and discovered this firefight. The identification of two craft registered on bonus chips, and the presence of so many targets within reach, had been enough to decide Nukiel's intervention: to take their target and clean space of the other vermin. But now Rifthaven knew they were there.

Some of those ships may have fired on the Mandala. His mouth tightened. *We ran a little wild there, but I can't regret it.*

❋   ❋   ❋

Ivard stared at the lock through which they would shortly walk to face the Panarchist forces. He swallowed, his shoulder aching with renewed fire. Montrose glanced down at him and touched his good arm. "We'll be all right," he rumbled.

Ivard rubbed a sweaty hand down the sides of his jumpsuit, carefully not moving his bad side.

His eyes turned toward the Panarchists. Only Osri looked pleased; his father rubbed absently at his left arm. Brandon stood behind them, his gaze on the ground, his face closed.

Marim and Jaim stood together, Jaim with the blank expression he'd worn since the day they found Dis blasted. Ivard felt the familiar flicker of grief deep inside when he thought of his sister. *I'm glad you didn't live to see us captured by nicks, Greywing,* he thought. It didn't help.

For once the whisper of voices inside his head was still, leaving him able to think about what was happening. Did that mean more danger—or less? Suddenly he shivered, feeling chilled. That happened a lot now; the Kelly surgeon had told him it was to be expected. *The Archon whose genetic material you bear came from a warm planet,* they'd said. *Try to stay warm.*

A sound outside the lock brought his attention from the past to the present, and once again panic made his heart race.

An amplified voice came through the hull: "YOU'VE GOT ATMOSPHERE NOW. OPEN UP."

Vi'ya looked up at the lock console for a long moment. Ivard could see the green light from where he stood, and his hands started to sweat again. He rubbed them nervously.

Vi'ya hit the control and the lock door opened. Ivard gasped as a blinding light smote his eyes, silhouetting the hulking forms of Marines in battle armor holding firejacs aimed directly at them.

One of the Marines' voices came through his suitcom, loud and slightly distorted: "Hands on your heads. Move."

Ivard winced as his half-healed flesh pulled, and his hand dropped. He clutched it tight to his chest, the other pressed against his head. A Marine stepped toward him, the servos in the armor whining, but nothing more was said as Ivard fell into line behind Marim.

Single file they crossed the joining into the chill air of the cruiser. Just beyond the glaring light, Ivard saw the squat form of a self-mobile plasma cannon. He swallowed convulsively.

Behind him, he heard Osri's steps ring on the steel decking. "Listen, my father and I—" he began.

"CUT THE YAP AND MOVE," came the amplified voice.

Osri gasped, and despite his gnawing fear, Ivard sneaked a look behind him. Osri looked mortally offended. A snicker at Ivard's shoulder brought his head around, and he glimpsed Marim's mirthful face.

"Be careful of that one," she whispered, jerking her head in Osri's direction while looking up at Marine, faceless behind the battle-armor visor. "He's the sort gives Rifters a bad name."

"Got a temper too," drawled Lokri. "Sometimes have to lock him up."

Ivard snickered at the outrage on Osri's face, and the wicked glee on Marim's. He moved closer to her.

"That's enough gabble," snapped a Marine. He turned and thrust the muzzle of his jac between Ivard and Marim, knocking Ivard back a step.

Ivard bit against a yell as the weapon brushed his bad shoulder, and his arm dropped. He brought the other down and clutched it tight against him, wincing against fresh waves of pain. The muttering voices suddenly mounted in his head and the fog of confusion that had been his lot so often of late closed in.

"Hands high—"

"He's wounded," Montrose said, his deep voice threatening. "Burn."

Ivard leaned against the wall, muzzily wondering where his other two voices were, as, one by one, the rest were taken into a small room.

❊   ❊   ❊

Osri fought against an ice-cold sense of shock as he stepped into the room to find at least four jacs trained unwaveringly on him. *Could* they shoot a citizen out of hand?

They don't know you're a citizen, the voice of reason yammered in his skull. *You were on a Rifter ship.* A fresh burst of rage shook him as he remembered Marim's and Lokri's comments. *They were trying to get me shot!* Well, the jac would be in the other hand, once this was straightened out.

Meanwhile a businesslike person ran a scanner down his body and stopped short at his armpit. "Hand it over," the amplified voice said.

"But I—"

"Now."

Pressing his lips together, he unzipped his suit and withdrew the coin and the flight ribbon, laying them in the steel box indicated by a pointed weapon. He began composing a formal letter of complaint as the searcher pushed him toward another door. As he stepped through he sensed the familiar flicker of a retinal scan.

Inside this new room he joined Vi'ya and Jaim, who had gone first. A few moments later Ivard stumbled in, his face pale and vacant, his good hand curled back defensively over his burned shoulder. His eyes moved restlessly, without focusing on anything.

Osri watched in angry silence as the Marines lined up the others one by one against the long wall opposite a console. Their movements were brusque and assured: some stood back, their weapons unwavering, while others pushed their prisoners into position, without violence but not gently.

Marim and Lokri were still chaffering with the Marines, despite the command to be silent. Vi'ya moved with the acerbic precision that he now knew disguised deep anger; Jaim was preternaturally still and watchful. And Ivard ... Osri stared at the boy, whose good arm began to twist in a sinuous pattern, his walk assuming an unmistakable though subtle triple beat. He felt nausea grip at him: what was the Kelly ribbon doing to him now? A nearby Marine pushed Ivard up against the wall more roughly than the others, but the boy didn't seem to notice.

Then Osri forgot the others when the Aerenarch came in. At first Osri felt a surge of hope that they would recognize Brandon and thus avert the danger of being shot—it was the first time he had ever hoped Brandon's position would save them. But as he looked at Brandon, he realized that even his father would have trouble recognizing him now. Though, Osri thought with that detached and astringent humor that took hold of him now and then, the disreputable condition of Brandon's clothing and the bruises on his face seemed to highlight the differences between his walk and the wary surrender that informed the movements of the Rifters around him. It affected the Marine guards: it could be that the guards were no more conscious of the difference than Brandon seemed to be as he watched Ivard, yet the Marine guiding him did not touch him as he took his position with the others.

The figures in the bulky armor stepped back a pace when the tiny Eya'a appeared, but their weapons remained steady.

A hatch hissed open, revealing a short man with slicked-down glossy black hair and a narrow mustache. His uniform—the insignia marked him as a commander—was crisply pressed, making Osri feel even grubbier in his shapeless Rifter clothing. He was followed by an ensign, a young woman. The older officer looked around for a moment, his face revealing nothing, and then seated himself with precise, almost mannered movements next to the console. Marim muttered a bawdy comment to Lokri, then both fell silent.

The ensign seated herself at the console, glanced at it briefly, and said, "Two of them identified." She looked up at the crew. "Ivard il-Kavic, step forward. Jesimar vlith-Kendrian, step forward."

A hiss of surprise brought eyes to Lokri. He was very still for a long moment. Ivard's face was as white as the wall as he stepped away from it. Osri noted a brief flicker of surprise from the Rifters as well as his father as Lokri then took a step forward, his eyes light with hatred and his lips twisted in derision.

The man at the console said dispassionately: "Ivard il-Kavic, bond-breaker, Natsu IV, year 960." Then, with a glance at Lokri, "Jesimar vlith-Kendrian: praecidens." He paused.

Disowned?

"Murder, both parents and four Polloi, crime registered in Torigan, year 951," the officer continued. "None of the others registered in criminal records."

They only scanned for registered criminals. "If you'll just listen—" Osri began.

"Quiet," the ensign warned. The commander said nothing, nor did he move.

A Marine motioned his weapon at Osri, and Omilov murmured, "Be patient, son."

A Marine swung his dark visor in Omilov's direction, and the gnostor fell silent, his breathing harsh.

"YST 8740 *Maiden's Dream*," the ensign behind the console said. "Registry transponder inoperative. Who is the captain?"

Vi'ya stepped forward, one of the Marines tracking her with a jac. "I am," she said.

"Someone else here you'll want to speak to first." Marim snorted with laughter.

"Quiet." A guard pushed her back against the wall.

Brandon had been watching Ivard, a slight frown of concern in his eyes. When Marim spoke, he straightened up from his relaxed posture against the wall. It was a very subtle movement, so unthreatening that none of the Marines re-aimed their weapons at him, yet somehow it drew the attention of everyone in the room.

Suddenly Osri remembered their arrival on Dis, and Brandon straightening up that very same way after the shock of hearing about Markham vlith-L'Ranja's death.

An old professor had said once to Osri of the Douloi, *Don't watch their faces, watch their hands.* It was not Brandon's hands, it was his whole body, that expressed his thoughts, Osri realized.

Marim's forcing him to assume the Aerenarch persona.

But that wasn't it, not quite yet. Remembering that day on Dis, and other occasions, reaching further back into the past, Osri had another insight: *There are two sets of prisoners here, the Rifters—and the Aerenarch Brandon vlith-Arkad.*

Osri stood stiffly, his heart hammering. Omilov merely looked tired: had his father seen that transformation too?

If so, there was no surprise in his face. Had his father known it all along? Osri needed to think, but there was no time; Brandon's gaze lifted, and Osri turned in time to see the hatch slide open once more. He recognized the man who entered from the image of him on the viewscreen of the *Telvarna*, the captain of the *Mbwa Kali*. Osri groped for the name, remembered: *Nukiel.*

Then the captain looked up at the crew and stopped as suddenly as if he had run into an invisible dyplast wall. He stared at them; his throat worked, and for a moment—and Osri refused to believe it of a high-ranked naval officer—he looked almost afraid. Then the mask of command tightened his features again and he turned to the commander, but his eyes kept flicking back to the captives as he spoke.

"Commander, I assumed you scanned them under regulations."

"Yes, sir," replied the officer, his eyes searching. He'd seen the captain's reaction too, and Osri realized that the commander—probably the first officer, he thought—had no more idea than he what Nukiel had seen.

"Release the jurisdiction lock on those scans."

Osri felt a surge of mixed relief and triumph. Now the computers would compare their retinal patterns against the general citizen rosters—normally forbidden without permission of the person scanned. Soon things would be back to normal, the Rifters imprisoned, and he, his father, and the Aerenarch free.

The console hummed and twittered as the discriminators went to work; it would take some time, Osri knew, for them to sift through the immense mass of data represented by the citizen roster.

Ivard swayed, and Brandon steadied him. "Cold . . ." Ivard whispered, the sound loud in the room, just before the Marines forced the two apart.

At that moment the console bleeped, and the captain, who was watching it, looked up, his startlement plain. "Ten-*hut!*" he barked suddenly, stepping around the console as the commander and the ensign leapt to their feet.

The Marines straightened up, ground their weapons briefly, then brought them to attention.

"Krysarch Brandon nyr-Arkad—"

"Aerenarch," Omilov corrected softly, his tired face quirking with rueful amusement.

"Aerenarch—" Captain Nukiel repeated, his eyes manic with shock, "I have the honor to welcome you aboard." He dropped on one knee before Brandon.

The Aerenarch held out his hands palms-up as the captain placed his, palms-down, over them. Then Brandon raised his hands, bringing the captain back to his feet.

Abruptly the room was a swirl of motion as the captain ushered the Aerenarch across the room. Osri stepped forward, only to be motioned back by a Marine; Brandon began speaking to Nukiel. A moment later the ensign motioned Osri and his father forward.

As they approached the hatch, the commander addressed Nukiel.

"Captain. Set course for Ares?" he asked.

Nukiel turned slowly. He suddenly seemed older, and Osri saw a certain pain in his features. He looked at the Aerenarch, then across the room at the Rifters, especially Ivard and the Eya'a. Then he shook his head.

"No, Commander," Nukiel said, almost inaudibly. "Set course for Desrien, maximum speed."

There was a moment's pause as the outrageous order fell into sudden silence among the small group of Panarchists, though in the background Marim and Montrose could be heard arguing strenuously with the Marine guards.

Osri's heart thumped painfully, he heard his father grunt with surprise, and the Aerenarch's blue eyes opened wide as his head snapped sideways to look at the captain.

At the console, the commander's mouth fell open.

Then, with a quiet sigh, Ivard slumped to the deck in a faint.

"See? See what you did, you blunge-eyed nickblits?" Marim yelled.

In the distance they heard Lucifur howl and hiss.

I know what's happened, Osri thought wildly, *I've finally gone mad.*

He slid his hands over his eyes and gave himself up to helpless laughter.

✳   ✳   ✳

ARTHELION

It was night, and the windows in the library of the Palace Minor reflected his image blackly as Eusabian moved along a wall of books, fingering their spines and drawing one out occasionally for a closer look. A floating lamp followed him as he moved slowly along; the rest of the room was mantled in unquiet shadows from a fire crackling on the hearth. The room was redolent of leather and glue and the less identifiable scents of an ancient technology that would never be entirely displaced by electronics.

The Lord of Vengeance pushed a book back into its place and turned away from the bookcase. After a moment he seated himself in one of the flare-backed leather chairs facing the fireplace. To one side was an elegantly fragile table made of some twisted, twining, highly polished wood, looking more like it had been grown than constructed. It held a number of record chips scattered around a small box with a data socket in it.

Eusabian picked up one of the chips and regarded it musingly. On its surface, in a bold, spiky, upright handwriting, was indited "Testamentary—Jaspar Arkad." The ink was faded, more visible by the indentation in the surface than any remaining pigmentation. After a moment he placed it in the socket and sat back expectantly.

There was a long pause, then a sudden flicker of reddish light and a subtle tingling in his bones. The Avatar of Dol sat up in momentary startlement. *It scanned me. Why?*

Then an image wavered into solidity in front of him as some unseen mechanism damped down the fire and the lamp, so that the only source of illumination in the room was the ghostly figure of the founder of the Arkad dynasty, Jaspar hai-Arkad. He was a spare man; his face echoed that of the Avatar's defeated foe, but it was old and seamed. Nonetheless, he stood rigidly erect, unyielding to age, and the force of his personality reached out undiminished across the centuries.

The image's eyes came to rest on him and seemed to focus. Eusabian felt a prickle of awe which he suppressed angrily; but for the first time, he understood the near-mythical stature the man had attained, and how it was that the polity he had fashioned had lasted so long. Behind him he heard the door to the library open quietly, but his mind was held in the thrall of a man long dead, and he ignored the interruption.

Then the image spoke.

"Since you are not of the house of Arkad"—now Eusabian understood the purpose of the scan—"you cannot know that this record is only viewed by the ruling member of the Family upon his or her accession. *That* message you will not receive; but, as I know, perhaps better than most men, that nothing in Totality lasts forever, I now address myself to whoever, or whatever, has usurped my descendants."

Barrodagh stood indecisively in the doorway, his exultation dying out of him, replaced with a shiver of awe as he watched his lord lectured by a ghost.

" . . . only when the counterbalances of civilization are flung awry by great misery and massive suffering, so that a touch in the right place can redirect the upwelling energies that drive us toward the Telos into a new path, can one man or woman make a difference in his or her own lifetime. I was one who was both fortunate and unfortunate enough to be so placed . . ."

Barrodagh crept forward, hugging his arms to his sides to keep from shivering. He'd been among Dol'jharians too long, he thought, with their ghosts and demons. Now, unbidden, the legends of his Bori childhood rose up from the dark corners of his mind. He remembered the terrors that had made his nights a misery, especially the tales of the Vengyst, most famous and horrible of all Bori haunts, told him by his unspeakable older sister just before she turned off the lights and locked him in the darkness. The Vengyst, which cries *Willa-Drissa-Will* from the corner before it pounces and sucks out its victim's eyes with its purse-like mouth.

He shook off the memory and listened. The image spoke in an archaic accent that made it hard to understand; but somehow he couldn't will himself to take another step forward. Anyway, he rationalized, he could tell from the position of his lord's head that he was listening intently—so intently that interruption would be dangerous.

". . . be that my house has failed of wisdom, and your usurpation is a just one. If so, do not be too quick to discard what has worked, while sweeping away that which has not; and do not ever forget the tremendous inertia of society. Humanity has a basic wisdom of its own; resign yourself to working slowly—and do not misunderstand their resistance to change . . ."

When the message ended, there was silence for a long time.

The fire crackled to life again as the ghost of Jaspar Arkad, favoring the Lord of Vengeance with the appearance of a long, measuring look, faded back into invisibility.

Finally Barrodagh reluctantly moved forward to stand some distance to the side of his lord's chair. The firelight painted the Avatar's strong profile in colors recalling the karra-fires of his homeland; his eyes were fixed on infinity. With a tingle of anxiety Barrodagh noted the dirazh'u lying limply in his hands.

The Bori suddenly remembered the simple words engraved on the stone in front of the statue in the garden: "Ruler of all, ruler of naught, power unlimited, a prison unsought." Now he realized that Eusabian was struggling with the magnitude of the burden his successful paliach had imposed on him—not that he would feel the obligation to his subjects that the ghost's speech had assumed. No, thought Barrodagh uneasily, it was the lack of control expressed by that quatrain that the Lord of Vengeance would resent most keenly, as evidenced by his initial miscomprehension, there in the garden, of its meaning.

Even as he thought this he saw the Avatar rouse and throw off the mood that had possessed him, visibly rejecting the counsel of the ghost with every bit of the absolutism his ancestors had bequeathed him. He turned and looked at Barrodagh.

"Lord, we have the Heart of Kronos."

The dark eyes widened, reflecting the flickering light from the fireplace. "Where?"

"It was recovered on Rifthaven by the Karroo Syndicate." Barrodagh swallowed, reluctant to go on but knowing he could hide little or nothing of this from the Avatar. "Along with two of the stolen items from the palace."

Eusabian stood up and looked down at him.

"It was evidently the same gang of Rifters." Barrodagh hesitated, still weighing how much to tell Eusabian. He decided that an item of less importance but nonetheless intriguing might take the sting out of worse news still to be revealed. "The captain is an escaped Dol'jharian slave—a tempath."

One of the Avatar's eyebrows quirked. "And the Arkad?"

"The Arkad was still with them. They escaped and were intercepted by a Panarchist cruiser."

Eusabian stared at him for a long beat. Then the Avatar turned back to the fire, his fingers slowly beginning to work at the silken cord. "A slave and a deposed prince." He laughed softly, a cold sound. "I wonder what the Panarchists will make of that combination?" He pulled at the cord; it did not yield, the knots now braided into it resembling the links of a chain. "Hekaath . . . they do not understand. No slave ever fully escapes its master. The bond is stronger than freedom."

He shook himself out of the reverie. "Have the Panarchist prisoners transferred to the flagship. Divert the nearest Ur-equipped vessel to Rifthaven to pick up the Heart, for a rendezvous with the *Fist*." He smiled, visibly relaxing from the strain of the strange interview with the first Arkad.

"We will make an exchange. The Heart of Kronos will return to the Suneater after ten million years, and the Panarch—truly the ruler of naught—will go to Gehenna."

He looked at where Jaspar's ghost had stood. "And nothing can resist me now."

PART THREE

✻

TWENTY-FIVE

✴

ARTHELION

Barrodagh stared after the Avatar as he strode out of the library. Then he tabbed the communicator on his belt and roused Juvaszt on the *Fist of Dol'jhar*, who confirmed his suspicions. There was no point in embarking immediately: the spatial relationship between Rifthaven, Arthelion, and the Suneater meant they would merely wait in space for several days to rendezvous with the *Samedi*—the ship closest to Rifthaven, which Juvaszt was even now dispatching to pick up the Heart of Kronos.

Well, he would explain that to the Avatar tomorrow. Despite Eusabian's boredom, Barrodagh doubted he had extracted all the pleasure to be had from possession of his enemy's palace—and he would be even more bored, and thus more dangerous, on board the *Fist* while waiting for the rendezvous. And the delay would be useful: it seemed that Ferrasin was making great progress toward extracting critical information from the computer.

The thought drew his eyes to the table next to where Eusabian had been seated. He walked over to it and bent over the data socket, trying to decipher the faint writing on the datachip.

Unable to make it out in the dim flicker of the firelight, he reached down to pry it out of the socket.

There was a faint pop and the datachip disintegrated with a spurt of flame which stung his fingers. Barrodagh whispered a curse as he snatched his fingers away and stuck them in his mouth.

A faint glow in the corner of his vision caught his attention. He turned just in time to see the ghost of Jaspar Arkad shimmer back into visibility, not an arm's length away from him.

Its eyes seemed to focus on him. Barrodagh's breath caught in his throat and he stepped back; the arm of the chair caught him behind his knees and dumped him sprawling across it, unable to retreat further as the phantom slowly advanced toward him.

The ghost stopped in front of him, too close, and slowly a terrible, sly smile possessed its face. It bent over; Barrodagh could see clouds of darkness moving behind its eyes.

"Willa-Drissa-Will!" the ghost hissed suddenly, and its face distorted for a moment as its lips shot out on the end of a glowing stalk and lunged at Barrodagh's eyes.

Warmth flooded Barrodagh's breeches and he gave a strangled shriek. The ghost stood back, as if surveying the effect of its attack. Then, once more wearing the stern visage of the founder of the Arkad dynasty, it chuckled quietly and turned away. Moments later it glided through the wall and out of the library.

Suddenly furious, the Bori pushed himself out of the chair and sent the carven table spinning across the library with a vicious blow. "I hate you!" he cried; then stopped, appalled. Just so had he screamed at his horrid sister when she locked him up those nights so long ago. But she was long dead, almost his first victim when he had come into power in the Dol'jharian bureaucracy. There was no reason to remember her now.

He exhaled shakily and looked down at the stain spreading across his crotch. Something would be to be done about that Ur-be-damned palace computer. It must have known he was Bori, known the legends . . .

Then he shrugged. *It doesn't matter now.* In a matter of days they would leave for the Suneater, away from the Mandala and its hateful, archaic machines. Then things would return to normal.

But as Barrodagh·left the library, he thought he heard a chuckle from the air behind him—a sound and a memory he could not escape.

❈   ❈   ❈

Morrighon didn't know at first what had awakened him. With the facility born of long practice, he scanned the whispers coming from the communicators on the table near his bed, staring up at the ceiling now faintly lit by the glow of false dawn. There was nothing but the normal chatter of the channels he'd chosen to monitor this night—no, he suddenly realized, the Tarkan channel was more active than usual.

Then he caught a single word: *karra.* Another haunting, then. Perhaps it had been a mistake to monitor that channel; he didn't need to know about Tarkan encounters with the computer-generated hologram that was making their duty such a misery. He closed his eyes.

False dawn?

His eyes snapped open. Barrodagh had transferred him to a lower level of the palace after Anaris' first meeting with Eusabian, as an indication of his displeasure. There were no windows in his quarters.

He rolled over, propping himself on his elbows and looking over the end of the bed into the room. His breath stopped.

The faintly glowing form of an old man in a Panarchist uniform stood looking at him from against the opposite wall. After a moment, Morrighon recognized the face as belonging to the first bust in the Phoenix Antechamber: Jaspar hai-Arkad. Despite his thorough materialism, the Bori felt a chill seize him.

It must be the computer. This was a new level of manifestation; he had to contact Ferrasin. The thought didn't help: he found, with a mixture of fear and disgust, that he still couldn't bring himself to move.

The ghost—*It is* not *a ghost,* his mind insisted fiercely—smiled at him and faded back through the wall, leaving behind a faint pool of light that shivered and crawled along the surface for a moment before fading out.

Morrighon got up and padded out of his bedroom into the working portion of his suite. The lights came on in response to his movement, banishing the darkness and with it much of his disquiet. He seated himself at his desk, laying his palms on its smooth, cool surface for a moment, and then tabbed his com.

"Ferrasin here." The response came more quickly than he expected, and there was no trace of sleep in the technician's voice.

"This is Morrighon. The apparition . . ."

"We are working on that now, serach Morrighon," interrupted Ferrasin, the faint emphasis on the word "we" warning the Bori that the technician could not speak freely. A light glowed on his com, indicating a download waiting. He tabbed the accept key. "We will have a full report by morning."

"Very well," Morrighon acknowledged, and tabbed off.

He keyed up the file that Ferrasin had sent him under cover of their conversation.

A few minutes later, frightened to the edge of nausea, he yanked on yesterday's clothes and summoned a Tarkan escort to take him to Anaris.

❈   ❈   ❈

The chiming of the annunciator brought Anaris out of deep sleep. He fought away confusion and looked at the chrono: 02:38. Alarmed, he reached for his wrist and then his hand fell back when it encountered bare flesh. He was among his own kind again—and Dol'jharians did not use boswells. Annoyance mixed with amusement as he remembered tossing his own boswell into the disposer just before he returned to his father: what Dol'jharian would ever entrust his thoughts to a machine that could be taken away?

Leaning over, he tabbed the com. "Who is it?"

"Morrighon, lord." The Bori's voice was fearful. "You told me to . . ."

"Come in." Anaris sprang out of bed and threw on his dressing gown as Morrighon entered.

The Bori looked even worse than usual, Anaris thought, facing the trembling man. His clothes were rumpled and smelled faintly, his thinning hair stuck out in wispy spikes in every direction, and the paleness of his face exaggerated his bad complexion.

"My lord," he said as the door slid shut behind him, "we have received word from Rifthaven." The Bori stopped, swallowing convulsively.

Rifthaven! Had Snurkel been right, then? Was Brandon there?

Better, was he now captive? He bit back a shout of triumph; now he would have the last word with his laughing enemy of old. And, in completing his father's *paliach*, would take another step toward the throne.

Morrighon's expression became even more woeful, and some of Anaris' exultation faded out of him. "Widespread fighting has broken out on Rifthaven among the Syndicates, even within some. It appears to have been triggered by the discovery of the Aerenarch, as suspected by our primary contact there." Morrighon stopped again.

"And?"

Morrighon's words emerged in a rush. "In the confusion, the Aerenarch escaped. His ship was intercepted by a Panarchist battlecruiser. We can only assume he is now on his way to Ares."

Rage replaced triumph. Anaris felt his face distorting into the *prachan*, the fear-face, as, once more, the laughing Arkad third-son evaded him.

Morrighon stepped back, pressing against the wall, his face a sickly hue. For the first time, Anaris could see his eyes entire, so wide were they.

Then a tendril of fear stilled the rage. What a report had been made to his father? He forced himself to relax. "What does the Avatar know?"

It took Morrighon a moment to find his voice, his larynx working. "Snurkel recovered the Heart of Kronos," he squeaked at last. "The Avatar has accepted his explanations concerning the Aerenarch. No hint of our role has emerged: Snurkel's position on Rifthaven is precarious and depends entirely on the Avatar now—he cannot afford any suspicion of double-dealing."

Anaris' anxiety began to fade. With what the Avatar regarded as his key to complete victory now in his hands, Eusabian would have a mind to little else. Still, it might be best to arrange accidents for the seconds that he and Morrighon had suborned, especially Snurkel—from now on Rifthaven would be of little importance, and they could only be a source of embarrassment.

Then a thought struck him: his machinations on Rifthaven, through Morrighon, had been the key to the Aerenarch's escape. Savoring the acidic bite of irony, he relived the many times Brandon and his brother Galen had used his Dol'jharian instincts against him in their despicable games, until he finally learned to think as they did.

It was you, as much as your father, who taught me to think as a Panarchist. The realization shocked him; with a kind of perverse pleasure he recognized that Brandon was becoming a worthy foe. And he knew that they were not finished with each other.

He noticed the Bori looking at him in utter horror, and realized that he was smiling, a rictus that made his face ache.

"Sit down," he ordered. Morrighon flopped bonelessly into a chair, staring up at him, still fearful.

Anaris looked at him thoughtfully. It had taken some courage to bring him that news; fear, the underpinning of the Dol'jharian state, was often as much an impediment to knowledge as a lash to efficiency. He had sensed that between Barrodagh and his father—he could not afford that between Morrighon and himself.

"You did well to awaken me, and you need not fear my wrath. I bear the blame for this."

He saw the astonishment replace fear in the Bori as he continued. "We are not finished on Rifthaven . . ."

Just as he finished outlining his plan the com chimed, signaling the deposit of a recorded message. He crossed the room to it and tabbed it on.

"This is Barrodagh, speaking for the Avatar. The Heart of Kronos has been recovered; preparations are beginning for departure to the Suneater. The Panarch and his remaining councilors will be transferred to the *Fist of Dol'jhar*. Your father desires you to hold yourself in readiness to accompany them."

Anaris tabbed the acknowledgment key and turned away from the com. "He was rather vague about the schedule."

"He probably doesn't know it yet," replied Morrighon. "That will be for Juvaszt to figure out."

Anaris nodded, but his thoughts had already run ahead, following the implications of the Avatar's decision. His father would be the last to leave the planet, as required by Dol'jharian custom. But the face that filled his mind's eye was not Eusabian's, but Gelasaar's. Did his father intend them to meet face-to-face? What would he say to him? Barrodagh's message had been vague—deliberately, he was sure—concerning the nature of his escort duty. Would he see the man who had fostered him or not?

As he turned back to Morrighon, to begin planning their response to this new development, Anaris didn't know which he would prefer.

✳   ✳   ✳

ARTHELION SYSTEM

Anderic's fingers jerked spasmodically. He forced himself to control his hands as he sidled a glance around the bridge. No one was watching him. His fingers snaked out and he tabbed the keys to make certain the logos was turned off.

Then he tried to calm his slamming heart as he watched sho-Imbris lay in the course that Anderic had just required—a course suggested by the logos.

But did I turn it on first or not?

He couldn't remember. He squeezed his eyes shut, wondering if he was going mad—or maybe Tallis' eye, transplanted into his body against his will, was forcing him into madness. Three times now, he had spoken to find the logos on already, and he did not remember turning it on. Now he convulsively tabbed it off every few minutes, trying to make certain. And what about the flickers? Was guilt imposed by his Ozmiront upbringing creating those half-seen movements, like disapproving faces, that thronged the corners of his vision when he was fatigued, which was most of the time now?

The logos . . . and the crew. He felt more isolated from them than ever. It seemed lately that everyone on the *Satansclaw* was involved in the secret orgies—everyone, that is, but its captain.

A pang in his eye reminded him of one of the reasons they shunned him. The main reason? He flickered a look around, wondering how they could not know about the demonic presence of the logos haunting him, waking and sleeping.

"Emergence pulse, Captain."

Anderic jerked up in his pod and slapped the go-key. The fiveskip burped.

"Signature, frigate—it's the *Golden Bones*."

Anderic relaxed. A moment later, the long-nosed, unlovely visage of the frigate's captain appeared on the screen.

"Besvur here," she said. "Barrodagh says they're expecting the nicks to try a counterattack on Arthelion. Any news?"

"We've been patrolling here, and we haven't seen anything but our people," Anderic said, striving to sound bored. "I think he's been juicing down too much of the Panarch's best fume."

Besvur cackled. "Hope you're right," she said. "We need some time to count our loot; don't need t'tangle with a buncha hothead Navy chatzers."

They talked a while longer, cautiously probing each other for information. They were using ordinary EM, so they didn't have to worry about the Dol'jharians listening in over the broadcast-only hyperwave.

Anderic cut the connection and chewed a nail, wondering if Besvur would be an ally or a rival in the increasingly desperate maneuvering for favor with the Dol'jharians. He looked around the bridge; half the pods were empty, their monitors on Z-watch. He'd promised sho-Imbris extra points in whatever action they might meet if he'd do longer hours, and Ninn didn't seem to mind being in his pod most of the time.

But neither of them could help him deal with the increasing chatter on the hyperwave. It was getting harder and harder to sift the useful data out of the flood of rumor and braggadocio flooding the system.

Lennart could, though.

Jealousy burned in Anderic. Too bad if he interrupted her usual fun and games. She was the worst of them, the ugly toad—seemed like every time he spied on one of his crew, he interrupted bunny fun, and she was almost always in it.

He smiled meanly. *Too bad, Lennart. Time to work.*

He tabbed the locate.

Luri's full red lips parted in a soft laugh. She hefted the pot she'd brought out from the galley, and Kira Lennart smelled the scent of fresh-melted chocolate.

"What's that for?" she said.

"You shall see," Luri murmured. "Luri has fun in mind."

Kira laughed, her heart squeezing inside her. She couldn't help it; she knew Luri was not even remotely constant; in fact the only reason why she saw as much of her as she did was that Kira participated willingly in Luri's plots to get rid of Anderic, but she didn't care.

When she bunks me out I'll hurt, and the rest of my life I'll probably bore people with the tale of my one great romance, she thought with rueful irony as they hurried down to the bilge area.

Tallis looked up with painful expectancy in his one remaining eye when they entered. Luri set down the pot carefully by her side, and as her perfume and the chocolate chased away the faint, unpleasant tang of bilge pervading the room, Kira realized why she must have brought the chocolate.

It certainly had no part in their plans.

Kira tapped her boswell; it flashed green. No monitors active in the room.

"It's clear. I've got the com console rigged. If Anderic runs a locate, we'll have a few seconds' warning."

Luri touched Tallis' cheeks. "Tal-lis must remember that he doesn't want Luri here, hmmm? If Anderic spies."

Tallis sighed as the woman's hands ran down his body, then caressed the metal ball hanging on his member, hidden by the thin fabric of his trousers.

"Luri will find out how to remove that," she added softly.

Jealously stabbed at Kira, and to banish it, she said, "Should we get to our planning? Tallis, you said next time you might have something to tell us." She added doubtfully, looking around the bilge chamber which Tallis was unable to leave, "What have you found out?"

Tallis Y'Marmor rubbed his forehead. "It's nothing I've found out, it's something—" He stopped, then said abruptly, "There's a logos on board."

"A what?" Luri asked.

Nausea clawed at Kira's insides. "A *what*!"

Tallis looked from one of the women to the other, then said to Luri, "It's a—an artificial intelligence." He got it out quickly, avoiding looking at Kira. "I had it installed. Barcan-made. One of the ways it communicates is through an eye implant, which is why Barrodagh did that to me."

Kira fought back her revulsion, thinking quickly. "Anderic's an Ozmiront," she said. "He won't use it—"

"He already has," Tallis said.

"How do you know that?"

Tallis shrugged, indicating his console. "I think it has tried to contact me," he said, looking distinctly greenish around the jowls.

Kira repressed a shiver. Only Luri seemed supremely undisturbed; whether because she was ignorant of what the logos was capable of, or merely because anything which did not relate to her immediate plans was automatically insignificant to her, Kira did not know.

"This makes things different—" Kira began. Then her boz'l buzzed against her wrist. "Locate."

Luri laughed, stood up, and in one magnificent gesture ripped her gown free of her body. "Kira, you too." As Lennart complied, excited and confused at once, she turned to Tallis. "We shall return," she murmured to him, leaning forward to kiss him. "Now, remember: you are miserable, we are teasing you with what you cannot have."

And before either of the others could speak, she picked up the chocolate pot and held it in both hands. Kira felt another buzz from her boz'l; the imager had now activated.

"Tal-lis," Luri said in her breathy singsong. "We are here to alleviate your bore-dom. You get to watch while Kira and Luri have fun." She lifted the pot and spilled the half-congealed dark liquid down the front of her naked body, then stepped forward and spilled more on Kira, who jerked as the liquid flowed down her chest, kindling an answering warmth. "You get to watch and see if Kira and Luri can lick each other off in . . . would you like to guess how long it will take?"

Tallis gave a low whimper.

❋   ❋   ❋

Anderic groaned. *Again!* He watched, fascinated, his nacker painful as the two women writhed, glistening with streaks of chocolate in fascinating accents against Luri's amber and Lennart's coffee-colored flesh, in front of the miserable one-eyed Tallis. Anger, jealousy, lust burned in him.

Then a thought struck. Quickly he got up and crossed to the communications console, ignoring the curious looks from sho-Imbris and Ninn. He opened a record bank and started storing the image from the bilgebay.

Then he watched until Luri and Lennart reached the climax of their chocolate romp, squealing with delight.

Smiling, Anderic sealed the record under his own personal code and then patched it into the hyperwave for random replay. Lennart would find it and cancel it despite the coding, he was sure, but by then someone—several someones, no doubt— would have recorded it. He was sure that it would become staple entertainment on the Rifter bilge-banging session that formed an increasingly large part of the traffic on the hyperwave.

Then he tabbed the call key. "Lennart, I need you on the bridge." He cut the connection without waiting for an acknowledgment and returned to his command pod.

He was looking forward to Lennart's reaction to her newfound fame.

TWENTY-SIX

MALACHRONTE SYSTEM

"And what do you intend to do if I refuse?" said the Aegios.

Hreem glared at the viewscreen as the man continued.

"We've got the teslas up, and soon we'll have the weapons systems powered up as well. You have no time left, Rifter." Ferniar Ozman laughed, his heavy jowls shaking. "Best you flee now—my engineers tell me the drives will be the last system on-line, so we might not even chase you."

He held up his hand as Hreem made to speak. "Oh, we've heard of your superweapons. But you want a battlecruiser, not a cloud of gas, am I correct?"

Without waiting for a response, he terminated the connection.

Hreem swore as the screen flickered back to a view of the Malachronte Ways, and stalked across the bridge of the *Flower of Lith*. His crew was silent, eyes down. Norio, standing near the aft hatch, made no move toward him.

Hreem glared at the viewscreen again. Here, at the inner edge of the system's asteroid belt whence came the raw materials for the Ways, framed in the spidery complexity of construction machinery, the deadly symmetry of a battlecruiser glimmered in the

light of the distant sun. Beyond it the Rifter captain could see
other docks with ships in various stages of construction, but
they held no interest for him.

His eyes ranged greedily over the battlecruiser's seven-
kilometer statement of invincibility, the contours of the silvery
hull interrupted by the thorns and turrets of projecting weaponry
and sensors, blurred slightly by the faint shimmer of an activated tesla field.

It looks ready to go. He swore again. Obviously it wasn't,
quite, or the Aegios would have ordered its weapons turned on
the *Lith*.

"Cap'n? I'm getting faint readings from the cruiser's ruptor
systems." Erbee spoke up from the sensor console. "It looks like
a low-power test."

"That'd mean about twenty hours or so till they bring them
up to full power," Piliar at Fire Control commented.

Hreem gnawed his thumb as he sat down again. Pili was ex-
Navy, cashiered for something he wouldn't talk about, but he
knew weapons systems.

It had been easier than attacking Charvann, up until now. His
forces had quickly blown away the Malachronte defense. But
with the Archon gone—he'd been on Arthelion when it fell—
there was no one with sufficient authority to order Ozman to
surrender.

Faced by Ozman's obduracy, he had only two choices. He
could blast the cruiser into atoms, or he could flee. What he
couldn't do, as long as that chatzing Aegios held the ship, was
force his way on board.

At least the Dol'jharians haven't shown up yet. Once they
did, there would be no way to explain away his failure to the
Lord of Vengeance. A brief pang of anxiety shook him.

Then the Rifter captain felt the pressure of two strong, narrow
hands on his shoulders, probing for the shakrian points.

"Chatzing nick," Hreem growled. "He'd laugh out his
blungehole if I just had him here." He flicked the heel-claws on
his boots out, scoring the deckplates.

"No, Jala. I think he is courageous, and no doubt possesses
other virtues as well." The tempath gave a soft sigh. "At least,
the Douloi call them virtues, but you and I . . . we can call them
weakness."

Hreem looked up at Norio, whose eyes glittered with malice.

"For instance, as one in the Ranks of Service, he is trained to place a high value on human life." The tempath smiled. "It would be so very delightful to see how he balances his oath of fealty against . . . say, fifty thousand lives."

The maximum population of a Highdwelling. And there are hundreds of them around Malachronte.

For a moment the enormity of what Norio was suggesting made Hreem waver. In the long history of the Thousand Suns, no ship had ever targeted a sync. What Norio was suggesting was orders of magnitude beyond anything he'd done so far in his long and bloody career. He looked back at the battlecruiser, and the familiar image of himself on its bridge possessed him wholly.

"And the *novosti* will be so very eager to share the spectacle with all of Malachronte system," Norio added softly

Hreem laughed. Norio was right. The newsfeeds would do most of the job for him: the battlecruiser was as good as his. And if he timed it right, he could be back here laughing at Ozman's reaction as he watched the news from the syncs in realtime.

✳   ✳   ✳

Norio savored the novosti's fear as the man stepped onto the bridge of the *Lith*, his larynx bobbing as he subvocalized his commentary through his boswell. His head swiveled smoothly as he surveyed the bridge, the *ajna* on his forehead reflecting the status lights on the consoles as the semi-living lens adjusted its focus. The tempath wished he could feel the emotions of the billion-plus viewers the device was relaying its images to. *Like falling into the sun, embraced by the cleansing flames . . .*

He shook off the mood and glanced over at Hreem as the novosti approached him. The captain lounged in his command pod, casually picking his nails with a dagger, but Norio could feel his excitement, a fascinating compound of anger, lust, and—Norio laughed silently—stage fright.

The bridge was silent. Riolo, the Barcan computer tech, nervously hitched up the belt supporting his absurd codpiece as the newsman's gaze swept across him.

"Stop that. Now." Hreem pointed with his knife at the man's throat.

The novosti stammered, "S-stop what?"

"If you're going to talk, do it so we can hear you." Hreem started flipping the dagger in the air, catching it by the blade. The novosti's eyes followed it; Norio enjoyed the way his anxiety pulsed in time to the weapon's glittering course. "Well, genz Bertranus, you're the lucky chatzer that won the draw. So ask your questions."

"If you please, genz chaka-Jalashalal, I need . . ."

"Just call me Captain." Hreem was smiling broadly, his emotions now approximating those of a cat toying with its prey. Norio felt the skin on his arms tingle with pleasure.

"Captain, I need to finish setting the background for my viewers, if you please."

Hreem waved one hand negligently. "I please."

The man's eyes focused on distance for a moment. "Yes, I'm ready to continue," he said, apparently speaking to his relay on the ship that had brought him to the *Flower of Lith*. Then he began, picking up from where he had been interrupted.

"Following the defeat of the system defense forces, the attackers disappeared, leaving behind only a growing crescendo of rumors, fueled by the unbelievable reports carried here by refugees from Charvann. Now they have returned.

"I am now standing on the bridge of the *Flower of Lith*, flagship of the Rifter fleet occupying Malachronte system. Its captain, Hreem chaka-Jalashalal, known throughout the Thousand Suns as Hreem the Faithless, has agreed to an interview."

The novosti faced Hreem. "Captain, refugees from Charvann say you forced the surrender of that planet with some sort of superweapon. Is that true?"

"Yes."

"Do you intend the same here?"

"No." Norio could feel Hreem's amusement growing.

"Why are you treating the two systems differently?"

"My orders were unequivocal concerning Charvann. I have considerably more latitude here." Norio smiled. Never before had Hreem an audience so large for his words, and he was making the most of the opportunity.

"Orders? From whom, if I may ask?"

"Jerrode Eusabian, Avatar of Dol, Lord of Vengeance and the Kingdoms of Dol'jhar."

There was a momentary silence. Norio knew the refugees from Charvann must have reported this as well, but its confirmation by the captain of a Rifter destroyer had to be a shock despite that.

"Then, Captain, if you will, tell us your intentions toward Malachronte."

"I have no intentions toward Malachronte," replied Hreem, with all apparent mildness.

Bertranus blinked.

"Then why are you here?"

"I've come to take possession of the battlecruiser under construction in the Ways," replied Hreem. "Unfortunately the Aegios, Ferniar Ozman, has not been entirely cooperative."

"And that is why you asked to speak to his mother, on Sync Ozman?"

Hreem smiled. "It was you who suggested his mother. I merely requested contact with someone close to him, who might give me an insight into his character, to ease the negotiations. There is very little time before the contingent from Dol'jhar arrives, at which point I will no longer have very much control." He paused and attempted a sorrowful look, which was only partially successful. Norio suppressed a snort of laughter as Hreem continued. "They have far less patience than me."

The novosti looked into distance again. "Do we have her online?" He paused. "All right."

The captain looked over at Norio, who nodded fractionally. As they had discussed, the mention of Dol'jhar was intended to cast Hreem in the position of an almost ally of Malachronte. The novosti's emotions indicated that it was working. The tempath shivered with anticipation; this would make the coming whiplash of emotions even more violent. He wished again he could experience the feelings of Bertranus' viewers, even though it would probably kill him. *But such ecstasy . . .*

"Beam incoming, Cap'n," said Dyasil.

A window expanded on the viewscreen, revealing the head and shoulders of a white-haired woman against an elegant background, her dark eyes and hooked nose like those of the stubborn Aegios.

Norio could feel the instant surge of hatred and resentment that the woman engendered in Hreem. He also sensed unease in the newsman as the background to the window revealed that the ship was coming about and accelerating toward the ring of Highdwellings around Malachronte.

The novosti spoke to his viewers. "We now have Lady Vite Ozman on-line." He sketched a deference to the screen. "Lady Ozman, thank you for agreeing to speak to us."

"I am not sure your role in this affair reflects well on your character or your organization, genz Betranus," she said, her voice neutral. "Please. You requested an interview?"

Bertranus didn't reply for a moment. His larynx bobbed slightly. "Excuse me," he said to the image, and turned to Hreem. "Captain, my relay ship is having difficulty keeping station. Why are we moving?"

"Tactical reasons," Hreem replied. "Nothing to worry about."

The novosti licked his lips, then turned back to the screen. "I apologize, Lady Ozman." He looked up at Hreem. "You had some questions for Lady Ozman, Captain?"

Hreem smiled, and Norio could feel the unleashed cruelty rising in him. "No questions. I just wanted to see her face."

The woman's brows drew together as she considered this, then she reached toward something under the screen as the novosti stammered, "But, Captain, you insisted on this contact . . ."

"Leave off, you blungesucking nick," Hreem snarled at the screen, leaning forward and holding the point of his dagger to Bertranus' throat. "Cut that connection and this chatzer dies."

The woman was silent, her face grim. Huge drops of sweat oozed from the novosti's forehead as he froze in place.

"Missile armed and ready," said Pili at Fire Control.

"Captain!" the newsman squeaked. "What are you doing?"

"Target acquired," continued Fire Control. "Sync Porphyry, plus-one spinwise of Ozman, as ordered." Norio could hear the stress in his voice, and sense his unease at what he was doing, along with his greater fear of defying Hreem.

"This is just to convince you, and your chatzing son out of the Ways, that I mean what I say."

Just as Hreem spoke, Norio realized the flaw in their plan. "Captain, wait." Norio bit his lip, holding back laughter as relief billowed from the newsman. *So you think I'm going to prevent this, do you?* "I suggest a change in target."

Hreem looked at him, frowning.

Norio leaned close. "Consider. Ozman's oath of fealty will forbid him to consider his Family first. If he yields, he will be disgraced." Norio nodded toward the Douloi woman on the screen. "Do you think she would hesitate to disown him for such weakness? Or fail to embrace death in the service of her liege? But if you destroy Sync Ozman now, you take away the glory and replace it with senseless death. The shock, combined with the threat to another sync with which he has no familial connection, and thus to which he actually has stronger obligations—that will weaken him considerably."

"Virtue as weakness," Hreem repeated, smiling in delight.

Norio smiled back, shivering with anticipation.

"You have imagers focused on Sync Ozman?" Hreem asked Bertranus, withdrawing the dagger from his throat.

The man's lips moved as he communicated with his relay. "We do now," he replied, his voice barely audible. Norio watched, fascinated by his sense of shame for the part he was playing. *Yet he continues.*

"Fire Control, retarget," Hreem ordered. "Sync Ozman."

Lady Ozman's Douloi assurance faded. "Captain, I ask you to spare the innocents of Ozman. I will come to your ship."

"Target acquired, Sync Ozman." Pili's voice was flat.

Hreem stared at the Douloi woman, unspeaking.

"Do you want me to beg for our lives?" she asked.

"No," he finally replied after a long beat. "I don't want you to beg. I want you to die."

He brought his hand down on the firing pad.

❊   ❊   ❊

". . . I want you to die."

Norio watched Ferniar Ozman avidly as Hreem's image, relayed by the newsfeed from the inner system twenty light-minutes away, brought his fist down on the firing pad. The image from the novosti vid switched away to an exterior view of Sync Ozman: a finger of light reached out from the dragonfly angularity of the *Flower of Lith* to impact near one end of the habitat. A brilliant flare of light was followed by a spew of fragments and a billow of haze from the rupture in the shell of the habitat. Nearby, the deadly thorn-studded shape of a Rifter frigate hung motionless; beyond it loomed the fragile immensity of another sync.

"I'll save you the time of listening to the gabble from the novosti channels," said Hreem. "Sync Ozman has about six

hours before it goes chaotic and starts to come apart. You wanna
be there for the end, like a good nick?"

Ferniar Ozman looked out of the viewscreen at them in silence for a moment, his features tight. Norio wished he could
feel the man's emotions. *Such a feast of pain and regret.*

Finally the Aegios spoke. "You will give our ship safe conduct?"

"We'll exchange ships," replied Hreem, suggesting an ancient
and well-known protocol for surrender. "Here's how it will
work . . ."

The negotiations concluded, Hreem tabbed off the channel and
smirked in triumph at his bridge crew. Some smiled back, others
tried to hide fear and other complex emotions.

"You were generous with him," Norio said.

"No need to be greedy now." Hreem grinned. "I get that luxury yacht—a nice bonus."

Erbee's console bleeped. "Emergence pulse, bearing 109
mark 72, plus 2 light-seconds," shouted the tech.

Hreem jerked upright in his pod and slapped the skip pad.
The fiveskip burred momentarily, compounding Norio's discomfort at Hreem's sudden surge of fear. Unexpected emotions were
always hard to deal with.

Moments later Erbee spoke again. "ID established, the
Karra-rahim. It's the Dol'jharians."

"Beam incoming," Dyasil put in.

Hreem tensed as the arrogant, deeply seamed features of a
senior Dol'jharian Tarkan windowed up on the screen. "Have
you secured the battlecruiser?" she snapped, without preamble.

The tempath sense Hreem's anxiety shading into anger at the
woman's arrogance. "It has been arranged."

He explained the surrender agreement to the Tarkan, and won
her grudging agreement to wait until Ozman and his people departed from the inner system before approaching more closely.

"If you press them, they may decide to go out in a blaze of
glory, for the honor of their oath."

The Tarkan nodded and cut the connection.

Norio smiled. "Virtue as weakness. The Dol'jharians are
much the same as the Panarchists, with their oaths and loyal-
ties."

But Hreem pounded softly on his console. "Damn, damn, damn. If I could've gotten on board first . . ."

Across the bridge at his console, Riolo tugged again at his belt, causing his codpiece to wriggle ludicrously. Strangely, instead of the usual surge of disgust that the Barcan engendered in Hreem, Norio sensed instead a pulse of excitement.

"What is is, Jala, brightness? Have you seen a way out?"

Hreem nodded slowly and got out of the command pod. "Have Riolo meet me down in the aft bay. I've got some questions about the pinnace's nav computer."

❆   ❆   ❆

The silvery hull of the battlecruiser loomed immense beside the two tiny ships fastened lock-to-lock. As the last of the Panarchists squeezed past him into the *Lith*'s pinnace Hreem held out his hand to Ozman.

The Aegios slowly placed a datachip in the Rifter's palm, then looked momentarily past Hreem, at the thorns and spikes of the battlecruiser hull that formed a wall just outside, blurred by the energies of the electronic lock field that kept them all breathing. Hreem turned to Norio, saw his intent focus.

"Guilt and fear," Norio whispered.

Ozman's eyes snapped over to him.

"He's hiding something. I think he left someone behind."

"Is this all of you?" Hreem demanded.

"There's one missing," Ozman admitted, sweat lining his tense brow. "We couldn't find him. But he can do nothing—everything's locked down, and you have the codes."

Hreem considered, then shrugged. "He'll be sorry."

A few minutes later the two ships drifted apart. The Aegios' personal yacht, now carrying Hreem and a contingent from the *Lith*, moved toward the nearest bay of the battlecruiser. The pinnace moved away, slowly orienting itself for the jump into fivespace.

On the bridge of the yacht the viewscreen showed only the pinnace, and a portion of the battlecruiser's hull, looming like the limb of a planet seen from low orbit. Beyond were only the stars—the *Lith*, in accordance with their agreement, was on the other side of the cruiser, where it couldn't attack the pinnace.

Then Riolo touched a control, and a small targeting cross blinked into being in the starfield behind the pinnace.

"Any moment now," the Barcan said. His red-tinted goggles glinted, reflecting the status lights on the yacht's console.

The pinnace suddenly yawed about, orienting on the distant point of light that was the Dol'jharian ship. It began to accelerate.

"They've tried to enter fivespace. The program is engaged," said Riolo.

Hreem grinned as a green lens on the console lit up. He reached over and accepted the communication.

"What have you done?" Ferniar Ozman demanded. Behind him Hreem could seen someone frantically tapping at the nav console.

"You swore an oath," replied Hreem. "To hold your liege's enemies as your own, and your life as his to spend in defense of the Thousand Suns." He laughed, barely able to continue at the expression on the face of the Aegios. "Out there is a ship full of Dol'jharians—the Panarch's bitter enemies. I'm just helping you fulfill your oath."

Hreem paused as Riolo held up three fingers, then two, then one.

"Good-bye, Ferniar Ozman," said the Rifter.

The pinnace vanished in a pulse of light as its fiveskip engaged. Four seconds later a dim spark of light indicated the destruction of the *Karra-rahim* as the little ship's course intersected its position.

"Good work," said Hreem, seating himself in the control pod. "Let's get on board."

The complex fittings of the cruiser's hull slipped out of sight past the edges of the viewscreen as the little ship moved toward the immense bay yawning open for them. Hreem could hear Norio's breath rasping unevenly in his throat, and he grinned, knowing that his emotions were almost too hot for the tempath to handle. In truth, he could barely contain them himself—he'd never before felt such an intense happiness.

The green com light kindled on the console.

"Yeah?"

Dyasil's face windowed up on the screen. "Dyasil, here, Cap'n. Erbee says there's somethin' goin' on in the cruiser's engines, and he doesn't like it."

"What?" Hreem snapped. "I thought the engines weren't up yet."

"That's just it, Captain," came the scantech's voice, all traces of its usual drawl effaced by anxiety. A moment later his face pushed into view over Dyasil's shoulder. "It takes hours to bring the engines up safely, but the cruiser's are comin' on-line right now, and they're not stable." He jerked his thumb up. "You'd better get out of there."

Before Hreem could reply the image fuzzed and tore across in a pattern of zigzag lines, re-forming moments later into an unfamiliar face. Dark, deeply lined, with a high forehead and thin lips compressed into a snarling smile, the man glared madly out at Hreem and the other Rifters.

"Don't, Captain," he said, emotion distorting his speech into a guttural accent that Hreem immediately recognized. "I want you to join me for the final voyage of the *Paliach ku-Avatari*." He looked down momentarily, evidently checking some instrument not in the imager's field of view. "The Avatar's Vengeance, you would say in that puling tongue you Panarchists use."

The image jittered. Hreem felt a ripple of gravitational energy tug at his innards, and on the screen, the Dol'jharian's face distorted in a momentary flash of agony. Hreem slapped at the console, bringing the yacht about, fear screaming through his nerves. Behind him he heard Norio moan in pain.

"Now I take my name into the darkness, and with it your hopes of glory. *Attarh ni-grishun ta nemmir Hreem alla ni-Takha . . .*"

Hreem slapped the go-pad, cutting off the man's cursing in midsentence. The fiveskip burred, then cut out.

". . . say in that puling tongue you Panarchists use."

Hreem tapped at the console with wooden fingers, his mind numb. The viewscreen flickered to a view of the battlecruiser now several light-seconds distant. Unable to magnify the image as much of the better sensors of the destroyer Hreem was used to, it also revealed the *Flower of Lith* stationed nearby. As he watched, the destroyer suddenly vanished in a burst of light as it, too, fled.

Now the wavefront carrying the curses of the Dol'jharian agent had caught up with them, but the man did not lapse back into Uni before his voice suddenly cut off with a choking scream. A burst of glaring-bright vapor shot from the radiants of the cruiser, sending bits of the superstructure of its dock spinning away into space. Then, in the utter silence of vacuum, a network of cracks shot through the hull, revealing a growing brightness from within that grew and grew until the electronics of the yacht refused the overload and blanked the screen.

When the viewscreen cleared there was nothing left but a rosette of plasma, churning in a complex pattern that slowly faded against the stars.

Hreem sat in silence. Norio hovered in a corner, his face manic. No one else moved; Hreem knew that they all feared his anger.

All except Riolo.

The Barcan approached. Hreem saw his own reflection, distorted weasel-like in the little man's goggles. Riolo's breath was sweet with some unfamiliar spice.

"I know where there is something that Eusabian needs even more than a battlecruiser," he whispered. "And there are no Dol'jharians there—never have been, never will be."

Hreem considered this, rage suspended by curiosity.

"Take me to Barca with you," said Riolo, "and I will give you an army of such power that even the Shiidra wailed with fear at their appearance."

"Army?" Hreem croaked.

Riolo smiled and pulled his goggles up, his pupils instantly contracting to pinpoints and tears springing into his eyes. Hreem remembered Norio commenting that this was the ultimate Barcan gesture of sincerity.

"Yes," said Riolo. "I will give you the Ogres."

TWENTY-SEVEN

FIVESPACE: RIFTHAVEN TO DESRIEN

Osri Omilov stepped back and surveyed himself in the mirror. A haircut, a new uniform, and behind him the familiar dimensions of the standard lieutenant's bunk space and console, and he felt as if the universe had righted itself again. Looking at the reassuringly routine sight, he could almost pretend that the past weeks had not happened, that life was normal again.

But they had happened, and life outside this ship was not normal. Elsewhere in the same ship the Rifters, the Eya'a, and the big cat were imprisoned, and at another location Brandon prowled restlessly along the corridors.

And nearby, Sebastian Omilov, Osri's father, awaited him.

Osri turned away from the mirror and went to the drawer where he'd put the flight ribbon and the coin. There was no point in hiding them any longer: by now any Navy personnel who might be interested had heard about them. Osri had had plenty of experience with the near-FTL speed of shipboard gossip, and he'd seen the muted curiosity in the eyes of the Marine who'd restored the artifacts to him.

He took a perverse pleasure in the fact that the Rifters, safely housed in the brig, did not know that he had the two items, nor would they be likely to find out. Nor did Brandon know—or Osri's father.

Osri's mood sobered as he contemplated his father.

It was time to join him; the captain had invited them both to breakfast, which would take place not in the Senior Officers Mess, but in the new quarters that Sebastian and Brandon shared. Osri did not know why his father had insisted on this, though he spoke of health reasons. Perhaps it was to gauge how cooperative the Navy really was—and perhaps it was just more of his oblique diplomatic sidestepping.

Just before retiring, Sebastian had asked his son to join him early.

Osri's fingers groped at his left wrist, a convulsive movement that reached consciousness when his fingerpads hit the tabs of the standard boswell he'd been issued. He fought back the urge to record his thoughts, instead with a quick movement pocketing the ribbon and the coin.

Walking quickly up the corridor, he thought about telling his father about the artifacts. Why was he resistant?

Perforce they had spent more time in one another's company lately than they had since Osri was the schoolboy that the Rifters called him. And during that time, Osri thought he'd come to understand his father a little more, and even to appreciate the breadth of his perceptions.

But below that was anger. Now that Osri had had time to think through the events of recent weeks, he found that his mind kept returning to '55, and what had happened on Minerva. He had come by degrees to believe that there was more to what had seemed straightforward events than he had thought, and that in fact Markham vlith-L'Ranja and his father, the Archon of Lusor, had been unfairly treated by Aerenarch Semion for what amounted to political reasons.

What lingered in Osri's mind was resentment against his father that the whole truth should have been kept from him.

And the time, perhaps, had come to discuss it.

When the door slid open in the hastily converted storage bays known as "civ country," Osri saw his father and Brandon seated in two clean-lined, low Retro-Futura-style chairs. This central room was large, the tianqi set in the conventional spring-breezes mode, all the signs of the military being called upon unexpectedly to house VIPs from outside.

Both looked up at Osri's entrance. Osri's right hand slid into his pocket and tightened around the jumble of silk and ancient metal.

"Good morning, son," Sebastian greeted him.

"Good morning," Brandon echoed.

And before Osri had taken two steps into the room he saw the glance that passed between them. It was brief, but it took Osri straight back to their school days, and the maddening realization that his own father and the blank-faced Krysarch seemed to understand one another without the need for words.

And so he reacted as he had then, by striking out with the truth. "I'm interrupting a private conversation." And he backed a step, to retreat.

"We were discussing the detour," Sebastian said, his tone exactly the same mild, friendly one that Brandon had used a moment before. It functioned as a rebuke. "What could be Nukiel's reason for not going to Ares? Have you heard anything from the junior officers that can shed some light?"

Osri came in and sat down. "They are circumspect around me," he said. "As is appropriate. But I overheard some talk while I was in the quartermaster's, and when I was shown the wardroom, we interrupted some talk. They seem as surprised as we are. More."

Sebastian murmured, "Nukiel seems a by-the-books officer."

"He certainly doesn't seem the kind who'd run to a fogbound planet full of self-proclaimed seers for inspiration," Osri said acidly.

Brandon got to his feet and stretched. "Well, find out what you can. I will too, when my turn comes tonight." He glanced down at Sebastian, smiling. "Meanwhile, if I don't catch some sleep soon," he said, "they'll have to scrape me out of my bunk when we do reach Desrien."

One of the doors on the other side of the room slid open and shut, and Brandon was gone.

Osri saw his father's eyes narrow with the familiar considering gaze, as if he were thinking, "What do I do with you now?"

It was completely without anger, but somehow Osri preferred his mother's scorn and sarcasm.

He now saw his father considering his words, and he said quickly, "Don't use your diplomacy on me. For once speak straight."

Sebastian's bushy brows rose. "There is little danger of your interrupting anything of importance between Brandon and me." He hesitated, then added, "To my infinite regret."

The metal of the coin cut into Osri's fingers. "Is this to fix the blame on me for his future mistakes?"

Sebastian's hand stirred, a gesture setting aside irrelevancies. "Accusations of fault and blame have no value. The facts are—"

"The fact is," Osri interjected, "I accused him of desertion, which is the truth. I accused him of deserting out of cowardice, which I no longer think is true. But if it's not, then why did he abandon everything we believe in, everything we have sworn to protect? He was going to join that same gang of Rifters sitting in the brig right now!"

"He was going to find Markham vlith-L'Ranja," Sebastian corrected.

"You're trying to say that he didn't desert? On the day of his Enkainion, with half the government gathered in the palace to watch the ritual?"

"I don't deny it."

"To find Markham L'Ranja, a man ten years outside the law," Osri said. "A *Rifter*. True?"

"True."

"So where is the difference?"

"The difference is in the intent," Sebastian said slowly. "I wish there was more time ... before we reached Ares." He frowned abstractedly, then looked up. "Brandon's motivations and intentions I cannot second-guess. As we've established, he will not confide in me. But from conversations with Montrose, Ivard, and some of the others, I gather that Markham did not prey on Panarchists, only on other Rifters."

"This excuses desertion—the prospect of a Krysarch of the Phoenix House robbing other thieves?" Osri's sarcastic edge sharpened on every statement, but to the same degree his father seemed to grow more remote, more abstracted.

"I think ... I think his goal was to win justice from outside the system." Sebastian's gaze transferred to Osri's face, but the narrowed eyes seemed to look past him. "From Brandon's perspective—you have to admit—the system did not seem to work."

"Perhaps if he'd spent less time drinking and more in effort, he would have. . . ." Osri's words sounded weak in his own ears, weak and petulant. He remembered, as he knew Sebastian did, his own shock at finding out the truth: that Brandon's having been cashiered from the Academy was because he'd been caught trying to augment his training. *Semion wanted Brandon to be a Social Figurehead, just as Galen was the family Patron of the Arts,* Sebastian had said to him on one of their first private talks aboard the *Telvarna*. *Gelasaar's only mistake was in permitting Semion to supervise his brothers' educations. But how could he know it for a mistake? Semion was as fearsomely competent as Gelasaar himself, and we'd thought as truthful.* "I can't believe that the Panarch did not see any of this," he said finally.

"Then we get into the limitations of personality," Sebastian said, and with a faint return of his old irony, "Will you perceive this kind of discussion as treason?"

Osri opened his mouth to set his father straight on who had been committing treason, when, and how, but then he stopped. A year ago—a month ago—he would have been sure who was right, and who was wrong. But not now.

"You're saying that the Panarch is—"

Sebastian cut in quickly, with a shake of his head, "I'm saying that Gelasaar is probably the most hardworking, decent, innately truthful human being I have ever known, save only for his wife when she was alive. But after she died . . . I think a part of him went with her, and it was a relief for him to hand some jobs over to Semion, the overseeing of the education of Galen and Brandon being one of them."

Osri had only brief memories of the Kyriarch Ilara, but those memories were vivid. One was how she always managed to make everyone laugh, even children, whenever there was a gathering. A more personal memory was of her blue-gray eyes in a face round and smiling, bending toward him. *What are you learning now, Osri?* she'd asked, and she'd waited for the answer as most adults didn't, waited as if what he had to say took precedence over everything else. He couldn't remember what he'd said, but he did remember her sudden bright smile, and his own conviction that it was the *right* answer, and how happy that had made him feel all through the day—

Until he got home, and his own mother had questioned him closely on the interview, and then afterward said angrily, "That fool! Hadn't she the wit to invite you to stay? Or did you make a mistake and ruin your own chances?"

Osri knew his mother saw people in single terms—in one dimension. They were good or bad, stupid or smart, depending entirely on how they served her. He realized now as he stood staring at his waiting father that he had learned some of the same habit, and all Sebastian's efforts to educate him out of this narrow view had been fruitless.

I'm too like my mother, Osri thought with a bleak flicker of humor. *Quick to anger, and to judge.*

He felt an impulse, and gave in: "Why did you marry my mother?"

And saw the question strike Sebastian like a dagger in the heart. It was not an overtly obvious reaction—if Osri had been looking elsewhere he would have missed it—but his father's pupils contracted and he inhaled sharply.

Then Sebastian looked away, his Douloi mask hiding his thoughts. He said, "It seemed the right thing to do at the time."

"For whom?"

His father's eyes strayed to the holosim of space on one wall. "The family desired trade access to Ghettierus, and your mother wished a closer social connection to the Mandala. As for how successful—or how worthy—these goals were, you will have to answer for yourself."

Though Osri had heard his mother vilifying Sebastian so often he was inured to it, he had never heard anything negative about Risiena from his father.

"To return to Brandon's flight from Arthelion," Sebastian went on, "I think he had a purpose, of which he has not yet lost sight." He glanced at the discreet wall chrono, then stretched out a hand to touch Osri's sleeve. "They are due now," Sebastian said, "and I'd hoped to discuss something else of importance."

Osri looked down at the gnarled hand. His father had aged badly in recent weeks. "My report. You want me to ignore what happened? Or lie?"

Again the Douloi mask. "Do what you think best," Sebastian said in a pleasant voice, the cadence as slippery as water over rocks. "But I take leave to remind you that Nukiel and Efriq are also thinking ahead. Everything they have done or said since they took Vi'ya's ship on board will be raked over by those at Ares. They have striven mightily to make these quarters comfortable, to give us the impression we are guests, and that our meetings are interviews. But—"

"They are interrogations," Osri stated. "And our words are recorded. I'm familiar with Navy usage."

His father sighed, rubbing his hand over his temple. Osri felt the sting of remorse when he saw a trembling in the fingers. But then the door hissed open and Sebastian straightened up, his hands groping to the arm of his chair. Control was in place again.

The captain and the commander came in, both dressed in faultless whites. As salutes and greetings were exchanged, white-jacketed stewards brought in the covers for the meal.

Osri's mind was busy during the polite exchanges as they moved to the table and began. He knew his father would not sham weakness; though he was a diplomat, he had never been a fraud. Had he let his control slip for a reason?

Or had it been involuntary? He remembered his father's reaction to his question about his marriage. It had had a powerful effect, but why?

Osri took his place at the table, and other than returning answers to questions directed at him, he deferred to Sebastian. The talk ranged along safe channels: the comfort of the new quarters, the Aerenarch's wishes (Nukiel had insisted on giving up his quarters to the Phoenix Heir; Brandon had been even more insistent that he remain in civilian country; Omilov, speaking as Brandon's old tutor, had cast the swing vote. A complicated little dance whose outcome was a predictable as its steps—and as necessary, Omilov had said afterward).

While the other three talked, Osri retraced his way through his conversation with Omilov. The subject had been Brandon, but they had not stayed on him. Markham L'Ranja . . . Gelasaar . . . Risiena—no, that had been his thoughts only.

The Kyriarch.

Osri felt a subliminal jolt. *Ilara . . . and then my question: Why did you marry my mother?*

He felt clamminess on his palms and wished he were back in his own cabin, away from other eyes. His fingers slid over the metal Tetradrachm, rubbing over the unevenesses, but it afforded little comfort.

Don't ever take lovers, his mother had said to him once, in one of her rare confiding moments. *You'll find yourself bound by the chains of their greed.* He'd certainly seen the truth of that after some of the more spectacular fights. She'd always seemed to pick badly; Osri had cordially hated all his mother's lovers—a hatred he shared with his half siblings, even if they shared little else.

His father's house had always been a contrast much to be preferred: the quiet, monastic atmosphere. Music, art, learning. As a child Osri had assumed Sebastian's fidelity to Risiena; during his adolescence he'd speculated that his father did not care for women, but he had not sought male company, either. Later, he'd assumed Sebastian's celibacy was because he'd chosen to be wedded to his work.

Meanwhile Osri had grown up with the portrait of Ilara in Sebastian's study, never questioning its presence.

And from a conversation long ago, Sebastian saying of Gelasaar: *He is one of those rarities in our culture, a genuinely monogamous person. Having had the great fortune to find the ideal, I expect he'd feel that tarnishing the memory with casual intimacy would be intolerable.*

Osri stole a look at his father's jowly, big-eared profile.

The new insight did not change anything concrete. It couldn't even be talked of, Osri suspected. But once again he felt his perspective on the universe reeling.

Sebastian looked up and smiled. "I think I can elucidate the mysterious Eye-of-the-Distant-Sleeper, gentlemen," he was saying.

Osri knew that quirk to his mouth; he could almost hear Sebastian's voice, long ago: *The best way to keep people from talking about what you don't want to talk about is to get them onto a bigger secret.*

"Let me tell you what little I know of the Heart of Kronos."

OORT CLOUD:
ARTHELION SYSTEM

Metellus Hayashi drew a slow breath and let it out even slower. *I will not get angry. I will not even glance at my chrono. Armenhaut wants just that.*

The strategy meeting of the captains had been called at 12:00 standard. Hayashi and his subordinates had been here for hours; the frigate captains had arrived in the last quarter hour. Armenhaut and KepSingh, captains of the *Flammarion* and *Babur Khan* respectively, had waited until the last possible moment. And the couriers could find no trace of *Joyeaux*. That in itself was evidence of what the Navy faced—not, thought Hayashi, that that would make any difference to Armenhaut.

(Shuttle,) the officer of the watch reported, dry-voiced.

Hayashi put his hands behind his back, concentrating on keeping his demeanor impassive as he took the lift down to the forward beta landing bay. Margot had asked him to meet the captains.

He could hear her voice again: *Remember, Metellus, Semion is dead. From now on, Armenhaut and his kind can only be promoted on merit. Every time you look at Armenhaut's face, think of that and pity him. I will.*

With a hiss and a subdued boom, the shuttle's ramp came down. A pair of Marines tramped down, ground their weapons, then stood at attention at either side.

Two figures, one short and round, one tall and commanding, and both clad in faultless whites, their rank insignia visible from across the bay, appeared at the top of the ramp.

Metellus' eyes went to the chrono: 12:00 precisely.

"I have permission to come aboard." That was Armenhaut. KepSingh looked up suddenly, but he said nothing.

Metellus kept his face utterly blank as he stepped forward, uttered the formal greeting, then bid them follow.

As they entered the lift, he touched his boswell: *(Had permission: whites: KepSingh too—)* But as Metellus glanced at the shorter captain, he surprised a slightly pained glance on the man's face as he glanced at Metellus' own regulation daily-wear blues.

No one spoke as the lift spurted them upward; when they left, Metellus once again tapped Margot's private code and added: *(KepSingh came on Stygrid's shuttle, but no blockade there.)* That was all he had time for.

That gave Margot a few seconds' preparation as they walked down the spotless corridor. Marine guards snapped to attention outside the big conference room. Armenhaut, as senior in rank, went through first, followed by KepSingh and then Metellus.

They found all the captains waiting, everyone, including Margot's trim form, in regulation blues. Metellus saw Armenhaut's upper lip quirk faintly.

"If you'll be seated, we can get started," Ng said. And as everyone went for a pod, lighting up their arm consoles, she went on in her pleasant voice, "Good to see you again, Stygrid. It's been a long time since our Academy days, has it not?"

And now I outrank you: nice opening shot, right across the bow, Margot, Metellus thought appreciatively.

Armenhaut murmured something, his Douloi mask just hard enough to permit them to see that there was no friendship here.

But she'd already turned to KepSingh, and this time she held out her hand. "Captain KepSingh," she said cordially. "We've never met, but Admiral Horne has a great deal to say in your praise."

KepSingh's round face relaxed in a brief smile. "We were ensigns together in the Eighth Shiidran Expedition."

"The first use of the Ogres," Ng said. Metellus noticed a slight change in Armenhaut's expression. The Barcan battle androids came perilously close to infringing the Ban, something not likely to sit well with an old-family High Douloi like Armenhaut.

"We heard some tales about that action," Ng continued. "We even lived through some of them in the sims."

KepSingh laughed softly. "He did threaten to do that."

Now would be the time for Ng to offer them some refreshment. She hesitated, flickered the briefest glance at Armenhaut's white uniform, and said cordially, "You'll find all of our reconnaissance data in your banks."

Fire two—and two hits.

"Stygrid," she said, turning to Armenhaut, "you requested the interrogation tapes: have you had time to review them?"

"I have, Captain," Armenhaut said.

"Good." To the room at large: "We are at war, against Eusabian of Dol'jhar and a fleet of Rifters. Eusabian will be expecting an attempt to free Arthelion, that being what any Dol'jharian would do in our place. I suggest we use that as a subterfuge, but our true objective will be to capture one of the FTL communicators that Eusabian has equipped a number of his ships with. Questions?"

Armenhaut said, "Captain, have you obtained authorization from Ares?"

Broadside from Stygrid. Armenhaut was making it very plain that he respected only the uniform, and not the person inside it. Metellus saw KepSingh direct a hooded glance to his left. As first in, Armenhaut must have offered to share information with KepSingh—standard procedure. Metellus was certain that their old friend Stygrid had also used the opportunity to pour some poison into the older man's ears.

Older, Douloi, but not as high in rank, and every point he has he earned. I'll wager my ass KepSingh is Highdweller, and thus outside of Semion's birth-and-blind-obedience promotion fast track. And Stygrid doesn't even have the wit to see that KepSingh sees it all.

". . . sent the courier ship as soon as reconnaissance had verified the data we took during the interrogations," Margot was saying. "But we had to send the couriers to Ares' last known position and we have no way of knowing if that is still current. Best case, the couriers will not return for another nine days."

She paused as a mutter went around the room; several people looked down at their console insets. Metellus felt a light bloom behind his eyes. His hands were in his lap; without any visible movement he hit his boswell.

(Euan Macadee reports two more Rifters arriving in-system; could have taken them both—sloppy.)

Metellus looked up, saw Bea Doial's chin lift. They traded smiles, and then Bea looked across at Galt, the third captain of Metellus' squadron.

(And there is increased shuttle activity around the Fist of Dol'jhar—*all of it up from the planet. Tactical believes they may be making ready to depart.)*

Metellus flickered a glance at Margot. The Rifters captured at Treymontaigne had spoken of something called the Suneater, apparently a power source and communications center key to the

Dol'jharian successes. Margot and he had agreed that Eusabian's presence on Arthelion, instead of, as would seem strategically more sound, on this Suneater, was strong evidence that the Avatar was mired in Dol'jharian cultural patterns—making the tactics the two of them had developed to seize an FTL com even more likely to succeed. But if Eusabian left Arthelion, all bets were off.

Margot must have received the same news. She said, "We must act now, or lose this opportunity. Reconnaissance shows more Rifters moving in-system to defend—as Eusabian sees it—the Mandala. Worse, it appears that Eusabian may be preparing to depart, which will deprive us of our last chance to force battle on our terms."

"I must protest, Captain," Armenhaut said in his precise accents. "I can sympathize with the desire to win glory—and we all wish to see the Mandala freed—but the regulations were written for just such occasions as this. . . ." And he went on to outline the proper procedure for attack in undeclared war.

The implication was clear, and Metellus saw shiftings and downcast eyes around the table. Ng sat, smiling and to all appearances unmoved, throughout his lengthy speech.

At the end she reached casually and tapped her chair arm. Metellus saw Galt's face flushed; he and Ng were the only Polloi in the room, but Galt had never learned Margot's control.

Margot sat back, her fingers visible, laced peacefully on her console. "Any other questions?"

"Yes, Captain Ng," KepSingh said. "Have you a plan to put forward?"

"I do, Captain KepSingh," Margot replied, without looking at Armenhaut's rigid face at KepSingh's left.

He's using her name; this is merit talking to merit here. We've got him.

Ng tabbed a control and lit up the battle tank, showing the system, with Arthelion at the center. "The goal of this action is not to free the Mandala—it is to obtain a hyperwave. What I propose is this. Eusabian has only the one cruiser, the *Fist of Dol'jhar*, in orbit around the Mandala. We will pin it there by threat of Marine landings, using decoys disguised as lances, and Captain Hayashi's squadron will harass it. At the same time we'll send our frigates in to seek out the Rifter destroyers and frigates—the ships most likely to have the hyperwaves, according to the Treymontaigne interrogation—and try to isolate them for us. Our job will be to destroy all escort craft and disable the destroyers' drives. We'll then launch Marines for boarding and seizure of the hyperwave."

Just then a jacketed steward came in, bearing the magnificent silver coffee service that Margot's patron had given her when she was posted to her first ship. All eyes went to it; Ng lifted her fingers, and the steward set it at the side table, then took up a stance next to it. The aroma of real coffee filled the room, and Metellus felt his mouth water.

"Any questions?" Margot said.

Again Stygrid spoke, using the tonalities of voice-of-reason addressing lack-of-control. "Might I remind you, Captain, that there is a standard procedure for this kind of action: as you have posited it, we will be scattering our fleet. Also, using frigates against even Rifter destroyers is to invite heavy losses. We'd do better to strike at once, with minimum risk to our forces, and once we've cleaned the skies of the Rifters, find one of these putative FTL devices where it is most reasonable to expect it: in whatever Highdwelling now serves as the Node for Arthelion."

"And thus risk civilians, Stygrid?"

"They are not our civilians—"

"We don't know that. It would be typical of the Dol'jharians to use civilians as hostages. Remember also that the Dol'jharians are thoroughgoing Downsiders, and thus unlikely to put such a valuable device anywhere other than on the surface."

Oh, ho! Fire three, thought Metellus. *I wonder if Armenhaut knows that his Downsider patronage is gone for good.*

"I am not willing to attack a Highdwelling on the off chance we might find one. The risk must be to ourselves."

A murmur went around the room. Armenhaut's arm muscles jerked; Metellus wondered whom he was bozzing—and if it was defense or attack. *He really thought he was going to come in here and take control from Margot.*

"In any case," Armenhaut went on, "the discussion is hypothetical. Without authorization from Ares, you cannot order us into attack."

"You'll find the Standing Orders in your comp," Ng said, nodding to the steward. "If you'd care to refresh your memory, please tab down to section 10, paragraph 19."

She paused, and again a subdued murmur went around. Meanwhile, the steward came forward and placed a china cup at Margot's elbow, and expertly poured out a stream of gently steaming brown liquid. The aroma of real coffee strengthened in the room. *Concession?* Metellus wondered. Much as he wanted coffee, he wondered if Stygrid would read the sudden offer of refreshment as an attempt to placate.

But then Margot said, "Thank you."

And the steward went right back to the table and took up his stance again.

Metellus fought fiercely against a bubble of laughter inside. He heard a muted gasp from Doial, but he refused to look at her.

Margot went on calmly, "Pursuant to section 10, paragraph 19 and following, of the Standing Orders (Wartime, undeclared), I hereby declare the ships assembled here a Provisional Fleet and assume its command." She paused to take a delicate sip of coffee.

And a broadside from Broadside; he's vapor. Metellus bit his tongue inside his dry mouth and sat back to appreciate Margot's unspoken but lethally effective reminder of whose ship they were gathered on—and who really had the power here.

KepSingh suddenly grinned and folded his arms. "It's good, Ng," he said. "Good."

No one asked him to elucidate. Armenhaut's neck turned brick-red.

Margot said, with her sweetest smile, "Would anyone care for some coffee while we discuss the details?"

TWENTY-EIGHT

✳

FIVESPACE: RIFTHAVEN TO DESRIEN

Mandros Nukiel stared moodily into the depths of the mug in his hands, grateful for the warmth its gold-green contents radiated into his fingers. He raised it to his lips and sipped; the tangy, sour spiced tea pricked his tongue as he swallowed. Around him his brightly lit cabin was silent except for a faint susurration from the tianqi. They were simulating the warmth of high summer on Sync Ferenzi, balmy breezes carrying the scent of oranges, but he was still cold.

It was an iciness of the mind, not the body. Soon they would emerge over Desrien to face—what? Nukiel set the tea down on the table next to his chair. He had never felt more alone.

And it wasn't just Desrien. The interception of the Rifter ship with the Aerenarch aboard had plunged Nukiel into the midst of high politics, with no precedents to guide him. Had the Aerenarch indeed, as the Rifters insisted, given them leave to loot the palace? How had the Aerenarch escaped Arthelion in the first place? And then there was the Lusor affair, rearing its head again. It didn't help that the two Douloi had refused noetic questioning, as was their right.

Odd, though, that the younger Omilov had been so unforth-coming. He was Navy, and so Nukiel could have ordered him to talk. But it was better to leave that to the Ares command; he had no desire to get tangled up in the maelstrom of intrigue that would swallow up the Aerenarch and his companions once they reached the station.

In the meantime, he had the not-very-believable stories from the Rifters, who couldn't, of course, refuse noesis—except the one from Timberwell, still technically a citizen. But you had to know what questions to ask, and their answers only revealed what they believed to be true, not the truth itself. Whatever *that* was. Nukiel groaned.

He rubbed gently at the com button set in the arm of the chair, suddenly aware of the focus of forces it represented. A slightly stronger pressure on the tab, a few words, and he could loose more firepower than all the armies in all the wars of Lost Earth. So why did he feel so helpless?

The annunciator chimed, rescuing him from his thoughts.

"Enter."

The hatch slid open to reveal the slim form of Commander Efriq.

"Come in, Leontois," said Nukiel, signaling the informal na-ture of their meeting before the other man could salute. "Can I get you anything?" He waved toward the chair facing his.

Efriq seated himself. His nose above the debonair mustache wrinkled and he pulled his collar a little looser. "You're drink-ing that vile tea of yours, with the heat up like this?" He fanned a hand near his face. "Nothing for me, thanks." Then, looking more closely at Nukiel, "You catching a chill?"

Nukiel chuckled, a humorless sound. "You might say that."

"Ah." Efriq looked around the cabin for a moment. The light-ing sparked highlights from his glossy, close-slicked black hair. "The magisters'll do that to one."

There was silence for a time, the companionable quiet of two friends who feel no particular pressure to speak.

"You've been to Desrien, haven't you?" Nukiel said finally.

"Low orbit," replied Efriq, "as close as'll do for a lifetime, for this one." He shrugged. 'Not much to tell, really. I was an ensign on the *Thunderous* when it was assigned to map

Desrien." He sighed. "The government never gives up, does it? Every thirty years or so, like a stable orbit." He waved a hand dismissively. "Well, that's as it is. They fitted that old frigate with every kind of sensor you can imagine. I was on the bridge when the captain hailed Desrien Node and the machinery patched him through to somewhere on the surface."

"He asked permission?"

"After what had happened in '99, he didn't dare otherwise."

"And what did they say?"

"They just laughed. Not jeeringly, no arrogance, just—well, rather bemused, like they couldn't understand why we couldn't get it through our heads that it just wouldn't work." Efriq shook his head. "They told us to go ahead, but not to attempt to land." His brows went up. "Not that anyone wanted to."

"What happened?"

"Nothing, at first. Captain Enneal put us in a low polar orbit that took us over the entire surface. Everything ran smooth as woven monothread."

He fell silent again. Nukiel took another sip of tea. "And then?"

"And then SigInt tabbed in the command for the discriminators to go to work on the data. Everyone was watching the screen for the first coordinates to come up. Next thing we knew, the lights just flickered a bit and SigInt's console started squealing like a wattle with its tail caught in a hatch. The computer had crashed."

He shook his head again. "We kept trying. Got the computer back up—next time it crashed, the bit-rot somehow spread into Environmental. Air started to smell like old socks."

Efriq got up and walked over to the shelf displaying Nukiel's awards. He laid an index finger gently against one plaque, and continued without turning around. "Captain didn't give up then, either. We ended up limping home on one engine, with gravitors that couldn't maintain a constant gee-force from one section to another, and worst of all, the galley refrigerators broke down and the food synthesizers would only deliver stale beer and Pnahian jiggle-cheese."

Nukiel choked on a swallow of tea and his sinuses stung. Gasping, he laughed out loud.

"Pnahian *cheese*? That's the stuff that—"

Efriq turned around and nodded, his upper lip lengthening in prim disapproval. "Smells like a corpse's armpit."

"Well, that, but the chatzing stuff *moved*, constantly, right on their plates, the one time I saw it."

"It moves even more when you try to swallow it," Efriq said with morose humor. "It being all we had, we did try. Now I know why no one but a Pnahi can stomach it."

"But I was told they can't get enough of it."

"Which is why they are about as popular in small, enclosed spaces—like a ship—as a case of Medlybbi Fungusdrool." Efriq walked back to his chair. "But we got off easy, compared to some."

Nukiel nodded, the urge to laugh dissolving like the steam from his tea. The expedition of '99 had simply vanished.

Efriq reseated himself and leaned forward. "Mandros, why *did* you order us to Desrien?"

Nukiel carefully replaced the mug on the table. "I was summoned, I believe—it has something to do with the Aerenarch, and the others—"

The com chimed softly.

"Nukiel here."

"Captain, emergence at Desrien, three minutes."

"Thank you, Mr. Pele. Have Communications patch the Node relay through to my cabin."

He tabbed the communicator off.

"We'll soon know for sure. I want you here for this, Efriq—if I've blown up my career, I'd like at least one person to understand what happened."

Efriq nodded and settled back in his chair. There was nothing more to say, until the Magisterium spoke.

DESRIEN

As a fitful summer breeze tossed the branches of the trees shading the cloister garden of New Glastonbury, a stray sunbeam struck through the half-open window of Eloatri's study, refracted by the beveled glass into a rainbow segment dancing on the polished wood of her reading desk. A portion of her mind noted the quiet clicking outside the window that marked the progress of the gardener with her shears, ministering to the gardens with the severe love of her calling. Then the chuckling mimicry of a mockingbird drew Eloatri fully out of her book—*tick-tack-tick, too-wit, too-wit, birdie, birdie, birdie*—followed by a snatch of amazingly accurate bell sound that made her laugh.

She put the book down and stretched, inhaling deeply of the scented morning air, cool yet heady with orange and jasmine, jumari, and hints of rosemary and less familiar scents from the knot garden outside her window. The the bells of Glastonbury clamored in reality, striking eleven times.

One hour before Sext, she thought. Unbidden, a bit of pedantry from the book bubbled up: *Sext is the hour of Peter's vision at Joppa, in which the universal mission of the church was revealed* . . .

Eloatri sighed. As helpful as the books and chips were, it was the routine of the Daily Offices that was doing the most to settle her into her responsibilities in this, regrettably, still somewhat alien faith. She tugged at her clerical collar, then, suddenly aware of the motion, dropped her hand into her lap and swiveled about to look out the window.

What was the name of that ancient bishop in Rome, that her clerk had told her about? Peregrinus, Pellerini? *Selected bishop by a pigeon landing on his head when he wandered into a church out of curiosity.* She knew what he must have felt like; and wondered briefly what kind of bishop he turned out to be.

Her mouth quirked. Her clerk Tuaan had a sly sense of humor sometimes, but without him she'd be lost.

As if in response to her thoughts, the communicator on her desk chirped for attention.

"Yes?"

"A battlecruiser has emerged and taken position at the Node," came Tuaan's voice. "They're not entirely clear on why they're here, but I think they were Summoned."

Eloatri sat up, a shock of anticipation coursing through her. Was this what she was waiting for?

"I'll be right there."

When she reached the holo room, Tuaan was waiting for her, his face alight with humor and curiosity. Without a word he tabbed the holo alive and stepped back out of its field of view.

The image wavered into solidity, revealing a tall, lean, dark-complected naval officer with a short, square, salt-and-pepper beard. He stood stiffly, not quite at attention; she could see little of the room around him, but judged it must be his cabin. Certainly it wasn't the bridge.

His hard eyes suddenly focused on her, then widened. He hesitated. *He recognizes me!* she thought in amazement. She didn't recognize him—he matched none of the dream images that had made her nights so restless since she left the vihara. *Perhaps he* was *Summoned.*

"This is Captain Mandros Nukiel, of His Majesty's battlecruiser *Mbwa Kali*, commanding," he said finally.

"Welcome to Desrien orbit, Captain," she replied. "I am Eloatri, by the Hand of Telos High Phanist of Desrien."

The captain's heavy eyebrows converged on the bridge of his nose as his forehead wrinkled in perplexity and doubt.

"Tomiko was on Arthelion," she said, hazarding a somewhat oracular statement in the hopes of eliciting some confirmation of the rumors that had reached Desrien. Despite her visions, and those of others on the planet, there was still no hard news of the convulsion that was sweeping through the Thousand Suns.

Then, as she saw the statement strike home with all the force she could have wished, she raised her hand, displaying the weal burned into it by the Digrammaton.

Captain Nukiel sighed, an unwilling but entirely human reaction. "Then you *did* summon me."

"I believe you were Summoned," she said carefully. Seeing the captain's confusion, she continued, "But we are not talking about a link on the planetary DataNet." She chuckled. "You and I have some things in common, Captain. We are both under orders—but yours are, usually, far clearer."

A hint of impatience showed in Nukiel's face. "Forgive me, Numen," he said, using the formal term of address that belongs only to the High Phanist, "but I have hazarded my career in the midst of war to come in response to your summons. I request you do not toy with me."

War! Despite her visions, the visitation of Tomiko, and everything else, the bald confirmation of her forebodings rang like a tocsin in her mind.

"Forgive *me*, Captain," she replied. "I can only tell you this: that my mind has been much troubled of late by visions of a young man, red-haired, with the pale skin of an atavism, who may be wearing an emerald ring. There is also the matter of a small silver sphere, which may be related to him."

The captain looked at her for a moment, his indecision plain. There was a murmur from off-screen that she couldn't distinguish, and then Nukiel's face cleared.

"I see what you mean about your orders," he said. "I think I know what you are referring to . . ."

With growing amazement, Eloatri listened to the captain's story, and as she did the frisson of the numinous settled deeply into her bones.

Truly, she thought, *we stand at the hinge of Time.*

Eloatri pushed open the tall door at the west end of the cathedral and walked down the long aisle through the nave. The vast interior of the church glowed with light, prismatic splendor striking through the multitude of stained-glass windows that pierced the heavy walls, transforming them into an impossibly light tracery of stone.

Eloatri smiled. Something in her responded strongly to ancient Christian architecture—it was perhaps the facet of this faith that most helped reconcile her to her new life. *Like walking through the mind of Telos, all light and space and structured beauty . . .*

There were others in the cathedral, of course—it was never empty—but they all moved in their own orbits, dwarfed by the immense space, intent on their own communion with Telos and the triune holiness of an ancient faith. There was, she was beginning to see, a rhythm to this life, a dance-like structure, wherein the faithful moved at times in solitude, and then were drawn together in the solemn measures of the Mass and other rituals, and then apart again, but never really separate.

But now she herself desired solitude, to meditate upon the words of Captain Nukiel, now waiting impatiently in orbit above Desrien. And on what her advisers had told her. The xenologist had been especially insistent. *That ship is almost certainly their hive now. Without it, they very likely will not survive Desrien.*

She slipped into the sanctuary and genuflected deeply before the altar. She stood quietly a moment, looking up at the carven agony of the crucifix. She still found it deeply disturbing, almost repulsive.

You did not think you drank this for yourself? The words of Tomiko in the vision came back to her, almost a rebuke, and she forced herself to look at the man on the cross as others might see him—those others, for instance, who waited in orbit, each with their own pain to bear, past and future. Even though, as High Phanist, she was the defender of all the faiths of Desrien, this one had been chosen for her to live, now, but not for her alone.

The image's eyes were calm beneath the crown of thorns. *He is all of us, as a thousand years of peace dissolve in agony.* And the words of an ancient warrior of Lost Earth resounded in her inner ear: *It is humanity, hanging on a cross of iron.* Then, looking around for a moment longer, she settled into the lotus position and breathed out slowly.

Clearing her mind, she entered into her own communion.

❈   ❈   ❈

Some time later, Nukiel stared at the holo of the High Phanist, almost unable to believe what he had heard. "You want me to what?"

Eloatri sighed. "Put them on their ship—all of them, including the Aerenarch and the other two Douloi, and the Eya'a—and send them to me."

Nukiel looked over at Efriq, out of view of the High Phanist. Efriq shrugged and spread his hands.

"I'm sorry, Numen," Nukiel said finally. "That would be an abrogation of my oath and my responsibilities. You are welcome to interrogate them here, but I cannot release them."

"I don't wish to *interrogate* them, Captain," she replied, a hint of irritation creeping into her voice, bringing up the image, from his vision, of her head crowned in a flaring corona as Ferenzi disintegrated around him. "In fact, it is not for my benefit at all that I make this request, although I must admit to more than a little curiosity about their adventures, after what you have told me."

She paused, considering. Then her face hardened into a greater severity as she apparently saw that Nukiel would not yield.

"Captain, I assume you have a console there in your cabin."

Nukiel blinked, taken off guard by the sudden changed in direction. "Of course."

"Good. I hereby invoke the Gabrieline Protocol and command you to do as I have requested. You will find the protocol under code Aleph-Null in Fleet Standing Orders."

Nukiel snorted, suddenly convinced he was dealing with a madwoman. "There is no code Aleph-Null in the Standing Orders, and no such protocol." He heard Efriq tapping at the console as he glared at the gray-haired woman in the holo, wondering if he would be allowed to take the *Mbwa Kali* out of orbit after defying her. Efriq's story, funny in the telling, was now assuming a different, altogether unfunny dimension.

There was a sudden inhalation of disbelief from his first officer and Nukiel wheeled about to face him. Efriq looked up at him, no trace of his customary insouciance remaining in his expression. Without a word, he swiveled the data console around to face Nukiel. There, glowing under the Sun and Phoenix, was a protocol he'd never seen before.

He looked at Efriq. "It's authentic," said the first officer. "Countersign matches."

Nukiel read quickly—the Gabrieline Protocol was short and succinct—and then turned back to the High Phanist. She watched him calmly, a hint of sympathy in her expression.

"It seems I have no choice," he said.

Then, suddenly, Efriq spoke in the tones of a quotation, although Nukiel had never heard the words before: "This has been willed where is willed must be."

To his utter astonishment, the High Phanist laughed in delight. Nukiel glanced over at Efriq, whose demeanor was expressive of rueful amusement as he stepped forward into the view of the holo imager.

"You have a classicist on board, I see," Eloatri laughed. "Well said, ah"—she peered more closely at Efriq—"Commander. But some would say that applies to the Mandala, as well as Desrien. Certainly I make no claims to omnipotence."

"You might as well," Nukiel said grumpily, motioning at the console, "for all the choice that leaves us."

"No choice, but I do not expect you to leave your ass swinging past the radiants."

Nukiel choked and Efriq smiled as Eloatri laughed again. "I'm sorry, Captain," she said. "But you need to know we're not all folded hands and stained glass down here. My father was a career Navy man—chief petty officer on the *Sword of Asoka*. So I take your responsibilities seriously. You may assign two Marines to accompany them as guards, and to take whatever other precautions you deem necessary." Her face sobered. "But mark this well: no one else of your crew is to leave the ship."

Again the image of the Goddess amidst the destruction of Sync Ferenzi possessed his mind. "But I thought . . . I was summoned."

And then the woman's face, formerly soft and almost grandmotherly, settled into an expression of almost inhuman pity. Nukiel couldn't say why, but he was suddenly terrified—and as she spoke, the reality of Desrien reached out and grasped him in a grip that he knew would never be relaxed.

"I'm sorry, Captain, but the Goddess has given us no message for you. Your time is not yet come."

And the image dwindled away like a flame and vanished.

❊   ❊   ❊

Marine Solarch (First Class) Artorus Vahn stood at his post against the wall, thinking about the circumstances that had made him probably the only person alive to have served as an honor guard for all three Krysarchs.

The last living Krysarch sat in front of him now, eating dinner with the captain and Commander Efriq. Vahn's post right now was no accident: Nukiel had obviously done some excavating in the personnel records, and found out that Vahn had been stationed on Talgarth before being shifted to duty on the *Mbwa Kali*.

It had been no accident, either, when he'd been detailed to serve at Talgarth, a posting that had seemed a sinecure until he discovered that he was not meant to be a guard, but a spy. His request for transfer had been granted a year ago. The accident was in his being put on this ship at all.

Laughter interrupted his thoughts. The Krysarch Brandon—now Aerenarch—dropped his napkin back in his lap and reached to move some of the silver about on the table as he illustrated his story.

"So then the Kug jumped the Draco at this intersection, and while they enthusiastically tried to quarry each other's innards, we fell into an access hatch here—and into the waiting arms of a gang of feud-bent Yim, who were hoping we'd be Draco . . ."

The Aerenarch was describing his run through Rifthaven before he and the Rifters lifted off in the Columbiad. He made it vivid, and funny, and Nukiel and Efriq seemed to be enjoying it. The tone of hilarity also, Vahn noted, appeared to inspire a joking answer to the occasional direct question from captain or commander. There was certainly nothing overtly evasive in the Aerenarch's manner, and he readily described in detail certain things they asked for.

"My younger brother is the smartest of us," Krysarch Galen ban-Arkad had said once. He'd added thoughtfully, "I hope he discovers it before anyone else does."

The *anyone else* had to refer to Semion, then Aerenarch, the one who had posted Vahn to Talgarth with orders to report every conversation he overheard. *For security reasons*, he'd been told. *The ban-Arkad's mind is always on music and he wouldn't know if an assassin or a spy was among the loyal.* It had taken almost half a year before Vahn could see past the distorted lens of the training he'd received on Narbon, to appreciate Galen's freedom of thought and speech not as weakness but as something quite different. But he also had realized that the only people permitted around Galen for any length of time were Semion's spies—and that the older brother was the only inimical thing in Galen's life.

Though that turned out not to be true, Vahn thought, as the men before him refilled their glasses and toasted the Panarch yet again before drinking. The news from the *Grozniy* ate at him sometimes, at night: could he have saved Galen if he hadn't transferred away from Talgarth?

" . . . so these Rifters have no allies, as far as you are aware, Your Highness?" Commander Efriq asked after a pause. The dapper man's finicky manner hid a very acute mind.

"Their allies were killed when one of Eusabian's Rifters found their base," the Aerenarch answered. "I don't suppose you've ever heard of Hreem the Faithless?"

The captain shook his head, and Commander Efriq murmured, "Would we find the name on the bonus chips?"

"Safe bet," the Aerenarch replied.

"Judging from the vids the *Grozniy* captured at Treymontaigne," Nukiel said, "it appears these Rifters Dol'jhar has armed are embarking on a sacking spree that Eusabian has done little to control."

"That's what rumor said on Rifthaven," the Aerenarch agreed. "No controls at all."

"He probably encourages it," Efriq put in. "Makes sense: while his allies prey on hapless planets, or each other, he can consolidate his position."

Nukiel nodded, setting his wineglass down and steepling his fingers. "Your Highness, do you know what Captain Vi'ya planned to do once the *Telvarna* was safely away from Rifthaven?"

"That was under discussion right before Karroo sent half the ships in orbit after us," the Aerenarch said, smiling. "I believe her intention was to fall back to a second base and hide out until things got resolved one way or the other—or supplies gave out."

Efriq said mildly, "Did those plans include you and the Omilovs, Your Highness?"

Vahn wondered if the Aerenarch perceived how carefully the question was worded. He didn't seem unduly worried as he drained his third glass of wine and reached for the decanter.

They had yet to establish whether the Aerenarch was with these Rifters by accident—or by design.

"Perforce," Brandon said presently. He grinned over the cut crystal in his fingers. "One of the other things they discovered while on Rifthaven was that the Dol'jharian taste for thoroughness in revenge had inspired Eusabian to put a price on my head worth a few dozen planets. I get the impression that some of Vi'ya's crew wavered between the dreams of trying to collect and the reality of how long they'd live under Dol'jharian ministrations if they did try to turn me in. Right before your ruptor finished off their drive, we had just established that Vi'ya was disinclined to put us down anywhere—thought we'd be easy targets."

Which answers the superficial question and sidesteps the real one, Vahn thought appreciatively.

He'd been born on Arthelion—both parents had been Marines—and he'd grown up absorbing the lacework of protocol that dictated life there. The problem here was a potentially messy one: there was not only the matter of civilian hierarchy, but military vs. civilian, augmented by the Aerenarch's sudden departure from military life ten years before. *If he held even nominal rank, Nukiel could order him to talk and be protected by regs.*

"True," Nukiel said, nodding soberly. "And she'd be afraid that you'd lead the Dol'jharians right back to her and her crew."

"Willingly or not," Brandon said, again putting a spin on the direction of the questions. "Sebastian would not live long under one of their torture machines again, despite their best efforts."

"So the medics tell us, Your Highness," Efriq said softly. "One thing I feel safe in promising: as soon as we reach Ares he'll get the reconstructive care he requires."

A glance went between captain and commander, no more than a flicker. Brandon was watching the play of light on the liquid in his glass, his face with its myriad healing bruises hard to read.

"But I'm afraid our arrival at Ares has been delayed," Nukiel said, sitting back in his chair. "We are presently in orbit about Desrien."

"Ah. Desrien," the Aerenarch said, looking up. "You have business here first?"

Vahn realized that this was the first time *he* had asked a question. *He does know. He won't ask anything that might require Nukiel to define his status first—as citizen or prisoner. What is he trying to protect?*

"We do," Nukiel replied, and then smiled slightly. "Or to be more correct, you do. The whole matter is still mysterious to me, but the High Phanist was quite clear in her orders—"

The Aerenarch cocked an eyebrow and Nukiel paused.

"'Tomiko was on Arthelion' was what the Numen said to me," the captain interjected. "She now has the Digrammaton."

The Aeranarch blinked, the humor vanishing from his expression, to be quickly replace by the same bland mask that Vahn had seen Galen assume whenever discussion of Semion arose.

"In any case," continued Nukiel, "you, the Omilovs, the Eya'a, and the Rifters—she didn't mention the big cat, who, by the way, seems to have been adopted by the junior officers—are to be sent down, in the Columbiad."

Vahn saw the skin around the Aerenarch's eyes tighten very slightly—a subtle sign that he wasn't sure either the captain or the commander noted, or understood if they did. It momentarily increased Brandon's resemblance to his eldest brother.

He's not pleased, not pleased at all. Vahn could hardly blame him. No royal had set foot on Desrien for nearly 150 years; not since Burgess III at the end of his long reign. He had abdicated in favor of his daughter, taken the robe of an Oblate, and vanished forever among the shrines of Desrien. No Arkad was likely to be comfortable with a power that didn't follow the equations of authority that Jaspar had established a millennium before.

"Have you told the Rifters?" the Aerenarch asked after a moment.

"I have not," Nukiel said. "My interview with Eloatri—the new High Phanist—was not long before we gathered here." He looked at Efriq again, who looked back with dry humor. "It appears you have been more successful at communicating with them than we have, Your Highness. Would you like to be the one to tell them?"

"I will," the Aerenarch said slowly. "I wanted to check on Ivard anyway. Unless he's housed elsewhere?"

"He's with the others of the crew. Insisted on it most strenuously, and the medics felt it was best to consider his wishes." He glanced again at Efriq. "I'm afraid they can do little for him. Perhaps on Ares—" He let the statement die unfinished.

The Aerenarch nodded. "When do we shuttle down to the planet?"

"At oh eight hundred."

And I'll be with them, Vahn thought, with no particular pleasure. What he'd heard about Desrien did not appeal to him at all.

"Thank you." The Aerenarch rose. "Perhaps I'd better do it now," he said. "So we can all get what sleep we can before the ordeal." His tone made a joke of the word "ordeal," which deflected attention—at least superficially—from the fact that he, and not the captain, had brought the interview to a close.

The captain and commander also rose, and after they exchanged politenesses, the Aerenarch left the captain's quarters, Vahn falling in step smoothly just behind him.

The ability to jeeve, to be invisible until required, had been drilled into Vahn during the intensive training he'd received on Narbon. He knew how to judge to the centimeter just how far a person's breathing space extended. To go unnoticed and unremarked was the highest praise one could expect in Semion's personal service: if he spoke to you, it was invariably to your detriment. Galen had been the opposite—it had been disarming, and sometimes unnerving, the profound interest he took in everyone around him, rank notwithstanding.

As they walked toward the lift, Vahn wondered whether Brandon would emulate Semion and stand a meter away, ignoring him as if he were alone—or would inquire, as Galen had, into his family, likes and dislikes?

They reached the lift—the Aerenarch first, and he raised his own hand to tab it open, instead of waiting for Vahn to perform the service. One for the Galen column.

When they got into the lift, the Aeranarch turned to him, as if they'd known one another for years, and said, "Efriq told me you were on Talgarth."

"Yes, Your Highness," *He is like Galen, then.* And he braced for the personal questions.

But they didn't come. The Aerenarch smiled faintly and said, "You must have been in Semion's private army beforehand."

It was not a question, so Vahn did not have to answer. Still, he felt his heart give one sharp rap against his ribs, then start racing.

He hazarded one look at the oblique blue eyes, caught the end of an assessing glance, and then the Aerenarch said, "I hope you know the way to the brig. My two official tours of cruisers somehow neglected to include that."

Vahn swallowed. "Yes, Your Highness."

The lift opened, and Brandon indicated that Vahn should lead the way.

He gained a brief respite during the necessary protocol for obtaining clearance to enter the brig area.

No one ever called it a private army in my hearing, but that's what it was. Vahn had been selected out of his initial training for being bigger, stronger, and faster than the other recruits, with an added knack for arcane weapons. And the training on Narbon had been hard, with fierce competition for promotion. Such an atmosphere for someone with ability and ambition was exhilarating, and for a long time Vahn had reveled in the private slang, codes, and rituals only known to the special detachment of Marines on Narbon.

The were Marines, they used the same rank system, yet there came a time when Vahn had perceived the differences: this detachment was trained to owe their loyalty to the Aerenarch's person, not his place in the greater schema ... and all of the men—and they were only men—had come only from Tetrad Centrum planets. No Highdwellers, no one from the Fringes.

But calling what had amounted to a private army by "private army" wasn't as hard a hit as the assumption that he'd had to have been on Narbon first: that Semion controlled placement to Talgarth with his own men.

It was a truth that had taken Vahn time to figure out—and the knowledge had driven him to dump a promising career and side-step into the mainstream. At no time had he ever stated, or heard stated, the bald truth.

Until now.

For a moment he felt a strong urge to justify himself, to tell the Aerenarch why he was here—except one didn't speak while on duty unless spoken to.

And if he knows that much, wouldn't the conclusion be obvious? No one transfers from Narbon by accident.

The unsettling sensation that an entire conversation had taken place in that brief exchange distracted Vahn, so it was only long familiarity with procedure that carried him through.

He has me placed, but I don't know what he thinks about it—or what he'll do with the knowledge.

"Level 3, block 5," the watch officer said.

Vahn forced conjecture from his mind and indicated the way. He saw the Aerenarch glance back at the watch console. "Seems to be a full house," he commented. "Nukiel's been busy."

Again it was not a question, so no answer was required. Still, Vahn was glad when they reached their destination, and the Marines on guard saluted, then keyed the blast door open.

The Aerenarch paused to glance around swiftly. Vahn looked at it as if with new eyes: the main room was much like an ordinary rec room, slightly smaller in dimension, featuring much the same scattering of tables, library-and-game consoles, and two vid tanks. Two rooms led off either side.

The inmates looked up at their entrance, all eyes going from the Aerenarch to Vahn and then back. Vahn stood in the doorway at parade rest for just as long as it took for them to scan him, and then jeeved.

"It's the Arkad!" An amazingly pale, skinny boy jumped up from one of the game consoles.

"Come to gloat?" a small blond female asked, her face and voice edgy. She did not rise from her chair.

Neither did the heavy man by the vid tank, or the tall, dark-haired woman at another console. A tall man with Serapisti mourning braids down his back did not move, either, but his posture went still with the poise of an Ulanshu master, and his gaze was unblinking.

The lack of polite usage jarred at Vahn, but the Aerenarch did not react, even when the red-haired boy bounced near him, sniffing audibly, and reached a skinny freckled hand to pat his face and then his arm.

"Came as emissary," the Aerenarch said. "Message from the captain."

The small blonde looked up at the ceiling and said, "The food stinks. You people ought to hire Montrose here as galley-chief."

"Br-r-r-rp! Blat," the boy gibbered, waving his arms in fluttering movements. Then his face crimsoned, and he hunched his shoulders.

The Aerenarch gripped the boy by his thin shoulders. "I walk the halls in perfect freedom," he said, so softly that Vahn might not have heard it without the augmentation devices implanted in his mastoids. "Try not to worry," he added. Then he lifted his head and said to the room in general, "We aren't going to Ares, at least not right away. We've stopped at Desrien, and it seems that you and I, and the Omilovs, and even the Eya'a, will be making a landing."

Vahn felt a lightning jolt down his nervous system when without any warning two small white figures glided from one of the rooms, their twiggy feet scratching the deckplates.

Eya'a, Vahn thought. He'd seen them once, prowling the decks—as a newly discovered sentient species, not yet neatly categorized by the bureaucracy on Arthelion, the Standing Orders accorded them automatic ambassadorial rank, though no one had attempted to communicate with them. Or at least if they had, he hadn't seen it, or heard about the outcome. Obviously they preferred being here. *I wonder if they even know it's a brig?*

The Aerenarch was on the move, and Vahn had to pay attention. But he just walked around to look at each player's game set. Then he turned to the big man—Montrose.

"Anything I can try to get you?"

Montrose shrugged massive shoulders, his ugly face amused. "More music, perhaps?" He waved at the library console.

"Jaim?" The Aerenarch turned to the Serapisti.

The man looked down at his hands, tense and flat on the table. Vahn felt readiness for action tighten his back muscles; the man looked on the verge of flight, or fight. But he looked up, and then down again, at his empty hands, and merely shook his head.

"Ask 'em why we can't have Lokri with us," the little blonde put in. "And when are we out of here? They have nothing to charge *us* with."

'I'll be meeting you at oh eight hundred," the Aerenarch said. "I'll try to have some answers for you by then." He stepped back, then turned. "Vi'ya?"

Large, dense black eyes lifted to the Aerenarch. The rest of the woman's face was smooth and cold, unreadable as stone.

That one's the Dol'jharian, Vahn thought. He should have known; weren't they supposed to be bigger than most humans?

The woman was certainly tall, with a strong build. There was grace in the line of her neck, and in one visible hand; he realized that she, too, knew Ulanshu kinesics. *A lethal combination.*

"The captain tells me that Lucifur is well—he's adopted the junior officers for the duration," the Aerenarch said.

"I know." She turned back to her console.

The Aeranarch faced Vahn, smiling with faint inquiry. They left.

TWENTY-NINE

✳

DESRIEN ORBIT

"Beacon acquired," Lokri said, voice soft and eyes angry.

There was a brief twitter as the data leapt to Vi'ya's console; Montrose watched as she set up their course.

The rest of their flight down to Desrien was accomplished in silence. On a viewscreen assigned to the aft imager the massive battlecruiser dwindled as they fell toward the planet; the stars faded as the glowing limb of Desrien slowly filled the forward view.

The entire crew was on the bridge, even the Eya'a and the Omilovs. Jaim stood at the com console, working with Marim to repair the damage caused by Nukiel's ruptors. For him, at least, there was no other place to be: the captain of the *Mbwa Kali* had ordered the fiveskip of the *Telvarna* disabled and the engine room sealed shut.

Montrose looked slowly around the bridge as the atmosphere of the planet began to whisper over the ship's hull. Vi'ya sat still at her console, only the unusual precision of her movements giving any hint of how angry he knew she must be. Nearby the Eya'a stood, absolutely unmoving, facing her. They appeared entirely uninterested in the viewscreen, or anything else on the bridge.

Marim seemed uninterested in their destination; instead, her attention was divided between Jaim and Ivard, the latter seeming to inspire her with fascinated disgust.

Montrose sighed. It was unlikely that the boy would survive to return to the *Mbwa Kali*. The cruiser's medics, despite their best efforts, had been unable to arrest the deterioration of his immune system, or the increasing dementia that the Kelly ribbon had triggered. The visit of the Aerenarch the night before had been the occasion of Ivard's last coherent words. Now he sat on the deck, rocking back and forth and buzzing quietly to himself from time to time; his skin was almost translucent, greenish yellow and badly bruised, like that of a victim of a blood cancer, and his arms and head writhed ceaselessly in spasmodic movements.

At the fire-control console, sealed and dark, the Aerenarch sat looking down at the ring on his hand. Behind him and to each side the two Marines assigned to accompany them stood against the bulkhead, alert and silent.

Sebastian Omilov sat at Ivard's station, his eyes closed, his aspect tired. Beside him his son stood, radiating distrust.

Montrose looked up at the viewscreen, feeling curiously empty. It was as though the planet now filling the viewscreen had sucked some vital essence from him. Bleakly he realized that alone of all those on the bridge, he knew that there was no limit to the changes this planet could ring on the human spirit.

For Tenaya, his wife, had been a haji. He had seen the change in her, in the few short weeks they'd had between her return from her pilgrimage and her death. She had been different, vastly different: even more loving and vital, yet somehow distant, as if ever hearing some music that was inaudible to him. They had had too little time for him to fully come to terms with that: he would never know what life might have held for them after she was touched by the Dreamtime.

He blinked, fighting back memory. A once-familiar voice seemed to whisper in his ear: *But in the Dreamtime there is neither past nor future . . .*

The ship shuddered and the plasma jets whined to life as the *Telvarna* entered aerodynamic flight, arrowing across the face of Desrien toward their unknown goal.

✳   ✳   ✳

As the engines spun down into silence, Vi'ya cleared her board with a swipe of her hand, and without a word, stood up and stalked off the bridge toward the midship hatch. Osri moved hastily aside as she passed him. Silently the others followed, the two Marines shadowing the Aerenarch. He seemed to take no notice.

The ramp whined down and thumped onto the ground, and a brisk breeze whirled into the open lock, bringing with it the scent of grass and damp earth, overlaid with a heat smell from the hull of the *Telvarna*, now pinging softly as it cooled. No one moved for a moment; then Lokri snorted and pushed past Marim. He trotted down the ramp, the metal booming underfoot.

Outside, the sky was a rich blue-green between towering clouds, gray underneath and blinding white above in the light of the yellow-white sun. Before them a long meadow stretched up toward a hill crowned with a few twisted trees. As Osri watched, a racing cloud shadow sped across the slope toward them; a chill fell on him as the sun vanished.

A sudden peal of bells rang out from the other side of the ship. They followed the sound around the bow of the *Telvarna*.

He heard his father inhale sharply, as if in pain and wonder. "New Glastonbury," he said, staring at the vaulting lacework of gray-white stone. Osri swayed, suddenly dizzy: against the moving sky the twin spires of the edifice looming above seemed to topple toward them.

Sebastian's face was gray. "The god who died," he whispered. "Is that why we're here?"

Osri put out a hand to steady his father, who grasped his arm. Then, looking down at Osri's sleeve, he touched the embroidered emblem of the Phoenix there, ringed in flame. On his other side, Brandon suddenly appeared, concern in his eyes. Then the older man's face cleared.

"Ah, I lost more to Eusabian's henchman than I knew, if I've so thoroughly forgotten my mythology."

"What do you mean?"

Sebastian shook his head. "No matter." He moved off, seemingly lost in private thoughts. Osri looked at Brandon, who watched with narrowed eyes.

"Let's get this over with," Brandon murmured. Osri fell in step beside him, the Marines trailing after them.

Ahead, Marim kicked savagely at the low shrubs defining the gravel path they were following; Ivard honked and moved toward her, his arms writhing even more strangely than usual. She ignored him and he fell back behind her again.

As they approached, the cathedral gradually swallowed the sky, shouldering it aside until it defined the world for them. Osri reflected on little he knew of this faith. His only recollection was a dim wonder, in a history class long ago, that humanity should have remembered so long a brutal death by torture more than four thousand years past. *Torture? Was that why Father reacted so?*

He studied the cathedral as they walked into its shadow, puzzled at the exuberant architecture, the sense of turbulent joy embodied in the frenzied explosion of figures and carvings of trees and beasts and other, more abstract forms, trying to reconcile it all with that image of violent death. He touched the crumpled ribbon and the coin through the fabric of his pocket, remembering the warmth they had held, and the slippery feel of blood, when he had picked them up from where they'd fallen out of Ivard's grasp.

They had caught up with the others now. Vi'ya strode up to the massive doors, towering high above them, and grasped one handle. The muscles in her back bunched; the door swung out silently. She walked through the slowly widening opening, followed by the Eya'a, and then the others.

As the door swung open behind the Dol'jharian captain, Artorus Vahn placed his palm against it, gauging its heft, and was astonished as it pushed his hand away even as he leaned into it. He looked thoughtfully at the Dol'jharian woman, suddenly conscious of the weight of the neurojac hanging on his belt. He looked over at Roget; the other Marine formed a silent whistle with her lips and rolled her eyes.

They followed the Aerenarch inside and stopped, held, like all the rest of them, by the majesty of the cathedral's interior. All of them, that is, except the little blond Rifter. *Marim. Raised on an unchartered habitat. Gennated for plantar free-fall adhesion.*

Artorus shook his head as the information bubbled up unprompted. His brain still buzzed with the effects of the memory enhancers he'd taken to study the interrogation chips on the Rifters and the others.

Marim trotted forward a few steps, then turned back and looked at them exasperated, hands on her hips. Artorus realized that sheer size and height meant little to her.

Then he forgot her. The rest of them were Downsiders or Highdwellers and the Cathedral of New Glastonbury held them in thrall. The towering windows, explosions of color and complex form, transmuted the uneasy sky into restless beams of light sweeping through the interior. To either side tall columns marched toward the distant front of the cathedral, drawing the eye toward the elevated dais with the white-clad altar on it, and above and beyond it, the glorious mandala of colored glass that dominated the east wall. Faintly the sounds of voices came to them, raised in a chant of eerie beauty, too faint for words to be distinguished. There was a sweet, resiny smell lingering in the air—Vahn heard a tinkling in a minor key and looked over to see Jaim's nostrils flare as he gazed around.

Then something else caught his eye, a small figure in black walking toward them. Slowly it resolved into a short, stout woman with gray hair and a grandmotherly face, wearing a long, multibuttoned garment with a curious high white collar.

Somehow she seemed to gather the majesty of the cathedral around her as she neared them, assuming an aura of power quite at variance with the smiling openness of her face.

Vahn watched as the group drew together. His focus narrowed to three figures: Vi'ya, her stance radiating obduracy as she stared at the woman in black. Brandon vlith-Arkad: slim, elegant, his pleasant face utterly unreadable as he, too, gazed at the older woman. And the focus of all, the stranger in their midst.

"I am Eloatri," she said. "Welcome to Desrien."

Although her gaze passed quickly over Vahn, he felt the weight of her full attention on him, but without any sense of judgment or appraisal—she had simply seen him, in a way that made him, despite his training, feel like a blind man.

Finally her eyes came to rest, not on the Aerenarch, as protocol would demand, but on the skinny, red-haired boy, whose limbs and head even now moved in a ceaseless rhythm with a subtle triple beat. She smiled at Ivard and moved toward him;

and the Marine watched, shocked by the fierce, uncompromising love that suddenly shone from her worn features.

"Ivard il-Kavic," she said, in a voice so soft that Vahn triggered his augmentors to hear her more clearly, "be at peace here, and find your heart's desire, in the name of the Father, and of the Son, and of the Holy Spirit." As she spoke she reached out and traced a cross on the boy's forehead, lips, and over his heart.

For much the same reason that underlies their appreciation of the waltz and the Abbasiddhu triskel, the Kelly appear to find only Christianity, with its triune image of holiness, intelligible among human religions.

Vahn shook his head again as the memory drugs served up another dollop of data—he had no idea what a "triune image of holiness" referred to. But whatever it was, it seemed to reach the ugly, pale-skinned Rifter. Ivard's eyes focused on Eloatri and he smiled hesitantly; the movements of his arms and head quieted, but did not disappear. Nearby Montrose pursed his lips—and he glanced over at the Aerenarch, who returned his gaze with a lift of his eyebrows.

But moments later the boy's spasmodic movements resumed and his face settled back into vagueness. The High Phanist appeared untroubled: she caressed his cheek and then stepped aside as he loped forward in his bizarre fashion and wandered off toward the distant altar.

Eloatri's movement took her a step closer to the tall Dol'jharian woman and the tiny, white-furred beings. Vi'ya stared down at her, expressionless; the two Eya'a looked up at the older woman, their diamond-bright eyes gathering the soft light of the cathedral into lambent prisms.

The tableau held a moment, then a shrill, ear-stabbing trill erupted from the Eya'a. They threw their twiggy hands over their eyes and cocked their heads back at a jagged angle that made Vahn uncomfortable, exposing their throats to the High Phanist. She reached forward and touched each of them in turn beneath the chin with a single finger; then, as their heads came down, she bowed deeply to them.

"In the name of Telos, and the Fulfillment of Humankind to Come, and of the Magisterium, I welcome you, Second Mind of . . ." she trilled on a high note, "to the Thousand Suns. May you find what you seek." The Eya'a moved forward and ran their slender, attenuated fingers over the woman's wrists and forearms for a moment, making high chirping sounds.

Vahn saw a flicker of—disbelief? anger? surprise?—cross Vi'ya's face, but she said nothing.

Eloatri looked up at the Dol'jharian. For a long moment there was silence. "It is there, deny it as you will," Eloatri said at last. Vi'ya looked down at her, her face cold. "As the 'one-who-hears' you will not be able to avoid it."

Vi'ya turned on her heel and left the cathedral. Vahn jerked his head at Roget; she slipped out the door after the Dol'jharian, but Eloatri shook her head and called her back. "Do not disturb her. She merely returns to her vessel."

The Eya'a remained in place as Eloatri turned to the Aerenarch and executed a formal deference: a bow exquisitely judged, conveying recognition of his formal status with the reservation of judgment concerning its permanence. Brandon's lips curved into a wintry smile not reflected in his eyes and he returned the deference: the unique Royalty-to-Numen mode paid only to the High Phanist, but with the conditioned-on-proof modulation. Vahn suppressed a desire to laugh. That, too, was exquisitely judged—there'd been much speculation on the *Mbwa Kali* on how the Digrammaton could have gotten from Arthelion to Desrien.

Eloatri smiled and held up her right hand, displaying a white raised weal—now fully healed—burned into her palm that echoed the shape of the Digrammaton on her chest. "It was white-hot when I received it from Tomiko—and even now it is not entirely safe to wear."

The Aerenarch's face blanched; gone for a moment was the Douloi mask. Behind him Montrose looked up, startled, at the High Phanist.

Vahn felt his stomach griping with an empathetic response to the ugly weal seared into Eloatri's hand. But his mind was even more disturbed: only if she had received it at the moment of her predecessor's death on Arthelion, hundreds of light-years away, would the wound have had time to heal.

"Go to the north transept," Eloatri continued, addressing Brandon, her voice brooking no objection. "Await me there."

She turned to the others, who had drawn away slightly, and the Aerenarch, after a long, thoughtful gaze at her back, obeyed.

❋   ❋   ❋

The ramp of the *Telvarna* thudded open and the rich smells of Desrien crowded into the lock and shouted in Ivard's skull. The blue fire around his wrist pulsed in delight; images fountained from two small flames nearby, quicksilver brightness, multiple flashes that broke through the veil that hung between him and the world he had once known. The muttering pain slashing across his back hung red behind him, pushing him forward as the other, taller flames around him moved onward. Their anxiety and fear clawed at him, borne outward by the complex stew of chemicals they generated without a trace of control.

He tasted the clangor of metal. One of the flames spoke; this time the words broke through to Ivard.

"New Glastonbury."

Ivard didn't know what that meant, but the blue fire leapt higher, a warm pudding of satisfaction welling from it. Around him small flames flickered in a web of life and movement, slow and fast. Around the base of one of the tall flames—he'd exchanged life-stuff with that one—some of the tiny flames changed color, some flickered out. He danced a protest, but received no response.

Abruptly the veil cleared for a moment, revealing a tall building intricate beyond any he had ever seen. It tugged at him, rhythms in stone and glass drawing him forward. He responded with a dance of celebration and recognition. One of the others had shown him, had played this—no, there was no room on the *Telvarna*. The momentary confusion dropped the veil across his vision once more; he tasted comments from the others but did not understand, wandering forward in a blue-shot haze, following the flames as they resumed their progress.

Coolness wrapped him round as the light dimmed and changed, echoes pressed on him, a sweet scent clanged in his skull—where were the cymbals, then?

. . . love is stronger than death . . .

One had sung that.

And then there was a woman's face, gray-haired, kindly. Ivard tasted love, felt coolness, delicious, on forehead, lips, and chest. The blue fire leapt up, delighted, and withdrew a measure, and he returned to himself.

". . . find your heart's desire . . ." Memory echoed from a

moment just past. He smiled at the woman. Then the haze returned, blue and smothering, but Ivard fought it desperately. The woman caressed his cheek and stepped aside, and Ivard moved on, hating the worm-like movements of his body. He was glad Greywing couldn't see him.

His anger pushed back the veil that ate at the corners of his vision, leaving clear the vaulting space around him. The part of him consumed by the blue fire conjured up crowds of people around him; he could see—or was it smell? taste?—them moving in patterns of grace and courtesy, all centered on the white table far ahead. There was a glint of silver on it.

He moved forward. The air around him felt strange, as though past and present and future were all rolled up together in the subtle light from the colorful windows, under the vaulted ceiling so high above. A sudden swell of music filled the air; he looked around and saw, further toward the front of the building, a man sitting at a tall console of some sort raised well above the floor.

As he drew closer to the table the splendor of his surroundings reminded him of the palace and all the beautiful things they'd taken. They were going to be rich, until the nicks caught up with them. He saw Greywing's face again, and the little metal disc with the bird on it, that he'd lost. *Heart's desire* . . .

The music ceased, was replaced by a discordant series of tones. He looked back at where they had entered the building; there was no sign of the others.

He limped up the steps of the dais on which the white-and-gold-clad table stood. The cloth covering it was richly embroidered; on its surface were two tall candleholders, intricately worked in gold and silver.

Ivard blinked. In the back of his mind the blue fire muttered. There, in the center of the table, was a battered old silver goblet, looking entirely out of place. He reached out and touched it with one trembling finger, suddenly conscious of his unnaturally pale skin, the rusty blotches and scattering of reddish hairs.

"If you are thirsty, drink."

Ivard spun around and almost fell, pain shooting through the unhealed wound across his back. A few paces away, an old man stood, watching him.

"I wasn't going to steal it!" he blurted.

The man smiled gently. "I know. Drink, if you desire. That, none of your treasures could buy for you."

Ivard stared at the old man. He was sure he'd never seen him before, yet he felt he knew him. For that matter, why did he think him old? There were no lines on his face, his hair was dark and glossy, but he was very old, of that the boy was certain.

Then he realized: he *was* thirsty. He turned and grasped the cup. It was cool in his hand; inside, the clear water caught the light from the huge window at the end of the building, shimmering with mysterious color. The blue fire mounted in his head, but this time it did not swallow him, but rose parallel with his own thoughts. A rich scent welled from the cup, he tasted life, multitudes, and flames flickered at the corners of his vision, watching him, murmuring, approving.

He drank.

It tasted like the old woman's fingers had felt on his forehead, like the approval in Greywing's eyes when he got something right without prompting, like the gentle rumble of Markham's voice, joking and helping, like the genuine interest in the blue eyes of the Aerenarch ...

Ivard put the cup down, carefully, and turned to look straight into Greywing's eyes.

He opened his mouth, but no sound came out. She put out her arms and caught him in a fierce hug as he stumbled forward.

"Greywing, you were ... in the palace ..."

"Hush, Firehead." She pushed him out at arm's length, smiling; he suddenly noticed that, like the old man, now nowhere to be seen, she looked old, but still just as young as when he'd left her, under the palace, lying ... He pushed the memory away. It didn't fit here.

"I lost your coin," he said.

"No, it's here," she said, and then smiled her old special smile. "I'm proud of you, Ivard."

And somehow he understood: that in truth she stood a long way off, even as she was here, now, and when she spoke his name she meant all of him, as he had been, was, and would be. To the blue-fire part of him it was perfectly clear, for its memory reached far back in time; but for the part of him that was a young and tired human boy, it was too much, and darkness shot through the blue fire like veins of smoke, whirling him away from her smile into an echoing peace.

THIRTY

✳

Osri stayed close by his father, looking about him with increasing uneasiness. He watched the small woman talk to the others,
first Vi'ya, who promptly turned and stalked out. Osri watched,
envious—he wished he'd thought of it first. Last she addressed
Brandon, and Osri felt a bleak stab of humor at his automatic
reaction of outrage at the inversion of precedence.

"I wonder how long we'll be forced to stay here," he murmured behind his hand, conscious of how the stone overhead
made sounds carry.

His father did not reply, and Osri jerked around, irrationally
afraid. Sebastian was gazing off toward the altar, his gaze tense.
Osri turned to look, just in time to see Ivard, whose face was
upraised, stumble forward one step and crumple slowly to the
ground.

"Telos," he breathed. "What happened?"

"He was drinking, I believe," Omilov replied in a curiously
absent tone. "I only saw him from the back."

"Well, I would say that drinking or eating anything here
seems an invitation for drug-poisoning. How else could they in-
flict their ill-famed nightmares on people?"

Omilov did not answer. Osri saw that he hadn't even heard

instead he was watching one of their Marine escorts bend over Ivard. Annoyance burned in Osri, but he said nothing. A moment later a pair of dark-robed figures appeared from one of the shadowy corners and approached. The Marine and the monks held a short converse, at the end of which Ivard stirred.

Sebastian let out a sigh of relief as the boy sat up, his face turning upward toward the railing where the organ music came from.

Then Sebastian blinked. "What's that, son?"

"I *said*," Osri raised his voice slightly, "we'd be wise not to eat or drink anything here."

"We poison people, of course," an amused female voice came from behind them.

They both turned quickly. Osri felt his neck burn.

"We poison them so that they freeze into statues, which we put out in the gardens. Then we send back in their places clones made from carnivorous fungoids." The small, grandmotherly woman in the many-buttoned robe smiled, here eyes crinkling to slits of silent laughter. "It was a great story. I saw it on a serial chip when I was a girl."

Sebastian chuckled, and Osri felt the old rage again—just as he had as a boy when his father had found Brandon's and Galen's meaningless jokes so funny. "Why were we brought here?"

His voice sounded a little louder and ruder than he'd meant it to, but the woman merely raised her hands a little. "I do not know," she said. "It is for you to tell me."

Osri gave a sigh of annoyance.

Sebastian spoke quickly, as if to draw attention away: "I'm worried about young Ivard. If we don't get him to proper medical attention on Ares soon . . ."

The woman smiled. "I do not think that this diversion in your path will have harmed him any. We shall see."

Osri felt a stab of irony, which must have showed in his face, for the woman looked up at him in inquiry.

"We started out for Ares weeks ago," he said. "Every nightmare since has been a diversion not of our choosing. This is just another."

The woman smiled, but she looked past him at his father.

Sebastian shook his head. "If something about this place does that boy any good, then I will consider this diversion well worth the time it took."

It was a diplomatic reply, in a peacemaking tone of voice. The woman nodded to them both, then moved on toward the stairway to the organ loft.

Sebastian sighed again, then looked up at one of the huge wall murals. "Some of the Panarchy's finest artists have given of their best here," he murmured. "I don't want to miss this opportunity to examine their work."

Osri nodded, trying to swallow down his anger. He recognized this as another peacemaking gesture, one just for him. By giving them something rational and intellectually worthwhile to do, it acknowledged Osri's point. So even though Osri had little interest in artwork of any kind, much less religious, he followed along with his father and obediently looked at the paintings, mosaics, and statues along one wall.

And indeed, some of them began to absorb his attention. If nothing else, one had to admire the way the painters could use a few splotches of synthetic color to paint figures that seemed to live and breathe, to move in three dimensions. He could appreciate with his aesthetic sense the way light and dark were used to infuse the figures with power and majesty.

He moved, on, but his father lingered, looking intently at a painting of a dark forest, with a man in archaic costume confronted by some sort of beast. Osri moved back to his side and heard him speaking softly, reading an inscription on a small plaque below the canvas, but he couldn't catch the words.

"What's that, Father?" Osri asked.

His father shook his head again, as if something pained him but did not reply.

Osri walked on purposefully, determined to get something out of this imposed diversion, but some of the art defeated him utterly. He turned to make an observation, only to find that his father had vanished.

Osri craned his neck, trying to see into the alcoves along the wall. He looked around; strangely no one else was visible at all, not even the Marine guards. Then he turned and started back, but a flicker in the corner of his eye caused him to jerk around, wariness tightening his shoulders. The twinkling of stars in a broad field make him blink. Vertigo caught at him; for a moment, the painting he stood next to almost looked real.

But he laughed at himself, forcing the image to stay a painting, a panorama of a galaxy. Something made him look close at it, and he saw that in its foreground, tiny against the swirl of stars, was a small asteroidal habitat, a bubbloid, like Granny Chang's, lights glowing from viewports scattered over its craggy surface. Near it hung a decrepit ship painted in garish colors.

Rifters again, he thought in disgust. Then he bent lower.

Below, a small brass plate gleamed at the bottom of the picture's frame. "The stone rejected by the builders has become the chief cornerstone."

He snorted, only to find he couldn't pull his eyes away, and the Dreamtime took him.

❋   ❋   ❋

Roget didn't see the others leave, but suddenly she became aware that she was alone in the cathedral. Alarm burned through her; what had she been thinking about?

She ran toward the back of the cathedral, where the High Phanist had greeted them, then slowed as she caught sight of the two Douloi, the gnostor and his son, against the south wall. As she walked toward them, she heard a sound behind her, and turned to see the Serapisti Rifter approaching. Beyond, in the north transept, she caught sight of Vahn. Her heart eased its slamming.

The two Douloi did not notice her approach. The younger man put out his hand and touched his father's arm, whose face was drawn and haggard. She halted a short distance away, unwilling to intrude, but curiosity led her to trigger her enhancers.

"What have they done to you?" Osri asked.

The gnostor closed his eyes, then raised his hands to shade them. "It is what I have done," he murmured, his voice hoarse with repressed emotion. Then he dropped his hand, his face working into a semblance of a smile. "Or what I did not do." A tear jumped down the furrows of his face and splashed onto his tunic.

"I had a kind of dream," Osri said. "I knew it was a dream, but I could not break it until it was done with me."

"Tell me."

But Osri stopped as the tall Serapisti, Jaim, walked past. He paid no attention to Roget or the two Douloi.

"It was the usual jumble, like any dream," Osri said, looking over at the Rifter.

Then Roget's boswell burred in her inner ear. *(Roget! I've*

lost the Aerenarch!) The passionless tones of neural inductio
couldn't disguise Vahn's near panic. The others forgotten, Roge
whirled around and ran toward the north transept.

❊   ❊   ❊

Osri was startled by the sudden movement of the Marine, whom
he hadn't noticed standing nearby. He watched as she ran acros
the cathedral, then looked back at Jaim, who was watching he
too.

Unwanted, the dream image of the dead Reth Siverknif
echoed in Osri's thoughts. He wondered suddenly how often th
man must have relived the image of Reth's body in th
Sunflame engine room.

Jaim was looking for someone, Osri realized. His face wa
pensive, his eyes tired.

Seeing him as a human being for the first time, rather tha
merely as another Rifter enemy, Osri felt the impulse to sa
something.

But his father spoke first. "Whom do you seek?"

Jaim stopped, facing them. "The High Phanist," he replied. "
want permission to return to the *Telvarna* and they"— a nod i
the direction of the north transept—"won't let us go without it.

"We saw her last walking toward the organ loft," Omilov re
plied.

Jaim nodded and went on his way.

When he had disappeared from view, Osri said, "I though
the main thing that marked Rifters from our own culture wa
their insistence on living outside our laws—their insistence, i
you will, that virtues of loyalty and service are meaningless."

Omilov rubbed his thumbs along his upper eye sockets. "Yo
ought to know by now," he said finally, "that speaking for all o
them is a dangerous thing. But one generality I will allow:
think some of them are as capable of loyalty as anyone else
should they perceive something worthy of their loyalty."

Images from his dream echoed: *"They need leadership."* Osr
fingered the ribbon and coin in his pocket. *"They have re
sources."*

He stepped out, looking for Jaim. The tall Rifter stood di
rectly before the cathedral altar, his head back. He seemed to b
lost in contemplation of the steady flame that flickered on a re
candle in a golden lamp suspended from the ceiling.

"Lend me your arm, my boy," Omilov said tiredly. "Perhaps the Marines will allow us to return to the ship. I am afraid I am badly in need of rest."

✳   ✳   ✳

Jaim saw the flame the first moment they entered the sacred place, but he kept his distance.

For a time he stayed at one side of the great stone building, watching. He saw a small woman, whose commanding presence pointed her out as leader, enter. He watched the Eya'a respond to her as they never had to any other human, and he saw Ivard briefly come out of his Kelly fugue when the woman touched him in a ritual pattern. He watched Vi'ya react with challenge and then retreat; he watched the woman dismiss Brandon, like an erring child, to another portion of the building.

He saw Marim skip away, no doubt on the lookout for anything not nailed down that she could conveniently fit into her pouch. He watched Lokri, whose anger at the Panarchists for baring his past had not diminished, look about for an exit and leave.

He saw Montrose drawn to the music and heard his familiar style on the organ. And he watched Osri, who prowled around like something being stalked, while his father wore his diplomat face: neither trusted this place for a heartbeat.

Jaim sympathized; he did not, either. Like the supposed shadow side of the Path, the rituals were beautiful, but they were all essentially false.

He saw one of the Marines take up her station a short distance away. On impulse he walked over to her, noticing as he did the splashes of reddish light from the windows overhead. Once he turned his head and looked up—he had always liked vitrine art. The ruby lights were from patterns in the glass, and as he watched them, words flickered through his mind:

The Rouge Gate, whose aspect is actuality.

What was that? But the familiarity was gone.

He dismissed conjecture and approached the Marine. "I would like to return to the ship," he said.

She shook her head. "We'll keep you together, at least until I get orders not to."

"But Vi'ya went back."

"The High Phanist spoke for her," was the response.

The obvious course, then, was to get the High Phanist t speak for him. Yet he was reluctant to seek the woman out. H had no wish to argue truth and nontruth with a shaman; no mat ter what they said, he knew the truth was that Reth was gone There was no joining of spirits—despite the years of ritual, de spite the unswerving love they had had for one another . . .

He winced, trying to shake the images. If anyone should hav been able to bridge the Valley of Mystery, it was Reth. He ha never known anyone so serene, so strong with the Flame.

He looked down the length of the building toward the flicke in the lamp. Actuality: a flame existed here, but nothing There Here it burned you.

He saw Omilov and Osri closely examining the artwork an decided that this would be a good way to occupy his time.

Turning his back on the flame, he walked westward, lookin up and down at the displays, absorbing the sacred art of an un familiar branch of the Path. The triune imagery, the depiction of a human suffering a hideous death, seemed strange to him. A first he wondered if this might be a Dol'jharian religion, but ex cept for the one image of a man being tortured on a cruciform the other symbols evoked different responses.

Indeed, he noted that triune symbols were overlaid by th more familiar balance of fours: even the building itself was lai out in a rectangular form.

Looking up at the light slanting in the west windows, agai the words came to him: *The Phoenix Gate, whose aspect i irreversibility.*

Appropriate, he thought, smiling as he turned to walk east ward along the northern wall. Phoenix: the bird that was de stroyed in flame and then reborn. Another splendid fantasy. Jair shook his head. Irreversibility: she was gone, and there was n going back. *Except I shall send Hreem after, that I promise.* Th Ulanshu Path—that one also promised irreversibility. The flam of anger, that one burned steadily for vengeance. That one wa no fantasy.

He paused and looked down toward the altar. The strong ligh from above cast the east end in shadow; the flame was no mor than a tiny gleam. Anger burned brighter than spirit.

Flexing his hands, he walked on.

More art to look at, then he saw the Omilovs again. The ol man seemed sick, and Osri's eyes did not strike hatred as the always had. Had the Dreamtime gripped them with unsheathed talons?

All to little purpose—be at peace, he was inclined to tell them, but of course he did not. Except for Brandon, the nicks had never tried to look past the facade of Nick vs. Rifter. His opinion would mean less than nothing to them; he would not waste time or breath in offering it.

He did ask them where he'd find the High Phanist and they replied courteously enough, then he walked on. Nick manners— Douloi. Ivory—

The Ivory Gate, whose aspect is autonomy.

Now he had it: the Mandala. The nick art treasures had been kept in the Ivory Hall's antechamber, and Ivard had looked all this up. Jaim remembered the boy talking about it while doped up, just before they reached Dis.

Autonomy. He liked that.

Breathing in the scent of incense, he walked eastward toward the altar. The huge rose window at the east end gleamed with muted color. Its shape was the eternal circle, which corresponded with the last of the Panarchist four: *The Gate of Aleph-Null, whose aspect is transcendence.*

Beauty with no meaning, he thought, stopping directly before the altar. But then beauty was beauty—he could appreciate it for itself; it did not, in the final analysis, have to have meaning. "Transcendence" simply meant that one could look away from the bone and grit of everyday life for a short time, and contemplate grace and color and joy in form, but when the eye turned away, it was gone. As when the body died, the spirit was gone.

Gone.

The flame burned steadily. Gazing at it, Jaim felt the lure of the Dreamtime and willed it away. Exulting in his victory, he became aware of the sound of slippers whispering over stone.

Looking over his shoulder, he saw the High Phanist. When she raised her eyes to his, an expression of expectation, he spoke on impulse: "This is a nick religion—a Douloi religion."

She smiled. "When it began, it was for the lowly, the poor, and the outcasts."

Jaim shrugged, not wanting to hear a history.

The High Phanist said, "There is an enclave for the Serapisti at the other end of this continent."

Jaim shrugged again, glancing at her before turning back to his contemplation of the flame.

Her eyebrows had lifted a little. "Mourning braids?"

The question was oblique enough to make an answer possible. "The rituals bring someone closer in memory for a short time, and they are beautiful."

"You treasure beauty," she said, not quite a question.

He nodded, watching the steady tongue of fire. How still the air was that high! The flame rarely flickered.

"But now you have chosen the Path of the Warrior."

Surprise made him turn to face her at last. "If I have?"

She smiled, her whole face merry. "Bear with me, Ulanshu flame-seeker," she said. "I think you are the very person I was just hoping might exist . . ."

He crossed his arms.

She touched his wrist with one finger. "It is not a game. But I'm going to intrude, and I sense that privacy has been your armor. With your permission, then?" She gave him a short, antiquated bow, dignified, but her eyes were still merry.

"Go on."

"You have denied the spiritual Path, because access to someone's presence seems to have been denied you. This suggests to me that you have chosen the Warrior's Path because you've found a worthy leader. Yes?"

"Why?"

She gave a short sigh of relief, then turned and took a few steps, looking northward. Curious, he followed. In the north transept, shafts of light from high western windows illuminated a familiar profile: the Arkad.

"Where he is going next," the High Phanist said, "he will be alone among many dangers. He has to steer a course through these shoals, but I would find someone to guard his back while he sleeps."

The objections came to Jaim's mind first, all of them having to do with their relative positions. But he voiced nothing, because he saw in her face that she knew them as well, but saw past them. A moment passed, during which neither of them spoke, and then she nodded once, a short movement, suggesting covenant.

Solarch Vahn stretched his aching neck and exhaled slowly. The Aerenarch had stood a long time before the cathedral altar, then he'd moved to this side room, the "north transept" the Numen had called it, contemplating the statues in wall niches as if he were going to buy one.

Vahn followed for a time, checking his surroundings. He knew all the exits, so he fell back, giving the Aerenarch more space. After a time, bored, his mind still buzzing from the memory drugs, he looked back into the nave of the cathedral. No one was visible save Roget, watching the two Douloi, and the tall Rifter with the mourning braids.

He shrugged. His responsibility was the Aerenarch; the captain had made it plain that if only one person returned from Desrien, it must be Brandon vlith-Arkad. Roget would take care of the rest.

He turned back. Terror gripped him: the transept was empty. *A trick of the light.* He ran forward, but there was no sign of the last Arkad heir. He slapped his boswell.

(Roget! I've lost the Aerenarch!)

He heard her footsteps racing toward him, then, suddenly, Brandon vlith-Arkad was there, against the opposite wall, his face sweat-sheened and his eyes wide and shocked.

(Cancel that. It's the light in here.)

He felt rather than heard her sigh of disgust via boswell, but didn't take his eyes off the Aerenarch as he approached him, tightening his grip on his weapon. It wasn't the light; and more now than ever he didn't trust anything about Desrien. Nothing would take him from the Aerenarch's side, from now until lift-off.

He heard footsteps behind him and whirled around.

The Numen came directly toward him, the tall Serapisti Jaim right behind her. Vahn jeeved as the woman passed him and went right for the Aerenarch, who stood where he was, back to the wall, blinking rapidly. Vahn followed; neither the Aerenarch nor the High Phanist took any notice of him. Jaim glanced at him, his gaze somber, then focused intently on the Aerenarch.

"Highness," she said, her hand brushing her long robes as she bowed, "I crave a boon." It was said in a grand manner, but not at all disrespectfully.

The Aerenarch gestured for her to speak, a flourish which matched her tone, but his fingers were tense.

"For my own peace of mind," the High Phanist went on. "I feel I owe it to your esteemed father."

This time Brandon seemed to find speech. "What can I do?" The light voice was almost lost in the huge room.

"You can stay alive," the High Phanist said, still in that tone of slightly pompous humor. "And I propose to offer you this fine young man to see that you do."

Brandon's eyes went from Eloatri to Jaim, his expression uncomprehending.

Vahn felt a flash of annoyance; that was *his* job.

A moment later the High Phanist turned his way. "Your place is at the official functions"—she turned back to Brandon—"but there is a need for someone within your own walls."

The humor was gone now, and Vahn got the distinct impression that two conversations were going on here, one whose meaning was opaque to him.

The Aerenarch looked past the woman. "Jaim?" The question was directed at the Serapisti.

"My life," Jaim said, "for yours."

Brandon winced. He said in a hurried undertone, "But my life is—"

He did not finish. With unprecedented rudeness, the High Phanist cut in, still in that odd tone blending humor and formality: "You may not leave Desrien until I am assured that every precaution will be taken."

The Aerenarch's eyes narrowed. "Leave? Desrien?"

"You are free to go," the High Phanist said, smiling. "Whenever you wish. After I have my assurance."

The Aerenarch bowed, the sovereign granting the petitioner's boon. The irony in the gesture silenced Jaim and made Vahn hold his breath, but the High Phanist seemed pleased.

"Well, then," she said, "why don't you find your companions and see what they wish to do? Of course, you are all free to stay here as long as you desire."

The Aerenarch's eyes moved to Vahn's face, and the Solarch said woodenly, "Shall I summon Roget?"

THIRTY-ONE

ARTHELION SYSTEM FALCOMARE

On the viewscreen the *Barahyrn* vanished in a pulse of reddish light. Beyond, the *Lady of Taligar* hung unmoving, its angular form barely discernible against the stars—one of which, barely brighter than the rest, was Arthelion's primary.

"*Barahyrn* away," reported the first officer. "One hundred fifty seconds to skip."

Metellus Hayashi took a deep breath, savoring the air of excitement and satisfaction that pervaded the bridge of the *Falcomare*.

This was the kind of action every destroyer captain dreamed of, the violent, high-speed slash-and-parry that only these vessels could deliver. Not for him the ponderous, near invulnerability of a battlecruiser, bludgeoning its opponent into scrap with the ripping terror of a ruptor beam, against which the teslas offered no protection.

The thought momentarily sobered him. That was what they would face in the action that would commence in mere minutes. For the first time in twenty years, the Thousand Suns would see an engagement pitting three destroyers against the kind of ship they'd been designed to kill.

Only without our best weapon. They couldn't use their skip-missiles on the *Fist of Dol'jhar*, not so long as it hugged the planet. Would the Dol'jharian captain realize this?

"D'you think we're up against Juvaszt?" asked Orriega, his first officer, echoing the direction of his thoughts.

"Who knows?" Hayashi shrugged. "With their fondness for purges we might get lucky. I just hope whoever it is doesn't figure out what we're really up to."

"Not likely," replied Orriega, her tone a mixture of triumph and laughter. "He'll be too busy tracking down and vaporizing drones full of vatbeef."

Hayashi chuckled. That had been Margot's suggestion: to load the drones masquerading as lances with slabs of vatbeef, to simulate the right mix of organic and metallic debris when they were blown apart by the defenders. *"Just an old-fashioned Dol'jharian cookout,"* she'd laughed. But they only had enough meat for the first three waves of drones, one from each destroyer in turn. The *Barahyrn* was first; it would emerge over Arthelion moments after their attack on the *Fist* commenced, on the opposite side of the planet.

Orriega glanced at her console. "Fifteen seconds."

"Well," said Hayashi, raising his voice for the benefit of the entire bridge, "let's show them what's wrong with battleblimps. Engines to tac-level five, arm missiles, lock down for full-ruptor drill."

He heard a muted clank as the hatches to the bridge engaged their locking bolts, and the faint echo of nearby accesses doing the same as the *Falcomare* segmented itself into self-sufficient domains in preparation for ruptor attack. Hayashi's stomach knotted—if anything qualified as a terror weapon, the ruptor was it—but let nothing of his disquiet reach his voice as the countdown reached zero.

"Engage."

The fiveskip burred harshly, making his teeth ache, but Hayashi felt only an almost breathless excitement.

"Emergence minus twelve, eleven, ten . . ." He could hear the same excitement in Orriega's voice, sense it in the postures of the other crew at their consoles. In mere moments they would emerge over Arthelion at nearly one-quarter light-speed, hurling shaped-charge missiles at their vast enemy, while in the middle system, the real battle would be fought . . .

He had a brief image of Margot's face, their last night together; a brief stab of regret, and then the fiveskip disengaged, and there was no time for anything but the fierce concentration on the here and now that is the experience of battle.

✳   ✳   ✳

FIST OF DOL'JHAR

The shuttle slid through the lock field, throwing off rainbow rings of light, and settled to the deck, seemingly cushioned by the spray of static discharges from its hull. Outside, another shuttle slowly approached the *Fist of Dol'jhar*, silhouetted against the limb of Arthelion vast beyond.

Guardsman Tanak grounded his weapon briefly, presented arms, and snapped to attention with the others of his squad as the shuttle door slid open, revealing the form of Anaris rahal'Jerrodi, the conditional heir. Tanak shivered and would have straightened up even more, had there been any slack in his posture—unlikely, in a survivor of the savage Tarkan training regimen. This was the one spoken of in whispers, favored of the ancestors—Arzoat, second in the squad, had seen that with her own eyes. Even the shades of the Panarchists, down below in the haunted precincts of the Mandala, obeyed him, they said.

Anaris stepped to the deck to receive Kyvernat Juvaszt's salute. Taller and stronger-seeming even than his Tarkan honor guard, he paused a moment. His dark eyes swept across all in the hangar bay, piercing above the strong nose and firm lips that recalled his father the Avatar. Behind him, ignored, a short, astonishingly ugly Bori scuttled out of the shuttle, glancing nervously around.

Juvaszt took them aside, joining a small group of officers, as a group of men in plain prison garb began to disembark. Tanak watched with avid curiosity—these were the enemy, who'd humbled the Children of Dol a generation ago. He wondered for a moment which one was the Panarch, and then a short, slender man emerged, and all doubt fled. Not just the way the others deferred to him, not even the sudden alertness shown in the postures of the conditional heir and those around him, but the man's own carriage, announced him as the defeated ruler of the Thousand Suns. And yet, Tanak could see, there was nothing of defeat in him; he stepped down onto the deck as though he owned the ship and the loyalty of everyone within.

As their guards led the Panarchists past, Anaris held up his hand commandingly. The guards halted, and the Panarch stopped and looked up with an air of inquiry into the face of the conditional heir. Tanak strained to hear, not daring to move or even change the angle of his head.

Only long years of discipline, then, prevented him from jumping when a whooping siren pulled all heads around.

"Emergence pulses, two, closing at point-two-two cee, missiles detected!" The voice boomed even louder than the siren.

Juvaszt grabbed his communicator and began shouting orders even as he ran for the inner hatch to the transtube that would take him to the bridge, followed closely by Anaris and the Bori. The guards from the shuttle began herding the Panarchists through another hatch; Tanak saw a sudden smile on the Panarch's face, reflected as pride and excitement in the others around him.

The immense doors of the bay began to slide shut with startling speed. Outside, the curve of Arthelion blurred suddenly as the ship's defensive fields energized, seizing the hapless shuttle still outside in a merciless grip and shredding it into a haze of debris under the lash of the teslas' momentum transformation. Beyond, as Druashar, their squad leader, double-timed them to another hatch, Tanak thought he saw a spark of light, swelling rapidly. Then the shuttle blew up silently with a blinding flash just before the bay lock slammed shut.

Tanak was the last Tarkan through the hatch. As Druashar tabbed the go-key, long habit turned Tanak with the others to face the door.

Afterward, his memory sorted the events into order, but at the time, it all seemed simultaneous. The doors began to slide shut as a frantic technician ran toward them, shouting, but his voice was drowned by a shattering compound roar. Tanak saw the massive lock door begin to bulge, then burst into a flare of white light. The technician flared brightly and vanished in the burst of ardent heat that struck at them through the narrow slit as the transtube doors slammed shut. Tanak felt his skin prickle sharply, like a sunburn, as the concussion knocked them all to the floor. After an agonizing delay, the module jerked into motion, accelerating them away from the wreckage of the hangar bay, now dissolved into a plasma hotter than the sun.

❊ ❊ ❊

The roar of the sequenced missile strikes on his ship drowned the tinny shout of Juvaszt's communicator as his transtube accelerated toward the bridge three kilometers away. In his mind's eye he could see vividly the multiple strikes at the same spot, each detonation cumulatively weakening the shields until only bare metal stood in the way of a million-degree plasma moving at a quarter-cee.

Then the concussion wave caught up with them. The module shuddered and squealed as it hit the sides of the transtube, throwing them to the deck, then reaccelerated. Juvaszt climbed to his feet and spat out a tooth. He shook his communicator experimentally, but the impact with his mouth had crushed it. He looked around, but the junior officers with him had coms that couldn't access his command channel—a standard precaution against mutiny.

Then Anaris' Bori secretary stumbled forward and pressed a communicator into his hand. Juvaszt noticed three more communicators dangling from the Bori's belt as he snarled at the man reflexively, irritated by the useless gesture. But then he recognized the voice of his second squawking from it.

". . . Juvaszt! Are you able to respond?"

It was tuned to the command channel! He glanced speculatively at the Bori and caught a glimpse of a slight gleam of irony in Anaris' eyes, of a sort he'd never seen from the Avatar.

"Juvaszt here. Report." His tongue probed at the hole in his gum as he noted the mushiness of his inflections.

"Two destroyers, sir," responded the voice of so-Kyvernat Chodalin. "Gone now. Tactical skip executed, ruptors on-line, skipmissile charging . . ."

"Cancel that, you . . ." Juvaszt bit down on the next word before it emerged, chagrined at his loss of control. "Cancel that. Neither we nor the Panarchists can afford to use skipmissiles. Arthelion is unshielded, the Avatar is in the Mandala. Damage?"

"Aft second bay not reporting, minor damage to forward ruptor one . . ."

Then the damage wasn't severe, except for the bay. "And the Panarchists?"

"Safe, on their way to the brig."

Now, as the surprise of the attack dissipated, Juvaszt began to speculate. *What are the Panarchists up to?* Without skipmissiles they could do no more than sting the *Fist of Dol'jhar*, although, he admitted ruefully, their first sting had been a telling one.

The module began to decelerate. Juvaszt looked up to see Anaris regarding him coolly. He noted with approval that the conditional heir appeared completely in control, in contrast to his Bori attendant, whose fear-paled brow was oozing oily sweat.

The module halted; the doors jerked open. Juvaszt smelled the tang of heat, caught a glimpse of seared metal on the outside of the module—a fraction of a second longer and they would have been vaporized. He ran down the short corridor onto the bridge, followed by Anaris and the others.

His second jumped out of the command pod and saluted as he approached. "Kyvernat Juvaszt, observers report a destroyer emerged on the other side of Arthelion during the attack and discharged a wave of small vessels. They are decelerating into the atmosphere at high speed." He looked grim. "Their signatures match that of Panarchist Marine lances; their courses appear to intersect the Mandala."

"Weapons!" shouted Juvaszt, seating himself and tapping on his console. "Ready missiles for atmospheric entry, ship-to-ship. Target lances and fire upon emergence." He wiped his lips and swallowed; his mouth ached and his speech was becoming less intelligible.

He looked up at the plot screen that echoed graphically Chodalin's report. A targeting diamond appeared in response to his input. "Navigation, take us in, two skips, maximum safe angle." They would have to skip out and then back in to go around the planet in the least time, and the larger the angle formed by the two legs of their route, the closer they would be to radius each time. But the Avatar was in the Mandala.

Juvaszt had a sudden, vivid image of the deadly, needle-shaped lances closing in on the palace, disgorging their cargo of battle-armored Marines. He had no illusions about their efficacy: trained in a tradition of small-squad, independent action, they would slice through the rigidly hierarchical Tarkans like monothread through flesh.

"Nonsense," Anaris snapped as the fiveskip burped in the first skip. Juvaszt turned, startled, as his mind threw up a brief image of the spectral hands of Urien hovering over the conditional heir's head at the ghost-laying ceremony; but Anaris was looking at the viewscreen. *Favored of the ancestors, yes, but not a telepath.*

Anaris glanced down at him, his dark eyes still gleaming with cool irony. "The Panarchists wouldn't waste their time attacking the Mandala. It makes neither tactical nor strategic sense. It must be a ruse."

The fiveskip burped again.

"They are striking at the Avatar, who has usurped their ruler and claimed his palace," said Juvaszt, turning back to the viewscreen. Now he was irritated. This was his ship, he was responsible to the Avatar, not to the heir. *No, conditional heir.*

On the viewscreen the green spears of laser-boosted missiles leapt away; moments later coins of light blossomed above the nightside of Arthelion as they found their targets.

"Sensors, scan those explosions."

"They don't think that way," said Anaris.

"Spectrum indicates organic debris consonant with human remains," reported the sensors officer after a moment.

Anaris said nothing more, and Juvaszt, after a moment's reflection, decided not to follow up on his advantage. The sensor report said it well enough.

"Communications, raise the *Satansclaw*, the *Kali*, and the *Mojyndaro* and patch them through for orders." A destroyer, especially one equipped with a logos, and two frigates, should be sufficient to deal with further lance attacks. He'd like more, but he needed the other Rifter forces to locate the Panarchist forces. How would the Panarchists follow up? More of the same? And from where? *At least I know they had to be clumped within a few light-seconds, to start with, with their lightspeed communications.* That would make it easier.

"Then contact the Mandala and request an audience of the Avatar." Better that he call down—even thought he couldn't really spare the time—than have the Avatar call him demanding an explanation.

He tabbed his console, summoning a medic to give him

something to cut down on the flow of saliva and blood from the empty tooth socket so he could speak clearly, then motioned his tactical officer over as he continued giving orders. He had no doubt they had very little time before the next attack.

Anaris felt the old familiar rage mount up behind his eyes, but he rigidly controlled himself, letting nothing of it show. The report from the sensors had been a blow, shaking his certainty that the lances were a feint. *Would the Panarchists throw away lives like that?* Then he remembered the looks on the faces of the men and women around the Panarch in the hangar bay during the missile attack, and the Arkadic Marines he'd known while a hostage. That was the wrong question. *Would they* spend *lives like that?*

For a brief moment the fear of defeat seized him, even there on the bridge of a ship armed with the unstoppable power of the Suneater. The Panarchists would pay whatever price was asked of them, if they thought the prize worth it. *So what is the prize?* One thing he was sure of: it was not the Mandala. The fact that the other Dol'jharians around him saw the Mandala as the logical goal of the Navy's attack merely confirmed the deception. *They knew we'd believe it.*

He listened to Juvaszt snapping out orders, the consonants of his speech mushy from the missing tooth, impressed with the man's command of himself and the situation; but all the while his mind worried at the question of their enemy's real purpose. What was worth such a high cost?

Then so-Erechnat Terresk-jhi turned around from the communications console, a mixture of fear and awe on her face that told Anaris immediately what her next words would be.

"Kyvernat Juvaszt, the Avatar will speak to you," she said, confirming Anaris' conjecture.

Juvaszt motioned her to open the channel, and a window swelled on the main viewscreen, revealing Eusabian's face and shoulders. The image was slightly rough; Anaris could see Terresk-jhi tapping at her console, but it didn't help. He guessed that the useless chatter and images loading down the hyperwave from their Rifter allies were stressing the discrimination and decoding circuits.

Anaris did not recognize the room Eusabian was in, but from the furnishings guessed it was an intimate chamber in the Palace

Minor. He noted a gleam of excitement, almost satisfaction, in his father's eyes; he doubted anyone else could see it. He glanced covertly at Morrighon and something in the Bori's stance moved him to amend that thought—he was sure that his secretary saw it too.

Then Eusabian's eyes focused on Juvaszt. "Kyvernat Juvaszt. Your report."

As Juvaszt gave Eusabian a précis of the attack and his surmise of its goals, Anaris studied his father and saw the same culture-blind assumptions distorting his judgment as well. *He studied them for twenty years, but he still thinks of them as weak versions of Dol'jharian. There must be some way to use this blindness, but how?*

And then his father handed him the lever he needed in full view of everyone on the bridge.

"Bring the Panarch to the bridge and show him to the attackers—hold the sword of their oath against their own throats."

You fool! They live and die by symbolism; it is the foundation of their culture and their lives. Do you think they swear their oath to nothing but a living man?

Even as Anaris exulted silently at this incredible mistake, his father's eyes moved to him.

"Anaris *ji-rahal*," he said formally, using again the conditional form, "I lay my paliach in your hands for a time. Return my enemy to me, or kill him."

Anaris bowed deeply. "As my father commands, so it is done," he said. He heard an intake of breath from Juvaszt as he straightened up. He had claimed the kinship without the conditional form, a response both respectful and defiant. On the screen Eusabian stared at him a moment, that strange gleam still flickering in his eyes, and then the image vanished.

"*Satansclaw* reports in position," said Communications after a moment's silence. "No contacts reported by any ship."

Taking advantage of the slight pause in activity following the Avatar's call, Anaris stepped forward. Juvaszt turned to him.

"Kyvernat, you must obey my father, but I tell you now, it will not work." He spoke to be overheard, but not to draw attention to their conversation.

Juvaszt said nothing for a moment. Anaris could feel the weight of his regard, his dark eyes steady and considering.

"You are right," said the man finally. "I must obey the Avatar." The faintest of stresses on the title was the only indication of his disbelief.

Anaris nodded and stepped back. That was enough for now.

✳   ✳   ✳

GROZNIY

"Target pattern confirmed," announced Rom-Sanchez with satisfaction. "We've got them." He looked over at Ng.

The tactical plot showed a god's-eye view of the middle system, with the *Grozniy*, its attendant ships, and their target, the Rifter destroyer *Finality Jones*, in the ecliptic just sunward of the asteroid belt.

"They haven't changed their tactical algorithm since the last update to the signature banks," he continued. "They're still using the Salim set . . . at leg five now." On the viewscreen the Tenno shifted, echoing the new information.

"Weapons, prepare for narrow-beam lazplaz attack," Ng said. "Target the engines and accelerator only. Fire on emergence. Navigation, take us in to point-five light-seconds." She paused, savoring the moment. "Engage."

The fiveskip snarled momentarily; it was set to a high tac level for precise control and high real velocity.

"Retargeting . . . firing," said Harrick at the weapons console as the fiveskip fell silent. On the viewscreen a thread of light marking the complex beam of coherent light and near lightspeed plasma speared out, intersecting a minute spark of light distinguished from the stars around it only by the targeting cross imposed upon it by the computer. It vanished, then lanced out again, then finally ceased altogether.

Then the viewscreen flickered to a close-in view. Plasma sparkled from a rent in the destroyer's aft section; its radiants flared, then guttered out. There was a blast of plasma from midway along the ship's missile tube; it bent, its complex struts crumpling as the stricken ship began to yaw.

"That's got it," said Ng. "Begin evasive pattern."

The fiveskip burped again as the navigator engaged the programmed drunkwalk designed to avoid surprise attack by ships responding to the distress call of their victim—if it had a hyper-wave.

They waited. Rom-Sanchez essayed a few jocular comments about the Rifter ship's attempts to regain control, but his comments fell into a silence compounded by Commander Krajno's grim concentration on the screen, and he desisted. Finally, as the commander stirred impatiently in his pod, Ng shook her head.

"That's it, then. No hyperwave on this one." She paused, distaste flooding her at the necessary next order. The heat of battle was the proper setting for death—she had never enjoyed executions.

"Weapons, shoot ruptor, one turret, full power."

Moments later the *Finality Jones* disintegrated into a blast of light and glowing particles that dissipated rapidly.

"Communications, signal the squadron. Target two. Dispatch this engagement record for tacponder recording, full-sphere burst."

After a brief delay, the communications console twittered briefly. "Record dispatched, Captain."

"Navigation, take us to the next battle coordinates."

As the fiveskip engaged, Ng wondered briefly what kind of luck Armenhaut and KepSingh were having. With three squadrons, each composed of a battlecruiser, three frigates, and assorted corvettes, the odds were they would encounter what they sought fairly soon—especially considering how thickly strewn with tacponders the Arthelion system was. Even Ng had been surprised at their density. *But then, they've had almost a thousand years to place them.* The combination of thousands of tacponders and efficient use of courier ships gave them communications almost as good as if they had one of Eusabian's FTL coms in each ship. But not quite.

And Eusabian has that advantage across the entire Thousand Suns. The thought reassured her again of the rightness of her actions, but that didn't stop the ache at the thought of the cost they would doubtless pay. Her thoughts went out to Metellus, even now slashing at the *Fist of Dol'jhar* above Arthelion.

"*. . . and I will pay whatever price demanded by my oath and honor . . .*" The fragment of the Naval Oath struck at her with renewed force, and Metellus' face, glowing with passion at the end of their last night, floated before her mind's eye for a moment. They paid the price of honor with each separation, but she knew that only the last one, known too late, would reveal the true cost of loyalty.

❋   ❋   ❋

FLAMMARION

Stygrid ban-Armenhaut sat stiffly in his command pod on the bridge of the *Flammarion*, glowering at the viewscreen.

"Ready for the skip to first coordinates, Captain," came the voice of Bar-Himelion at the navigation console. "Ten light-minutes out for long-ranging."

Armenhaut blinked. "Engage."

The fiveskip hummed briefly, ceased. The screen cleared and a few moments later SigInt reported acquisition of their target.

"Signature ID'd. *Ghostmaker*, frigate."

His tactical officer began tapping at his console, analyzing the movements of their quarry, looking for a pattern that would enable them to emerge with enough precision to put a narrow beam through its engines, rather than relying on the broader, deadlier stroke of the *Flammarion*'s ruptors.

Armenhaut bit his thumb moodily. Ng's provisional assumption of the rank of commodore, fully within the Standing Orders as it was, still rankled with him; being under her command was even worse. And nibbling at the back of his mind was the near-constant worry that with the Aerenarch dead, his career might truly have reached its zenith.

The silent activity on the bridge stretched out to minutes. Armenhaut had no doubt that the bridge of the *Grozniy* was full of chatter. He sniffed. What could you expect of a jumped-up Polloi? *She cultivates that image of hers, of promotion through pure merit, but I'd like to see where she'd be without the Nesselryns behind her.* He still remembered vividly his encounter with the long arm of her patron family, back just after their graduation from the Academy. Only his burgeoning connection with the Aerenarch had saved his career from a nasty setback. A traitorous part of his mind—perhaps liberated by the stress of recent days—reminded him that he'd struck at her politically because he'd found he couldn't compete on any other basis, but he slapped it down.

Politics is the continuation of war by other means. That had been a favorite epigraph of the Aerenarch. Merit could take you only so far, Ng would find someday.

Or would she? Semion was dead.

Armenhaut shifted in his pod and was grateful when Lieutenant Commander Rajaonarive's voice interrupted his thoughts. "We've got a pattern, sir," said the tactical officer. He snorted. "He's using the Omega tactical algorithms, with the destroyer optimization sets. Telos knows what good he thinks that'll do in a frigate."

Commander Gormen leaned over toward Armenhaut. "Some noderunner got lazy," commented the first officer.

Armenhaut grimaced. He really didn't care about some nameless Rifter computer tech right now. Gormen turned back to his console and tapped at it before speaking.

"Attack profile is now entered, sir. Tac-level four, narrow-beam lazplaz attack, engines only, then drunkwalk skips while we wait for a response."

"Very well, Commander. Navigation, take us in to point-five light-seconds. Engage."

The fiveskip snarled. The the screens cleared, a narrow thread of light lanced out toward their target. One second later a rosette of light bloomed where the frigate had been, churning as it faded away.

"Bloody hell," snapped Armenhaut, jumping to his feet. "Weapons, I wanted a Rifter frigate, not a Telos-damned ball of plasma."

"Yes, sir."

Armenhaut stood a moment longer, glaring at the sublieutenant at the weapons console. She looked back at him, her face properly expressionless. Then he turned to Commander Gormen. "Commander, take Weapons for the next attack. We can't afford that kind of sloppiness."

Armenhaut saw protest, quickly stifled, in the woman's eyes, but didn't let it touch him.

"Communications, signal the squadron. Target two. Dispatch this engagement record for the tacponder recording, full-sphere burst."

The communications officer complied. "Record dispatched."

"Navigation, take us to the next position, ten light-minutes out. Engage."

He sat back down, resentful at the *Flammarion*'s failure, watching as the sublieutenant walked stiff-backed to a sub-console at Commander Gormen's direction.

But what was she to him? Just another Highdweller, from some minor family on some obscure habitat out in the Fringes. He sensed a heightened tension in the bridge officers and smiled. His action would serve as an excellent reminder who was in command.

Armenhaut dismissed them all from his mind and bent his attention to the next attack.

THIRTY-TWO

FIST OF DOL'JHAR

Gelasaar hai-Arkad stood between two Tarkans as the transtube decelerated. The prison tunic the Dol'jharians had issued him itched, but that was not half so distressing to his fastidious nature as the smell—his captors' ideas of hygiene fell well short of his own.

It hadn't been so long ago that his worries were planetary economies and millions of lives; now his concerns had narrowed to bad laundry practices and unpalatable food. Gelasaar felt a soft laugh escape as he remembered his former longings for a simpler life.

"Prayers which heaven in enormous vengeance grants."

He spoke out loud, provoking a change from alertness to wariness in one of the Tarkans. He glanced up and was amused to see a glint of fear in the man's eyes. *Do you understand Uni?* Perhaps only the word "vengeance": that, a Dol'jharian might be expected to understand in any tongue. *Probably thinks I'm curse-weaving against his master.*

He laughed again as the module came to a stop. Eusabian's

success had cursed the Avatar worse than any enemy could wish, had he but the wit to see it.

Then the doors opened, and Gelasaar realized again how far short of understanding his victorious enemy fell as the Tarkans pushed him forward down a short corridor to the bridge of the *Fist of Dol'jhar*. He knew what was coming now, and he looked forward to its inevitable denouement.

The bridge of the Avatar's flagship was quieter than a Navy battlecruiser's would have been under the circumstances, and lacking the tianqi, it reeked of anxiety-tinged sweat. Gelasaar thought he also somehow tasted the harsh tang of Dol'jharian discipline, perhaps sensing it in the stances of the men and women moving purposefully about.

Suddenly the activity on the bridge intensified. The main viewscreen split into two windows, echoed by others. In each a point of light swelled rapidly. He strained to understand the rapid-fire Dol'jharian, catching only fragments. Two destroyers in a fractional-cee attack, no skipmissiles, and something going on . . . He felt a momentary shock of surprise. An attack on the Mandala? With lances? *Ridiculous. It must be a ruse.*

Then he noticed Anaris standing with a short, dumpy Bori a few paces behind the captain's command pod. The young Dol'jharian was engaged in conversation with the Bori—no doubt his secretary—and hadn't yet seen him.

The attack ceased. On another screen the lance attack on the other side of the planet dwindled under an onslaught of missiles from a destroyer and some other ships. He caught a fragment of a report—organic debris confirmed—and looked away from the screen, feeling sick.

Then he remembered, and had to fight hard to suppress a smile. He knew this maneuver: Jaspar had used it against the Torigan Demagogues. It was still known by an acronym—BBQ—whose meaning had been lost. Apparently the Dol'jharians hadn't figured out yet what was happening.

Relieved, he looked back at Anaris and studied him for a moment. His amusement at the Navy's successful ruse faded, and a certain melancholy took its place. *Poor amphibious spirit.* Caught halfway between two worlds that were nearly poles of the human experience, iron and ice against elegance and generosity, Anaris was neither Dol'jharian nor Douloi. Not for the first time the Panarch wondered if his fosterage had done the boy a service, or scarred him beyond healing.

Boy no longer. Gelasaar remembered the aborted meeting in the hangar bay before the attack, saw again the pride and certainty of purpose in Anaris' eyes. *What did he intend to say to me?*

Then Anaris turned and saw him at last, as the Tarkans escorted him toward the captain. As Juvaszt stood up with the easy courtesy that the military life demands for a respected enemy, Gelasaar watched Anaris. Eusabian's son had always been hard to read, but the Panarch had long been a careful observer, and he thought he detected signs of ambivalence, of pride and uncertainty, which would seem to confirm the polarities of the young man's spirit.

Like a Dol'jharian, he'd carefully constructed a set piece for the meeting in the hangar bay, and now was at a loss for words in this unplanned meeting. But, Gelasaar was sure now, the Douloi in him had seen the failure of Dol'jharian understanding that his, the Panarch's, presence on the bridge implied, and was ready to profit from it.

Yet Anaris did not speak, he only nodded, smiling faintly.

He says nothing. Is he then my enemy or not?

Anaris' smile widened, and now the Panarch detected irony, an emotion learned from his fosterage days.

Gelasaar recognized the irony, appreciating its sting: Anaris was not going to speak.

Gelasaar looked away, feeling anew a wave of grief for his dead sons. At the same time he recalled his insistence that his own people treat Anaris not as a prisoner, or as a hostage, but as his own sons were treated. The gesture had been a gift, then, intended as a bridge. Would it now aid his own people?

Perhaps there is a fourth son, safe from the Avatar's paliach. Though Anaris would face dangers of his own.

Gelasaar looked up thoughtfully at Anaris' face as the young man watched the screens. What, then, were his plans?

DEATHSTORM

Aziza bin'Surat shifted in her pod, monitoring the ceaseless flow of messages from the Urian relay webbed and bolted to her console on the bridge of the Rifter destroyer *Deathstorm*, now patrolling the middle system a light-hour out from Arthelion. Most of them were coded, from the Dol'jharians to other ships throughout the Thousand Suns, but many were sent *en clair* or in various Brotherhood or Syndicate codes, from other Rifter ships. That no doubt galled the Dol'jharians, but there was little they could do. And some of the images . . .

She forced her attention back to the task assigned her by Captain Gnar-il Qvidyom: filtering and forwarding everything from the *Satansclaw* and the other two ships fighting off the Panarchist attack on the Mandala.

That should stop pretty soon. She looked down at the small windowed image from the *Fist of Dol'jhar* that her console was echoing to one of the secondary screens on the bridge. The image was almost surreal: the Panarch of the Thousand Suns, in a tunic she wouldn't let a wattle nest in, surrounded by hulking Dol'jharians on the bridge of his enemy's flagship. It was like something out of a serial chip. She wondered how the Panarchists receiving it via ordinary EM felt.

She knew how her fellow Rifters felt. The volume of messages had increased dramatically since the Panarch's image went out over the Urian com system. Some were comments and jokes about the Panarch, others were suggestions on how to wage the battle, aimed at the *Satansclaw* and the two frigates, or even at Juvaszt on the *Fist*. Any moment she expected that slug Barrodagh to show up on the com and threaten them all with various horrid Dol'jharian punishments if they didn't shut up. *Lotta good that'll do.* But she had to admit, it was getting pretty hard to filter out all the blunge on the hyperwave—she wondered briefly how the Ur had done it.

Maybe they had eyes and ears all over their bodies, or something. She snickered at the image, then stifled it as the captain, slouching broodily in his command pod, shifted irritably, not taking his eyes off the viewscreen. Something about the Panarchist attack obviously bothered him, but he wasn't the sort to confide in his crew, and should anyone be stupid enough to ask, he might alleviate his boredom by carving ears or other extremities with one of his knives. Why was he worrying? The nicks'd have to stop now, they couldn't shoot the Panarch.

She looked back at her console and busied herself with unnecessary keytaps as Qvidyom caught her gaze and glared at her.

"Lipri," she heard the captain demand, and caught a glimpse of the astrogator straightening up in his pod. "Take us to our next position." She heard the fury in his voice at the necessity of following that stiff-nackered Juvaszt's patrol orders, but they had little choice. The Dol'jharians controlled the Urian power source, their own reactors were cold and dark—it would take hours or days to bring them back on-line. And the Dol'jharians wouldn't stop there; they'd be helpless to resist when a ship showed up to carry them off to the torture chambers. Obedience was their only course.

On the viewscreen the long lance of the ship's missile tube swung across the starfield as the ship came about. Aziza quashed another snicker. It was typical of Qvidyom to leave the launcher visible in forward views. She doubted that the one between his legs worked.

A message from the *Satansclaw* dragged her attention back to the task at hand, but it was just a status report, noting the destruction of the last few marine lances from the second attack. They were better off than those poor blits, anyway, she thought, and obedience had been rewarding, so far. Aziza began to drift into pleasant memories of their looting of the Achilenga Highdwellings. Then the reality of war suddenly intruded.

The sensor console bleeped. "Emergence!" Odruith's voice was practically a shriek. "Big one!"

The captain slapped at the go-pad on his console, but nothing happened. The lights flickered, and moments later there was a low rumble, transmitted through the fabric of the ship.

"Damage control!" Qvidyom yelled; then a beam of plasma so bright the viewscreen transformed it to a finger of blackness limned in light traced a line of destruction along the missile tube, billows of gas and gouts of flaring metal erupting from its point of contact.

"Engine room not reporting!" Eglerda stabbed at his console. "We've got power, but no drive."

The beam ceased; plasma leaked from the wreckage of the missile tube.

"Skipmissile not charging," Eglerda continued.

"I can see that, you chatzing nackerbrain!" Qvidyom screamed, tobacco-stained spittle spraying from his mouth.

"Skip-pulse," reported the sensors tech. "They've skipped out." His voice shook, a mixture of fear and confusion.

"What? Are you sure? What in the name of Prani's Nine Bronze Balls is going on?"

Aziza's brain started working again as the imminence of death receded a bit. What were the Panarchists up to? Why hadn't they used their ruptors, and more bewildering, why hadn't they followed up? Then a horrid certainty possessed her: they were going to be boarded.

"Bin'Surat, you stupid chatzrip, stop dreaming and put me through to Juvaszt on the *Fist*."

The captain's insult jerked her out of a fearful vision compounded equally of serial chips and her too-vivid imagination, of Arkadic Marines, invulnerable in battle armor, rampaging through the ship. The Panarchist attack was failing, with the Panarch as hostage, but it was too late for the *Deathstorm*. She patched in the channel with trembling fingers, hoping it wasn't also too late for the *Deathstorm*'s crew.

FALCOMARE

To the unassisted eye the naval staging point looked empty. Only the small circles drawn by the computer around otherwise undistinguished points of light enabled Metellus Hayashi to detect the other two destroyers of his squadron, now preparing for the third attack on the *Fist of Dol'jhar*. Now it was *Falcomare*'s turn to deliver the mock lances, while the *Barahyrn* and *Lady of Taligar* slashed at the enemy battlecruiser.

"Look at this, Captain," said Mbezawi at SigInt. "Got a great shot of the *Fist* during the last pass." He tapped at his console as Hayashi nodded. "Couldn't have done better with a skip-missile."

A window bloomed on the viewscreen, revealing a close-up

of the aft portion of the Dol'jharian battlecruiser, shifting rapidly in perspective. There was a low whistle from someone on the bridge; Hayashi smiled broadly. They'd hit one of the ship's hangar bays; a notorious weak spot, it was now a glowing pit lined with snarls of metal, glowing puffs of gas and dust billowing from it at random intervals. The image flickered out.

"Good work, Ushkaten," said Hayashi. The weapons officer beamed. " 'Zawi, pass that image along to the armory, with my compliments."

The lieutenant turned back to his console, but as he started tapping at it his motions suddenly slowed, then stopped. He stared at his screen for a moment before speaking.

"Captain," he said, all the triumph now gone from his voice, "you'd better take a look at this. There's a broadcast from the *Fist of Dol'jhar*. From the bridge."

"What, is he asking for terms?" said Hayashi, but the joke fell flat against the alarm the communications officer's sudden change in tone had engendered in the others on the bridge. "Put it on-screen," he continued.

The starfield on the viewscreen yielded to an image of the bridge of their opponent; Hayashi recognized the Dol'jharian uniforms and realized that they were possibly the first naval personnel in twenty years to see such a view. Then shock replaced his interest with anger as he recognized the man standing between two hulking Dol'jharian guards, next to the *Fist*'s captain: Gelasaar hai-Arkad, forty-seventh of his line, holder of Hayashi's oath and that of every person on the *Falcomare*.

Dressed in ill-fitting prison tunic and trousers, the Panarch stared straight out of the screen at him, as though they were standing face-to-face, and his expression had nothing of defeat in it. Despite the fact that he knew this was a one-way link, Hayashi almost saluted, so commanding was the man's presence.

He heard indrawn breaths from several on the bridge, and a muttered curse.

"Communications," he said, not taking his eyes from the screen, "signal *Barahyrn* and *Lady of Taligar*. Hold position."

There was movement in the image, and as Hayashi watched, barely hearing the acknowledgments from the other destroyers, he became convinced that this was not a recorded loop, but an ongoing broadcast, a window onto the bridge of the *Fist of*

Dol'jhar from only minutes in the past. And then he smiled as he realized the message implicit in the Panarch's stance, a message the Dol'jharians had no chance of intercepting. It was a command no less compelling for being unspoken.

Metellus Hayashi laughed, a bitter sound that strained his throat. "Those Telos-damned fools," he said, as the others on the bridge looked from the screen to him. "They think they'll bind us with our oath of fealty. What does a Dol'jharian know of loyalty? They understand only fear."

He tipped his chin at the image. "You know what he expects of us."

He looked around the bridge, seeing understanding and sober-grim agreement in the crew.

"Communications, raise *Barahyrn* and *Lady of Taligar*. Conference."

Ensign Mellieur tapped at her console briefly; two windows popped up on-screen, revealing the faces of Doial and Galt. Hayashi could see the same mix of anger and resolution in their faces that he was feeling, and wondered momentarily how even a Dol'jharian could so misread an enemy.

"Captain Juvaszt has made a terrible mistake," he said. "I propose we explain it to him." He paused, tapping up a tactical plot and echoing it to both of them, as a snort of laughter escaped from Captain Doial.

"I propose we execute the third attack as planned, but instead of meeting at the next staging point, the *Falcomare* will skip behind Lunaire. The moon's mass will hide us but we can relay a beam through a drone to talk to Juvaszt, and watch him as well. In the meantime, both of you deliver a fourth load of mock lances here." The tactical plot responded to his touch as he sketched out the geometry of the attack in relation to the position of Arthelion's moon.

"We'll be talking to him at that point and powering up in a Katy Wheel, so when he skips up on the first leg of his circumplanetary jump and starts to come about, we can wheel past him and get off a shot at his radiants without endangering Arthelion or the Highdwellings."

A ship always emerged from skip on the same heading it entered on, with conservation of any rotation. By imposing a yawing spin on the *Falcomare* and skipping at just the right moment, the ship would emerge with the missile tube already swinging into alignment with the *Fist of Dol'jhar*.

He held up a hand as he saw the objection on their faces. He knew it wasn't to the danger of the maneuver—the *Falcomare* would emerge headed more or less straight for Arthelion, since that was the only way they could get off a shot aiming safely away from the planet.

"Sorry, Bea, Jarnock. Rank hath its privileges." He smiled. "This one's mine."

"Pretty iffy," Galt growled. "That's a double Katy you're planning. *Falcomare* up to it?"

"Green thoughts, Jarnock." Hayashi laughed. "The *Fistula* didn't lay a beam on any of us, so we're as ready as you are."

They laughed at him. He knew they didn't begrudge him the shot.

It was too bad, though, he thought, that there was no safe way to plan a follow-up attack on the battlecruiser. This close to the planet the risk was unacceptable. Only one ship could deliver their response, and that ship would be the *Falcomare*.

They conferred a few minutes longer, fine-tuning the attack, and signed off. Moments later, the *Falcomare* skipped out toward Arthelion to begin the third attack.

✳   ✳   ✳

FIST OF DOL'JHAR

The radiants of their two attackers dwindled, vanishing in twin bursts of reddish light as the third attack ceased.

"Possible ruptor hit on one destroyer during the last attack."

Anaris noted the obvious relief in Erechnat Chikhuri at the weapons console as the sensors officer reported. Dealing with a fractional-cee attack was difficult, especially from two directions at once, but so far the *Fist* had dealt nothing to its enemies to compare to the destruction wrought on the aft second hangar bay during the first attack. It didn't help that since the Highdwellings around Arthelion were now the Avatar's possessions, their use of the ruptors was severely constrained.

The Panarchists are probably aware of that too. So far, the enemy's tactics had shown a thorough understanding of

Dol'jharian thought patterns, an understanding unmatched by Juvaszt and the other officers on the *Fist of Dol'jhar*.

It galled Anaris that though he recognized a ruse, he did not yet comprehend the purpose of the attack. A battlecruiser was capable of absorbing this kind of warfare indefinitely; since the destroyers couldn't use their skipmissiles, they couldn't hope to disable the *Fist*. But there was no sign of any other activity, although he was certain there were other Panarchist ships out there.

He looked over at the Panarch, who stood at ease between his Tarkan guards, intent on the viewscreens, a faint smile on his lips. That was the only other person on the bridge who realized that this was all a sham; but did he know what the Navy's real thrust was?

The fiveskip snarled as the *Fist of Dol'jhar* made the first of the skips that would take it around Arthelion to assist the Rifter contingent in dealing with the latest wave of lances.

So-Erechnat Terresk-jhi suddenly straightened in her pod, tapping at the communications console. "Realtime message from *Deathstorm*," she reported. "They are under attack by a battlecruiser . . ." Her brow crinkled in puzzlement. "They did not use ruptors, and skipped out after disabling the drives and the skipmissile accelerator."

And then it all crashed together in Anaris' mind. *Realtime!* They had realtime communications at any distance through the Urian communicator, and the Panarchists hadn't. *That's what they're after.*

He stepped forward to stand beside the command pod. "They want an Urian communicator," he said. "This attack is merely a diversion."

Juvaszt gave him a brief glance, tapped at his console, and then looked up again consideringly. "Diversion it may be, but we cannot leave the Avatar undefended."

He turned away. "Communications, I want a realtime feed on that secondary screen"—he tapped his console briefly and one of the smaller screens near the main viewscreen flashed briefly—"for all Rifter vessels in-system."

The communications officer worked at her console, and a number of windows began popping up on the indicated screen. They flickered, the images were grainy, and Terresk-jhi's movements became steadily more jerky and frantic, her posture sig-

naling severe stress. Occasionally another image would bleed
through for a moment. Anaris realized that the discriminators
were having trouble dealing with the overload caused by the
comments and images flooding in from all over the Thousand
Suns as the Battle of Arthelion engaged the interest of their
Rifter allies.

Juvaszt began issuing orders, dispatching all the Rifters in the
system to converge on the *Deathstorm*'s position. His speech
was clearer now; the medic had packed his wound with an ab-
sorbent, but Anaris could hear growing irritation in his tones as
he dealt with the increasingly unclear communications with the
Rifters in the Arthelion system.

When he was finished he leaned back in his command pod.
"If that's what they want, then they will commit all their forces
to gaining it," said Juvaszt. "Now we can force the engagement
and use the full weight of our weapons against them."

"Message incoming," said Terresk-jhi. "From the captain of
the Panarchist attack squadron. He's hiding behind the moon,
relaying the signal via drone. Two-point-five-second delay."

Juvaszt glanced up at Anaris again, his expression difficult to
read. "Navigation, hold position. Put him on."

The viewscreen flickered to reveal a powerfully built man
with a strong, hawk-nosed face, seated in his command pod.
The bridge around him was out of focus. Anaris studied him
momentarily while the lightspeed delay elapsed, then looked
over at the Panarch. The smile was gone from his face, replaced
by the mask of command. The Dol'jharian felt a spark of anticipation; it would happen as he expected.

After five seconds the image spoke. "Captain Metellus
Hayashi, of His Majesty's destroyer *Falcomare*, commanding. I
assume, as is your nature, that you intend His Majesty as a hostage against the safety of your ship. I will need to confirm his
well-being before speaking further."

Anaris saw Juvaszt smile thinly in triumph as he motioned to
the Tarkans. They prompted the Panarch forward, as Juvaszt
said, "That, and cessation of your attacks against the Mandala,
and of the action in the middle system . . ." He broke off as the
communications officer motioned to him.

"A fourth wave of lances has been launched antipodal to our
position."

"Dispatch the *Satansclaw* and the frigates to deal with it," Juvaszt ordered.

As Juvaszt's reply reached him the Panarchist captain's eyes shifted from the kyvernat to the Panarch. He saluted, but remained seated, within reach of his controls. "Your Majesty. I regret the circumstances. Are you well?" Then, as the system relayed the communications officer's report as well, Anaris saw Hayashi's lips quirk slightly.

Anaris looked away from the screen and watched the Panarch as he replied. He wondered if Juvaszt had even an inkling of the formal emptiness of the exchange between the two, an emptiness that hid a fullness of meaning that needed no explicit statement.

"As well as can be expected. I congratulate you on your tactics; I'm sure Kyvernat Juvaszt here will confirm their effectiveness."

Anaris felt a flare of conviction, but hid it. The lightspeed delay made the conversation seem even more dance-like and ritualistic: it was utterly Douloi. He could see Juvaszt's eyes begin to ferret between the two Panarchists. *He senses something wrong, but doesn't have a chance of figuring out what it is.* Exultation accelerated Anaris' heartbeat. This Hayashi was giving him the keys to power on the *Fist of Dol'jhar*.

"Thank you, Your Majesty. That is good to know." His eyes moved back to Juvaszt. "Well, Captain, you leave me no choice. Please stand by."

"By no means," replied Juvaszt quickly, his uncertainty evaporating. "We will not stand by while your fourth wave of lances attacks the Mandala. We will discuss terms after we have dealt with them." He motioned decisively and the image flickered and froze.

Looking past Juvaszt, Anaris saw the Panarch watching them. Gelasaar's eyebrows lifted fractionally, and somehow the gesture, freighted with meaning that no one else on the bridge could grasp, even if they saw it, left Anaris feeling even more alone than usual. For the one man who saw and understood his coming triumph was one with whom he couldn't share it.

❊   ❊   ❊

FALCOMARE

The engines of the *Falcomare* groaned on a rising note, accelerating the ship into a yawing spin that was taking it dangerously close to the stress limits imposed by its elongated form.

On the viewscreen the image froze. Next to Juvaszt, the Panarch, standing between the two larger Dol'jharian guards, looked out of the screen directly at Hayashi, his gaze as compelling as if they were still in contact.

Metellus Hayashi laughed, a savage sound; looking around the bridge he could see its echo in everyone present.

"Skipmissile charged and ready," reported Lieutenant Ushkaten.

"Engage," Hayashi said.

There was a momentary pause—the computer would actually decide the moment of skip. Then the fiveskip burped, taking them out from behind the moon on the first leg of the skip that would take them in for the attack. It ceased, and the stars whirled madly across the viewscreen. Hayashi could feel the ghost of inertia pulling at his inner ear; the gravitors were not designed to compensate for this dramatic a rotation.

Moments later the fiveskip burped again, not so harshly. They couldn't afford too high a real velocity, since they'd emerge headed at the planet. The lower speed would leave them exposed to the enemy's ruptors all that much longer, but Hayashi was counting on the Dol'jharian inability to believe that they would fire on a ship carrying their liege.

Fools! A Dol'jharian'd be shot—if he was lucky—for doing so. I'd be shot, and rightly so, if I didn't.

"Emergence," said Navigation. Arthelion bulked huge ahead, fleeing across the screen as the ship yawed, exposing the stars above its limb, and then the bright star of the *Fist of Dol'jhar* came into view. The screen flickered to maximum magnification; the huge ship yawed noticeably as it came about for its second skip to deal with the fourth lance attack. Its radiants flared brightly, then were suddenly overlayed by the reddish pulse-wake of a skipmissle. There was a gout of light that momentarily blackened the screen.

Then, as the nose of the *Falcomare* swung past their enemy, the computer engaged the fiveskip, hurling them away from the engagement.

✳   ✳   ✳

FIST OF DOL'JHAR

The viewscreen cleared from skip and stars fled across it as the *Fist of Dol'jhar* came about for the second skip that would take it over Arthelion to assist the *Satansclaw* and the other Rifter vessels.

Juvaszt stretched in his command pod. Anaris perceived the gesture as the assertion of control that it was and smiled slowly in response, letting the captain see his expression. Juvaszt's brow knitted, and he opened his mouth.

"Emergence pulse!" shouted Durriken at the sensors console. "One-seventy mark 8, destroyer, course 262 mark 33, coming about for skipmissile attack . . ."

"What?" shouted Juvaszt, looking over at the Panarch, his eyes wide with disbelief. "Ruptors! Fire at will . . ."

A savage blow jolted the bridge. The lights flickered and a wave of gravitational distortion from suddenly unstable gravitors threw several officers off their feet or out of their pods. Even as he clutched at the back of the captain's pod for support, Anaris exulted. *Captain Hayashi, your timing is impeccable!*

Juvaszt's mouth snapped shut. He stared at Anaris a moment, his face echoing the expression he'd worn at the *eglarhh hreimmash*, the ghost-laying ceremony. Then he slapped at his console.

"Damage Control!"

"Skipmissile impact on radiants, severe damage to engine one, automatic shut down sequence engaged; engine two destabilized. Skip aborted."

"Enemy vessel has skipped out, no other traces detected," reported the sensors officer.

"Engineering, report!"

The bright sound of delighted laughter turned the heads of everyone on the bridge. The Panarch was staring directly at Juvaszt, and following his gaze, Anaris very nearly burst into laughter himself. He saw Morrighon's lips twitch as well; Juvaszt wore an expression of utter outrage, almost betrayal.

"He told you the truth," said Gelasaar, his Dol'jharian distorted by a heavy accent, and by his smile. "You left him no choice, nor did his oath."

The Tarkans on either side of him looked on, confused, not knowing what to do until Juvaszt motioned to them with a savage slash of his hand. They grasped the Panarch by each elbow and marched him toward a hatch.

Anaris waited until they reached the hatch before he gave in to impulse and signaled them to halt.

They obeyed, dropping back when he walked over and nodded, so that he and the Panarch faced one another alone.

Anaris waited, studying Gelasaar's face. There was no hint of defeat, only the well-bred inquiry that indicated perfect control.

Anaris pitched his voice so that only Gelasaar could hear, and said, "Brandon is alive."

The physical reaction was all he could have wished; the Panarch's head jerked up, one of his hands going to his heart before dropping to his side.

He opened his mouth to ask a question, but Anaris waved to the Tarkans, who stepped forward, one of them clamping a hand on the Panarch's shoulder.

But before Gelasaar was taken away, he shook off the Tarkan's hand and bowed, the graceful and deliberate deference of unalloyed gratitude.

Then he was gone, leaving Anaris to face the unsuccessfully repressed curiosity of Juvaszt and his bridge officers. Anaris knew they would have misjudged the meaning of the Panarch's reactions, seeing defeat there. The wary respect with which they watched him follow the Tarkans made that abundantly clear.

But they had not seen the Panarch's face, which had so freely expressed his emotional reaction. Anaris had not been sure what he expected, but what he saw was hope, and unshadowed joy.

Anaris examined his own reaction to that, which had surprised him a little, and laughing to himself as he turned back to the bridge, began exploring ways to use it.

THIRTY-THREE

✳

GROZNIY

Margot Ng closed her eyes briefly as the subtle pulse of the ruptors died away. On the viewscreen another Rifter ship dissipated in shreds and tatters of glowing debris.

"It's your empathy that makes you such a good captain," Metellus had said to her once. *"You can put yourself in their minds, see as they see ..."*

And feel as they feel, she thought. Maybe it was the core of her success, but she sometimes wished it didn't hurt so much.

"That's another empty," grumbled Commander Krajno. "I wonder if KepSingh or Armenhaut is doing any better."

"Evidently these FTL coms are less common than those Rifters thought," said Rom-Sanchez.

"That's good news, of a sort," rejoined Krajno.

"Navigation," said Ng, "take us to position three."

As the stars slewed around on-screen, Ng wondered if their luck, or lack of it, would hold. As the battle progressed, if you could call such a spread-out, cold-blooded hunt by that name, their information on enemy positions became older and less accurate. They'd jumped right on top of their first victim; the second one had taken almost ten minutes to locate. They could expect an even longer search for the next one, and eventually their chances would be no better than a random search.

"Emergence pulse, courier," said SigInt.

"Navigation, hold position," Ng snapped.

"Message incoming," Ensign Ammant said. "*Flammarion's* got one, a destroyer; two frigates and a destroyer have already responded. Coordinates transferred."

Ng checked the timing on the message. The courier had taken less than ten minutes to find them.

"Navigation, take us in, eight light-minutes out at forty-five degrees, your discretion." She tapped her console plot-pane to clarify her request.

The fiveskip burred harshly for a time, fell silent. The viewscreen cleared, and a tactical plot windowed up. She studied the information as the Tenno shifted and stabilized, hearing without attention the twittering from the communications section as tacponder information flooded in: reports from Armenhaut and others in his squadron. Rom-Sanchez' fingers blurred on his console as he sorted them out, applying temporal filters; she noted Warrigal at her console, backing him up.

She sighed. Armenhaut was fighting with his usual unimaginative style; he'd not yet gotten his lances away. KepSingh hadn't shown up yet.

"Let's take this one," she said finally, tapping at her plot-pane. A red circle ringed a Rifter frigate. "We'll stay out of Armenhaut's way for the moment." She turned to Rom-Sanchez. "I want updates to and from the tacponders as often as you can handle it."

"Navigation, take us in to these coordinates, three light-minutes out for an update. Prepare for high tac-level attack. Weapons, charge skipmissile."

She paused, feeling the lift in spirits on the bridge. Not for the first time, she wondered momentarily at the human preference for danger to boredom, a failing—if that's what it was— that she fully shared.

Then Ng pushed the thought aside. "Engage," she said, and there was no more time for philosophy.

❊ ❊ ❊

SATANSCLAW

Anderic moved his hands over his console, trying to keep up with the actions of the logos as that cold intelligence fought the ship for him. On the viewscreen green fingers of light reached out and clawed at the last few lances of the third attack, transforming them into bursts of plasma that shredded instantly away in the upper airs of Arthelion.

His hands ached, both with the tension of keeping up appearances and with the effort he was expending to keep them from shaking uncontrollably. He remembered the exultant expression on Tallis' face, over Charvann, and during the pursuit of the courier; loathing filled him at his former captain's stupidity. *What credit is there in following the motions of a machine? I'm just a chatzing puppet.*

He was beginning to think that nothing the Dol'jharians could do to him would be as bad as what he'd done to himself. He was damned, in inescapable slavery to the machine that haunted the *Satansclaw.*

"ALL ATTACKING VESSELS DESTROYED," reported the logos in his inner ear. Anderic slumped back in the command pod, wringing his hands in his lap, trying to relax them. At least they were here potshotting lances, instead of dueling with Panarchist battlecruisers in the middle system, or sitting dead in space like the *Deathstorm.*

He noted Lennart looking at him, her face a studied blank that he found vaguely threatening. Something in her demeanor toward him had changed. He snorted and dismissed it; no wonder, that image of her and Luri had become a favorite of every Rifter ship with a hyperwave. Anderic fought a smile. Some inspired tech had dubbed in a new sound track with outrageous noises; just thinking about it made his sides ache all over again.

Lennart turned away as her console beeped. She listened a moment, her head cocked. "Signal from *Fist of Dol'jhar.* New attack, coordinates transferred."

"Take us around," said Anderic, his heartbeat accelerating again.

The fiveskip burred, ceased. The ship came about, skipped again. As the screen cleared, targeting crosses sprinkled the limb of Arthelion below, while above, tiny with distance, threads of light lanced out toward the planet from the blocky form of a frigate.

Wearily Anderic began his deadly charade anew as the logos began its merciless slaughter of the lances diving toward the surface they would never reach. He wondered how long the Panarchists could keep this up.

"DEBRIS SIGNATURE INCONSISTENT WITH HUMAN OCCUPANCY," said the logos suddenly. *"INSUFFICIENT ORGANIC TRACES."*

Anderic frowned. That was strange. Were they throwing empties now?

"Sensors, scan the debris for organic residue again."

After a moment the tech replied: "Different signature, Captain. Not enough organic molecules." He looked up, brows raised. "I think they're empty."

"Communications, signal the *Fist*."

Moments later the harsh features of Kyvernat Juvaszt windowed up. "Report."

"Scans indicate the lances are now unmanned," said Anderic, too weary even to attempt an ingratiating manner.

Juvaszt stared at him for a moment; then the image froze. A few moments later it jumped to a new view of the Dol'jharian as transmission resumed. "Cease fire and skip to these coordinates," said Juvaszt. "You will cooperate with the destroyers *Hellmouth* and *Bloodknife* and the frigate *Golden Bones* to destroy the Panarchist battlecruiser attacking the *Deathstorm*. Stand by for further orders after emergence. Juvaszt out."

The screen blanked. Anderic stared at it for a moment, empty of emotions, and then began issuing the commands that would take them into battle, conned not by flesh and blood, but by the crystalline incarnation of warriors long dead. Did they care, he wondered, if they died again?

※　　　　　※　　　　　※

FIST OF DOL'JHAR

Anaris watched Juvaszt issue orders to the Rifter destroyer and frigates that had been defending Arthelion against the lance attacks. Despite the hammerblows the man's assurance had taken in the last few minutes, his actions were precise and accurate.

It helped that the reports from Engineering were fairly hopeful. One engine was down for at least forty-eight hours, but even so, the *Fist of Dol'jhar* was still a formidable engine of war, even more so with the Urian-enhanced skipmissiles. Now that there was no threat to the Avatar, events would turn rapidly against the Panarchists in the middle system.

As for his own campaign, Anaris was fairly sure that he now had the upper hand with Juvaszt. He hoped so. *It would be a shame to have to purge him.*

Well, that was still in the future. There was much to do in the meantime. He motioned to Morrighon, then held up his hand and stayed him as he heard the next orders.

"Navigation, take us in to ten light-minutes out from *Deathstorm*'s position. Weapons, charge skipmissile."

He means to deny the hyperwave to the Panarchists by destroying the ship.

Anaris stepped forward. Juvaszt turned to him, and the conditional heir felt satisfaction at the hint of deference in the man's expression.

"Kyvernat," said Anaris, pitching his voice for Juvaszt alone, "that may well be necessary, but I would suggest delaying it as long as possible, lest our Rifter allies lose heart." He smiled, inviting Juvaszt to share his joke. "They are not, after all, Dol'jharians."

A short bark of laughter escaped Juvaszt. Anaris sensed his appreciation—never to be expressed in words—at the lack of gloating on his part. "No more than I am a Panarchist, it seems." He turned away for a moment.

"Navigation, hold position."

Anaris felt a wave of triumph. That was the equivalent of surrender in a proud Dol'jharian noble like Juvaszt. He waved his hand, dismissing the subject. "I'd be a fool if I lived on Arthelion as long as I did and learned nothing of their ways." He paused for effect. "And even more a fool if I learned too much."

Juvaszt laughed again. "A fool, or dead," he agreed. "Among the Children of Dol it's usually the same thing, which is our strength."

He turned back to his console. Anaris could see the realtime feed changing as he queried various Rifter ships fighting around the *Deathstorm*. Then Juvaszt issued new orders and the *Fist of Dol'jhar* skipped out of Arthelion orbit to join the battle.

✳   ✳   ✳

EISENKUSS

Dyarch Ehyana Bengiat watched as the *Flammarion* fell away behind her lance and then vanished in a pulse of reddish light. She switched the viewscreen to the forward view; ahead a dim spark of light marked their target, a Rifter destroyer, dead in space.

There was no other sign of the battle raging all around them. Space was too large, and human ships, even battlecruisers, far too small. She couldn't even see the other lances; even had she known where to look, their dull black hulls would have defeated her eyes, just as their other countermeasures defeated the far keener senses of enemy ships. In silence, against diamond-sprinkled velvet, the *Eisenkuss* lunged toward its prey.

It would be several minutes before they reached the sprint point, where the engines would trigger into overload to take them through the destroyer's shields, past any weapons that might be brought to bear. *And they must know we're coming for them.* As Meliarch Abrams had pointed out in the briefing, the fact that Captain Armenhaut hadn't used the ruptors was a dead giveaway.

Well, there was no use worrying about that. She stretched against the dead weight of her battle armor, not yet energized, and then triggered the diagnostic sequence.

"Again?" came a dramatic groan over the general access channel.

"You'd look pretty funny wallowing around in half a ton of inert dyplast and battle alloy, Jheng-li," she replied. "Yeah, again." She grinned. Solarch Jones Jheng-li affected an aversion to any effort that went beyond the usual Marine avoidance of scut work, but his squad was consistently near the top of the ratings in simulations and exercises. A few mocking comments followed, but quickly subsided. A Marine's battle armor was serious business: the thirty men and women on board—five squads—busied themselves confirming the status of the servo-armor that made them the deadliest fighters in human history.

A web of colored lines swept across her faceplate, followed by a flux of alphanumerics as the eyes-on display cycled. All AyKay there.

The diagnostic sequence completed just as the navcomp warned of the approaching sprint point, just as she'd intended. Now the Rifter destroyer had a shape, long and angular, slightly blurred by the gas and debris leaking from its wounds.

Bengiat tapped the big go-pad with one gauntleted hand, the only part of her yet powered up, and that at only five percent. Her faceplate sealed; she felt the clamps engage around her armor.

"Time to shut your face or suck vacuum, Mary," she said, observing the ancient tradition. "Prepare for gees."

"Will you respect me in the morning?" yelled Jheng-li, his voice near manic in the equally traditional response, provoking a flurry of similar comments as her five squads pumped themselves up for attack.

Then the brightly driving trumpets of the Phoenix Fanfare filled the com channel. A few moments later the navcomp triggered the engines, and no one had any breath left for talking. Everything in a lance was aimed at one goal: taking it safely through the spacetime distortion of a fully driven tesla field behind the fierce jet of a shaped nuclear charge. Only the bare minimum of energy was spared to cushion the Marines from gee-forces. It was a ten-gee ride all the way in.

On the screen the destroyer swelled alarmingly, filled the view, and vanished in a flare of light that blanked the viewscreen as a shattering roar rattled her bones. The lance's hull rang like a vast bell struck by an avalanche as the engines were triggered into destructive overload, carrying them through the savage deceleration of an impact that would otherwise have reduced them all to twin blobs of jelly in their armored boots.

There was a moment of ringing silence, then another roar as the front of the lance exploded outward. The interior filled with smoke for a moment, which whipped into madly rushing streamers of gray that were pulled around the edges of the opening into the destroyer, escaping back toward the vacuum of space. They slowed into random eddies as white sealant pumped out.

"Was it good for you?" yelled Jheng-li, provoking a wave of laughter and bawdy comments. Bengiat's faceplate flashed, the clamps on her limbs disengaged with a rattle, and her suit came to life. The gee-tank elevated and she stepped out.

"Let's go," she yelled, waving the five other Marines in her squad forward.

FALCOMARE

"The starboard hangar bay's pretty much done for, but we're still fit, otherwise." Bea Doial grimaced. "We got off lightly, considering."

Hayashi nodded. Captain Doial and her crew had learned something that often killed the student: that no simulator could duplicate the real impact of a ruptor. But he saw only eagerness in her face now, and in Galt's too, in another window on the screen. They were at the fifth staging point, preparing for the fifth attack on Arthelion.

"Courier report incoming," said Ensign Mellieur. Her console twittered. She looked up, startled.

"From Captain Ng. The *Fist of Dol'jhar* has joined the battle around *Deathstorm*. The Marines have boarded."

"Damn," said Hayashi. "They must have scanned that last wave of lances."

On the screen a tactical plot windowed up; he saw Doial's and Galt's eyes move as Mellieur echoed it to them.

"We've got to keep the *Fist* away from the *Deathstorm* until the Marines get clear with the FTL com. Give him no rest, keep him hopping. Eventually he's going to figure to deny us the com by destroying the Rifter ship—we can't give him the time."

He started sketching on his plot-pane, the screen echoing his movements with bold slashing lines of color.

"Here's how we'll start . . ."

DEATHSTORM

Bengiat's squad spilled out the front of the lance in drill-perfect form, covering each other, but as was almost always the case, there was no one waiting for them. It was impossible to predict just where a lance would impact. Her squad deployed, positioning themselves to defend the other four squads as they emerged.

Her eyes scanned the wreckage of the hold they'd penetrated, noting without effect the gruesome blotches of shattered flesh decorating the twisted bulkheads. The hatch to the corridor outside hung by a single hinge; a Marine grasped it with one gauntlet and wrenched it off, sending it spinning to one side.

She felt a grinding shock as another lance struck the destroyer, then another. Her com crackled to life.

"Bengiat, status," came the voice of Meliarch Abrams. Behind her the rest of the lance's contingent spilled out into the hold.

"Secure the corridor," she commanded, then switched to the command channel.

"Breach secured, sir. No casualties, all full effective."

"Good. You're furthest forward and up. Proceed to the bridge and secure the FTL device. Extract the codes and grab the comtech if you can." A tactical map spidered up on her faceplate. "Secure these points on your way." Circles bloomed on several corridor junctions and stairs—they couldn't use the transtube. The map shifted, with other points highlighted. "We'll secure the port and starboard hangar bays and the ships for evacuation, and shut down the power room."

"AyKay, sir. Understood."

"You heard the man," she shouted. "We haven't got much time—when the Dol'jharians figure out what we're after they'll try to blow up the ship. Move it!"

They double-timed down the corridor, following the green traces in their faceplates supplied by their tactical computers. Every Navy ship had the plans for every type of vessel ever built; thanks to their tac-comps, the Marines probably knew this destroyer better than most of its crew.

From time to time red targets flashed on the bulkheads or overhead, answered by bursts of plasma from the jacs of the Marines: imagers and other sensors identified by the tac-comps.

At the critical points identified by Meliarch Abrams she deployed small groups of three to hold them—half a squad. A lance contingent, five squads of six, was an almost infinitely adaptable force. They moved as a unit, effortlessly coordinated by years of training, and yet as individuals, immediately responsive to any situation. Nothing could match them, and they knew it.

As they approached the bridge her suit discriminators picked up sounds indicative of some sort of defensive effort. She halted the two squads short of the last corner and popped a Scuttler out of her suit. The little device shot around the corner, relaying a clear picture of the six Rifters in half-armor clustered behind two plasma cannons before a flare of energy from a jac vaporized it.

"Jheng-li, deployed two for splash-n-burn, smoggers at minus three. Sniller, stun-bombs to follow up; Amasuri, you and I with the wasps." She looked around as the other Marines scrambled into position, the two Jheng-li she had assigned for splash-n-burn dialing their jacs to wide aperture. The rest not called out took up positions to cover their rear. She called up the wasp setting with her eyes-on, felt the little missiles click into readiness below her wrists.

"AyKay. Five, four, three . . ."

FIST OF DOL'JHAR

Kyvernat Juvaszt could feel a titanic headache building. The grainy flickering of the realtime feeds from their Rifter allies in-system gnawed at his eyes; his irritation was compounded by the ghost images and jeering voices from other Rifters throughout the Thousand Suns that the discriminators couldn't entirely eliminate.

He glanced at Serakhnat Mekhli-chur at the tactical console. Was he keeping up with the flood of information? The tactical plot was jumpy, but appeared to be updating properly. It was hard to tell. Juvaszt dismissed the niggling thought. He had no choice but to rely on his officers' competence; and they all knew the price of failure.

The presence of the conditional heir didn't help, either. Anaris had refrained from gloating, and his suggestions had been genuinely useful, but having him standing behind the command pod was almost as bad as having the Avatar there. *Except that his understanding runs deeper.*

Juvaszt shifted in the command pod, mildly shocked by the dangerous direction of his thoughts.

His tactical officer leaned toward him. "I suggest these new coordinates for the *Satansclaw* and *Bloodknife*," he said. Above, a screen echoed his comments graphically. Juvaszt nodded. Serakhnat Mekhli-chur turned away and began issuing the orders.

"Sensors indicate boarding in progress on *Deathstorm*," said the sensors officer.

Juvaszt glanced at Anaris, who shrugged fractionally.

"Navigation, after next tactical skip, new heading, 44 mark 272, prepare for skip, *Deathstorm* minus ten light-seconds. Weapons, status?"

"Skipmissile charged, all ruptors on-line . . ."

The ship shuddered. The fiveskip moaned in a tactical skip.

"Skipmissile, glancing impact," said Damage Control. "Minor damage in forward third."

"Destroyer signature, skipped, reading 145 mark 13."

That was the first sign of Panarchist destroyers in the battle around the *Deathstorm*, thought Juvaszt. Evidently Captain Hayashi knew they were no longer to be fooled by the lance attack on Arthelion. Well, he and his squadron would have to be dealt with first.

He raised his voice. "Navigation, new course . . ."

DEATHSTORM

Jheng-li tossed the smoggers around the corner. In her mind's eye Bengiat could see them scuttling toward the Rifters, then bursting into thick clouds of energy-absorbing particles, cutting down the efficiency of the plasma cannons. He slapped one of the Marines waiting at the corner, Suza; she dived across the corridor, her armor deflecting the coruscant burst of one of the mobile jacs for the brief time she was exposed. Then she swiveled and with the other Marine Jheng-li had chosen for the splash-n-burn triggered her jac into the corridor, aiming at the deck, creating a wash of intense heat that rolled down toward the Rifters, under the clouds from the smoggers.

". . . two . . ."

Sniller stepped forward and lobbed the stun-bombs around the corner. Their faceplates automatically filtered out the visual stutter-pulse, the audio in their suits stopping down at the same time to save them from the stunning ultrasonics.

". . . one, *go!*" Bengiat launched herself into the corridor, twisting in midflight, extending her arms toward the Rifter positions hidden in the smoke and flipping her wrists palms-up. Plasma splashed off her armor in a burst of radiance and she felt the little wasp missiles discharge as her momentum carried her into the cross corridor. The coolant system of her suit whined. Twin explosions slapped at the air as Amasuri followed. Two more explosions, then silence.

She stepped cautiously back into the corridor. Nothing happened. She moved forward, her jac ready. The smoke from the smoggers cleared, revealing the cannons as twisted wreckage, surrounded by dead Rifters, mostly in pieces, armor melted around cooked flesh.

"All clear. Let's blow the hatch."

The tac-comp flashed charge-points on her faceplate, outlining the weak points in the sealed hatch onto the bridge. She motioned Jheng-li forward; he slapped two hand charges onto the spots that his tac-comp, too, was showing and stepped back.

"Clear."

There was a muffled whomp, twin spurts of light, and the charge casings fell away, revealing neat holes with blue-white edges. Bengiat stepped forward, using her eyes-on to bring up a new setting in her armor. This time, flipping her wrists ejected two stout hooks which she pushed through the holes, along with a fiber-optic probe. A quick scan of the bridge revealed nothing their armor couldn't handle.

She retracted the probe. "AyKay, Mary. It's showtime." Four Marines turned to hold the corridor, the rest poised themselves in readiness.

She pulled smoothly, reveling in the incredible amplification of her strength lent by the servos, and pulled the hatch out of the opening. Stepping back, she waited as the other Marines pounded past her, yelling fiendishly with amplified voices that boomed from the bulkheads, then threw the hatch down the corridor and followed them onto the bridge.

✻   ✻   ✻

FLAMMARION

"Hit on *Babur Khan*," said SigInt.

The viewscreen flickered to extreme magnification, Armenhaut saw plasma billowing from a glowing gash on the flank of KepSingh's battlecruiser before the big ship vanished in a burst of bluish light.

"Severe damage; he's skipped. Enemy destroyer bearing 82 mark 66, 6.2 light-seconds, skipped, heading 234 mark 16."

Armenhaut scanned the tactical plot. Hayashi's destroyers were harassing the *Fist of Dol'jhar*, keeping it away from the *Deathstorm*. He wondered momentarily when Juvaszt would give up and order one of the other Rifter ships to destroy the crippled ship, and if they would obey.

"Emergence pulse, battlecruiser—" The moan of the fiveskip modulated SigInt's voice as the *Flammarion* executed a tactical skip. "ID *Fist of Dol'jhar*, 34 mark 208, heading 65 mark 40, firing skipmissile . . ."

A gout of light erupted on the screen. It flashed to a close-up, revealing a sphere of light expanding against the stars, with the missile tube of a destroyer spinning away from the explosion. SigInt's voice went tight.

"*Barahyrn* destroyed." Then, "*Fist of Dol'jhar* coming about to new heading, firing ruptors . . ." He paused. "Skipmissile impact on *Fist of Dol'jhar*, minor damage, engines destabilized, estimate back on-line fifteen seconds."

Another spark of light flared. "*Falcomare* hit. Severe damage, skipped . . ."

As SigInt continued, Armenhaut realized that the fog of battle had swept away the Panarchist defenders of the crippled ship and the Arkadic Marines on board. Juvaszt had seen his opening; there was nothing standing between the *Fist* and the destruction of the FTL com that so many lives had been sacrificed for already. Nothing except the *Flammarion*.

"Launch all corvettes," he commanded. "All ships to converge on *Deathstorm* to assist Marine evacuation. Navigation, new heading." He snapped out the heading that would take them in against the Dol'jharian battlecruiser. "Weapons, status?"

"Skipmissile fully charged, all ruptors on-line and tracking."

"Communications, tactical full-sphere burst." He quickly dictated a situation report, then, as the stars slewed to a halt on the viewscreen, "Engage."

THIRTY-FOUR

DEATHSTORM

Aziza cowered behind her pod, shaking with terror, her jac forgotten in her hand as the hatch ripped away and the Marines thundered onto the bridge of the *Deathstorm*. Their amplified battle cries tore at her ears, jac-bolts sizzled overhead, a console exploded, someone screamed tearingly, a horrible sound that ended in a gurgle.

It was over in a moment. The surviving members of the crew, including Captain Qvidyom, who'd dropped his jac almost instantly, were quickly rounded up by the Marines, faceless in their bulky armor. Aziza could feel heat radiating from the armor of the one who pulled her from behind her pod, the only sign of the jac-bolt that had hit him.

Three of the invaders went directly to the Urian hyperwave, glowing weirdly against the communications console. Tools extruded from their gauntlets and began to gnaw at the fittings holding down the device. Another began tracing its cable connections, while yet another went to the main computer console and began working at it. Aziza watched in fascination, her terror slowly subsiding, at the delicate whisker-like feelers that sprouted from his suit.

"Which one of you chatzers is the comtech?" came a booming voice. Aziza stared as the faceplate of the suit from which the voice issued popped open, revealing the face of a woman who wouldn't have looked out of place in one of the fancy fashion chips her mother had been so fond of.

"Well?" said the Marine, her voice more human without amplification.

"I am," Aziza squeaked. Captain Qvidyom glared at her.

The Marine swiveled and stomped toward her, her armor whining. Suddenly Aziza giggled. She couldn't help it—she knew she was on the edge of a hysterical fit—but she had a sudden image of the woman in a fashion show, stumping down the runway in her armor. *What kind of lingerie does the well-dressed marine wear, or is she naked in there?*

"You know how to work that thing?" the woman asked as two other Marines herded the others a short distance away and made them sit down on the deck. Aziza nodded, swallowing. The smell of burned flesh was making her nauseous. The woman's eyes scanned her face, her expression softening slightly.

"What's your name?" she asked, her voice somewhat less brusque.

"Aziza. Aziza bin'Surat."

"AyKay, Aziza. Where are the codes?" The Marine at the computer looked up. "Can you identify them?"

"Yes."

The woman pushed her toward the main computer console. Aziza was astonished at how gentle her touch was, despite the heavy armor. "Help him find them."

She turned away as another Marine entered the bridge. Qvidyom stared at Aziza, her eyes full of hate. He mouthed an obscene threat at her, shocking even for him. She shuddered and concentrated on the console, stealing a glance at the Marine standing next to her. His face was craggy, his expression tense.

As she worked she heard fragments of a conversation: ". . . can't pick us up, corvettes on the way . . . out of time . . ."

"That's it," said the Marine finally, straightening up from the computer. The console twittered and went dead, and he disconnected his probe.

"Dyarch, we've got . . ." A sudden gargling noise from the

front of the bridge interrupted him. Aziza looked up to see a hideously burned figure suddenly flop out onto the deck from behind a pod, moaning. She guessed it was Nigal, though she couldn't be sure; evidently the Marines had thought he was dead. She hoped he soon would be, no one should suffer like that; he'd actually been pretty decent.

The Marines guarding the prisoners turned to look. Suddenly Captain Qvidyom rolled onto his side, reached for his boot, and jackknifed to a sitting position as his hand cocked back. His arm jerked forward even as the woman Marine swiveled toward him. Aziza shrieked as a knife sprouted from her shoulder.

"Chatz!" the woman shouted, took two long steps toward Qvidyom, and lashed out with her foot. There was a wet crunching sound, followed by a squelching thud as the Rifter captain's head bounced off a bulkhead and came to rest in the middle of the deck, staring upward. The eyes blinked twice, the mouth worked briefly and was still as his headless body toppled over, spouting blood all over the luckless Rifters around him.

"Medic!" shouted the woman, and then, "That's it! We've got what we came for. Prepare to evacuate, we're going straight out."

The bridge blurred around Aziza as the medic pulled the knife out of her shoulder and packed the wound with synflesh. He slapped an ampoule into her upper arm; the pain abruptly fuzzed away. Another Marine strode toward her, shaking out a silvery bag. Her mind suddenly, horribly clear, Aziza shrieked again and tried to scramble away as they started to stuff her into it and the bridge buzzed into darkness and whirled away.

GROZNIY

"Skipmissile impact, aft beta section, aft beta ruptor off-line and not reporting, fiveskip destabilized . . ."

The grim litany of the damage-control officer rose above the pulse of the ruptors as they fired. Ng scanned the tactical plot rapidly, snapped out the orders for a new ruptor barrage.

". . . estimate twenty seconds to skip . . ."

"Skipmissile charging, forward gamma ruptors in harmonic cycle, shutdown in fifteen seconds."

The battering the *Grozniy* was taking from the Rifter skip-missiles was alarming, but the battlecruiser had a long way to go before it was no longer a danger to its enemies.

A flare of light erupted on the screen. "Multiple ruptor hits on *Bloodknife*. Target destroyed."

That was one less Rifter destroyer to worry about, she thought. Then a sudden shift in the Tenno drew her attention back to the viewscreen. She superimposed a tactical overlay, then gritted her teeth. *Armenhaut, you fool.*

He'd managed to hold off the *Fist of Dol'jhar*, deflecting it from its attack on the *Deathstorm* but taking tremendous damage in the process. And now he'd passed up his last chance to withdraw. Had he even seen it?

A wash of pity welled up in her, partly for him, mostly for his crew. Armenhaut was not an imaginative man; she thought he knew it, and was sure the knowledge had always been a part of his resentment of her. But neither was he a coward.

"Ten seconds to skip capability."

Even though she knew it was futile—they were seeing the action many seconds in the past, at extreme skipmissile range—she snapped out a new heading, watching the screen intently. "Shoot on acquisition."

"Tacponder message, relay from *Deathstorm*," said Ensign Ammant at Communications. "The Marines have the FTL com and are withdrawing. *Flammarion* has dispatched all corvettes to attempt pickup."

That was good news; but it made all the more bitter the solemn inevitability of the tragedy unfolding on the viewscreen. Slowly the *Fist of Dol'jhar* came about on its new heading. A targeting cross sprang up across its image, suddenly overlaid by the skipmissile wake.

"Target acquired, skipmissile away, skipmissile charging."

The *Flammarion* yawed desperately, trying to bring its skip-missile to bear on its opponent. The chain-of-pearls trace of a skipmissile lanced out from the *Fist*; the *Flammarion* vanished in a flare of light. When it dimmed, the ship was still there.

A blast of light washed out the image of the *Fist of Dol'jhar* as the *Grozniy*'s skipmissile impacted, too late. Moments later the Dol'jharian battlecruiser skipped out.

Ng held her breath.

"I think ..." began Commander Krajno; then a billow of bright plasma shot out of the radiants of the *Flammarion*. Small dots of light shot away from the stricken ship; some of its personnel were escaping—Armenhaut had evidently given the order to abandon ship. Then there was nothing but a sharp-edged sphere of light fading against the stars.

Ng shook her head, then straightened up in her pod. "Navigation, new heading ..." she began. The Marines were still on the *Deathstorm*, their lives so far bought and paid for by *Flammarion* and many others. She would do whatever she had to to complete the transaction.

BEREITTE

Lieutenant Gristrom tapped at the nav console of the corvette *Bereitte*. The little ship responded handily, crabbing closer to the stricken destroyer less than half a kilometer away. The voice of the Marine dyarch came through the com; in different circumstances he'd have fantasized about the owner of such a voice.

"We're ready here."

"Still clear," said Ensign Appleby, crouching intently at the another console, set for SigInt functions. A sudden flare of light washed through the con from a distant explosion.

"Big one," she said. "One of theirs, I hope."

Gristrom ignored her, concentrating on the targeting cursor for the corvette's lazplaz. If he was off by as much as a meter he'd fry the Marines and their prize.

Finally satisfied, he locked in the setting. The fire-control computer would handle it from here.

"Beam incoming," he said. A brilliant lance of plasma glared out, metal puffing away in brilliant coruscations where it hit the destroyer next to the bridge. He tapped the internal com.

"Stand by at the locks."

The lazplaz beam dimmed and ceased, its job done. He glanced at the viewscreen. Nearby, other corvettes hung in space, waiting for the Marines. Beyond, another coin of light bloomed in the darkness, now shot through with new-made nebulae marking the deaths of ships.

"Emergence pulse," shouted Appleby. "Big one, a cruiser, I think."

The viewscreen flickered to full magnification. Gristrom stared at the silvery hull looming a few hundred kilometers away, the red fist clutching thunderbolts bold on its side.

They were already dead, he thought. He wondered what a ruptor felt like.

DEATHSTORM

Aziza came back to consciousness almost immediately, but for a moment she was unable to orient herself. Then memory flooded back, and the thin, slick fabric around her resolved into the interior of the rescue bag the Marines had stuffed her into. One of them had slung her over his back. Aziza squirmed around, feeling the tug of the synflesh in her wound, until she could see through the semitransparent dyplast.

Sounds came through the fabric blurrily; she heard the woman say to her fellow Rifters, "Go." They scrambled to their feet and vanished through the ruined hatch. The Marines dogged down their faceplates and turned as one to face a bulkhead.

The lights failed, came back in the red of emergency power. Gravity failed. Aziza heard a sizzling roar, and the creaking of metal stressed beyond its limits. The roar grew louder, Aziza twisted, trying to see over the shoulder of her captor. The rescue bag torqued up, leaving her suspended upside down, but able to see what was going on over the Marines ahead of her.

The roar ceased. Two Marines stepped forward, placed a number of small objects against the bulkhead. They stepped back; jets of flame spurted from where the objects were leeched to the metal.

Aziza heard the screech of escaping air as the two Marines triggered their jacs at the weakened bulkhead. The rescue bag crinkled and expanded around her; her nose began to bleed as the pressure dropped. Something started popping at her feet; she felt tiny stings on her calves. *Oxy-poppers.* As the crystals re-

leased the precious gas she took a deep breath and wiped her
nose. Everyone knew how a rescue bag worked; no one ever expected to use one.

The bulkhead blew out with a suddenly silenced roar. Now
she couldn't hear anything except the crinkling of the dyplast as
the Marine towed her out of the hole. She stared in astonishment: instead of more ship, there was only a tangle of wreckage,
and then space.

Her captor launched himself away from the ship, small thrust-
ers flaring at the sides of his armor, aiming for a small ship not
far off. A reddish pulse of light bloomed beyond it. Abruptly the
Marine twisted, putting himself between her and it. Then the
ruined bulk of the *Deathstorm* lit up with the reflected light of
a distant explosion. Aziza felt her right foot tingle, the skin
burning, and jerked it toward her body. She was in the middle
of a battle in space, with nothing between her and the vacuum
but a plastic bag.

She considered the thought for a moment with a kind of quiet
hysteria and did the only logical thing. She fainted.

✳   ✳   ✳

GROZNIY

"Target identified, nine light-seconds, 62 mark 19, coming
about."

"Skipmissile charged."

"Fire on acquisition," said Ng.

The *Fist of Dol'jhar* hung near the ruined Rifter destroyer,
dwarfing the little corvettes swarming around it. As she
watched, several of them puffed into dust and glares of light.

"A little bit of target practice, the chatzer," said Krajno, his
teeth gritted.

"That's odd," Ng commented. "You'd almost think he'd lost
track of us."

"Target acquired, skipmissile away."

"Navigation, new heading, 30 mark 10, skip ten light-
seconds, tac-level five. Weapons, fire all bearing ruptors on
emergence."

The *Grozniy* came about, the viewscreen flaring with the impact of the skipmissile on the *Fist of Dol'jhar*. With all the dust and debris from the battle its impact would be severely diminished. *But then, so will that of the Dol'jharians' skipmissiles.*

The fiveskip snarled, ceased. The ruptors pulsed.

"Ruptor hits on *Fist of Dol'jhar*. Target coming about . . ."

The squeal-rumble of a ruptor pulse shuddered through the ship.

"Tactical skip, now," said Ng.

They'd bought the Marines a little more time, she thought, and then issued new orders to continue the attack.

※   ※   ※

FIST OF DOL'JHAR

"Ruptors, fire at will," said Juvaszt. On the screen, the Panarchist corvettes began to disintegrate.

He glanced at the tactical screen again to reassure himself. Yes, the last remaining Panarchist battlecruiser was still reported . . .

The tactical screen jerked, froze momentarily, then blurred into a new configuration. The overload on the hyperwave had caught up with them.

"Mekhli-chur!" he snarled, then stopped, his mouth open as the significance of the new information registered.

"Navigation! Tactical . . ."

A soundless blow jolted the ship. The gravitors hiccuped, Juvaszt felt his stomach lurch. The lights flickered.

"Skipmissile impact, forward first segment, forward first ruptor turret not responding, fiveskip destabilized, estimate ten seconds to skip . . ."

"Ruptors fire on heading 135 mark 16, wide barrage, now!" Juvaszt shouted. He glanced again at the tactical plot. One of the Rifters would have to deal the deathblow to the crippled ship; then together they could deal with the last battlecruiser. "Communications, give me clean channels to *Satansclaw* and *Hellmouth* . . ."

The shuddering squeal of a ruptor pulse shook his voice into silence. A gravitational eddy ripped open a bulkhead at the front of the bridge, spinning a luckless crewman away in a tangle c broken limbs as a console exploded.

"Multiple ruptor hits, engine two destabilized, fiveskip stil stabilizing . . ."

"Tactical skip when able," Juvaszt snapped. "Fifteen ligh seconds. Communications, where . . . ?"

"Coming up on subscreens one and two."

There was a flash of sparks from the ruined console as th fiveskip engaged. All the screens went dead for a moment, cam back, their images bouncing. Terresk-jhi stabbed frantically a her console, was rewarded by an image on the main screen.

Juvaszt's jaw dropped.

Anaris stared in amazement at the image on the main view screen. Two naked women, one dark, one honey-light, writhe on the deck of a ship, covered in some viscous dark liquid, fran tically licking each other in a tangle of limbs while a one-eye man looked on, clutching his bulging crotch and whimpering. I Dol'jharian terms it was unspeakably depraved.

Static crackled. "Whip me, beat me, make me speal Dol'jharian," a voice said lasciviously, while others moaned an panted in the background.

"Hey, Juvaszt, send that to the Panarchists! They'll be s busy flipping their nackers you can blow 'em away easy," shouted another. Anaris realized that Rifters throughout th Thousand Suns were now looking on, indulging, in total safety in baiting their Dol'jharian masters.

And so did Juvaszt. After a moment of frozen astonishmen he leapt from his pod and strode over to the communication console, knocking Terresk-jhi to the deck. He stood over her, hi mouth working for a moment, but he couldn't find words.

The unknown Rifter onlookers, however, could.

"Jump her, Juvaszt!"

"Ooh, Dol'jharian sex! I love it! Hurt me, you beast!"

"Juvaszt kim Karusch-na bo-synarrach, gri tusz ni-synarr perro-ti!"

Anaris bit his lip against a fierce desire to laugh. The un known Rifter had an excellent command of Dol'jharian, and hac concocted perhaps the worst insult imaginable, equating Ju vaszt's performance in the conquest-rituals of mating with soli tary sex.

Juvaszt slammed both hands down on the console, shattering it. Sparks flared, smoke rose from the ruined console as the image vanished. He motioned to the luckless officer's second, who took over on his console, and then to the Tarkans posted by the second aft hatch. They ran over and hauled the dazed woman away.

Anaris glanced at Morrighon, who made a note. If Terresk-jhi was still alive after the battle, he would intercede for her—another ally would be useful, especially in communications.

After a moment, Juvaszt straightened up. He looked around for a moment, then returned to his pod and seated himself.

"Communications reestablished with *Satansclaw* and *Hellmouth*," reported the second communications officer.

Juvaszt began issuing orders in a voice that gave no hint of the events just past. Anaris watched, thoughtful. The kyvernat's loss of control was another lever for the machinery of power he was building.

Moments later, Anaris noted with some perplexity the feeling of relief that washed through him, as Damage Control reported that the section of the ship housing the Panarch and the other prisoners had escaped damage.

To distract himself, he looked up at the tactical plot, slowly reading the information there. The Panarchists were taking tremendous losses.

He smiled to himself. On more than one level, the Battle of Arthelion was going very well.

BEREITTE

Dyarch Bengiat pushed her burden ahead of her into the lock of the corvette, easing it to the deck as gravity grabbed at it. She looked thoughtfully at the unconscious woman within.

Woman? She's barely more than a girl. The girl's short curly hair was matted down, her olive skin smudged; Bengiat could see a vein throbbing in the translucent skin of her temple. *How'd a child like that end up with a ship full of blungebags?*

Then she shook her head as the inner lock door cycled open.

For all she knew this Aziza could have grown up with the like of Qvidyom.

She pushed through the hatch into the corvette and triggere her com.

"Sound off, Marys, I need a head count." Anyway, she ha more important things to worry about now. She looked over . Jheng-li, who cradled the alien machine in his arms. They ha what they came for; all that remained was to get the hell out . the system alive.

✳   ✳   ✳

SATANSCLAW

"But, Kyvernat," Anderic stammered. "There might be . . ."

"Do not argue with me, unless you want to be left powerles to face that Panarchist battlecruiser," Juvaszt cut in. "Destro the *Deathstorm* immediately and stand by for further order Juvaszt out." The image disappeared, leaving stars in its plac

Anderic looked around the bridge, sensing the pressure of th crew's attention, even though none of them looked directly . him. *Don't they realize I don't have any choice?*

But it made no difference; it wasn't a matter of logic. Eve as allies of Dol'jhar, Rifters still thought in terms of us versu them, and the Dol'jharians were more ferociously *them* tha even the highest Douloi.

For a moment the image of the Panarch standing on th bridge of his enemy's flagship, clad in rags yet unbowed, hov ered before his eyes. He had every reason to hate the nicks, bu somehow the Panarch, despite his commanding presence, ha looked like someone you could actually talk to, who would ac tually listen.

Anderic snorted. He'd talked to Eusabian instead, who woul never hear anything but what he wanted to from the fearful scu tlers around him.

"Navigation," he said. "You heard him. Take us in to thre light-seconds. Fire Control, status?"

"Skipmissile charged," came the answer. Anderic could hea resentment in the man's tones.

"Course laid in," said sho-Imbris.

"Do it."

The fiveskip hummed for a moment. The screen cleared, stars swung across it. The screen flickered to a close-up. The *Death-storm* was a wreck, great holes punched in its hull where the lances had penetrated, its missile tube bent and torn, plasma leaking from a rent near the engine room. Several small ships hovered nearby. As he watched, they began to vanish, leaving behind the spherical pulses of the fiveskip. A targeting cursor bracketed the dying ship.

"Target acquired."

"Fire," said Anderic. Nothing happened.

Anderic looked hopelessly around the bridge, seeing no friendliness anywhere. He realized that the only thing that would keep him alive from this point on was the logos, which he hated. With a snarl of self-hatred he transferred control to his console and brought his hand down on the firing tab. Three seconds later the *Deathstorm* blew up, fragments spinning away through a scintillant cloud of dust and glowing gas.

A short time later he reported to Juvaszt and received his new orders. While the Dol'jharian was questioning him about the Panarchist ships, Anderic suddenly realized he hated the Dol'jharians even more than the logos. What would happen, he wondered, if they thought the hyperwave had been destroyed, but it hadn't? He'd seen some ships leaving; maybe the Panarchists had it now.

He smiled, knowing Juvaszt would misinterpret it. "They were all destroyed in the explosion," he said.

GROZNIY

Captain Ng watched again the replay from the courier. As the remains of the *Deathstorm* faded she tapped her console. The image vanished.

"That's it, then. Communications, any news?"

"Nothing new."

She sighed. The battle was evaporating now. The Navy had taken too many losses to continue. *Flammarion*, *Barahyrn*, and

Lady of Taligar destroyed, *Babur Khan* missing . . . Her thro tightened. *Falcomare* missing . . .

And they didn't know if they had the FTL com or not. The could only wait, staying out of the way of the victorious enem while the slow pulse of relativistic communications sprea through the tacponder net, invisible to their opponents.

"Emergence pulse," said SigInt. The fiveskip burped in a automatic tactical skip of 2.5 light-seconds. "Corvette, th *Bereitte*."

"Message incoming." Ammant put it on the screen before N could respond.

The viewscreen cleared to an image of a very small, ver cramped bridge. A Marine, a dyarch from the insignia on h rumpled jumpsuit, stood beside a small olive-skinned woma with a bloody nose. But Ng's eyes were fastened to the Marin next to them, standing with his hand possessively on the weir est piece of—what? Her heart slammed.

The naval lieutenant in the foreground saluted. "Lieutenan Gristrom reporting, sir, attached *Flammarion*." He smiled weary and proud. "We got it." And he added grimly, "Paid i full."

The bridge was pandemonium, a release of emotion greate than anything Ng had ever experienced. And rightly so. They' paid a terrible price for that red-glowing lump of metal, but no they had the key to the greatest of the enemy's two advantage

They now had a chance.

After a time she became aware of Ammant trying to sho above the tumult.

"Tacponder update incoming. We've found the *Babur Kha* it's in bad shape."

The noise died away abruptly.

"Get on board, Lieutenant," she said. "We've got more do."

❊   ❊   ❊

It was almost a day later that they finished evacuating the *Bab Khan*, which had been battered into scrap by three Rifter de stroyers. Captain KepSingh transferred his command to a frigat and volunteered to wait for any remnants of their forces tha might still find their way out of the battle area.

"I think we can even manage a few search-and-rescue runs,

e said. "With the tacponder net still running, we should be able
o find just about anybody with a functioning com."

Ng nodded wearily. Her duty was clear: the FTL com had to
et to Ares as soon as possible. A courier was one way, but
here were hundreds of wounded that needed medical care that
ow could be found only on Ares. Only the *Grozniy* could get
hem there.

"Very well, Captain KepSingh. We'll be on our way, then.
You have everything you need."

The older man nodded. His face softened. "We'll keep an es-
ecially sharp watch out for Metellus and his crew." He smiled.
That pirate's got a lot more light-years' travel in him, I'm
ure."

"Thank you, Captain." She paused. There was so much to
ay—but not now. She took refuge in ritual. "Light-bearer be
vith you; *Grozniy* out."

"And with you, Captain Ng."

The connection terminated.

"Navigation," she said after a moment, "take us to Ares."

As the fiveskip engaged, she stood up and left the bridge,
urning the con over to Commander Krajno. The transtube took
er to a hold deep within the *Grozniy*; the Marine on duty sa-
uted and let her in.

The lights sprang on, revealing the rounded glowing form of
he Urian communicator set on a table. They'd decided not to
ttempt any use of it—there were techs better fit for that on
Ares.

Margot Ng walked over and laid her hand gingerly on the
veird device, then snatched it away. It was warm, body temper-
ture, and felt uncannily like human flesh. Like muscular human
lesh, hard yet yielding.

Like Metellus.

A tear tracked down her cheek, then another. She was alone,
he let them flow, remembering him, the twenty-five years
hey'd had together, snatched in moments here and there.

Twenty-five years. She remembered his teasing about their
et. It had seemed a long time then. She'd been so sure she'd
rack down the port wriggle long before that. She knew she
vouldn't now. A sob caught in her throat. She'd give anything
o have him there to claim the forfeit.

It wasn't that she thought him dead; she wouldn't think that.

It was worse than that: she might never know. Space was larg
and human lives were short.

. . . and I will pay whatever price demanded . . .

The Urian device blurred as the tears came freely, but s
didn't look away.

"You'd better be worth it," she whispered fiercely.

THIRTY-FIVE

*

DESRIEN

Brim walked through the high doors of New Glastonbury into the cool night air.

He had no idea how much time had passed while they were within the cathedral. The night sky was clear, the brilliant constellations unfamiliar, and time seemed curiously suspended, as it had within the stone walls.

He looked about him, his senses heightened to an almost unbearable degree. The scents of loam, of trees and herbs, the sounds of whispering leaves and feet crunching the gravel, all were clear and distinct. Breathing deeply, he relished the dust and the chilly breeze. Each sensation moored him incrementally stronger to this world, veiling that other world with its false shadows and seductive dreams.

He looked at the others, observing the subtle signs that indicated the restoration of their perception of the here and now. Most of them talked, in the quick, laughter-punctuated, relieved voices of people who have endured something terrible and are temporarily drawn together in its aftermath.

The Aerenarch walked alone, his eyes contemplating the stars

overhead. Jaim knew that his mind had gone ahead to what h
to come next: Ares.

Will the nicks help him find his father?

A step beside him made him look up, glad for the distractic
The faint light outlined the familiar bony cheek and jawline
Lokri.

"Do you think they use drugs?" he drawled, pointing lazi
back toward the cathedral.

Jaim heard the bravado in Lokri's voice and guessed at t
fear that probably lay just underneath.

"Nothing so simple," he said.

"I take it you saw—things—too. Is that what they hit ever
one with who lands here? No wonder it has a rotten rep."

Brandon looked back, laughed.

"I can't figure out how they do it," Lokri said. "I know
can't be real, though it seemed so. If I had time to look for t
sim-machines . . ."

"I tried," Osri's acerbic voice broke in on their other side

"Discussing the medium," Omilov put in, "is as good a w
as any of avoiding the message."

Brandon was smiling. Jaim wondered if he, too, question
the physical reality of whatever it was he saw within the cath
dral. He seemed uninterested in the discussion whether they
imagined the whole as a result of some smokedrug slipped in
the altar censers, or if they'd stepped through the stone wal
into some other dimension.

"The truth is in the experience" is what Reth Silverknife us
to say.

The familiar pain gripped him.

Then the Aerenarch spotted the *Telvarna,* and he flexed h
hands; whatever was on his mind, he was preparing himself f
a confrontation.

And the only one there is Vi'ya.

Osri's voice splintered his thoughts. "If what I saw was re
then we'll all have to go back to school to relearn math."

Everyone laughed, even Montrose, who was carrying t
sleeping Ivard. Then Montrose frowned, shifting his grip on t
boy. "Say, where are the Eya'a?" he asked, looking around.

"They went back to the ship just after the captain did," Rog
spoke up. She added in a dry voice that raised a laugh, "We ha
no orders concerning them."

When they reached the *Telvarna*, Brandon paused, and as the others moved past him to go up the ramp, he gazed down at Ivard's face, now illuminated by the lights inside the ship. Jaim silently stepped behind him, watching. He'd expected to see the boy on the edge of death; though he still was bruised and thin-looking, and still feverish, there was a changed quality to his breathing, and in the eyes that suddenly opened, clear and blue, to smile upward before closing again.

"I almost think," Montrose said, "that he will live. He spoke back there, before he dropped off again, and he actually made sense."

"What did he say?" Jaim asked, aware of the others stopping and looking back.

" 'Got a bad case a' vacuum-gut. What's to eat?' "

"Very profound," Omilov said. "As well as cogent. In fact, his suggestion has a great deal to recommend it."

Montrose laughed. "If Nukiel's minions haven't raided my stores, I shall see what I can contrive. Let me get him settled first."

"C'mon, Lokri," Marim said, tugging on Lokri's good arm.

"What?" The comtech looked down into her merry bright eyes. "You're coming back with us?"

"*Anything's* better than this place," she said with a shiver. "I'll take my chance with the nicks."

"So will I, it seems," Lokri said, his voice edgy.

Marim said fervently, "This place is crazy, and maybe it'll be worse where we're going. So right now I want to hole up in our bunk, and until that chatzing cruiser grabs us let's bunny till our eyeballs steam."

Lokri choked on a laugh and they disappeared, hand in hand.

Most of the others headed slowly for the rec room, accompanied by the two Marines. The mood was akin to after-battle exhaustion, a peculiar mix of euphoria and sadness. No one had the energy to plan anything, and the Marines seemed to know it, functioning less as guards than as extra passengers.

Brandon said to the nearest Marine, "I'll be on the bridge." She nodded, and he turned, pausing when he saw Jaim just behind him.

"A moment," the Aerenarch said.

Jaim nodded, stopping.

"Is your offer—don't think I do not value it—something Eloatri forced onto you?"

Jaim shook his head. "No."

"Then . . ." Brandon lifted his hands. "Why?"

Jaim did not immediately answer, wondering how much to say—or if he should say anything.

Then the Aerenarch said directly: "It seems that everywhere I go people die, and I can do nothing to halt it."

"That will change," Jaim said. "You will change it."

Brandon looked up, his expression somewhere between a soundless laugh and a wince. "Maybe you'll tell me how," he said.

Jaim smiled, then moved on past to go into the bridge, aware of Brandon following.

Vi'ya was alone on the bridge. She sat in her pod, calm and smooth-faced as always, the strength of her body hidden by her dark jumpsuit, the midnight hair banded back in an uncompromising long tail.

Jaim quietly took the communications pod. Brandon leaned against a bulkhead just inside the access hatch, to all appearances unnoticed, his eyes on the captain. *Waiting?*

Vi'ya had just begun her status check when Jaim grunted in surprise, then tabbed a key. "Sensors—someone's outside," he said, transferring the image to the big screen.

They all looked up to see Eloatri standing on the green, a patient-faced clerk by her side. Both held small valises. "Captain," she said, smiling, "permission to come aboard?"

Vi'ya hit the com. "What is the problem?"

"It's not a problem," Eloatri said. "It's a joining of paths: mine and yours converge at Ares for a time. It would be simpler if I could share your vessel."

Vi'ya's hand hovered over her console. She looked across at Jaim. "I wouldn't want to make her angry," he said.

"No," Vi'ya agreed. She tabbed the key. "Lock opening." Then, looking over at Jaim with decided irony, she added, "Jaim will be right there to conduct you through the ship."

Jaim slaved the com console to hers with a swipe of his hand.

"Put her with the others," Vi'ya said. "I don't want her on the bridge. Arkad, you go with them."

Brandon hesitated, then said, "No."

Jaim's eyes lifted. *I was right.* He looked once toward Vi'ya, then nodded and went silently out. In the outside corridor he paused and looked back.

Brandon straightened up and walked onto the bridge.

Vi'ya closed the hatches, then started the flight sequence. On the screen the grassy knoll fell away, backlit by the *Telvarna*'s radiants, then the forestland raced below, rapidly vanishing in the darkness.

She did not look up from her work, but she was aware of the Arkad moving from the hatch to the nav console. Even without sound and sight, she could track him by the energy of his distinctive emotional spectrum. It took effort to block him out under the best of circumstances; she felt tendrils of vertigo around the edges of her senses, a little like inadequate window-fittings against the sear of Dol'jhar's sun.

She looked past him at the screen. The stars brightened as the ship accelerated, a subsonic whispering under the hull. The Arkad sat, motionless, as she located Nukiel's battle cruiser and locked in a course.

Then he spoke. "There are fewer women than men on Dol'-jhar?"

It was a strange sort of opening salvo, causing her to glance at him. The pose, the vocal intonations, were so familiar; she turned her gaze back to her console.

"Perhaps not at birth, but more of them are exposed," she said.

"Defects? Or just low birth weight?"

"Weakness." She hazarded return fire.

It forced a laugh out of Brandon, and she felt his focus sharpen, narrow-beam, laser-bright. An answering echo reached her from the Eya'a in their cabin: . . .*one-who-gives-fire-stone, is there danger for Vi'ya?*

No danger. She shaped the words in her mind, but her inner thoughts, too fast for them to scan, amended, *No tangible danger.* Out loud she said, "It's true enough on the mainland, though in some of the island Matriarchies, things differ." She crossed her arms. "It's a harsh planet. Early in our history the females—burdened by their own weight—were often crippled by joint disease at an early age."

She glanced up again. The Markham pose was still there, but this was not a lanky blond man with a lopsided face. Instead the head tipped to one side was defined in bone, the skin marred by healing bruises, the eyes wide and blue, the dark hair curling uncut these long weeks, on his neck. She could feel him listening intently, and she looked away.

"If this is a discussion of syntonics," she said, "we've adapted."

Brandon laughed again. A subtle alteration, no more than a ripple, flickered through his emotional spectrum, but still behind it waited a vast, dark pool. She did not want to define what lay below it.

"Do you always disarm before you destroy?" he countered.

"You sought this interview."

" 'Offense is the best defense,' " he said. And then, at last, a direct hit: "Why have you avoided me these past weeks?"

She realized belatedly that his initial indirection had been a gesture, not an attack. He knew how little Dol'jharians liked to give form to the intangibles by utterance. She said, "My priorities did not involve lengthy interviews with Panarchists."

"To avoid me," he went on pleasantly, "you left your crew to eat alone, train alone, and finally to lick their wounds alone." He waved a hand back toward the rec room. The movement caught the edge of her vision: the long fingers, the flash of the signet.

He knows us. She acknowledged the sense of threat she felt in his perception of Dol'jharian psychology.

"You avoided me at the risk of losing your crew," he finished. "I've been trying to figure out why." He got up and walked slowly about the bridge. "And the only answer that makes sense is that you wanted me to think that you'd betrayed Markham, arranged his death."

He was prodding at the tangential target that she'd offered him. A plaintive interpolation from the Eya'a distracted her: she caught reference to *one-who-gives-fire-stone* and *one-in-mask,* which was their old identification for Markham.

"Of course it could have been a purely philanthropic gesture," the agreeable voice went on. "Giving me something to do all those hours we spent in skip. And probably afforded you some entertainment, laughing from afar at my attempts to break into your system."

"It was entertaining," she agreed.

He looked up, an arrested expression in his blue eyes. The attempt to deflect failed: *This one did not emulate Markham, he was Markham's model.* Within the inner citadel, pain gripped her being. The time to deal with the implications would come. It was not now.

"I can't reconcile it," he said, no longer hiding behind the mask of politeness. "Mates. Not lovers: mates. What was that side of him, and why did I not know it?"

She could breathe again. He did not, after all, see the real issue; the shield had worked. She was safe. It was now possible to observe him, to endure the backwash of emotion—though just barely. From their hidden perspective, the Eya'a sent: *one-who-gives-fire-stone contemplates "trust" in sorrow.*

Trust: another of the intangibles. *What fools my ancestors were, to teach us that emotions were weakness, that everything could be conquered through force.*

"Who was he to you?" the Arkad went on, coming at last to face her.

She let the silence build, though she could feel the cost. Soon—minutes—he would disappear forever into *Mbwa Kali,* on route to Ares and the silk-and-glitter prison of High Douloi ceremonial. Those who were clever enough, or powerful enough, to have escaped Eusabian's clutches would be waiting on Ares to subsume him by whatever means. It was not, after all, her war.

But here, and now, she was alone with him, and she still had to decide what to say—whose integrity to protect.

A throb in her temple presaged the forfeit this interview would take from her, but that would be later. She said, "Why did you let him go?"

"Because I could not save him," Brandon answered, his eyes wide with pain.

"He warned you what Semion was."

"I didn't believe it—no," he amended quickly, "not the extent of it. How could I? All my life people shielded me from unpleasantness, from any hint that life on the Mandala was not gracious, perfect, the order that the universe strove for. The first break was when my mother died—"

The steady throb stabbed into her jaw; she was clenching her teeth.

"Life was a game." His voice was quick and soft, but the tide of memory-fueled emotion beat at her. "Semion was no more to me than a grim figure of authority, someone to play off. I had no real ambition—" He faltered, and the tide stilled. He looked across the bridge at Vi'ya. "Is that it? His ambition?"

He's fast. I keep forgetting it. Once again she waited, cursing inwardly at her inability to sustain this kind of duel. But once again there was reprieve.

"I had no ambition," Brandon went on. "He must have thought I was incapable of serious commitment. For I see now that though we talked about everything we did, we never talked about the future." He smiled, full of self-mockery. "Did he think it would bore me?"

The effort it took to withstand the battering of emotion made her mind begin to haze. But release came at last. The com flashed. She hit it with a fist, and a moment later acknowledged the docking order from Nukiel's comtech.

Brandon turned to the screen, his entire body radiating regret.

She felt the approach of the rest of her crew and the others, heard the rise and fall of voices.

And she could not, after all, leave him believing a lie.

"He trusted you," she said. "He always trusted you."

He looked up, the blue gaze intense. *He is fast,* she thought through the increasing red haze, but now events were faster. If at last he saw what it meant, it would be afterward, when they would no longer see one another: the repercussion, if any, would not be hers to deal with. The docking tractor seized the ship and there was nothing more for her to do; she deactivated the console and placed her hands on it.

"Hit the com," Montrose said, coming in first. "See if Nukiel will let me lift some of my tapes."

"How about the coffee?" Marim put in, appearing messy-haired and cheery as the *Televarna* set down in the docking bay, and the engines spun down into silence.

Chatter rose on all sides. Through it Vi'ya saw Brandon watching her, but he said nothing, and when one of the Marines addressed him low-voiced, he responded with an order concerning Jaim that she could not comprehend.

She no longer had to comprehend. Control had been taken away, for the last time; they were all someone else's responsibility.

She waited, sitting in the captain's pod, until the last of them had left the bridge, then she stumbled into the disposer and was rackingly sick.

❋   ❋   ❋

As the *Mbwa Kali* sped through fivespace toward Ares, Captain Nukiel entertained two of his guests—his newest, and his most exalted. He had out the best china, and everything was fresh.

The High Phanist Eloatri and the Aerenarch were the only ones who seemed at ease. Efriq sat, straight and still, and opposite him the Numen's clerk waited with folded hands for the others to finish their coffee. The young man's round face was impossible to gauge, but his eyes were never still.

Nukiel wondered if the magisters would be hashing over this conversation as closely as he and Efriq would be directly they left, and the thought made him smile.

Eloatri returned the smile. "Have I exhausted your patience with my questions?"

"That's all I know about Ares," Nukiel said, backtracking rapidly. "I was only there once, as a very green sublieutenant, and that was only in the Cap—the military sector. I never set foot in civilian country. Leontois?" He looked up at his first officer.

Efriq gave a quick shake of his head. Brandon looked from one to the other, his pleasant face completely unreadable. *Does the prospect of Ares mean triumph for him?*

"It gives us enough to go on," Eloatri said, sitting back in her chair. "I thank you gentlemen for your patience."

Nukiel hesitated, then essayed a gamble. The High Phanist had taken them utterly by surprise when she appeared along with the Aerenarch and the Rifters on their return from Desrien. Her appearance had thrown his crew into almost as much turmoil as the appearance of the Arkad heir on the Rifter ship had.

But she had been a perfect guest, self-effacing, content to remain in her own quarters after the official tour. She had not interfered in the various religious observances practiced by crew members who chose such things.

"I confess to curiosity," he said. "Is it the war that brings the Magisterium to Ares?"

Eloatri gave a small chuckle. "It's not war," she said. "It's your passengers."

Nukiel's breath caught, and he exchanged a quick glance wit Efriq. On his other side, Brandon just smiled.

"All of them," she said. Adding sympathetically, "The appearance—so sudden—must have been quite a shock for you crew."

Efriq choked on a sip of tea.

The clerk's lips thinned, obviously repressing a smile. Eloat did not hide her amusement. "I thought so. Well, it was no lea of a shock for us." Then a slight line appeared between he eyes. "But there's one more I . . . saw," she continued, her voic musing. "I don't know who he is."

Her face smoothed. "But no mind. For now, I find I must tr to communicate with the Eya'a better. And as for the youn bearing the Kelly Archon's genome . . ." She made a large ge ture. "I am delighted, by the way, that your medical techniciar report that he is on the mend."

"Well, his fever is gone," Nukiel said cautiously. "And h burn seems to be healing at last."

Eloatri nodded. "He has excellent care. I will have much t say in your praise when I do meet your Admiral Nyberg."

Nukiel felt relief balloon in him. In truth, he could hardl wait to hand them all over to a higher authority; he knew onc he had done so, every action, every conversation recorded an not recorded, would be picked over by anyone who had enoug clout to get clearance. On the surface the rescue of the Arka heir would be a coup, but he had no idea how it would transla into political terms.

Nukiel stole a quick look at the young man over the rim o his cup. Attempts to question Brandon vlith-Arkad about hi own experiences had yielded a fund of detail about inconse quentials, but the affable Aerenarch was more skilled tha Nukiel at the art of verbal dueling.

In a way he had made Nukiel's job easier; his tacit assump tion of civilian status gave Nukiel a clear path to follow. Bran don would be the civs' responsibility—the civs and the Nav high brass, he corrected silently. There were laws set up, just protect citizens against military encroachment, and these law would in turn protect the military.

"Tell me, Your Highness," Efriq said suddenly. "What di you think of Desrien?"

The Aerenarch looked up, his gaze abstract for a momen

then he smiled. "We only saw a small portion," he said. "But what we did see was unforgettable."

Eloatri chortled in delight. Even the clerk smiled.

"So I would imagine," Efriq murmured, his tone so devoid of innuendo the High Phanist laughed anew.

Brandon glanced at her appreciatively and then introduced an unexceptionable topic: the artwork in the New Glastonbury cathedral.

They were still on the subject of art when Nukiel signaled to the waiting steward to clear away the dishes. The interview was at an end; his job was officially over, all except for delivering them to Nyberg.

He resisted looking at his chrono, but he did glance at Efriq, to see understanding in his old friend's eyes. He was counting the hours.

THIRTY-SIX

ARTHELION

Morrighon stared into the darkness from his bed, watching the glow on the ceiling intensify.

Not again, he thought wearily. Several times since they'd returned to Arthelion after the battle, the computer phantom wearing the visage of Jaspar hai-Arkad had materialized in his room, watching silently for a time and then vanishing. He closed his eyes, waiting for it to go away.

Then he started as he heard his name.

"Morrighon." It was only a whisper, but the apparition had never spoken before. The Bori twisted, turning over and looking up over the end of the bed into his room.

"Listen," it said, and pointed one glowing finger at the communicators on the table near his bed. There was a crackle of static, and Morrighon heard the voice of Barrodagh, issuing a series of orders. As he listened, his eyes widened.

The eglarrh demachi-Dirazh'ul! The Avatar has decided!

Now Anaris would no longer be conditional heir, but heir in fact. After a short, predawn ritual of preparation, Anaris would be taken . . .

Predawn. Now. Remembering his private worry, he scrambled out of bed to begin dressing with frantic haste.

He'd seen the signs soon after their return. Anaris had become more irritable, more distant—signs, Morrighon was sure, invisible to anyone else. But to the Bori they presaged the conditional heir's disappearance into his quarters for a day and a night, not to be disturbed under any circumstances, and his eventual emergence looked purged and a bit haggard. This was the third time since his assignment to Anaris.

He had no idea what it meant. He hoped devoutly that it wasn't drugs or something similar; that would mean he'd tied himself to a fool, and the only outcome of that would be a horrible death at the hands of Barrodagh. But he couldn't believe that of Anaris.

He hopped around the room, frantically trying to balance as one foot became tangled in his trouser leg, peripherally aware of the ghost—*it is not a ghost*—watching him.

But it didn't matter what it was that Anaris did during those periods of withdrawal. *If Eusabian finds him in the state I think he might be in . . .*

Morrighon fastened his shirt tabs with shaking fingers, belted on his communicators, and hurried out. As he turned to close his door, he saw the apparition nod once, approvingly, and fade back through the wall.

His breath came in short rasps as he hurried down the corridors toward Anaris' quarters. He tabbed the annunciator frantically, ignoring the curiosity of the two gray-clad guards posted there. There was no answer.

Morrighon stared at the door in an agony of indecision. *Maybe he'll be ready for them, maybe . . .* No, he couldn't take the chance. He didn't know what Anaris would do to him for disturbing his retreat, but he did know what Eusabian would do, if his suspicions about Anaris were correct.

With shaking hands he entered the override code he'd pried out of Ferrasin.

Slipping through the door, he slammed it behind him, doing his best to block the gaze of the guards with his body. Inside, he stared, and his breath caught in his chest.

Anaris rahal'Jerrodi sat cross-legged in the center of the floor, his back to Morrighon, surrounded by a snowstorm of white dots. Peering closer, the Bori realized they were bits of the expanded foam used for packing, but what was impelling them in their frantic dance around the conditional heir? There were no air currents.

Acid crawled up his gullet as the bits of foam slowly coalesced into a tenuous representation of the features of Eusabian of Dol'jhar. For a moment the face held; then it melted into another: the Panarch of the Thousand Suns.

Morrighon began to shake. It was worse than he could have imagined. If Eusabian walked in at this moment and saw Anaris practicing one of the forbidden arts of the Chorei, he would have him killed instantly.

He stepped forward and timidly touched the Dol'jharian's shoulder. There was no reaction, save that the face of the Panarch melted into another, a woman. Morrighon gathered his courage, grasped the conditional heir's shoulder more firmly, and shook him.

Suddenly the bits of foam collapsed to the floor. Morrighon stepped back as Anaris sat still for a moment, then slowly got to his feet. He turned around. Morrighon stepped back further, terrified to the point of nausea. Anaris' nose was bleeding, his eyes bloodshot, the veins in his forehead distended and pulsing wildly.

He stared at the Bori without recognition for a moment. Then his eyes focused and the *prachan* slowly transformed his features. Morrighon felt death in the room.

"My lord," he gabbled, barely able to articulate the words. "Your father the Avatar has decided. They are on their way at this moment to begin your preparation for the *eglarrh demachi-Dirazh'ul*."

Anaris reacted as though he'd taken a blow. For a moment he stood facing the Bori, his eyes wild, his breath coming in ragged gasps. Then he rushed out of the room, and Morrighon heard him vomiting.

When he came back he sank exhausted into a chair, but his eyes were alert. No trace of the terrifying anger remained in his features.

"You have done well," he said softly. And with a grim smile, "There are no more secrets between us."

Then he stood up, and moving with sudden, feral grace he seized the Bori's shoulder. Morrighon barely restrained a cry of pain as the Dol'jharian's merciless grip compressed the bones and nerves.

"No one alive," said Anaris, speaking each word with precision, "knows of this." After too long he released him and turned away, crossing the room and stripping off his clothes.

As Morrighon watched Anaris reclothe himself in the unadorned black appropriate for the ceremony, he reflected on the emphasis the conditional heir had placed on the word "alive," and was amazed to find resentment in himself for that.

He suppressed the dangerous emotion. *But an unnecessary threat is a weak one*, he thought. That was a fault that would have to be dealt with, if Anaris was to gain the throne and keep it.

Then the annunciator chimed, and Morrighon composed himself to deal with the critical next few hours.

The shuttle took them out of predawn darkness into light as it accelerated toward the *Fist of Dol'jhar*, where the ceremony would be held, free of the taint of Panarchist weakness. Anaris gazed out the viewport, enjoying the symbolism of a course that forced an early dawn as they flew east.

The flight passed in silence; even had he been inclined to speech despite the throbbing headache that still gripped his temples, the presence of the Avatar forbade it. Next to him Morrighon sat quietly, making occasional notes on his compad.

An honor guard headed by Kyvernat Juvaszt and the senior officers of the battecruiser greeted them in the hangar bay. After a short passage via transtube, the module decanted them at the entrance to the gloomy chamber where the skull of Eusabian's father Urtigen guarded the Mysteries. Morrighon and Barrodagh stepped aside as they entered; only the True Men could witness the ceremony that would empower Anaris as a fit vessel for the spirit of Dol.

Inside it was cold; their breath smoked in the still air, echoing the twin pillars of incense twisting up from the altar below the skull. Between them a skein of black silk cord rested, animated to the semblance of life by the flickering light of the tall candles smelted from the flesh of Urtigen by his son Eusabian.

They arranged themselves in silence. Eusabian approached the altar, Anaris behind and to his right. The Avatar raised his

hands, the wide sleeves of his dead-black robes falling back to
reveal his heavy forearms, their wrists stippled with lancet scars
from innumerable ceremonial bleedings.

"*Darakh ettu hurreash, Urtigen-dalla. Tsurokh ni-vesh entasz
antorrh, epu catenn-hi hreach i-Dol . . .*" he began. Bestow
upon us your presence, great Urtigen. Turn not away your eyes,
for through you are we linked to the spirit of Dol . . .

The syllables resonated harshly in the cold air; from the corners of his eyes Anaris could see awe in the faces of Juvaszt and
the others gathered to witness his formal inheritance.

At the proper moment he stepped forward, joining his father
in the bloodletting that marked all high Dol'jharian rituals. The
hand-forged iron of the lancet was cold against his wrist, then
hot with pain as the steaming blood splashed onto the coals of
incense, adding the tang of heated copper to its pungent scent.

But even as he raised his voice in the austere antiphony of the
eglarrh demachi-Dirazh'ul, Anaris found his mind wandering.
Images, not of Jhar D'ocha and the wind-savaged rock and ice
of the Demmoth Ghyri, but of the marble warmth of the Mandala and the formal gardens of the Palace Minor, possessed his
mind. He tried to push the images aside, but they did not yield.
Even here, before the frigid sanctity of his family's altar, they
owned a power that could not be denied.

. . . hemma eg shtal . . . His mind fastened on a fragment of
the litany. Blood and iron. The image of Gelasaar's face hovered
before his mind's eye, expressing that very different amalgam of
gentleness and power that he had never fully understood. The
face melted into that of the Panarch's youngest son; Anaris felt
a surge of anger, and of anticipation. He knew that Brandon
would be taken to Ares; there he would assume his father's
mantle. Or would he? Could he? Did the two of them face similar struggles, each in the mold imposed by their culture and upbringing?

Suddenly Anaris felt his spirit expand beyond the confines of
the gloomy chamber; exalted, he perceived the Thousand Suns
as somehow wholly present to his senses, as something to be
grasped, like a game board, and across it the familiar, hated face
of his opponent.

Beside him his father had entwined his own dirazh'u with the
one lying on the altar, weaving a complex, lengthy knot. He

turned to Anaris, who faced him, the almost palpable image still holding his mind.

"Pali-mi kreuuchar bi pali-te, dira-mi bi dira-te, hach-ka mi bi hreach-te," the Avatar intoned. Be my vengeance entwined with yours, my curses with yours, my spirit with yours.

He touched the complex tangle of silken cords to Anaris' forehead, lips, heart, and groin in a fluid motion. Anaris took one end of the knot and pulled; the two cords separated, each now knotted in identical complexity.

Ejarhh! The sharp syllable from the lips of the Avatar shattered the silence. It is done!

Ejarhh! Anaris echoed.

Ejarhh! responded the watchers.

But as he and his father bowed before the altar, turned, and left the chamber, Anaris knew it was not done.

It was just beginning.

ARES

Osri Omilov held his arms a little away from his sides, hoping sweat wouldn't mark his uniform. His armpits were sticky and he felt a sudden, nearly overwhelming urge to pee.

They were here at last.

He stared out the viewport at Ares, the command station that every naval officer hoped someday to be posted to. Remembering the day he and Brandon had set out from Charvann with Ares as destination . . . he shook his head slightly. It seemed not weeks, but years ago. Another lifetime.

An ensign saluted him, a grin quirking his mouth. A flicker of amusement eased Osri's tension as he contemplated what must have been fierce competition to be assigned to the shuttle that would carry the Aerenarch, the High Phanist, and the captain who had brought them both safely to Ares.

A commander oversaw the transfer. Precise military ritual made the transition from cruiser to shuttle smooth. Now for the last journey: the transfer from naval control to civilian.

It was time to reenter Douloi governance.

Osri sweated, trying to distract himself. But his mind kept re-

viewing the past weeks as he wondered where the triumph was,
the elation he'd expected to feel when they finally reached
safety, order, justice.

He looked around.

All of them were on the shuttle, even the Rifters, although
Lokri was under guard. It had surprised Osri, until his father,
wearing a brand-new tunic, and looking haggard but alert, had
murmured as they left the *Mbwa Kali* and came on board: "It's
ostensibly on account of the Eya'a and Ivard. But no one knows
what to do about any of them yet, until Brandon tells them
whether he was rescued or kept prisoner."

It was both, Osri thought, sliding his hand into his pocket,
gripping the coin until his fingers hurt. *How does one secure
justice for that?*

He kept silent, aware how his own status had been falsely
raised by a few light words from Brandon. Somehow Osri had
been credited with saving the Aerenarch's life after they left
Charvann—though the truth was, Brandon had taken over the
piloting, and had chosen their destination.

But word had gone ahead the moment the cruiser emerged
outside the station, and while Osri was making ready, one of the
other lieutenants had appeared at his door, saying with a mix of
pride and envy, "High-end welcome at fifteen hundred on the
civ side. You're included, as Rescuer of the Heir. Com says
your family is in on the shuttle bay Greet List."

*Family. That means my mother. She's alive—and here. And
she'll be gloating over the social coup,* Osri thought, gazing out
the viewport as the shuttle slowly emerged from the huge
cruiser bay and started toward Ares.

He stared, fascinated, at the vast station. The military section
was a huge saucer of metal, tens of kilometers across, pocked
with depressions each large enough to moor a battlecruiser.
There were dozens of them. Depending from the underside of
the military saucer was a standard oneill habitat, giving the entire assemblage the appearance of a steel mushroom, whose
stem rotated against a stationary cap. Unlike a standard oneill,
however, Osri knew, the diffusers of the habitat derived their
light not from the dim red sun now serving as the station's primary, but from a vast fusion engine in the saucer, making Ares
entirely independent of location. The military saucer also
housed the largest fiveskip ever built, the field of which encom-

passed the oneill as well. Ares was the largest mobile construction ever built by humankind.

Normally, Osri knew, they would have docked on the saucer, but protocol demanded the Aerenarch and High Phanist be received on the civilian habitat.

As they approached the oneill, Osri saw a swarm of ships of every description. His eye was caught by an immense glittership among them, every line evocative of wealth and power.

Someone's breath caught. "*Whose* yacht is *that*?"

"Archon Srivashti's," the ensign said in a colorless voice.

Everyone looked up as Lucifur, who had been stretched out across Montrose's lap, gave a sudden low growl. Osri saw the Rifter's stiffened fingers stroking the big cat's raised hackles. The ensign turned and began going around to those of lesser importance, asking if anyone needed anything.

Osri watched the small group in the best seats before the big viewport. Brandon, in a plain white tunic, sat still and blank, with Jaim standing behind his chair. Nukiel on one side and Eloatri on the other exchanged low-voiced comments.

Ivard prowled around the little cabin, his thin face excited as he watched the bewildering display of ships through the various viewports. Suddenly his breath caught.

Osri switched his gaze to the viewport nearest, to see a battlecruiser, seared and pitted, huge holes blasted in its hull, choked with twisted metal. Osri gasped; it seemed inconceivable that a ship could take such punishment and still fly.

"That's *Grozniy*," the ensign said with pride. "Just got here ahead of you. Straight from the Battle of Arthelion."

Osri noticed a warning look from Nukiel; the ensign's face suddenly went blank and he said nothing more.

As they passed the long length of the terribly scarred ship Marim nudged up against Osri. "Sanctus Hicura," she said, and whistled. "Blits! Why didn't they skip out?"

Ivard appeared on her other side, his gaze intent on the *Grozniy*. "Blits?" he repeated in scorn. "Only cowards skip out. What I wouldn't give to fly one of those," he breathed.

Marim snorted, shaking her head. One hip bumped against Osri; he shifted away from her, his hand tight on the artifacts.

But for once she seemed to have forgotten about loot. As the shuttle's course took the cruiser out of sight, replacing it with the looming immensity of the Ares oneill, her sharp face tightened into uncharacteristic grimness. "Hell of a big prison," she muttered.

Ivard looked up at her, puzzled.

Marim jerked her thumb over her shoulder. "You think they're gonna have time for a bunch a' no-account Rifters, in the middle of a war? We're gonna be spending a long, long time here."

Osri realized it was as true for him as for the Rifters, and he felt an invisible vise settle around his heart. *It's a loss of control,* he thought. *When I was in the hands of the Rifters, I thought of this place as a haven, but now all I can remember is childhood, and feeling like a foreigner among my own kind.*

Marim sniffed in annoyance, plumping down near Lokri, whom she engaged in a muttered conversation.

The shuttle had curved around to the far end of the civilian habitat, approaching the center of the end cap where a vast bay loomed, a confusion of sensors and less identifiable protrusions around it. Osri moved up next to Jaim, looking out the viewport past the Aerenarch. He felt a shifting in his inner ear as the shuttle began to match spins with the oneill.

In front of him, framed by the viewport, the Aerenarch moved slightly, and suddenly the perspective of the scene shifted dizzily. For a moment, Brandon vlith-Arkad, the last heir of a millennial power, awaited by all aboard the station, each with their own expectations of him—for a moment he was the fixed point in space, while the ponderous, multitrillion-ton mass of Ares slowed to match its spin to his. Then the navigator in Osri reasserted itself and the shuttle was again but a sliver of metal approaching a man-made planetoid.

The glowing discharges of the electronic lock snaked across the viewports; an unexpected chitter from the Eya'a caused a ripple of reaction, nervous twitches and little laughs. A moment later a gentle bump in the shuttle indicated they'd grounded in the bay.

Everyone stood up, including Brandon. The Navy officers moved to the hatches, standing at attention. Murmurs of conversation went on around, but Osri watched Brandon, who stood still silent, his head canted slightly, as if he were listening. He seemed curiously isolated in the eddies of activity around him.

"You four will wait," a Marine said to Montrose, Marim,

Ivard, and Lokri. "Captain Vi'ya, as translator for the Eya'a, you are permitted to accompany—"

"I will remain with my crew," the woman said, her accent pronounced. "The Eya'a will know where to find me if they wish."

Brandon looked across the length of the cabin at her, but Vi'ya remained in her chair, her back to the main hatch and the people gathered there.

Osri moved slowly to the others, standing next to his father.

The hatch opened and the Marine honor guard presented arms. Beyond the ramp, Osri glimpsed a scattering of people waiting, their elegant clothing startling after weeks of either uniforms or cast-off flight suits.

To the uninitiated eye the scattering might seem random, but Osri knew that rigid hierarchy defined who stood where along the path; within the hierarchy the perilous minutiae of deference indicated who stood forward, and who behind.

Brandon gestured to Nukiel, and together they moved to the hatchway. Just before he passed through, Brandon turned his head slightly, and his eyes met Osri's. The perfect Douloi mask broke for the briefest moment and a flicker of a smile crossed his face. Then he looked past Osri, at someone behind, and his eyes narrowed.

A slight noise from Nukiel recalled his attention, and he started down the ramp, in step with Nukiel as peal after peal of the Phoenix Fanfare shivered on the air.

"Oh," Ivard sighed, leaning out of the hatch.

Osri suddenly remembered the nameless Rifter woman at Chang's station, and her priceless gift of passion and tenderness. *Priceless. She never even asked who I was.*

For once he acted on an impulse prompted by something besides anger. Osri grasped Ivard's skinny arm and stuffed the coin and the ribbon into the breast pocket on Ivard's suit. Then he zipped it, and before Ivard could say anything, he joined his father and walked down the ramp.

Looking ahead, he scanned the faces watching the Aerenarch's slow progress. He saw curiosity, politeness, interest, wariness, but no friendly eye anywhere in sight. These were the High Douloi; their ineluctable formality seemed to close around them like an icy force field—

But formality was not triumphant, after all.

A high, clear keening, like a wind instrument, beat the air above the formal music, and a Kelly trinity danced along the path, stopping before Brandon. As the Kelly performed a kind of obeisance, ribbons fluttering and headstalks whirling, Osri heard a snorting sound from inside the shuttle.

A muffled "Hey! You can't—" sounded, and then footsteps pounded down the ramp.

Ivard bounded past, nose twitching.

The Marines whirled, pointing their weapons, but Nukiel quickly raised his hand.

The Kelly then swarmed around Ivard, tweeting and blatting, touching and gently slapping him all over. He responded in kind, his arms writhing, hooting weirdly, joy informing every part of his body.

And a moment later the two Eya'a moved swiftly down the ramp, their twiggy feet scratching. A whisper went through the gathered humans there; several attempted bows, which looked foolish as the little white figures moved past without noticing.

Two people, a man and a woman, stepped up to Brandon then, dropping on one knee. Osri recognized the tiny, graceful woman: Vannis Scefi-Cartano, the former Aerenarch's consort. Her eyes, and her smile, were brilliant as gemstones. Next to her, in faultless Navy dress uniform, a man, older and suave: Admiral Nyberg.

Their obeisances were deliberate and graceful; together they managed to draw the eye away from the Kelly and Ivard. Once again, Douloi formality prevailed.

But it had been shaken, Osri thought, watching the silent stewards lead away the four figures. A hint that things were not, after all, the same, and could never be again.

Osri smiled.

THE END OF BOOK TWO·

BESTSELLERS FROM TOR

☐ 51195-6   BREAKFAST AT WIMBLEDON $3.99
                 Jack Bickham   Canada $4.99

☐ 52497-7   CRITICAL MASS $5.99
                 David Hagberg   Canada $6.99

☐ 85202-9   ELVISSEY $12.95
                 Jack Womack   Canada $16.95

☐ 51612-5   FALLEN IDOLS $4.99
                 Ralph Arnote   Canada $5.99

☐ 51716-4   THE FOREVER KING $5.99
                 Molly Cochran & Warren Murphy   Canada $6.99

☐ 50743-6   PEOPLE OF THE RIVER $5.99
                 Michael Gear & Kathleen O'Neal Gear   Canada $6.99

☐ 51198-0   PREY $5.99
                 Ken Goddard   Canada $6.99

☐ 50735-5   THE TRIKON DECEPTION $5.99
                 Ben Bova & Bill Pogue   Canada $6.99

Buy them at your local bookstore or use this handy coupon:
Clip and mail this page with your order.

Publishers Book and Audio Mailing Service
P.O. Box 120159, Staten Island, NY 10312-0004

Please send me the book(s) I have checked above. I am enclosing $ _____
(Please add $1.25 for the first book, and $.25 for each additional book to cover postage and handling.
Send check or money order only—no CODs.)

Name _____
Address _____
City _____ State/Zip _____
Please allow six weeks for delivery. Prices subject to change without notice.

THE BEST IN
SCIENCE FICTION

☐	51083-6	ACHILLES' CHOICE *Larry Niven & Steven Barnes*	$4.99 Canada $5.99
☐	50270-1	THE BOAT OF A MILLION YEARS *Poul Anderson*	$4.95 Canada $5.95
☐	51528-5	A FIRE UPON THE DEEP *Vernor Vinge*	$5.99 Canada $6.99
☐	52225-7	A KNIGHT OF GHOSTS AND SHADOWS *Poul Anderson*	$4.99 Canada $5.99
☐	53259-7	THE MEMORY OF EARTH *Orson Scott Card*	$5.99 Canada $6.99
☐	51001-1	N-SPACE *Larry Niven*	$5.99 Canada $6.99
☐	52024-6	THE PHOENIX IN FLIGHT *Sherwood Smith & Dave Trowbridge*	$4.99 Canada $5.99
☐	51704-0	THE PRICE OF THE STARS *Debra Doyle & James D. Macdonald*	$4.50 Canada $5.50
☐	50890-4	RED ORC'S RAGE *Philip Jose Farmer*	$4.99 Canada $5.99
☐	50925-0	XENOCIDE *Orson Scott Card*	$5.99 Canada $6.99
☐	50947-1	YOUNG BLEYS *Gordon R. Dickson*	$5.99 Canada $6.99

Buy them at your local bookstore or use this handy coupon:
Clip and mail this page with your order.

Publishers Book and Audio Mailing Service
P.O. Box 120159, Staten Island, NY 10312-0004

Please send me the book(s) I have checked above. I am enclosing $ _____
(Please add $1.25 for the first book, and $.25 for each additional book to cover postage and handling.
Send check or money order only—no CODs.)

Name _____
Address _____
City _____ State/Zip _____
Please allow six weeks for delivery. Prices subject to change without notice.